THE CARPENTER

THE CARPENTER

A Novel

Matt Lennox

The Carpenter

A Phyllis Bruce Book, published by HarperCollins Publishers Ltd.

First edition

HarperCollins Publishers Ltd
2 Bloor Street East, 20th Floor
Toronto, Ontario, Canada
M4W 1A8

www.harpercollins.ca

Library and Archives Canada Cataloguing in Publication

Lennox, Matt
The carpenter / Matt Lennox.

"A Phyllis Bruce Book."

ISBN 978-1-44340-734-2

I. Title.
PS8623.E5868C37 2012 C813'.6 C2011-905704-2

Printed in the United States of America

RRD 9 8 7 6 5 4 3 2 1

For my sister, Katherine Lennox

ONE

SEPTEMBER TO OCTOBER 1980

Leland King was back in town. He hadn't yet figured out what to make of that.

He'd arrived on the bus in the midafternoon on Labour Day, and had gone directly to a bachelor apartment that Pastor Barry had arranged for him. The apartment was above a variety store at the bottom of Union Street, near the south end of the town's lakefront. Across the street was the back of an A&P grocery. Beside the variety store, past a patch of grass, was a fence around a small scrapyard.

All of Lee's earthly possessions amounted to the clothes on his back and one suitcase and a wallet and cigarettes and a plastic lighter. The apartment contained some furniture abandoned by the outgoing tenant. A swivel chair. A pullout couch. A lamp with an anchor motif on the shade. There were pale patches on the walls where pictures had hung, and from the bathroom came a steady hiss. Nothing was square or level.

The variety store owner was also the landlord. His name was Mr. Yoon and he was one of Pastor Barry's congregants. Mr. Yoon curtly told Lee a few of the rules, how he didn't want loud noises or trouble. He wanted to know if Lee had a job.

—I have a job, said Lee. I'm a carpenter. Cabinets, counters, doors, windows, trim. All kinds of joining, you name it. I got my trade, boss. Barry got me working with a guy here in town. I start on Thursday.

Lee paid his month's rent in cash and Mr. Yoon gave him a new-cut key.

Thirty minutes later, Lee took a taxicab out to his sister Donna's house. He had a return address torn off an envelope. She'd not written often, and in the last few years almost not at all. It was Pastor Barry who'd done most of the writing.

The taxi driver had the radio on. Between songs, there was a news break recapping the events of the long weekend. The top story was an interview with that kid from out west . . . *Near the end of the day,* the kid was saying, *eighteen miles, I was coughing and choking, had pain in my neck and my chest . . .*

—You know who that is? said the taxi driver.

—Who?

—It's that one-legged kid who tried to run acrost the country. What's his name, Fox. Terry or what-have-you. He's been all over the news.

The kid on the radio: *All I can say is, if there's any way I can get out there again and finish it, I will . . .*

—What a crazy bastard, said the taxi driver. Trying to run acrost the country with one leg. Sounds like they're pulling him off the road.

—Sounds like it, said Lee.

The taxi driver droned on about other things, the weather, politics. Lee wasn't paying him much attention. What he was remembering of these parts was how August could be cold or September could be hot, as it was now, even when the leaves showed a silver edge that heralded the coming autumn. They passed a drying cornfield and a line of hydro towers. On the edge of the road was the crushed hull of a snapping turtle. It looked like someone had swerved to hit it.

The hometown to which Lee had returned was situated on the edge of Lake Kissinaw. Half an hour to the east was a smaller body of water called Indian Lake. The Indian River flowed back west from the smaller lake, pouring into Kissinaw, and dividing the town in half. Eighteen thousand people lived in Lee's hometown, and made their livings in manufacturing and farming and summer tourism. On the northwest edge of town was a CIL chemical factory that had produced munitions during the war years. Lee sometimes wondered what he might have ended up doing with himself, had he remained here. Coming back now, at this time in his life, was stirring up a lot of strange feelings.

The taxi driver was talking about hockey, what did Lee think of this season's trades. Lee had a vague notion to lean up between the seats and tell the driver that he sounded like a goof, talking all this bullshit. Instead he just muttered a noncommittal response.

Half a mile later they came to the house. It stood on two acres of shaggy lawn. It was sided in white vinyl with three wooden butterflies fixed to the front wall. The driver tallied a charge of six dollars. Lee opened his wallet. His cash felt desperately precious. He paid six dollars precisely. The driver gave him a strange look, expectant. The engine idled. Lee's mouth felt dry.

—Well, said Lee. Maybe that one-legged kid will get back on the road.

The driver just shook his head. Lee got out and the taxi moved forward and turned around and headed back the way they'd come. The buzz of a cicada rose and peaked.

As Lee made his way up the walk, the front door opened, but it wasn't Donna who came out. It was his mother, Irene. She came onto the stoop, pushing on a rubber-footed cane, and took the first steps down with great care. Lee could hear her long and shallow breathing. She stopped once to look at him. He arrived at the base of the stoop and they came together. She was panting for breath and her eyes were wet.

—Here you are.

—Hello, Ma.

She put her frail arms around him.

Behind her, Donna appeared on the stoop. Donna was thin and knobby-kneed in a pair of canvas shorts and a cotton shirt. Irene released him and stood back.

—I don't know what to say.

—Don't say nothing at all.

—You're working too hard, Mom, said Donna. You shouldn't of done the stairs.

Lee nodded and said: Donna's right, Ma.

—Come in, said Irene. It's too hot.

Lee led Irene up the stoop. At the top, Donna did not meet his eye. In a small voice, she said: It's good to see you.

And then, abruptly, she embraced him. She smelled of soap. Lee felt the fabric of her shirt over her shoulder bones.

As Donna helped Irene into the house, Lee looked at a wooden plaque on the front door: AS FOR MY HOUSE, WE SHALL SERVE THE LORD.

What he first saw in the living room were three different crosses. One was a simple rood. One was a framed needlepoint depiction of Golgotha. Finally, there was a cross of macaroni glued onto a paper plate, hung over the entranceway into the kitchen.

Two young boys, maybe seven or eight, hurtled into the living room, one chasing the other. They stormed past Lee, shouting, and angled down the basement stairs. Donna paled. She leaned over the banister and yelled after them: Boys, what are you doing? Don't run in the house. You'll upset Grandma's tubes.

She cast a helpless look at Lee and Irene. Lee badly wanted a cigarette but he'd heard you didn't smoke in people's homes any more unless they invited you to.

Irene struggled into an easy chair. Beside her was an oxygen cylinder on a slender dolly, with a nasal tube at the end of a hose. Lee went over and picked up the tube and held it. He felt stupid, holding the unfamiliar equipment. Almost immediately Donna came and took it from him.

—She's okay, Lee. She just shouldn't of done the stairs.

And then Pastor Barry came into the room. He was wearing corduroy trousers and a cotton T-shirt and tennis shoes. He was ten inches shorter than Donna. He spread his arms.

—Leland. Welcome.

—Good to see you, Barry.

Barry embraced him. Lee looked down at the top of Barry's head. Barry stood back.

—I'm afraid I don't have beer.

—No problem. You know I'm dry.

—I do. And it makes me happy to hear it. Was everything in good shape with Mr. Yoon? I had him leave some things in the apartment. I thought they might make you a little more comfortable. It's a simple place, but simple never harmed anybody. I can think of one guy in particular who didn't mind a simple bed.

—Simple as can be, said Lee.

Lee was given a glass of lemonade. Desperate for a cigarette, he went out onto a deck overlooking the backyard. There was a swing set and a sandbox and a wood-line on the far edge of the property. He wandered down to the grass. He put the lemonade down beside him and lit a cigarette. For the moment, he was alone. He took off his shoes. His big toe poked through a hole in his sock. He looked around and then he stripped off the socks and flexed his feet in the grass. He picked up his lemonade and walked down to the wood-line. He wondered how much he'd expected them to look different, his mother and Donna. To be different. Or had he expected them to be the same, somehow? What had he expected at all? Along the wood-line, the trees were pine and the smell of sap was strong, cut pleasantly by the cigarette smoke. Needles blanketed the ground. A chipmunk stuttered past and branches creaked and insects whined and a hawk circled overhead.

Coming back up the yard ten minutes later, Lee saw that his mother and Barry were out on the deck, his mother sitting with her oxygen cylinder beside her, Barry starting the barbecue. Lee also saw a young man napping in a lawn chair beside the house. Lee put his socks and shoes back on his feet. He went up the steps.

—Would you like one sausage or two? said Barry. Never mind. I'll make two for you anyhow.

Barry closed the lid on the barbecue. He turned to Irene. She was watching them intently and wearing the nasal tube. There was something obscene about it.

—Did you need anything, Mother?

—I'm fine, Barry.

Barry squeezed her hand. He went into the house.

—I can't believe you're home, said Irene.

—Me either, said Lee.

—Look at all those grey hairs you sprouted. But you're still skinny as a beanpole.

—Not so much any more, said Lee, patting the small pad of belly fat he'd grown.

A quiet moment passed.

—Don't be cross with Donna, said Irene. All this has almost turned her on her head.

—I didn't have to come for dinner.

—Everyone is glad to see you, Leland. Of course you had to come. We're your family.

—I know, said Lee.

A hornet buzzed around the rim of Lee's lemonade glass. He waved it away.

—I seen a kid snoozing around the side of the house, said Lee. I'd say that's Peter. I wouldn't of known him from the pictures you sent me.

—I sent those snapshots years ago.

—Is he a good kid?

—Yes. He disappointed me when he quit going to church and school both, but yes, he's a good fellow.

—He quit school?

—Yes. All he does is work at the gas station. Works and works. He left here at five o'clock this morning, and only got back here an hour ago. I can't guess what he wants.

—Maybe he doesn't know himself.

Lee drank down the lemonade. He crunched the ice cube between his back teeth and said: And I don't guess he knows about any of the other business?

His mother looked out over the backyard. A long moment passed.

—Leland, said Irene, quietly, there's no reason to stir up any of that old upset. Upset is all it would be.

Do you remember writing Christmas cards to your Uncle Lee? asked Donna.

The two boys did not respond. The elder was frowning at the tablecloth. The younger stared at Lee. Their names were Luke and John.

—Close your mouth, John, said Barry.

The boy managed to close his mouth for a short time and then it fell open again. From the other side of the table, Peter, older than his half-brothers by ten years, watched with amusement.

—They're afraid of outsiders, said Peter. That happens when you home-school.

—Peter, said Donna.

The two young boys looked like Donna and Barry, with Donna's high cheekbones and Barry's black hair and blue eyes. Peter had brown eyes and thin blond hair. He had Donna's high cheekbones but no other obvious suggestion of his parentage.

Luke finally spoke up.

—I remember you wrote some letters to us. You spelled *happy* wrong.

—Luke, said Donna.

—He put an *e* after the *p*.

—That's enough, said Barry.

—I'm sorry, Lee, said Donna.

—It's okay, said Lee. See, Luke, I didn't pay attention in school like you guys, so you'd think I'm a dummy if you read my letters. But I always liked to get them cards from you.

John stared at Lee. The boy's jaw remained unhinged. Finally, he said: Didn't they teach you to read and write in jail?

Donna clapped her knife and fork down.

—Maybe we shouldn't of done this.

—Mom said you had school in jail, said John.

—John . . .

Lee turned his plate with his thumbs. The meal was potato salad and two overdone bratwurst sausages.

—You're right, said Lee. There was school in jail. There was school for reading and writing, but that's not what I learned. Because reading and writing is more for you guys, who can be anything you want when you grow up. A guy like me isn't going to be a doctor or nothing like that, so I decided to learn something I was okay at, which was carpentry.

—You boys know what a carpenter is, said Barry.

—It's a guy who builds things, said Luke.

—That's right. That's what Jesus was. So Uncle Lee learned a pretty good thing. What do we say about school?

The two brothers responded in unison: The Bible says it's important to gain wisdom.

—Good, said Barry.

Lee nodded.

—You boys go to school right here at home? You're lucky. You don't have to wait for the school bus or nothing.

They chewed on through their meal and some quiet minutes passed. Finally, Barry said: Lee, Clifton Murray will be waiting for you on Thursday morning. He's going to be real busy right through the fall. You boys remember Mr. Murray from church?

—Yes, Daddy.

—He's given Uncle Lee a job as a carpenter.

—We're very proud, said Irene.

The boys kept looking at him between bites. John had not closed his hanging mouth.

—I can give you a lift, said Peter. I have a car.

—Say again?

—I'm guessing you don't have a car yet. I'll give you a lift on Thursday. I have an early start that day anyway.

—Well, thanks, Peter. You know where I live?

—Yeah. I saw it. Keeping the lamp was my idea.

After supper Luke and John went into the living room and sat on the floor in front of the couch. They swatted at each other when they thought nobody was looking. Barry had disappeared somewhere. Peter helped his grandmother over to her easy chair.

Lee watched all of this from the kitchen doorway, and then he turned back to Donna, who'd started the dishes.

—Should I go?

—You can stay for a bit, said Donna. They're going to do their after-supper thing.

—What, do they play Monopoly?

—No. Barry does a bible study with them. After that I think he's going to the church. He'll give you a ride back into town.

Barry reappeared carrying a cloth-bound study bible. He sat on the couch in front of the boys. Peter was leaning against the wall. He saw Lee watching him and he shrugged.

—Tonight we're going to talk about Jonah and the whale, said Barry.

Lee pulled a dishtowel off a hook above the oven. He started drying a plate. He saw Donna glance at him out of the corner of her eye.

—They do this every night?

—He's a good dad, Lee.

—I never meant nothing. He's been real good to me, sister. It was him who came to see me when I was in the city.

—I had the boys to look after. Mama too. It would of been pretty hard for me to go to the city.

—Look. I don't mean nothing. Anyhow, it can't hurt to learn about the Bible. I read it a couple times. I have questions about it, but you know me. The questions I have are probably for the experts.

He helped with the drying for a few minutes more. Then Pete was standing beside him.

—I can take over.

—I can do it, Peter, said Lee. Or do they call you Pete?

—Sure, I like that better, said Pete. Anyway, the dishes aren't any trouble. Usually I dry them. It's that or the bible study.

—You'd rather be in here?

—Yeah.

Lee handed him the dishtowel and moved over to the doorway. He looked at the boys and at Barry addressing them:

—It wouldn't take long for you or me to get real uncomfortable in a whale's belly. But not Brother Jonah. He just kept on praying and giving thanks. Saying his hallelujahs till the third day. So what does the Lord do? He tells that whale to let Jonah out of his belly. That's not the end, either. Jonah goes on to Nineveh, just like he was supposed to. This time he isn't afraid to preach the Word. He goes and tells those unbelievers what's what. And this time? The people listen to him. So I want you to think about being a brave Christian. About going out to spread the good Word. That's one of your jobs, boys. That's something the Lord expects in exchange for all the great things He's done for you.

By the time the lesson was done, Irene's eyes were closed. Lee went over and took her hand. Barry smiled at him and said: Come on, Brother Lee. I have to swing by the church. I'll drop you off at your new place.

Sometime after midnight, Lee woke from the same dream he'd been having for as long as he could remember. In the dream he was a boy again, venturing down into the basement of the boarding house in town where he and Donna grew up. The basement had brick walls and a dirt floor and towards the back was a coal furnace. A set of octopus pipes stretched up from the firebox and transmitted strange sounds through the house at night.

In Lee's dream, none of the dimensions were quite right and it seemed as if he approached the furnace slowly, over a great distance. He'd hear a sound and turn to see a crippled caretaker, bearing a spadeshovel full of coal, taking shape out of the dark. The caretaker always looked like he was about to say something but he never did. Lee would try to run, but would find his feet fixed to the floor, and with the certainty of dreams he knew the spadeshovel was meant for him, to lift him whole or in pieces and carry him over to the furnace and load him onto the burning coals.

The dream had come frequently to Lee through much of his childhood, through his years in prison. It troubled him. It always had.

A little later, he gave up on the idea of sleep. He got up from the pullout couch and walked around the apartment. Eventually he put on his jeans and undershirt, and he went outside and stood on the sidewalk. The street was deserted. A stoplight blinked overhead. Nothing was quite believable yet.

Judy Lacroix was dead inside a car, parked on the gravel patch where the drive-in cinema had burned down. When Stan Maitland found her, he had a feeling of all his long years as a cop dilating on him. He knew who Judy was. He knew her family. This was a particular burden he held entirely to himself. That it was he who should find the girl dead in the car was proof of what could not be outstripped by the passing of time alone.

Earlier that evening, Stan had been fishing with his granddaughter Louise. They'd taken Stan's boat north across Lake Kissinaw to a shoal in one of the back bays. Stan had brought along a carton of earthworms. Louise sat on the skiff's middle seat. Her rubber boots did not touch the floor.

They conferred between long stretches of affable quiet. He loved how she would ply him with questions as to the nature of things.

—Grandpa, what do the fish do when the ice comes?

—Different fish do different things under the ice. I don't know all of them, but bass—I told you how to tell which ones are bass—slow down and don't do much. They just kind of hang around till it gets warm again. Sometimes my friends and I used to ice-fish, and on a nicer day we might think we could catch bass, but we never could.

Over an hour and a half they caught two pickerel and a smallmouth bass. When it was time to go he pulled the stringer of catch up into the skiff. In his tackle box he had a hatchet-handle, which he used to crack each fish across the skull. Louise sat primly, studying his every motion. Stan laid the dead fish on the bottom of the boat and rinsed his hands in the lake water. He stood, feeling his back pop, and heaved the pull-cord on the motor.

It was two days past the new moon, and by the time they returned to Echo Point the dark had fully settled. He'd left a light on in the front window of the house.

A dark form appeared on the dock while Stan was tying up. It was Cassius coming to greet them. Stan pushed the old black dog's muzzle away from the fish. Louise trailed her hand along Cassius's back.

—Can I see you clean the fish?

—I have to take you home now. It's getting on to bedtime.

—Grandpa . . .

He knelt down beside her.

—You'll get Grandpa in trouble, said Stan. Come on, let's get your things. You can ride in the middle seat.

Stan told Cassius to stay in the yard. Louise climbed up into the cab of Stan's pickup and Stan got into the driver's seat and drove them out along Echo Point Road.

They talked about Louise's first day of grade three. She wanted to know if he remembered when he'd been in grade three. He told her it had been in a one-room schoolhouse. He'd had to light the woodstove in winter. The building was gone now, long gone. It had been on the edge of the piece of land where the town had put up a golf course fifteen years ago.

Stan drove them out of the bush and they passed through open country. Ahead of them dust rose in the headlights. Then they were coming up to the drive-in. A screen stood out against the horizon. The box office and the concession stand and one of the other screens had burned down the year before. Some people around town whispered about a collection on insurance. Stan had been able to see the glow of the fire from the second floor of his house. He'd gone in his truck. The town fire department and the volunteer firefighters had already had the burning screen and the concession stand cordoned off when he arrived, but he'd come ahead of the police. The cops, when they finally showed up, were young. He hadn't recognized them and they didn't know who he was.

Now, passing the drive-in with Louise beside him, Stan saw how the thin new moon shone on the windshield of a car. The car was parked halfway to where the burned movie screen stood in deeper black against the stars. The car was dark. He thought about it and did not think about it.

Then the drive-in disappeared behind them.

Before long he merged onto the highway. The lights of town lay ahead. Louise put her head on Stan's arm.

Mary and Frank Casey had a modern split-level house east of downtown. The windows were lit. Parked in the driveway were Mary's Volvo and a provincial patrol car. Mary opened the front door as Stan came up the walk, carrying Louise, who had fallen asleep.

He took her upstairs and put her into her bed, and then he stood back and spent a moment looking at her. He wondered, vaguely, how many more years he would get to see her grow up.

He followed Mary back down to the living room.

—I hope I didn't get her home too late.

—No, Dad, it's fine. Thanks. She loves it.

Mary sat in the loveseat and Stan sat down on the couch. Next to it, against the wall, was a Clarendon upright piano. Stan put his hand out and dallied his fingers over the keys but did not press them. Frank came out of the kitchen. He was wearing a grey T-shirt and his uniform trousers.

—Thanks for taking Louise, Stan.

—It's never any trouble. Where's Emily?

Frank sat on the arm of the loveseat and said: She's seventeen. You can guess where she's at.

—A new boyfriend?

—A boy. I don't know that I'd call him more than that. With her, it's the stray cats.

—She has good sense, Frank, said Mary, putting her hand on his knee.

—How's the detachment? said Stan.

—Labour Day is over. All the kids are back in school, let's put it that way. That makes me happy.

—Fall was always a quiet time, said Stan. A lot of people were too busy on the farms to mess around.

—Well, if things didn't change like they do, I wouldn't need half the cops I have now, fall or not. But that's how it goes.

—That's how it goes, said Stan.

Stan was back on the road a short while later. He was only eight years retired from the local detachment, despite what it had meant for his pension. At one time he'd known every street in town. He turned off the highway and five minutes later he passed the drive-in again. His headlights caught the same car he'd seen earlier.

Stan drove by. Then he pulled off to the side of the road. Gravel snarled against the underside of his truck as he moved from the hardtop to the shoulder. He brought the vehicle to a stop and sat holding the steering wheel. Then he got out of the truck and took out a D-cell flashlight that he kept under the seat. He didn't turn it on just yet. There was enough light from the stars and the moon to bring everything out in halftones. He walked into the drive-in lot.

The silhouette of the car resolved itself. Stan looked to see whether it was rocking and he listened for the creaking of springs. He sniffed the air for dope smoke. This would be better, he thought, if Cassius was with him.

He turned on the flashlight, at first pointing it at the ground. He waited for something to happen and when nothing did he brought the flashlight up and shone it on the windshield. He moved the light along the side of the car.

One of the back windows was rolled down a few inches. The space at the top had been stuffed with a towel. Stan could see a garden hose tucked through. The hose was looped down through the wheel well and around to the rear of the car. He moved up.

The flashlight cast a yellow glow into the back seat. The girl's face was slack, dismayed. Her eyes were marbled.

Stan stepped backward. He looked at the dark shapes of the drive-in, black against the stars and the frame of the old screen. When he looked again he knew who she was. Her name was Judy Lacroix. Recognition was a hand pulling at his shirt sleeve.

Not that he'd ever forgotten it, how it was his arrest and testimony that had hanged the dead girl's uncle.

At six o'clock in the morning on Thursday, Lee went into a diner called the Owl Café, a block away from his apartment. He took a stool at the counter. He was wearing his new work boots, carrying his new tool belt. These he'd purchased the day before. He'd also purchased a measuring tape and a hammer and a retractable knife and a small collection of pencils, which he'd carefully sharpened. He put the tool belt on the stool beside him. There was a colour television behind the counter playing a morning news broadcast. The picture was coming in and out. A waitress passing the set reached up and adjusted the antenna before she came over to Lee. Her face was warm and the name *Helen* was embroidered on her shirt. Her hips and breasts were round and full.

—Morning, hon.

—Morning yourself, said Lee.

—Anything catch your eye?

—You mean on the menu?

She grinned: Come on. You just got here.

He ordered eggs and home fries and extra bacon. She brought him a cup of coffee and then she moved away and passed his order through a wicket into a steaming kitchen. Lee lit a cigarette. Seated around him were a few other patrons. He didn't think he recognized any of them. There were a couple of truckers and a nurse along the counter, and four old men in a booth. A man with long dark hair and sharp features, wearing a down-filled vest and sitting near the window, might have been studying Lee if he allowed himself to think so. Lee tapped his cigarette into an ashtray. He flexed his toes inside his new work boots.

Helen came with his breakfast and refilled his coffee.

—Enjoy, Brown Eyes.

He slathered ketchup on his food and he hunched forward and dug into his breakfast. He sensed that Helen was watching him, amused. He looked at her.

—I don't know where you usually eat, said Helen, but nobody's going to steal your food here.

Before Lee could reply, she went back down the counter to take someone else's order. The man in the down-filled vest raised a hand at her, snapped his fingers, but Helen ignored him. It was a different waitress who went to refill the man's coffee.

Lee finished his breakfast. He got up and collected his tool belt and went into the washroom. When he came out, he saw Pete in a small car outside. The long-haired man with the sharp features was gone. Helen came over and Lee asked what he owed. After he'd paid, Helen said she hoped he'd come again.

He left the diner, feeling good and loose-limbed. Pete popped the trunk open and Lee dropped his tool belt beside the spare tire. He closed the trunk and got into the car.

—Morning, said Pete.

—Top of the morning to you.

—Ready for your first day?

—You bet, buck.

—I asked Barry to ask Clifton Murray where we're going, said Pete. It's out at the lake. Where all the new places are going up. My mom packed you a lunch. It's on the back seat.

They went south out of town and followed a road along the bottom edge of Lake Kissinaw. Lee remembered the geography of it, the aspect of the trees, a certain house. A sign advertised a lakeside subdivision to be built in the next year.

—I hear you don't go to school no more, said Lee.

—I . . . No, that's true. I quit.

—Wasn't to your liking?

—You could say that. I don't know how to explain it.

—So you work at a gas station all the time?

—Pretty much, said Pete. I'm saving some money. Before Grandma got sick, I was planning to leave.

—Is that right? Where were you going to go?

—West, said Pete. Out to the ocean. I thought I would figure it out from there. For now I just have to keep focused.

Lee felt an immense sense of strangeness with Pete, now that he'd met him and put a face to the name. It was not entirely comfortable but it was not as bad as Lee had expected it might be. Overall, it was just hard to believe that they were sitting side by side in a car all these years later.

—Was it sort of the same way for you? said Pete.

—Say what?

The kid was giving him a sidelong look, trying mostly to keep his eyes on the road as he drove.

—Staying focused. When you were . . . inside.

Lee thought about the question, and about the strange feeling he had sitting next to this kid. Nobody had ever asked him how he'd kept focused in prison. After a moment, he said: Well, there was this and that, I guess. The first couple of years it was all the wrong things. But later on I started looking in different places. I thought the Bible was okay. All that talk about lands of milk and honey sounded good. Create in me a clean heart and renew a right spirit in me. That's one of the Psalms.

—Yeah, I think I've heard that one, said Pete.

—I also had some dirty magazines. Those helped too.

They both laughed.

—There really wasn't all that much, said Lee. You've got to

get along with what you have. There was TV, which a lot of guys looked at, but I never cared for it. I thought a lot of the programs were bullshit.

—They mostly are.

Lee studied Pete's profile. He never would have believed it, but this was alright, riding along with Donna's son. This was alright. He had a fondness for the kid already.

—I haven't known you real long, said Lee. But I can see you're one of the good guys.

The job site was on the south shore of the lake, which was screened by a long, rocky point from the town waterfront. An orchard used to grow here and some of the apple trees remained yet, untended and straggling. A large cottage, four thousand square feet, was being built on the property. When Pete and Lee arrived, the building was just the framing and the roof and some sheathing. The ground was trampled mud. There were stacks of building material and a tall heap of half-inch crushed stone. A BobCat and two cars and two pickup trucks all stood in the driveway. Lee counted five men unloading tools. A wooden sign read MURRAY CUSTOM BLDG, CALL FOR ESTIMATE'S.

Pete parked behind the trucks. Lee got out and retrieved his tool belt from the trunk. From the back seat he took the lunch pail Donna had packed for him. Pete watched him.

—Do you know when you'll be done?

—No, said Lee. Anyhow I'll see if someone here can give me a lift back into town. Don't sweat it.

—Okay. Have a good day, Uncle Lee.

Lee's face quirked.

—Something wrong? said Pete.

Lee laughed. He said: How about, I'll call you Pete, and you call me Lee. There's no need for formal shit between the good guys.

—Okay. Lee.

Lee thumped his fist on the roof of the car. Pete gave him a little salute, rolled up his window, and drove away. Lee headed over to a man tying his bootlaces beside a truck.

—Are you Mr. Murray?

The man pointed to someone else, twenty feet away. He said: That's Clifton.

Clifton Murray was short and bowlegged, with curly red hair going grey. He held a pencil in his mouth and was frowning over an invoice. Lee crossed over and Clifton looked up, fixed him with a gnomish squint.

—Morning, Mr. Murray, said Lee. I'm Leland King.

Lee offered his hand. Clifton shook it once. He took the pencil, chamfered and moist, out of his mouth and said: Oh. Right.

—Thank you for the job. I've been looking forward to it since Barry told me.

—That's good. Pastor Barry might of told you this one: You will eat the labour of your hands, and happy will you be. So if hard work is something you like . . .

The man who'd been tying his bootlaces ambled by and said: Morning, Clifton.

—Good day, Jeff, said Clifton.

—Anyhow, said Lee. I got my trade. Cabinets, doors, all kinds of joining. You name it.

—Well, you can give Bud a hand getting the shingles up to the roof. I got 150 bundles that have to go up.

Fifty feet away was a gangly chap perhaps five years older than Pete. His hair was cut in a severe crewcut. He was hoisting a bundle of shingles from a stack onto his shoulder.

Clifton squinted at Lee.

—There a problem, mister man?

—No, said Lee. Just thought you needed a carpenter is all.

—I've got a carpenter. A darn good one. I subcontract out to him when I need to. Now what I need is those shingles on the roof.

—Okay.

Clifton spread his hands: Not five minutes you're here. I'm taking you on Pastor Barry's good word but I don't need any headache.

—No, sir. I'll get them shingles moving double-quick.

—That's better. Now. I don't allow profane language or idleness on my job site. You can smoke once an hour. Lunch is at noontime.

—Okay, Mr. Murray.

Lee started in the direction of the stack of shingles.

—Leland King!

Lee turned.

—A good thing to think about, said Clifton. Redeeming yourself doesn't happen all at once. One day at a time. Deeds, thoughts, prayer. That's from Pastor Barry and I believe it, every word.

Lee looked at the mud on the ground. He fingered the buckle of the tool belt on his shoulder. He found himself coming up against a depth of religious faith that he'd not expected. Clifton now, but also with his mother and with Barry and Donna. He should have expected it, he knew, given the letters Barry had written to him over the years. But knowing it from written letters, and finding it now in the world of free men, were two different things and he couldn't yet figure out what that difference might mean. There had been religion in prison, and it was on Barry's urging that Lee had sought guidance from the chaplain and had taken up reading the Bible. The chaplain, in turn, had spoken on Lee's behalf when his parole hearings eventually came around. But behind the cinder-block walls and the iron bars, the ideas of spiritual deliverance and a Kingdom of God had a much more basic appeal. Out here, it seemed somehow different. Less tangible. His mind coursed through a number of the bible verses he'd learned, but he couldn't seem to fix on one that might fit as a response to Clifton's comments. Clifton, for his part, had already gone back to examining the invoice.

Over at the stack of shingles, the gofer Clifton had indicated saw Lee coming. He flopped the bundle off his shoulder back onto the stack and he swaggered over to meet Lee halfway.

—I'm Bud, said the gofer.

—Hi, Bud. I'm Lee.

—I got to get these f-ing shingles up on the roof.

—I know. I'm here to help.

—F-ing A. Let's do this.

Bud had a small beer gut and lean muscles in his arms. He re-hoisted his bundle and carried it over to the building. An extendable ladder stood against the facer board along the edge of the roof. Lee looked around. He saw a big man gassing up the BobCat. Coming from inside the building were the hollow sounds of hammer-falls. Lee held his tool belt in his hands, considering it. Then he hid it between the top and bottom boarding of the skid beneath the stack of shingles.

He'd never done any kind of roof work. He lifted a bundle of shingles onto his shoulder and set out across the site. The mud sucked at his boots. He regarded the ladder dubiously. Overhead, Bud had disappeared onto the roof. Lee was nervous to climb the ladder with the shingles weighing heavily on his shoulder, but no other way was obvious, and Clifton was watching him, so he put his boots on the bottom rung and started up. The ladder flexed at the middle. He didn't like that much. Then Bud reappeared at the facer board to help him over the top and direct him to where he could lay the bundle across the peak of the roof. The roof was broad and pale, naked plywood, smooth enough that if the pitch were deeper it would be dangerous. Lee didn't care for it. He'd never even envied the guards in the penitentiary towers.

As the morning went on, bundle after bundle of shingles scraped Lee's shoulders raw. At one point, coming across the yard, he cut into the path of the BobCat. He heard the engine shift into neutral. The big man driving it leaned out of the housing and yelled: Anytime you want to get out of the way, okay?

Lee set his eyes forward and took another bundle up the ladder. Bud was there again, helping him over the top. Lee put the shingles down and stretched.

—Smoke break time, said Bud. You want a smoke?

—I'd have one, yeah.

Bud offered Lee a cigarette.

—Clifton doesn't like smoking, said Bud. He doesn't like drinking. Rick Flynn came to work hungover too many times and Clifton sacked him. You ask me, Clifton probably doesn't even like sex.

—Well, he's the boss. Long as he's got work for me, he doesn't have to like anything.

Lee passed smoke through his nose. Everything looked huge. The roof, the lake, the property around the building. The sky. The leaves on the trees had just started to change colour, but even this early contrast was vivid to his eyes. A flock of geese was traversing the sky out over the lake. All of this space, the colours, the autumn scent on the air. He closed his eyes and told himself the walls and bars were gone.

—Where you from, anyways? said Bud. Around here?

—I grew up here, yeah. Actually, when I was a kid I remember all this was just a bay. Me and a couple buddies used to catch steelhead out of season down here. There were some cabins out this way—you could rent them and whatnot—but there weren't any big motherfuckers like this one.

Bud darted a glance around and said: Clifton doesn't like swearing.

—Right. I forgot.

Bud grinned lewdly. He lowered his voice and said: Here's a good one. So the dick says to the rubber, Cover me, I'm going in!

—What?

—Oh. I mean, what does the dick say to the rubber? I frigged it up.

Bud shook his head briskly, as if to clear it of the frigged-up joke. Lee chuckled dryly. They finished their cigarettes and got back to the shingles.

When they broke for lunch, Lee went over to the skid to verify that his tool belt was still hidden. It irritated him to think of the dirt collecting on it. He then joined Bud and the others, who'd assembled themselves near the trucks and were sitting on building materials while they ate. Clifton wasn't around. Bud said he'd gone into town to see why a delivery was held up. Lee sat down and opened the lunch pail that Donna had packed. It contained a ham sandwich, an apple, a Thermos of tea, cookies wrapped in cellophane. He realized he had no idea what he would have eaten otherwise, and how he'd thought he could go the whole day on breakfast alone.

There were three men, not counting Clifton or Lee or Bud. Two of them looked much alike, brothers perhaps, maybe father and son. One of them was the man Jeff, whom Lee had seen tying his bootlace. He and his look-alike had a battery-powered radio sitting between them, and they had it set to a country station. Both of them were nodding to the music. Across from them, the BobCat driver was a big French guy. He was eating a chicken drumstick. If any of them knew who Lee was, they gave no sign of it. There wasn't much talk at all. Lee ate his lunch in minutes. Then he massaged his shoulder where the shingles had scraped it.

—Okay, said the French guy. You can move the shingles pretty good. But that don't mean you're strong or fast.

—What do you mean by that, said Lee.

The French guy grinned at him and said: I mean nobody wants all the good men to be held up because of the slow guy.

Did she mention my name, sang the radio. Lee stood up. He closed his lunch pail.

—I'm just here to work. I won't hold none of you up.

He carried off his lunch pail and found a tree at the edge of the property to urinate against. He was just bringing out his cigarettes when he saw a truck arriving, and then Clifton getting out.

Clifton clapped his hands and called out: Let's go, boys. We can't do it all in seven days, but we can try!

By two o'clock, Lee and Bud had moved most of the shingles up to the roof. They'd spaced them across the peak to distribute the weight. Then they heard someone hail them from below. They went over to the edge of the roof. Bud stood right at the drop, scratching his ass, and Lee hung back a few feet. It was the French guy calling to them.

They went down the ladder. The guy directed them to spread gravel into the driveway from the big mound of crush. Clifton was over measuring the foundation. He didn't seem to take any issue with this other man giving orders. Wordlessly, Bud went to fetch a wheelbarrow and shovels.

They spent the rest of the afternoon at the gravel. Lee wasn't aware quitting time had come until he looked around and saw the others packing up. Bud had gone off to piss somewhere.

Clifton waved to Lee and said: That's a day, mister man.

Bud and Lee stowed the shovels and the wheelbarrow against the wall of the building. The shadows had grown long and blue. Lee recovered his tool belt from under the skid and put it over his shoulder. He picked up his lunch pail and went to where the men were congregating at the trucks. Nobody had anything to say about the work that had been done that day, and to look at the building and the yard around it—other than the shingles having been moved—it was hard to see any difference since morning. Lee figured maybe with a project this big, you didn't see changes in the short term. You worked a day and then you worked the day after that, and only slowly did it all come together.

He cleared his throat and said: Could any of you give me a lift into town?

—Could always hitchhike, said the French guy.

—I suppose you don't have a vehicle, said Clifton.

Clifton scratched his neck. The two men who looked alike were over by their truck. The French guy was annotating his day's hours in a pocket notebook. All at once Lee felt helpless. Clifton squinted at him and looked like he was about to say something, but then Bud appeared, zipping up his fly.

He said: I'm goin' to town. You want a lift?

That evening, Lee was very sore. He'd stopped at the variety store downstairs to buy himself some provisions, and when he came upstairs, he packed himself a lunch in the lunch pail.

He could not remember when he'd last packed a lunch. For a time he'd lived in a halfway house in the city, working in a furniture shop, and he'd eaten every day from a truck that came around and sold submarine sandwiches. But this wasn't bad, packing a lunch. This was good. This seemed like the kind of thing you did when you had only yourself to look after and answer to.

Around eight o'clock there was a knock at his door. Mr. Yoon was in the hallway.

—How are you, said the landlord, flatly.

—I'm good, said Lee. Tired out. You know.

—You weren't here today.

—I was working. First day.

Mr. Yoon nodded and said: Is everything working here?

—Everything's working good.

—Okay.

After a moment Mr. Yoon nodded and left. Lee closed the door.

He got his tool belt and went back to the window, rubbing his sore shoulder. He sat there, watching the street. Indian summer evening—folks coming and going at the A&P across the way, a couple of high school kids acting like hoods on the street corner, boats out on the lake. While Lee watched, he cleaned the dirt from the tool-belt pouches and the hammer.

Bud had said he could drive him the next day as well, would pick him up in the morning. There was that. And it was good to be sore from a day of work, even if he couldn't see the progress at Clifton's job site the way he could see how a desk went together. It was good to not have much to think about at all.

Business was slow on Friday evening at the Texaco service station where Pete worked. The Texaco was on the highway bypass northeast of town. The sky above was turning dark and the night was going to be cool. Pete was sitting in a lawn chair, leaning back against the wall of the booth between the pumps, with a Louis L'Amour paperback—one of his Luke Short stories—open on his lap. A Ford Fairlane pulled in and drove over the bell-line and stopped at the pumps. Pete's co-worker Duane was at the edge of the parking lot, engrossed in conversation with a shift worker from the chemical factory, so Pete put his book down and got up from the chair.

He went over to the Ford. A thin old man, bald-headed, got out of the car and stretched and regarded Pete wearily.

—What'll it be, mister? said Pete.

—The unleaded, please. You folks have a washroom?

—Yes. Just go in the store and ask Caroline—she's at the cash-out—for the key.

The old man went into the store. Pete lifted the nozzle off the pump and pushed it into the Ford's gas tank. The smell of gasoline rose on the air.

—Working hard?

Pete was startled. He turned and saw a man of about forty who'd evidently been in the Ford's passenger seat. The man standing there did not appear to be all put-together. He had a wide grin and vacant eyes and sweatpants drawn high over his waist. He was wearing a baseball cap, but it didn't fully hide the edges of a scar near the top of his forehead. He was nodding his head in perpetual agreement.

—What can I say, said Pete. I'm keeping busy.

The man's head bobbed up and down. He laughed.

—And you? said Pete. Plans for the weekend?

—Oh, not me! I take it easy.

The old man reappeared from the washroom.

—For godsake, Simon. Get in the car.

Simon shuffled back to the passenger seat. Over his shoulder he told Pete not to work too hard.

—I'm sorry, said the old man. Sometimes he wanders away. It's frustrating.

—It's no trouble.

The old man didn't say anything. By way of something to break the quiet, Pete asked him if his car was the '79 Fairlane.

The old man blinked. He smiled, said: Yes, this is the '79. I was always a Ford man. I used to run a dealership. Do you have a car?

—I have a '73 Honda coupe I bought from my stepdad's friend. It gets me around. But I always wanted a Mustang.

The tank finished filling. Pete hung the nozzle on the pump.

—It'll be ten dollars.

The old man paid by credit card. As Pete took an imprint of the card, he caught sight of the man's name: *Arthur Grady.* Pete brought out a receipt and Arthur Grady signed it. He didn't leave immediately. He ran his hand along the roof of his car.

—I had a son who really loved the Thunderbird. The Bullet Bird, they called it. I bought him a 1961 brand new, the two-door with the hardtop and the 390. It was one of five I ever sold and I sold it to myself and I gave it to him when he turned eighteen. He'd made the first-round draft pick, see, and I didn't care what that car would set me back.

—How long did he have it?

—Not six months.

—Oh . . .

Arthur Grady flexed his mouth. He looked at the bypass and said: My son isn't with us any more. Anyhow, I apologize for taking up your time.

He got into the Fairlane. He pulled his door shut and started the ignition, but then he slid his window down and gestured to Pete. There was a smell of cigar smoke and leather upholstery. Simon, in the passenger seat, was fiddling with the radio. Without looking, the old man gently pushed Simon's hand away from the buttons.

—This is for you, said the old man.

He gave Pete a one-dollar tip. Pete thanked him. Arthur Grady slid his window up and started his car and drove back onto the bypass.

One by one the lights over the pumps came on. Duane had come back and was tapping Skoal tobacco out of a tin he kept in his pocket. He plugged the tobacco under his lip. He did this expertly, one-handed.

—Pete, man, I'm proud of you. You actually worked today.

Pete brushed past Duane and went into the store. At the cash-out, Caroline was working on a crossword puzzle. She smiled when she saw him. He brought her Arthur Grady's receipt and she put it in the ledger and then asked Pete if he wanted his paycheque. They went into the office. Caroline owned and managed the Texaco, and her office was small and neatly kept. She did not allow smoking. A geranium was potted on the windowsill. Caroline dug into the filing cabinet.

—That old man, said Pete. You know him?

—What old man?

—The bald guy that came in to get the key for the washroom.

—Him? I've seen him around, I think. Maybe. But I don't know him. Why?

—Just . . . kind of weird. Looked at me funny. Told me about his dead son.

—You'll hear all kinds of personal crap from people. Last week a woman in the store got real personal with me about her divorce.

All the legal details and so forth. Sometimes people just need other people to hear them. Even if it's just a stranger. You know?

Following his shift at the Texaco, Pete changed and got into his Honda. He picked up his friend Billy at a low-rise apartment building where Billy's older brother lived. Billy had a two-four of Labatt, which he toted around to the back of the car and put in the trunk. Then he came to the passenger side and got in.

—How's it hanging, Pete, said Billy. What time is it?

—It's seven, said Pete. A little after. What's the plan?

—We're going to church.

It must have been how Pete was looking at him. Billy grinned. He said: Music recital.

—What are you talking about?

—The girl I told you about, said Billy. Emily. She plays the piano.

Billy played piano across the dashboard.

—So we're going to church, said Pete. Jesus. I thought after I quit all that craziness at my stepdad's church that I wouldn't have to go any more.

—I'm being supportive is what I'm doing. It's what you have to do to keep the good ones.

—Okay . . . But if these people start talking in tongues, I'm leaving.

Pete had never been inside the United Church before. They parked across the street and they smoked a little bit of dope first. Then they went through a set of heavy oak doors and up a carpeted stairway into the church entryway. Pete was uncomfortably conscious of the hush around him. They found their way into the sanctuary and wandered between the empty pews. He did not quite know what to conclude about where he was. Galilee Pentecostal Tabernacle, where Barry preached, was an entirely modern building. The sanctuary at Galilee was almost like a concert hall or theatre. Here, in the church, the sanctuary was dimly lit and old-fashioned. It felt rigid, somehow.

Before long, a tight-browed woman in a beige pantsuit appeared behind them, wanting to know were they looking for somebody. They told her they'd come for the music recital. Billy added that they weren't there to steal bibles or anything. She gave them a doubtful look but she led them out of the sanctuary, past some offices, and finally to a banquet hall in the basement. There were four dozen classroom chairs arranged in the hall, facing a riser where a microphone and a piano and a music stand were arranged. Billy poked Pete in the ribs and pointed at the piano. Around them, most of the seats were already taken up. Families. Pete saw a mother holding a wad of Kleenex to her child's nose.

He and Billy took two of the seats at the rear.

—So where is she? said Pete.

—I don't know, she's here somewhere. She's small, man.

The woman in the pantsuit stepped onto the riser. She tapped the microphone and the scattered conversations around the hall went quiet. She said she was happy to welcome them to the September recital. The young musicians they were about to hear were all just really terrific. The three adjudicators were members of the regional board of the Christian Musicians Association, whose mission, for those who didn't know, is service to the Lord through good deeds, good words and musical talent. After the introductory remarks, an elderly woman in thick orthopaedic shoes came onto the riser and sat at the piano.

—So that's your girl, said Pete.

A man a few seats up turned around and looked at them over the top of his glasses.

The first performer was a girl of about fourteen. To the pianist's accompaniment, she played the flute—six or seven minutes of what they had been told was a concertino. She was very good. Next up was an adolescent boy who was indelicately carrying a violin and a bow. He was trembling and grinning frantically. The old pianist led him in with a slow piece. Pete thought he remembered it from the term of music class that he'd taken, but he couldn't recollect the name. Something by Bach or Mozart or some other long-dead composer. The boy drew the bow across the violin strings and a dreadful squeal of sound came forth.

—Oh shit, said Billy.

The boy shook, struggling through the piece. Every note cut like glass. Heads about the room lowered and people studied the floor.

—If I had my .22 here, I'd put him out of his misery.

—Shut up, Billy.

When the boy finished, he held his violin in one hand and the bow in his other hand and bowed stiffly from the waist. People applauded politely. A fat woman in a paisley dress stood up and clapped with furious resolve and looked around grimly. The boy ran off the riser and took the seat next to her.

Billy poked Pete in the ribs. He was gesturing.

A girl was standing up from one of the seats near the front. She was small. Pete could see nothing of her face. She walked with her back straight and her dark hair in a simple cascade, catching the light, down her shoulders. She had to tap the old pianist on the shoulder. The pianist gaped at her, startled, and then exited the riser. The girl sat down on the bench.

—What do you think? said Billy.

—What do I think? I think she looks respectable.

—I know. Wait till you meet her.

The girl's hands hovered over the keys for a moment, as if she was collecting herself, and then her hands moved down and she began to play. The tempo of the piece quickened, slackened, quickened again. She was playing from memory for there was no sheet music before her. Pete thought he could listen to the piece for a long time. Maybe it was the dope they'd smoked but maybe it was something more. He thought how not every feeling should be explained away. And when the girl had finally finished playing, and people were clapping, he was aware that it was over.

The girl traded off with the old pianist again. Two more acts followed, forgotten as soon as they finished, and then came the intermission.

They hung around the corridor outside the banquet hall and Billy told Pete about how he'd met the girl. There were three high schools in town. There was a small Catholic French high school called Sacré Coeur. There was Northside Secondary, where Pete had gone before he'd quit, and where most of the out-of-town kids came by bus. And there was Heron Heights, in town, where Billy said Emily had just started grade twelve. Billy had been at Heron Heights with the Northside lacrosse team, playing an exhibition game, the first of the season. He said he'd noticed Emily sitting with her friends in the stands nearby. After the game, Billy had thought she'd gone, but later, when he was coming out of the change room, he saw her in the corridor. He said he'd gone up and talked to her a little bit, and since then they'd been on a couple of dates. He was agreeable with just about everybody, but he was bold as well. Pete envied much about him.

—Hey, you.

They turned and saw her coming towards them. She walked with cool poise.

—That was great, said Billy. The piano playing. I didn't have any idea you could do that.

—Thank you. I practised that one for a long time. I didn't think you were coming. If I'd known you were here, I might have been nervous.

She reached out and took Billy's hand, then asked if he was going to introduce her to his friend.

—This is Pete.

—Hey, Pete. I'm Emily Casey.

—Hey, said Pete. What kind of music was that?

—It was a waltz, said Emily. Chopin.

—Well whatever, said Billy. It was great as hell. Anyway, when you're done here, you want to come with us? We've got a case of beer in the car.

—I can't, said Emily. I'm here with my family. But I've got some time in the week. And next weekend my friend Nancy might have some people over.

They would have talked more but just then a man appeared in the corridor behind them, some distance away. He was a slim man. Collared shirt and tie. The man was simply standing there, not moving towards them, but all the same Pete felt himself scrutinized. He occupied himself by examining some outreach tracts in a rack on the wall.

—Emily, said the man.

She gave the man a little wave, turned back to Billy, and said: That's my dad.

—The cop, said Billy, his voice low enough that Emily's father couldn't hear him.

—Yes. Anyway, call me.

She withdrew as coolly as she'd arrived, going through the doors of the banquet hall with them watching her, and her father watching them.

The case of Labatt made a full revolution of locations before it was opened. They ended up back at Billy's brother's apartment, where they smoked more dope and drank beer. Billy and his brother sat on the couch with their guitars and spent some time disagreeing over what song to play. Billy's brother had married just out of high school. His wife was watching television and didn't pay attention to Pete or Billy or even Billy's brother.

The hours passed and the beers got fewer. Pete went out on the balcony to get some air. The lights of town winked up at him, unchanging. Pete thought about the old bald man, Grady—or was it Gardy?—who'd come to the gas station earlier that night, with his one idiot son in the car and his talk of his other son, lover of Thunderbirds, long dead. Pete thought also of Emily, cool and collected, seated at the piano in the silent instant before she played.

Stan's cronies usually convened at Western Autobody & Glass a couple of times each week. The sign over the bay doors read FAMILY OWNED AND OPERATED SINCE 1934. Huddy Phillips, who'd opened the garage himself, had signed it over to his son Bob five years ago, but Huddy and the other old-timers still got together in the adjoining office to swap their stories. They stood around, drinking coffee, talking at length, sometimes talking over each other, often repeating tales they'd all told many times before.

—. . . I say if all them sons of bitches want to go their own way they can take everything east of the Ottawa River and go, is what I say, you know I was chums with Black Jack Stewart when we were young lads, turns out that chap she was going with was a queer, and they can take Trudeau with them when they go . . .

—Nothing is the same as it used to be, by Christ, said Huddy.

He sat under an official photograph of the 1959 Royal Tour, the Queen and her husband walking along a path beside Lake Louise. The photograph hung slightly crooked, and Stan could not look at it without wondering if the Queen had ever seen the inside of a place like Western Autobody, and what she might think if she had.

Dick Shannon filled two cups from the coffee maker. He was fifty-six years old, which put him much younger than the others, but he'd been married thirty-five years to the youngest sister of Bill Norman, who was one of the other old-timers hanging around the garage. Dick had been partnered with Stan at the local detachment for many years. He did not have long to go before he retired, but today he was uniformed and a marked patrol car was parked outside.

Stan was leaning beside a window into the service bay, watching one of the mechanics pump transmission fluid into an import. There'd been talk about the dead girl. He knew that. The circumstances of the discovery had not been published in the newspaper when the story broke last week, but word had got out quickly as to who'd found her. Stan had heard that her body was only now coming back from the coroner, so that a funeral could be held.

Dick brought Stan one of the cups of coffee. They listened to the gossip around them.

—Ferris's delivery truck, said Huddy.

—That old Chevy, said Bill.

—You don't know anything. It was a goddamn Ford. Panel built on the passenger chassis.

—How's the house? said Dick.

—It's standing, said Stan. It always needs this or that but I'd say it's got more winters to stand than I do.

—Word is that Frank and Mary might move out there.

—Maybe. Not just yet. I talked to them about taking it in a few years. It's been in the family a long time.

—I'll come out and visit soon.

—Anytime. I don't hide the whisky bottles any more.

They drank their coffee in silence. Then Huddy reached up and tugged Stan's sleeve. He said: Stanley, that gal.

—What gal.

—That gal they found out there, dead in her car. That gal was one of Aurel Lacroix's daughters, wasn't she?

Dick cleared his throat and examined his knuckles. Bill Norman and the other men in the office became quiet.

—Yes, said Stan. That's right.

—Aurel Lacroix, Christ Almighty.

—

On the evening before the girl's funeral, Stan went to the viewing. It was held at the unremarkable municipal mortuary. Light came from brass sconces on the wall and there were watercolours of nature scenes. He signed the guest book in the foyer. His good suit had been tailored of cashmere wool many years before. Now it was loose in the chest and shoulders. The last time he'd worn it was when his wife, Edna, died two years ago.

Judy Lacroix lay in a closed casket of varnished pine with autumn wildflowers arranged on the bier around her. There were twenty to twenty-five people in attendance, but Judy's only living immediate relative was her twin sister, Eleanor, not quite thirty years old. Their mother and father were no longer living, and their father's brothers had died before they'd had the chance to make any families of their own. Stan had never known a family more marked by loss. He saw Eleanor speaking to two well-wishers. It gave him an eerie sense to see Judy's twin sister here in the room, living, speaking, when the last time he'd seen that identical face, it had been frozen in dismay in the back of a car.

He went up to the casket and stood by for a respectful pause and then he stepped back.

—Thank you for coming.

Stan turned and saw that Eleanor had come to him. Her hand was extended. He shook it.

—I knew your family, said Stan. I knew you when you were just little girls. I suppose you hear that all the time, about how somebody knew you when you were yay old.

Eleanor looked at him steadily. Her eyes were bloodshot.

—It's the kind of thing you hear when you grow up.

He didn't think she recognized him.

—I'm sorry for your loss, said Stan. Your sister was a fine young woman.

She nodded her thanks. Stan directed a final look at the casket. Then he went back into the corridor and out into the twilight.

Across from the mortuary was a small trucking company. Three rigs were parked beneath a bright spotlight. Stan got into his truck and put his hands on the steering wheel. He hoped that the visitation would be the end of it.

It was raining when Lee woke for work, and he was soaked by the time he got to the Owl Café. He took the stool at the end of the counter. Over the last two weeks, the stool had more or less become his place.

The time had gone by quickly. He'd seen his mother and Donna and Barry just once. He wanted to see them more, especially his mother, but it was hard to get out to where they lived—and for all he'd had to come home to help his mother, she seemed to be taken care of, as much as she could be.

And it was not as if Lee's return did not cause his family some upset, especially Donna. He knew it. But given enough time, perhaps a month or two more, maybe he'd find his place with them. They just needed to see what he could do now, what he could make of himself.

Last week, he'd had a meeting with his parole officer, a foppish little man named Wade Larkin. They'd met in a room in the new municipal offices and all Larkin asked was how was work going and was Lee staying sober and had he had any run-ins with the police. Some girl in town had killed herself, right around the time Lee came back—the girl had made the news—and Larkin wanted to confirm that she was nobody Lee knew. She wasn't, Lee told him. Larkin said that was good, and made a note of it, and that concluded their meeting. They wouldn't have to meet again until next month. Larkin had given Lee his card with instructions to call right away if he got into any kind of trouble.

Helen came down along the counter with a mug of coffee and took his order.

—Give me your Thermos, Brown Eyes. I'll fill it up.

She took his order to the wicket and she filled his Thermos from a coffee maker behind the counter. Lee was chilled from the wet. He lit a cigarette.

He had just finished his breakfast when he saw Bud's car outside. The headlights were dense through the rainfall. Lee paid his bill.

—See you next time, said Helen.

Lee got up and took his lunch pail and tool belt. He went over to the door. Then he stopped. He went back to the counter. Helen looked at him and he gestured for her to come over.

—Something wrong?

—No, nothing's wrong. Look. My name is Lee.

—Okay, Lee. But I might keep calling you Brown Eyes, because of your pretty brown peepers.

—Your name is Helen. It's on your shirt there.

She smiled. Lee put his hand to the back of his neck.

—Anyways, I wondered if you'd want to get dinner.

—Sounds like a date you're asking me on, said Helen.

—A date. Yeah.

—There's a rule where I'm not supposed to go on dates with customers.

—Oh.

—But I don't really care about rules. So yes, Brown Eyes Lee. I would love to have dinner with you. Meet me tonight. Seven-thirty at Aldo's.

He was surprised that she'd named the place—wasn't that his to figure out?—but he supposed it was just one more thing that had changed while he'd been away. He said: That's the Italian place downtown?

—That's right.

She smiled. Lee stood back from the counter.

—Okay, said Lee. Seven-thirty.

—Rain before seven quits before eleven, said Bud. Just you watch.

Bud was correct. The crew sat in their vehicles for an hour but by eight o'clock the rain had tapered down. The air was cold and damp and Lee was glad to start moving his body again.

The big cottage was assuming form. The shingles had all been laid. They'd done that through some sunny days when the tar was soft and the flashing was almost too hot to touch. The sheathing had been house-wrapped and taped. Lee had never met the owners. He'd only heard speculation on their wealth. He did not even know their names. The bathroom on the second floor was bigger than two cells in the penitentiary put together.

Of late he was not having any dreams he could remember, and that was a relief. He would get up early and go to the café for breakfast and make small talk with Helen. Bud would pick him up and they'd head to the job site.

He was getting to know the crew. The two framers were father and son, Jeff and Jeff Junior. They would sing country standards, Buck Owens and Hank Snow tunes. They would work quickly to frame the walls and Lee and Bud would often have to trail behind them, moving studs a half-inch to the left or right before re-spiking them. The French guy's name was Sylvain. He was a subcontracted landscaper who'd worked with Clifton many times before and he was there to grade the property. He behaved with a kind of jovial hostility, and he would grin and ask Lee and Bud if they were extra lazy today, boys, or what? Clifton himself would move around the site with the sole purpose, it seemed, of wringing his hands and looking at his watch. He would invoke larger forces or biblical passages when any of the men appeared to be dawdling: Idleness! You-know-who likes to take advantage of idleness. I'm telling you for your own good.

By late morning Lee and Bud were both black with muck. They were in the midst of digging a drainage ditch around the foundation. Their hourly cigarette break came. Bud straightened up and stretched.

—This is a good one. A guy goes to see a doctor because his dick is orange, and the doctor says has he been eating Cheezies, and . . . Wait. No. It's what he tells the doctor. At the end. I frigged it up.

Bud gave his head the same brisk shake that Lee had seen the first time, and then shot him a hapless look. Lee just grinned, and they ground out the butts of their cigarettes and got back to work.

Clifton stayed for lunch that day. Conversation was usually muted when he was around. Clifton said that he hadn't seen any of them out at Galilee Tabernacle yet. The doors were always open. They could take their time, of course, but they ought not to take too much time. This Clifton said happily. God's patience runs out once you're at the gates. Then he looked at Lee and said: And how about you?

—How about me?

—I haven't seen you at Galilee. I figured you'd be front row centre, what with Pastor Barry being your brother-in-law and all that.

—Well, I'll get out there one of these days.

Clifton nodded, said: I'll be watching for you. You're getting along in town?

—Yeah. Matter of fact, I got a date with a gal tonight.

Lee was immediately sorry he'd said it. He didn't know why, except that it felt like he'd given something away. He looked at his hands.

—Is that so, said Clifton.

—Is she doing community service by going with you? said Sylvain.

Lee did not reply. He didn't know what to make of Sylvain, whether or not the man was a prick by nature or was just laying track with him, or if he even had bad blood with Lee from the distant past. It was possible, more so than he cared to consider. All he could think to do was to ignore the man's comments.

—Just you make sure you're up and at it for work tomorrow, mister man, said Clifton, digging at his teeth with a toothpick.

Later that afternoon, while Lee and Bud were digging, Bud said: You were in jail, were you?

—Yeah. I was.

—A long time.

—That's right.

Bud looked up from his shovel. He smiled.

—I knew. F-ing A. But you don't have to talk about nothing if you don't want to.

—I'm glad you say so.

Bud looked at him once more, then bent back to his work. It was okay. Lee liked Bud. Most of the time Bud stayed quiet. When they were on a smoke break or in the car he'd tell his jokes, or he'd talk about hockey or how he couldn't get his wife to go to bed with him unless he gave her jewellery.

The dirt they were digging was heavy from the rain. There were roots they had to carve through, and in places the soil over the bedrock was not deep. He'd drive the shovel blade down with his boot and feel it stop hard against rock.

—You been out for long? said Bud.

—Not real long. I was in the city for six months. I was on day release at a St. Leonard's Society house. I worked in a shop that built office furniture.

—And you're back up here in town for your ma? She's sick?

—She's got lung cancer.

—That's an f-ing drag. Same as that kid.

—Kid?

—That one-legged kid who tried to run across the country, Terry Fox.

—Oh yeah, said Lee. I heard of him.

—They say he's got tumours this big.

Bud made circles with his thumbs and forefingers and put them on his chest.

—Can you imagine that?

—No, said Lee. I see what's happening to my ma and I can't imagine nothing.

—Me neither. Hey, it's three o'clock. Let's have a smoke.

That evening Peter came by to bring Lee some leftovers Donna had sent. When Lee told him he was going on a date, Pete stayed to help him dress for it.

—You don't have anything other than jeans?

—No. I was at Woolworths on Saturday to get some new clothes. What you see in the closet. But I didn't think to buy nothing fancy.

Lee stood in his bathroom with the door open. He was wearing his undershorts and undershirt and he was shaving. Aqua Velva hung in the air. Pete selected a clean pair of jeans and a collared shirt and laid the clothes on the armrest of the couch.

—So who is she? said Pete.

Lee came out of the bathroom, patting his face with a towel.

—Her name's Helen. She works at the Owl Café. I see her most days when I go for breakfast. I'm taking her to the Italian joint up near the town hall.

—The town hall?

—The library. Used to be the town hall. I keep forgetting how they went and changed everything around. Anyhow, the Italian joint.

—Aldo's.

—That's the one.

Pete looked at the clothes again.

—Okay, well, I think you'll be good in these. We're not in Paris or anything.

Lee started to dress. He lit a cigarette.

—Do you smoke?

—No, said Pete. I never really took to it.

—Fair enough . . . You look like you got something on your mind, Pete.

—I was wondering something. But I don't know how to ask it.

—Why don't you just ask it straight? You don't have to talk careful around me.

—Well, have you ever really had a girlfriend before?

—What makes you think I don't have hundreds of girlfriends all over the place?

—I guess—

—Relax. I'm just hassling you. It's a pretty fair question, a guy like me who's been locked up forever. When I was a young buck there was a girl in town I went with pretty regular. We might of got more serious if I never went up. Then there was a lady who wrote me letters for awhile, maybe six, seven years ago. A church group put us in touch and for awhile she wrote to talk about God.

Lee was grinning.

—What happened with her? said Pete.

—I guess you're not so young I can't say this—this lady wrote to me about God at first, and then she started sending me snapshots of herself in her underpants. She was a big gal. She was a big big gal. She sent me these kinds of sexy snapshots for awhile, and then she stopped.

—Just like that?

—Just like that. It was another couple months before I heard from her again. It wasn't real surprising. She'd met a guy and she said she felt like God wanted them to get married. So that's what they did. I don't hold nothing against her.

—You didn't see anybody when you were living in the city?

—I was conditional in the city. I had to go back to the house every night. But there was a girl I'd go see sometimes, at lunch or maybe in the afternoon . . . Anyhow, that was kind of a business deal. You know?

—For sure.

Lee buckled his belt and said: How about you? Are you Sylvester the Cat?

—Not really. There was one I just met. She was pretty interesting. She goes to another high school, so I didn't know her before I quit. She plays the piano.

—Go show her a good time.

—It's not like that. She's . . . a friend. Maybe. That's what I think it is. It's not a problem. I'm not sticking around here much longer anyway.

Lee went back into the bathroom and ran a comb through his hair. He slapped on some more of the Aqua Velva.

—Think I look okay?

—Sure you do, said Pete. I'll give you a ride up.

—You don't need to do that.

—I don't mind. I like driving. I'm cut out for a long road trip.

Outside, the clouds had dissolved and there was a bright quarter-moon some distance above the horizon. They got into Pete's car and drove up to the restaurant. Not far away, up River Street, the limestone face of the library was lit by floodlights on the lawn. This was new. Across the street, Lee could see where his father's general store used to be. It looked like it had been turned into a place that sold household appliances.

—See that place? said Lee.

—What, the place where they have the washing machines in the window?

—Yeah. That was the place where your granddad used to have his store. Right there. I remember sweeping up and mopping the floor when I was a little kid.

—Grandma doesn't ever talk about him, said Pete.

—No, he's been dead a long time. Most of my life. He worked way too hard, was his problem. Now look at what they got there. Washing machines and vacuum cleaners and TVs. I'll tell you what, Pete. One of these days I'm going to walk in there and buy myself a TV.

—I thought you didn't like TV, said Pete.

—I don't. But I sure as hell like the idea of being able to walk into a store and buy one. One of these days. Hey, I'll see you soon, buck.

Lee got out of the car.

—Lee . . . , said Pete.

Pete was holding something out. Lee looked more closely and saw that it was forty dollars.

—What's this?

—I figured you might not have a credit card and maybe you don't have a lot of cash on you. This isn't the cheapest place.

—I don't need your money, Pete.

—It's, like, a loan. Pay me back later. It's no problem.

Lee set his teeth together, shifted them side to side. But he lifted his hand and took the kid's money.

Helen was already inside the restaurant, sitting at the bar, having a cigarette. She was wearing a dark jacket, a short skirt. She smiled as Lee walked up to her. Her lips were painted vivid red and her hair was puffed up big.

—It's the lady who's supposed to be fashionably late.

—You're right, said Lee. Goddammit. I'm sorry.

She laughed and tapped ash off her cigarette. He looked at how her legs showed in the skirt.

—Don't worry about it, Brown Eyes. Let's sit.

They took a table by the window. The interior of the restaurant was candlelit and only a few of the tables were occupied. A steward came to show them the wine list and to ask them about drinks.

—I'll have a Tom Collins, said Helen.

—For yourself, sir?

—Do you have Coca-Cola? said Lee.

—Yes, sir. We have Coca-Cola.

—That's what I'd like, boss.

The steward left them.

—I quit drinking, said Lee.

—So, you have some self-discipline, said Helen.

—Maybe I just wouldn't know what kind of fancy drink you'd get here.

—Never mind these guys. It's all for show. I'm sure I saw that same waiter at the mall in a pair of sweatpants.

They studied their menus. She made quiet hmms of consideration. Finally Lee put the menu down and pushed it away.

—What're you smiling at?

—Nothing, said Lee.

—Tell me.

He felt something brush against his ankle. It took him a moment to conclude that it had been her foot.

—Well, I think I'm in over my head. This is a nice place. But I don't know what the hell any of this stuff is.

She laughed loudly. She leaned over the tablecloth and touched his hand and said: You're an interesting one, Lee.

When the waiter came, Lee figured he'd follow Helen's lead. She opted for the prix fixe—a salad to start, a baked pasta with bacon and mushrooms for the main course, a slice of chocolate cake for dessert. The sequence seemed elaborate. Lee couldn't predict what would happen if he asked for a cheeseburger or a fried steak. Helen looked across at him and told him he might like the ravioli. He told the waiter he'd have the ravioli.

—Everybody likes ravioli.

—I was twenty-five the first time I ever ate spaghetti, said Lee.

They had some cigarettes. She finished her drink and was moving the ice in the glass.

—Tell me about you, Brown Eyes. What do you do after I see you for breakie every morning?

—I'm a tradesman. Carpentry. Windows, doors. Cabinets. Joining. You name it.

—But you haven't been doing that real long, have you? At least not here in town.

—What makes you say that?

—You've got a certain aura around you, said Helen. I'm good at sensing these things. I'm real spiritual. It's what you get with a Pisces like me.

—Well, okay. But what about you? You got a story outside the café?

—Oh my. I'm just an old soul, Brown Eyes. I just keep on keeping on.

She laughed again.

Her salad came and she ordered another drink. Lee went to the washroom. It occurred to him that she might be gone by the time he returned, that certain truths were evident no matter what, and that she need only to wait for an opportunity to slip out undetected. But she was still there when he came back, and he started to feel good.

They were into their suppers. He liked the ravioli and he liked the way she was smiling. She talked in a rambling fashion and came round eventually to where she'd started out, which was a mid-sized town in the south part of the province. She'd done a year or two of college, had quit to travel with some Hare Krishnas, and had at last ended up back in the big city. Where the action was, the city.

—The city, said Lee. Yeah. I lived there for awhile too. Right up till the end of the summer. That's a hell of a place. All kinds of action. Sirens all night long. I never thought of myself as ending up there, but I guess it's funny how it goes. Where you end up. Anyhow, if you were down there, how'd you end up here?

—Oh, the way karma plans things for you, you know.

She'd had four drinks by the time the dessert arrived. Her face was flushed. She carved a piece of cake and offered it to him on her fork. The waiter brought the bill and it ate up all the money Peter had loaned Lee and five dollars from his wallet besides.

—Where to now, Brown-Eyed Lee?

—I don't know. We could get a cup of coffee.

—Or you could show me where you live.

—Sure.

—You don't sound sure.

—I am sure, said Lee.

—I know. But you don't have a car.

—No . . .

She stood up from the table, weaving a little, and told the waiter to call them a taxi. Then she took Lee's arm and led him out of the restaurant. The sidewalk outside was quiet. She put a cigarette in her mouth and Lee lit it for her.

—You were in prison, weren't you, said Helen. You were a jailbirdie.

—How did you know?

—It's your aura. It's strong. I like it. Are you strong?

He smiled, still feeling good, and he rubbed at a spot on the pavement with the toe of his boot. He said: Am I strong? I don't know. I guess I'm no slouch.

A taxi came. The same cabbie who'd driven Lee out to Donna's house was behind the wheel. He ogled Helen. Lee told the cabbie where his place was. Helen pulled him into the back of the car and sat as close to him as she could. He could feel her nails on his thigh through his jeans. He put his arm around her and touched the big shape of her hair. She bit his ear and grinned.

When they got out at the variety store she came right out and asked him. He laughed.

—You don't ask anybody what they did, said Lee. You just ask them how long they're in for.

—Why is that?

—Because. It's just how it is. Most guys didn't do it, right? Like, they'll run their mouths about a lot of other things they did, or things they could do, but whatever they're in for, they didn't do that.

—So how long were you in for?

—Twenty years was what I was supposed to do. I got out conditional after seventeen.

—And? Did you not do whatever they said you did?

—No, said Lee. I did exactly what they said I did. But that was a long time ago.

Upstairs in his apartment, he told her he didn't have a drink to offer her.

—That's fine. I'm going to powder my nose.

—Say what?

—I'm going to use your washroom, Brown Eyes.

She was in there for a minute and she came out smelling strongly of perfume and she was on him quickly. She pushed him down and lowered herself onto his lap. The short skirt was bunched up and he had his hands on her big thighs and on the elastic of her underpants. She pushed her tongue into his ear.

—Let's see. Let's see just how strong you are.

He tore at the blouse she was wearing and then turned her against the couch and took her.

Afterwards, they lay together on the pullout. She lifted one leg up and flexed the toes.

—Oh my oh my.

He considered what he could see of the ceiling. He lit two cigarettes, gave her one.

—In the city you lived downtown, said Helen.

—I did, yeah.

He wasn't accustomed to talking about himself. What he was used to, for the most part, was the way people talked around what they wanted to know. But he told her what he had the words for. When he'd been conditionally paroled, he was moved into a halfway house on Sherbourne Street. From the outside you wouldn't be able to tell anything about it. It was a big house. It had a board fence around it, and there was an intercom at the front, and the gate locked electronically. There were twelve beds in six rooms. It was run by the St. Leonard's Society. The St. Leonard's people got Lee fixed up with a job at a shop that made office furniture. Lee did the woodworking. The man that ran the place was also an ex-con, twelve years out. Clean and sober. He had given a lot of jobs to people like Lee and he'd seen more than a few of them fuck everything up.

Helen was quiet. Then she said, slowly: Do you like what you do?

—Yeah. That's what I'm proud of. I make things. I see them come together.

A moment or two later, Helen was asleep. Her hand was on her chest and the cigarette she'd been smoking was burning down between her fingers. Lee took it carefully and dropped both hers and his into an empty cola bottle on the floor beside the couch.

He'd never been sure what he was going to do after his conditional release. He didn't care for the city all that much but he'd been told he could stay on at the furniture shop if he kept straight. He'd figured that was about as good as it was going to get, but then in July Barry came down to the city to visit. He'd never actually met Barry until then, he'd just known him from the letters they'd written back and forth. Those last few years it was Barry who had written the most and in early July it was Barry who came down to the city to tell Lee that his mother was dying.

The St. Leonard's people put in a recommendation to the parole board. The man who ran the furniture shop put in a good word. Barry found Lee work with Clifton Murray. And by Labour Day, Lee was on the bus going north. Homeward.

Lee felt good at the job site the next day. Just before noontime, Clifton called him over to his truck and gave him an envelope.

—There you go.

—What's this? said Lee.

—It's not a birthday card, Leland. It's your paycheque.

—Oh.

He opened it and took it out and looked at it. There was the cheque itself and a balance sheet of statutory deductions. He studied the numbers.

—Were you thinking I'd pay under the table? said Clifton. Because I won't. It's just not worth the headache.

—Like in the Bible, right? You have to give to Caesar what's his too.

—Well. It's just not worth the headache to muck around.

—Good with me, Mr. Murray. Everything above-board. That kind of thing keeps my parole officer happy.

—Yes, well.

—I'll get back to it, said Lee.

It rained that evening. Pete drove to the pizza joint over by the hospital. His work clothes were stuffed in a backpack in the trunk of his car beside a case of beer. He'd changed into jeans and a T-shirt and a jacket.

—There's my main man, said Billy.

Billy and Emily had a booth inside the restaurant. With them was a girl Emily introduced as Nancy. Nancy did not have the same poise as Emily, but she had an appealing nature. She laughed a lot. She and Billy did most of the talking.

They had pizza and frosted glasses of root beer. Conversation at the table threaded frenetically with Billy and Emily on one side and Pete and Nancy sitting across from them. Nancy talked with her hands almost as much as she laughed. Pete caught Emily's eye and she made a face at him. Billy's arm hovered over her shoulders.

—Billy said you quit school, said Nancy.

—Yeah, said Pete. Last May.

—The system doesn't trust guys like Pete, said Billy.

Nancy shook her head. She said how wild that was, Pete quitting school. Pete happened to catch Emily's eye. Her expression was mild and neutral, but all the same he reached up and scratched the back of his neck. He said: I was thinking I might go to community college at some point. I don't know.

He didn't say anything about his plans to head out west.

They had the rest of the pizza and sent for the bill. Nancy's folks were away for the weekend and she was having friends over to her house that night. She and Emily got up to go to the washroom and Billy winked at Pete as soon as they were alone.

—She's nice, said Pete.

—Sure she is. You bet.

The bill came and Billy burrowed about for his wallet until Pete put the cash down. The girls returned. Nancy came back and slipped into the booth beside Pete.

—Are you going to come to my house? I think you should.

—She thinks you should, Pete, said Emily.

Pete might have guessed there'd be trouble if he and Billy went to Nancy's house, school loyalty being what it was. By eleven o'clock, there were twenty people at the party, all of them from Heron Heights. Shortly after eleven a small group of guys arrived. They were all solidly built athletes. The biggest of them was six feet tall, and it wasn't so much that he was good-looking—he just had presence in the room. When he took off his jacket, he was wearing a Heron Heights varsity lacrosse T-shirt underneath. The air got tense.

Until that point it wasn't a bad scene. The house was nice—much bigger than the house where Pete lived—and there was lots to drink. He didn't know any of these people, except for Billy and

Nancy and Emily, and he was grateful just to take it all in. He spent a lot more time in Nancy's company than he'd predicted he would, given how it usually seemed to go for him when it came to girls. He'd noticed a picture of her on the wall: an ice rink, a figure-skating pose for the camera, a glittery outfit, thick stage makeup. He asked her about the picture and saw how she lit up. They sat on a couch in the living room and she told him how she volunteered as a coach when she wasn't training, how she'd gone to the nationals, was going again this spring. As she talked, Pete looked around. There were no crosses on the wall, and there was none of the medical equipment needed to keep an old woman alive. Nancy touched his leg. She asked him if he wanted another drink.

After a few more beers, Billy sat on the living room carpet with Nancy's father's Yamaha acoustic. He took requests. People sang. They opened the window and a joint made its way around. Emily sat beside Billy. She wasn't singing but she was watching Billy, smiling.

That was when the lacrosse player and his boys arrived. They came into the house bearing a couple cases of beer.

—Oh, said Nancy. I didn't know if you guys were coming.

—We got back from the tournament and heard you were having people over.

—Come in, then.

The athlete and his boys stood between the front door and the kitchen.

—Hey, Emily, said the lacrosse player.

Emily looked up at him. The guy smiled.

Pete guessed that the latecomers would put themselves in the living room, but they didn't. They disappeared elsewhere in the house a few minutes after they'd come in. A short while later Billy took a break from the guitar. He stood up and helped Emily to her feet. He weaved over and whacked Pete's arm.

—I've got to piss.

—No sense keeping it all bottled up, said Pete.

Billy went on his way. Emily approached.

—Are you having a good time, Pete?

—Sure, your friends are fun.

—Don't pay any attention to those guys who just got here. The big guy, his name is Roger. I think he's finding it hard to move on from certain things.

—It's okay.

Then Emily was gone. Her perfume hung behind her. Pete went to the washroom. When he was coming out he happened to look down the hallway. He saw Emily leaning against the wall, Billy in front of her. Laughing, both of them, her with her hand to her mouth.

Pete went down the hallway away from them. Then someone hailed him from a small den. It was the lacrosse player and his boys and a couple of girls. They were sitting around drinking, shoes propped up on a coffee table. Pete stepped into the den. They looked at him.

—So who are you, anyways?

—I'm Pete. I'm a friend of Nancy's.

The athlete put out his lower lip. He said: Pete, Pete. Pete Pete Pete. Okay.

Just then Pete heard the guitar strike up in the living room again. He heard voices starting to sing along.

—I'm going to have to talk to Emily, said the lacrosse player.

—I know you, said one of the others. You work at the gas station on the bypass.

The boys in the den laughed.

—I'm going to get a beer, said Pete.

He was trying to think of something to say, some sharp retort, but he couldn't think of anything. He was sweating under his shirt. As he turned away from the doorway into the den, he heard the lacrosse player saying: What the fuck is she doing with these . . .

Pete went into the kitchen to get a beer from the fridge. Two girls were talking at the table. Liquor bottles stood on the counter and paper cups oozed bad mixes. Pete opened a beer and went back into the living room. Nancy was standing near the kitchen entryway. She smiled when she saw him. She was sweating a little bit and it gave a high clear edge to her perfume. Everybody was singing the chorus to "Hey Jude" while Billy played, and Emily was sitting beside him again. They came to the end of the song and Billy plucked a final note from the strings.

—You guys are great, said Billy.

But then the lacrosse player and one of his friends appeared at the edge of the crowd.

—Hey, Emily, said the athlete. I want to talk to you for a couple minutes.

Emily gave him a serene look, told him no thanks. He made an O-shape with his mouth. Under other circumstances, it might have looked funny.

—I want to talk to you.

—I don't feel like talking right now, Roger.

—Emily.

—Hey, man, said Billy. She doesn't feel like talking right now.

—Who asked you, asshole?

The situation got ugly in seconds. Pete found himself standing side by side with Billy in the middle of the living room. In some ways, he had already been resigned to it. Voices were rising, challenging, protesting. Billy and Roger were almost nose to nose, trading brisk shoves to each other's chest. Then Roger's friend came on the run. He leapt over the couch and landed in front of Pete and gave him a push. Pete stumbled on an ottoman behind him and went over backwards. He hit the floor with the ottoman between his knees, his vision wheeling sickeningly.

A sharp whistle cut through the noise. Emily had her fingers in her mouth. She took them out and said: This is so goddamn stupid.

Beside Emily, Nancy nodded fervently. Her eyes were wide. She looked a little frantic, while Emily looked stern and composed and beautiful.

Roger and Billy had hold of each other's collar. Billy also had hold of the boy who'd pushed Pete over. Pete concentrated on the ceiling and then he sat up. His face felt hot and his head was spinning.

—What are you going to do, Emily? said Roger. Call your dad?

Emily lifted her hands: How did I know you'd say that. Really. How did I know.

—This is all bullshit, said Roger. You know we're only kidding around.

He and Billy warily unlatched and stepped back. Roger offered a tentative smile and a handshake. He came over past Billy and pulled Pete up.

—All good, right, Pete?

He put out his hand and Pete shook it.

Then Roger and his friends got their jackets and their beer. They took their time leaving, hanging around the front yard, talking, looking at the house. Finally, they got into a wood-panelled station wagon and drove away.

—Here, Pete.

Billy had brought him another beer. Pete opened it and Billy slung an arm around him.

—What kind of bullshit was that? You okay?

—I'm fine.

Peter drank the beer quickly. He went into the washroom. The toilet seat stood upright and dry vomit scum caked the bowl. Pete gripped the sides of the counter, breathing slow. He balled his fist and drove it into the wall. Once, twice, three times, until the knuckles were stinging and the skin was broken. He stayed in the washroom for a long time, letting the anger and the humiliation subside. Then he held a hand towel under a stream of cold water. He cleaned his knuckles with it and tossed the towel into the bathtub.

He came back into the living room. Nancy was on the couch. She got up and blundered forward and put her hands on his arms.

—I am so sorry about those guys.

—If Billy and me knew we'd cause you any problems we probably wouldn't have come.

—No, you're more fun than them. I am so sorry.

Pete looked around. The house had mostly emptied and only four or five people remained. All around were cups and beer bottles and small spills. The pictures on the wall hung askew. He did not see Billy or Emily. His earlier anger was gone, and in its place was a bitter taste of jealousy. He tried to shake it away, wondering what was happening to him. He said: Your living room is a goddamn mess.

—I know, said Nancy. But whatever. I'll make my little brother clean it up tomorrow. Come on.

—Where are we going?

—Just to talk, you know. Come on.

Nancy took him into her bedroom and closed the door behind them and turned on a bedside lamp. The room was many shades of pink and there were clothes strewn about and there was a rack of figure-skating trophies. Over the bed was a poster of Michael Jackson, and in the corner, she had a television. But then she had the light out again and she was groping at him and then he groped back and tasted the liquor in her mouth and the sweat on her breasts and her stomach. She sucked her breath in.

—I don't want you to think I do this all the time . . .

—I know, said Pete.

It didn't go very far. She was shirtless by the time they got into the bed, but after a few minutes of rolling around she seemed to slow down. Then she stopped responding entirely. He said her name. He touched her shoulder. She had passed out. Pete settled down beside her. It took him a little while to come down, to stop thinking about falling over the ottoman, to stop thinking of other things. He listened to the sounds of the house. He was listening for Billy and Emily and not hearing them.

—

In the early morning, Pete dressed in his work clothes. The light from outside was grey and cold. His knuckles were sore from striking the wall and his head hurt. He looked at Nancy. She was a stranger. She was snoring and was still wearing her jeans. Pete picked up her hand and put it down again. She did not stir. He shoved the clothes he'd worn the night before into his backpack.

He moved through the house. No one was around. He had no idea what room Billy and Emily might have ended up in, and he gritted his teeth against the idea of going door to door to find them. In the living room, he could smell burned carpet and spilled beer. It made his gorge rise. He went out the front door and down to his car and got his work jacket out of the trunk. It was a lined canvas jacket with his name stitched at the breast. He put it on and rubbed his hands together. He got into the car and started it. It was then that he saw Emily out on the front porch. She was wearing a cable-knit sweater and she had a steaming mug between her hands. She saw him and gave a little wave. He got out of the car and shuffled back to the porch.

—I was in the kitchen making tea, said Emily. I usually don't sleep the whole night through. But I would have a nap every single afternoon if I could. Where are you going?

He found himself looking at Emily's hair, looking for it to be askew, but it hung as dark and straight as the first time he'd seen her. At some point, she'd washed off her makeup, what little she had seemed to be wearing the night before, and though there were darker spots under her eyes, even in the early morning light she remained almost too pretty to look at.

—Well, some of us can't sleep at night because they have a guilty conscience, said Pete. And some of us can't sleep because they have to go to work.

—Guilty conscience?

—I'm teasing you.

—I know you are. You work at the gas station on the bypass, right?

—Yeah, that's right.

—How long have you been doing that?

—Since May.

—And what else? said Emily.

—What else what?

—What else anything, Pete. What's your story?

—Oh, said Pete. I don't know. There's not much to it. I was born in North Bay. We lived there until I was eight or so, then we moved back here, because this is my mom's hometown, this is where she grew up. She's married to a pastor now. I never met my dad.

—My mom teaches grade two, said Emily. My dad is a cop.

—And you play the piano better than anyone I ever heard.

—Thank you. My grandmother taught me. She could play like you wouldn't believe.

—My grandma lives with us, said Pete.

He did not mention anything about his grandmother's illness. For a moment he had a clear idea of how his story must sound to someone like Emily—his grandmother was dying, his uncle was an ex-con, he'd never met his father, and, as for himself, he was a dropout who worked at a gas station. Emily, meanwhile, had it good, and came from good people. At best, he thought, she might tolerate someone like him, as long as she was seeing his friend.

And yet, he was conscious of how he felt, standing here with her, watching her sip her tea. He said: Do you think you'll go with Billy again?

She shrugged. The mug was in front of her mouth.

—You never know. If he continues to be a gentleman, maybe I'll go with him again.

Pete rubbed the back of his neck: Yeah, Billy's a good guy.

—He's very good-looking, said Emily. He's got beautiful hair. And my dad would absolutely hate him.

—I see.

—Maybe you can see Nancy again. We could go out, the four of us. That would be fun.

He agreed lamely that they should all meet again. Then he went down the steps and got in his car, wondering what it was like to have a place where you fit in.

He pulled onto the street and watched Emily in his rear-view mirror until he'd turned the corner and lost sight of her.

Stan had a bad night. When he slept he dreamed he was awake but was unable to move. And when he was awake he lay looking around. All the ordinary features of the bedroom had new dimensions in the darkness. In the morning his whole body ached. He put on a track suit in preparation for his exercises.

Cassius was sitting by the woodstove when Stan came down. The last two nights had been cold enough to warrant a small fire in the stove, which Stan had kept because it was as old as the house itself and because it appealed to him in a way that electric heat did not. Stan scratched the dog between the ears and they went outside. Edna's garden was choked with weeds. The flowers were all dead. Stan and Cassius went down the embankment to the basement door under the house. Inside the basement, Stan kept a workbench and a selection of tools. Across from that was the exposed bedrock on which the house was built, coming up in one place to the bottoms of the joists. There was space for storage, extra siding, shingles, storm shutters, life jackets and fishing rods, a paint-spattered wooden ladder. In the opposite corner, an Everlast heavy-bag hung from the overhead beam.

He turned on an FM radio he kept on the workbench, tuned it to the news. He wrapped his hands and knuckles, aching as they were, and he put on a pair of old sixteen-ounce training gloves he'd had for many years. He shadowboxed for a few minutes and then he worked on the heavy-bag. In his youth, before his long tenure as a cop, he'd had four years as a professional boxer. His record was twenty-two fights, with seventeen wins, twelve of those by knockout. He'd been known as a good stylist and an outfighter, classing as a light heavyweight at a hundred and seventy pounds.

Stan had come back to exercising daily around the time he turned fifty and his doctor had given him some warnings about his blood pressure. So he'd quit smoking—which Edna had never cared for anyway—and had brought the fighting exercises back into his life. His knees and hips wouldn't let him use the jump rope much any more, but he could still work combinations on the heavy-bag. It used to be his cross, thrown with his right hand, that would win him a fight, if the victory was to be by knockout. Stan would strike his opponent's body until the guy let his hands and elbows down, and then he'd propel the cross from his hips and abdominals straight into the guy's jaw or temple.

After four three-minute rounds he stopped punching the bag to listen to the news. His sweatshirt was damp right through and he felt older than ever. Cassius lay with his muzzle between his forepaws. As a puppy it had upset him to watch Stan work on the bag and he would bark and snap until Stan would have to get Edna to call Cassius out to her. Now the dog only watched through half-lidded eyes. Stan steadied the bag. The news broadcast finished. He stood looking out the yellowed window-glass over the workbench, down past the cedar trees to the western shore of the point, which endured the worst of the weather when the prevailing winds blew.

He had a list of chores he needed to attend to. The outboard motor needed servicing. The toilet was making erratic sounds. He went at the chores in a distracted fashion. After lunch, he set a ladder against the side of the house and climbed up to clean the eavestroughs. The sun was warm on his face and the colours of the leaves were vivid against the sky. Somewhere, the sound of a chainsaw was buzzing through the trees.

He had been at this for twenty minutes when he heard the dog barking and a vehicle in the turnaround. He looked down and saw Dick Shannon coming to the base of the ladder. Dick was uniformed, carrying his cap in one hand.

—That's a long way up.

—I'll put that dog on you, Dick.

—That's fine. He could watch me all the way to my car.

Dick bent down and picked up a stick from the grass. He held it for Cassius to sniff and then he hurled it across the yard. Cassius trotted after it but stopped halfway and just looked. Dick shook his head and looked back up at Stan and said: I told you I owed you a visit. Them things you asked me about on the telephone a few days ago.

Stan came down. He got some beers from the fridge and carried two lawn chairs to the dock. They agreed there were not going to be many more days this year that they'd be able to sit by the lake and take in the sun.

—How's town? said Stan.

—Same as ever. Say, do you remember that business with Simon and Charles Grady?

—Christ, that's a lot of years ago. King, wasn't that his name?

—Leland King, said Dick. Anyhow, he's been paroled. He's back in town.

—I remember driving Leland King down to the provincial jail when his trial started. I thought he looked just like a kid. Remember how his dad—I think his name was George—dropped stone dead in that store of his one morning?

—Only from hearing about it later, said Dick. I think I was still overseas when he died.

—That's right. It would have been '44 or so. Anyway, it was better for him, I guess, to die long before he'd see what his son would make of himself.

—I expect Frank will pay a visit to Leland before long, said Dick. Tell him how things are.

—It was Frank who was first on the scene with the Gradys, if I remember right. Frank was new to town. Him and Mary hadn't even had Emily yet.

—I see Arthur Grady sometimes, driving around, said Dick. He still looks after the living boy. Hell of a thing.

—Yes, said Stan. When it happened, it was the biggest goddamn news in the county for a whole year. As big as the Lacroixes were . . . And Charles Grady, he was one hell of a hockey player, but I always wondered if maybe there wasn't a little more to the story than what came out at the trial. There were a whole lot of people not saying anything at all.

—Oh well, said Dick. I don't think it matters much any more.

They drank their beers and watched a boat cut across the lake two hundred yards out. The change in the colours had reached the point where there was an equal distribution of green and yellow and red around the shore. Edna had liked spring best because that was when she planted her garden, but she'd always said fall was the prettiest time. She came into Stan's head abruptly now, as she sometimes did, and just as abruptly he tried to push the thought of her away.

—So, do you still think you'll retire next summer? said Stan.

—You better believe it. They won't have any trouble getting me out the door.

—I was a few years past the thirty-five when I went. I lost money on my pension but I just didn't know what I would do with myself. I still don't.

—Is that what this is about? said Dick.

—What?

—We've known each other a long time, Stanley. I don't know anything else that's dogged your heels like the Lacroixes, and that was, Christ, I was a kid when that happened. Now this with Aurel's daughter, you being the one to find her.

Stan rubbed at a knot in the dock planking with the heel of his boot and said: It wasn't you on the investigation, was it.

—No, said Dick. It was Lenny Gleber.

—Look. I don't know what I'm thinking, Dick. Maybe I just don't have anything better to do.

—I don't think you owe that family anything. I don't think you ever did. Judy Lacroix was a pretty poor-off girl with her illness and all, anyhow.

—Did you get a look at the toxicology?

Dick took a folded paper out of his breast pocket. He held it out to Stan.

—You know what Frank would do, don't you.

Stan took the paper and unfolded it. He was looking at a photocopy. The reporting toxicologist's name was blotted out. Stan read the date of the test and the details. He looked at the drug notes, and he said: Look at this man's handwriting. Okay, that's carbon monoxide, just like how I found her. But, there's this, amitrip . . . What's this hen scratch here?

—Amitriptyline. I didn't ask Gleber about it because I didn't want word to get back to Frank. Gleber's alright, but he's a company man. So I rang up a pathologist I used to work with when I was down in the city. Anyhow it's a drug for a girl like Judy. It would make her feel normal, if you can call it that. It—what did he say about it—it can make you feel nothing at all. He said it could get you into a kind of mood where you don't give a fart if you're hurting or sad or even if you live or die. Judy was on that for her illness.

—This is goddamn hard to read.

—Or you just need glasses, Stanley. But what you're looking at is that she had close to four hundred milligrams of that stuff in her blood.

—She overdosed on it.

—No. It was the exhaust that killed her. Carbon monoxide. But four hundred milligrams of the amitriptyline is near three times the maximum dose for a full-grown man. With something like that, you might think all that work you had to do, putting the hose up from the tailpipe through the window, was just as easy as a Sunday drive.

—She left a note in the car, said Stan. I never got a chance to read it.

—There wasn't much. She just told her sister she was sorry is all. But one thing Gleber did find out is that there was a boyfriend. You only asked about how the girl killed herself, but I thought you might like to know what else I found out.

—Yes, said Stan. Just for curiosity, let's say.

Dick took out his notebook and flipped it open to a page he'd marked. He said: I knew I'd forget the boyfriend's name so I wrote it down. Gilmore. Colin Gilmore. Seasonal worker, not too much on him. I guess Mr. Gilmore didn't let on they were as serious as Judy thought they were. He said they'd stopped seeing each other a couple weeks before you found her.

—Maybe that had something to do with it?

—Maybe, said Dick. The gals that Judy worked with said she'd stopped showing up for work for a week or two. Her sister works at the National Trust downtown. She'd gotten Judy on with an after-hours cleaning crew.

Stan nodded. He drank his beer. Dick sat back in the lawn chair and rolled his cuffs up from his wrists. After a long moment, he said: People, when they take their own lives . . . You remember when we got called out to—What was his name?

—Templeton, said Stan. I knew him when I was a boy but I don't remember his first name. But yes, I remember that call. You hadn't been around real long.

—If he'd only had sense enough to put that .303 into his mouth instead of under his chin like he did. He must of lived forty-five minutes with his face like that. Between the two of us we could barely hold him in one place.

—Here's a thing I'll tell you about that call, said Stan. When we got back to the station that morning, Edna had left a message with the dispatcher. I was to go over to the butcher and pick up an order she'd put in before I came home. When I got to the butcher the order was a pound of ground beef. I took one look at it, and . . . Well, I made it outside around back before I was sick, but just. I just made it.

—That's one you told me, Stanley. You weren't sick at the scene. You didn't even blink, but later when you got to the butcher.

—You're lying. I never told anybody that.

—That's one you told me a time or two. It was many years after that call, but you told me all the same.

—Well.

Dick was quiet for another moment. Then he said: I can see it, Stanley. I can see the flywheels working in your head. But the Lacroixes are all gone except for Judy's sister. You don't owe them anything.

—Another beer, Dick?

—Oh. I guess not. I better get back to town. I've got some stuff for that fat bastard of a J.P. to sign before the court closes.

Stan walked with Dick up to the patrol car in the turnaround. Cassius was sleeping nearby in a patch of sunlight.

—I appreciate it, said Stan.

—I know you do. But I don't want you to work yourself too hard over questions that already got answers, sad as they are.

—It's just something for me to think about. More than those eavestroughs up there, let's put it that way.

—I'll keep my ears open, said Dick.

The National Trust was on Confederation Avenue, south of the river, a few blocks up the hill from the lake. A little way up, on the other side of the street was the shabby face of the Shamrock Hotel. Woolworths was around the corner. Eleanor Lacroix had a photograph of her sister on her teller's desk in the main room of the Trust. In the photograph, Judy was laughing, eyes closed. On Eleanor's finger was an engagement ring.

At that hour the bank was not busy, so after Stan had asked her, Eleanor leaned over to one of her co-workers and said she'd be back in a minute. She came around and they went to some chairs by the front window. An old woman with a plastic kerchief over her hair was writing a cheque at a table close by and outside a fine rain was slanting through the air. Eleanor sat and composed herself.

—So, if this is about Judy, I don't know why you haven't received the full payment. I sent it last week.

—I'm sorry, I don't understand.

—Aren't you with the funeral home?

—No—

—Are you from the church? If you are, you can tell that priest that what he said about what happens when you take your own life, how nobody knows where Judy is now, how could anybody say that?

Stan could see that Eleanor was shaking, fighting to keep a quiet pitch to her voice.

—Miss Lacroix, I'm not here for the church or the funeral home or anything. I'm not here for anybody except myself.

—You said this was about my sister.

—That's right. Maybe you'd go somewheres else to chat about this? If you've got a coffee break or when you're done work?

—I already used up my break and I've got errands to run after work. I've got maybe five minutes to talk.

Stan looked around. The old woman had gone over to one of the tellers and there was no one immediately close to them.

—Well, I was the one who found your sister.

He could see how Eleanor was thinking about this. She sat back.

—It was me who found her, said Stan. There's some things,

some questions, like, maybe for your peace of mind, that I'd be in a good position to ask.

—Listen, whatever this is, I don't even know who you are.

—My name is Stan Maitland, Miss Lacroix. Maybe you'd remember me.

One of the other tellers came by, close enough to get Eleanor's attention, and said she wanted to go on her break in a minute.

—I'll be there, said Eleanor. Sorry.

The teller moved on. Eleanor wasn't looking at Stan. She seemed to be looking at a point over his shoulder.

—I thought I'd start with you, Miss Lacroix, said Stan.

—I know who you are, Mr. Maitland. Are you still with the police?

—No, I'm retired now. Like I say, I'm not here on anybody's behalf but my own.

—Mr. Maitland, I know people used to talk about my family, how my dad was a drunk who couldn't keep a job. But I also know how my dad lived his whole life picking up the pieces after you sent his brother to be executed. So yes, I know who you are. You talk about wanting to ask some questions, but is it really for my peace of mind?

—It's not so straightforward as that.

Eleanor stood up. She wouldn't look at him. She was shaking again.

It occurred to Stan what Edna would say about all of this. She would likely tell him to leave it be, that digging around in anybody's fresh upset wasn't going to resolve anything. She would tell him he was acting like an old man who was both bored and lonely.

—I have to get back to work, said Eleanor. This is the worst thing I've been through in a long time. I'd appreciate it if you'd give that some thought. Can I ask you that much?

—I . . . yes, said Stan. I'm sorry to bother you.

—Have a good day, Mr. Maitland.

Lee liked to take walks, a weekend afternoon or a weekday evening if Helen wasn't around. Walking, you could just go, give your head all the latitude it might want. Strangers' houses interested him, what he'd glimpse in the yard or through the front window as he passed by. A man raking leaves, a woman setting out the dishes for supper. One time he stopped to watch some kids playing ball hockey on a side street. There were four of them, two goaltenders and two forwards, and they scrambled around each other and shouted and their sticks scraped on the roadtop. Lee leaned against a lamppost, taking in the game, until he realized the kids had stopped playing and were just looking at him. He gave them a little salute, and when none of them returned the gesture, he shrugged, pushed himself off the lamppost, and went on his way.

All things considered, he felt alright. He had the freedom to open his own door and go out walking for however long he wanted. He liked what he saw—the dinners being set out on tables, the kids playing ball hockey on the road—but he reckoned they were outside his reach. For now, at least. In the meantime, it was okay just to watch. And if it was evening when Lee went walking, he would go right to sleep when he came home.

A block away from Lee's place was a poolroom called the Corner Pocket. He'd noticed it on a walk. One evening at the end of September, he went up the steps of the poolroom and went in. A layer of cigarette smoke hung below the lights, and he heard country music playing. There were six eight-ball tables and two snooker tables and two of the coin-operated decks, and four of the tables were in use. A couple of rummies perched at the bar. There was the sharp-featured man in a down-filled vest who Lee recognized, but could not remember where from. He was shooting pool by himself at one of the coin-op tables.

Lee wandered between the tables and watched what games were going down until the man behind the bar asked if he could help him.

—No, said Lee. Sorry.

Lee went back to the door and opened it halfway. Then he turned and went back to the bar.

—Could I get a table?

The barman gave him a tray of balls and marked his start time on a chalkboard behind the counter.

—Are you thirsty, my friend?

—I could do with a Coke.

The barman popped open a can and filled a glass and handed it to Lee. Lee took the drink and the tray of balls over to a vacant table. The felt on the tabletop was worn dark and smooth in patches. Lee picked a straight cue and chalked the tip of it. He racked up the balls and broke them and studied where they'd moved to.

He'd played some as a kid, and they'd had a table at the halfway house in the city. The game pleased him, the variations of it, the precision, the interactions between players. He took on the parts of both opponents. Once when he looked up he found the sharp-faced man at the coin-op table looking back at him. Or so he believed. Lee bent down again to bank the nine ball into a pocket. Playing pool by himself was like the walks he took. His mind unfettered. Almost an hour went by. Then there were sirens outside and a flash of red lights against the windows. The sound of the sirens fell away but Lee had already replaced the balls on the tray. He carried the tray over to the bar.

—What do I owe you?

—Seventy-five cents for the table and the same for the Coke, said the barman.

Lee stacked a note and some coins on the bartop.

—Maybe I'll come on back sometime.

—Make sure you do.

Lee passed by the sharp-featured man on his way to the front door.

—How are you? said Lee.

—. . . What? How am I? said the man. Never better is how I am.

—Hey, John.

—I'm Luke, said the boy.

—I knew that, said Lee. I was just checking to see how switched on you are.

Clifton's crew had only worked until the early afternoon and Lee had hitched a ride with Jeff and Jeff Junior out to Donna's house. The older of Lee's two little nephews had come to the door when he knocked. Donna appeared behind her son. She was drying her hands on a dishtowel.

—Luke, who's at—Oh, Lee.

—I thought I'd come visit you and Ma.

He set his lunch pail and tool belt down by the front door and followed Donna and Luke into the kitchen. Donna went to a cutting board on the counter and Luke went back to the table where his brother was sitting. They had notebooks in front of them. Irene was there as well, slumped on a chair where she could watch the room. She breathed heavily, rhythmically, and her clothes hung loosely from her. It had been only a week and a half since he'd last seen her, but even since then she'd lost handfuls of hair. What remained was as thin as mist.

She smiled when she saw him, said: You look like you came from work.

—Thought I'd come to visit.

—What a nice surprise.

Lee looked down at John's notebook. He saw child's writing in big, cumbersome characters. He put his hand on the boy's shoulder.

—How's your school work going, buck?

Before John could reply, Donna told them: Boys, you can take a break. Go on down to the basement. No horseplay.

Lee watched the boys charge out of the kitchen and disappear down the stairs. Only once they were gone did Donna ask if Lee would sit and have a cup of tea and a piece of rhubarb pie. He sat.

—How's it going, Ma?

—I'll see the doctor tomorrow. More treatments.

—You let me know if you need me to go with you.

—Barry takes her, said Donna.

Donna put a piece of pie before Lee. She poured tea for Lee and Irene and then she stood near the counter.

—Well, like I say, it's what I'm here for, said Lee. I'll help you out, Ma, any way I can. I didn't move back up here to get rich and famous. Would you sit down, sister?

Donna scooted into the chair Luke had vacated. She examined what the boy had been writing in his notebook. Lee forked off a piece of the pie.

—To tell the truth, I don't know so much about the treatments, Ma.

—The doctor says it's going good, said Irene. He uses words I don't understand, but. He's foreign. Coloured.

—Chemotherapy and radiation, said Donna. They can't just remove the tumour at her age. You want to know, you take one look at all the pills in the bathroom. And you see what the chemotherapy does?

Irene grinned and said: I won't win the beauty pageant at the fall fair.

Donna looked hard at her son's notebook.

—You got the same thing as that kid, said Lee.

—Kid?

—That one-legged kid who tried to run across the country. I'm betting on you, Ma. We're a bunch of survivors is what we are.

He reached across the table and grasped her hand.

—How is work going?

—Couldn't be better, said Lee. You should just see the size of this place going up out there. It's bigger than the boarding house where we used to live.

—People with money are buying up and down the lake, said Donna.

—I'm starting to make a buck or two myself. Before long I'll buy a big godda— a big G.D. place like that and we'll all move out there.

—Listen to you.

—You and Barry can have the east wing. We'll send the boys to private school. Is that—Ma, take a look—is that Donna cracking a smile?

—Oh quit, would you?

But Donna was smiling. It changed her whole face.

The next day, Lee went to see the boarding house where he and Donna had grown up. It was a Saturday and the fall air was crisp and the sky was off-white. He walked up Union Street breathing in the smell of creosote from the rail crossing. Cars passed him trailing radio sounds. At the Owl Café he stood at the window. He cupped his hands around the sides of his face to block the light. He looked inside until Helen spotted him, as did a number of the patrons. She gave him a little wave. He waved back and went on his way.

The boarding house was on Merritt Street, on the north side of the river, a half-hour's walk from downtown. It was a timber-frame structure from the turn of the century, and it had been variously added to over the years. There had been six rooms to rent when they lived there. Tenants had to share the bathrooms. Now, while the house retained its old exterior look, it appeared to have been renovated for business interests. He read a sign for LUCKY TAILORING & DRY CLEANING in a main floor window and a sign for CHAPMAN SOLICITORS on the second floor.

Lee was only six when George King died. The boy had been confused by what was going on, and so he'd wandered away from the house, from the policemen who'd come, from his mother lifting her cigarette and trying to light it, asking over and over how she could be left like this, how he could do it, leave her alone with these two kids. George's heart had seized fast in his chest in the early hours of the morning when he had gone to open the store. The driver of a delivery truck had found him. And by noon his widowed wife, Irene, sat demanding, first from the policemen, then from her meagre surroundings, how it could be so.

The boy could go anywhere, he knew, with his mother so distraught. He could go to the lumberyard or to the river. But he didn't even end up going across the street. Instead, he went to the back of the house and down the basement steps. It was understood that the basement was not to be ventured into, particularly by the children of tenants. The boy went anyway, pushing at the solid wooden door and finding it unlocked and watching it swing open into a place he had lived above his whole life, yet never glimpsed.

The basement floor was packed dirt and the walls were brick, once whitewashed. Knob-and-tube wiring was tacked into the cavities between the overhead joists. The basement smelled of earth and wood-rot. Against one wall was a cabinet choked with items: pipefittings, light bulbs, copper fuses, an ankle boot with a busted heel. The boy picked up a ball-peen hammer from the cabinet and turned it and felt its weight in his small hand.

He was drawn to the furnace, to see what made the noises in the vents at night. He was curious about the sullen glow inside the firebox. But then he heard something. He saw the crippled caretaker coming from the direction of the coal bin, carrying a load in a spadeshovel, walking heavily on his bum leg, not saying anything. The boy turned and ran.

—

The general store his father had operated on River Street now had Victory Home Appliances on the front signboard. Much of the interior had been rearranged, walls knocked out, the space made bigger. Lee stood where the grocery counter had been. There was a display of used televisions almost exactly where his father had been found dead by the delivery man.

A salesman came around.

—You look like a man who's thinking about how to improve his house.

—No, just looking around. I'll get going.

—No need to run off. Looking's always free.

Lee left the salesman and went out onto the street, but then, abruptly, he went back into the store and over to the televisions. The salesman rematerialized quickly. Lee scratched the back of his head and said: Look, what I was thinking about was a television.

—You're in the right place, sir. We have good colour sets. Brand new. Here we've got a whole selection of used outfits. Great condition each one. Inspected. Really good bang for your buck. This one is a '72 Emerson, eighteen-inch. The colours are still bright as can be. Hundred thirty.

—Hundred thirty? I don't know about that. Maybe I'll come back again some other time, see what you got.

—I could go you a hundred. Cash. Right now.

—A hundred bucks.

—A hundred bucks and it's yours. Delivery included.

As usual, Lee had a sense of the money he'd earned passing out of his hands. He only had the hundred dollars on him because he'd cashed his paycheque the day before. But for the first time he could think of, he could bear the cost. Before he left the store he shook the salesman's hand.

—This used to be my dad's place.

—Is that right?

—It was a general store. He sold all kinds of things. There was a grocery counter right here.

—Well, there you go. I do some business and learn a little history in the bargain. Our delivery van will come around by five o'clock.

Lee went down the hill and into the A&P to stock up on food. He was thinking about the television he'd just purchased, and he was thinking about his long-dead father, what he could remember of the man, and he was thinking about the boarding house where he'd grown up. He didn't know why he'd waited a month, after moving back to town, to go see the house. It had felt a little like a confrontation, somehow, one that he'd been putting off. It seemed to him his last tangible memory of town, prior to going to jail, was the boarding house—even though he'd been at a friend's place when the police tracked him down and arrested him. All the same, he realized he would have been bothered if the old boarding house, with the basement of his recurring dreams, had been demolished.

When he was coming out of the grocery store now, carrying a paper bag of groceries, he saw they'd come for him. One of them was a constable, young. The other was a sergeant. A thin man, precise. They were standing alongside a patrol car. Lee was aware of people stopping to watch.

The sergeant said: Mr. King. Thought we'd have a word.

—Word about what?

—Why don't you come along with us. Just for a bit.

It had to be out front of the grocery store. It had to be the middle of the afternoon when people could watch. The constable took Lee's grocery bag and put it on the front seat. Then he patted him down. Just for procedure, he said. They didn't handcuff him, but they did seat him in the tightly caged back seat.

Lee looked out at the people standing around the front of the A&P, and a bitter flame, anger and humiliation, flared in his gut. The constable got behind the wheel and the sergeant got into the passenger seat, partly crushing the grocery bag beside him. The way the rear-view mirror was angled, the sergeant's eyes were in it.

They drove through town and Lee didn't say anything. It was the sergeant who finally spoke. —Your parole officer, what's his name?

—Wade Larkin.

—That's right. I know him. He's a nice chap, Wade Larkin. He's really a nice chap. How often do you see him?

—Once every six weeks.

—Once every six weeks. You see what a nice chap you got for a parole officer?

—Listen, boss, I get seen like this I could lose my job.

—What I can't figure out is why you're back in town at all. After they saw fit to cut you loose and set you up with a really nice chap like Wade Larkin, you came back here.

—My mother is sick with cancer.

Nothing was said in reply.

They drove for a short while until they were cruising past a long brick building with a curved roof. They rounded the corner and there was a baseball diamond, deserted except for some high school kids smoking at the bleachers. The kids saw the patrol car and got up and left. The car pulled around in front of the building and Lee saw the sign over the front doors: CHARLES GRADY MEMORIAL COMMUNITY CENTRE – HOME OF THE DYNAMITE! He looked at the eyes looking at him in the rear-view mirror.

—Kind of funny, don't you think?

—I don't think it's real funny, boss, said Lee.

—Myself, said the sergeant, I was just brand new here. I know that wasn't my very first call but it was one of them. I was sick when I saw it. What you did. I was sick right there on the driveway. I don't care what you think of that. If a man tells you he's got the stomach for it, first time he sees something like that, he's a goddamn liar. Maybe I was sick because the other boy was still alive.

—What do you want from me?

—I guess you get this idea, maybe, because there're all kinds of people who will tell you just how misunderstood you were, how what you really needed was this and that, how you deserve good things same as anybody else, so I guess you get this idea that you can put mileage between then and now. But I know you.

—I told you, I'm here to work and look after my mother. I haven't been bothering anybody. I don't even drink.

The eyes in the rear-view mirror. The man hadn't even raised his voice. He said: I know you and I know all about you, my friend. You remember that.

Then the sergeant told the constable to let Lee out of the car. The constable came around and opened the door. He gave Lee his bag of groceries and he grinned and said he hoped he'd see him again. The car pulled out of the parking lot and was gone.

Lee was breathing hard. His thoughts raced. He wasn't surprised that they had come for him, but nevertheless it burned him, far more than he had thought it would. He'd gotten out of prison, but his life was still under the thumbs of men with badges and guns. He'd been foolish to think it might ever be otherwise.

He put the groceries down and found himself a cigarette. It seemed ridiculous that he'd bought a television an hour ago. That he'd presumed to buy it, had presumed to buy groceries, had presumed to visit the house where he'd grown up. That he'd presumed at all.

He picked up his grocery bag and held it at his midsection while he walked. The ash from his cigarette drifted down. He passed a chain-link fence and a mean-looking dog came at him, barking, gnashing its jaws, until it hit the end of its chain. It stood with its forelegs splayed. He looked at it.

A short distance later the grocery bag was getting heavy. He put it down on the curb, and thought again of the day his father died, thirty-five years ago, but the man was present now more than he had been in a long time. He thought of the basement, the caretaker with the shovel. How he'd fled. How the crippled caretaker never said anything to him, never called him out.

TWO
OCTOBER TO NOVEMBER 1980

Thanksgiving came with a cold snap. Stan was invited to Frank and Mary's house for turkey dinner. He drove over on Sunday afternoon, bringing Cassius along with him. After he got to the house and said hello, he walked Louise up to the park so she could collect leaves for a school project. The dog went with them. Louise dug through the leaves on the ground at the park and brought her findings for Stan to inspect.

—What do you think, Grandpa?

—I'd say that one's a beech. It's just a couple inches. There's not so many of the little edges on it.

—They call those teeth, said Louise.

—That's right.

—Beech, said Louise.

She took a small plastic bag out of her jacket pocket. She'd already collected a maple leaf and an oak leaf. She put the beech leaf in and added a check mark to her notebook. Stan sat on a park bench and watched her. Cassius was over sniffing the base of a tree. After Louise had found a birch leaf, she told Stan she'd collected enough and now they could go.

Back at the house, they saw an older-model red Camaro parked at the curb. Emily was standing alongside it, speaking to the driver. Louise hung close to Stan as they came into the driveway. They weren't close enough to hear whatever was being said, but they caught sight of a boy behind the wheel. He had a look of raw pain on his face.

—Do Grandpa a favour and take Cassius around back, said Stan. Make sure the gate is latched. We don't need him running down the street.

Louise went with the dog and Stan started up the front walk. Emily came over and kissed him on the cheek.

—Hi, Grandpa. I'll be inside soon.

Emily went back to the Camaro and Stan caught a few words: I'm sorry if this doesn't make sense to you. And the boy saying: Hey, baby, please.

Inside the house Frank was watching from the front window.

—I was about to go outside.

—I think she's got it in hand, said Stan.

—Goddammit. Look at the hair on him.

Stan went into the kitchen. The smell of roasting turkey brought juices to his mouth. Mary was drinking a glass of wine and studying her mother's recipe book. It occurred to Stan that it had been a long time since he'd seen the book. He saw Edna's neat cursive—*Gravies etc.*—on the page and he looked away.

—The turkey is huge, said Mary. We'll have leftovers for a week. I'll send a bunch of it home with you.

—Sounds good to me, said Stan.

—You seem distracted, Dad.

—I'm just woolgathering.

—Okay . . .

—When you were Louise's age there was only the one public school in town, said Stan. Do you remember?

—River Street P.S. Sure, I remember.

—And do you remember if your school friends knew who I was?

—What made you think of this now?

—Nothing.

—There weren't as many cops in town back then, so yes, my friends knew what my dad did. But I don't think it ever really came up in public school. High school was a bit different. I started to hear more about you. There was an old phys. ed. teacher who coached girls' field hockey. Mr. Pritchard. I remember, after he figured out who I was, he would talk to me about your boxing days. Endlessly. He'd say, Maitland, come here! It didn't matter how practice was going or what the other girls were doing. He'd go on and on. He talked a lot about Windsor, some guy you fought. Sharkey?

—Sharkey, said Stan. He was a heavyweight from the States. He had quite a good run, had the title for awhile. When we fought, I didn't beat him. I drawed. I was lucky to do that, even. That was one of my only real big fights. Ha, Pritchard wasn't even there.

—He talked about it like he was. He must have told me that Windsor story a hundred times. I was only in grade nine or grade ten when I played field hockey. After that, I was more aware of it if I heard things about you. They always said you were a fair cop. They said you didn't do things by the book but that you were really fair to everybody. That's not Frank's way.

—Frank's a good policeman, Mary. He knows his job inside and out.

—He's got a lot of ambition for his career.

—Good on him. I never wanted that responsibility. I never thought I was up to it. Anyhow, was it hard for you if there were folks that weren't so happy about things I'd done?

—Everybody knew about the man that got hung, if that's what you mean. But nobody talked about it much. Was I even born when that happened?

—You weren't much more than a baby.

—What makes you think of this now, Dad?

—That family, in particular, had a lot of hard times. Anyhow, never mind. I never wanted to expose you or your mother to any of that.

Mary laughed.

—Oh God. You and Frank, you've got that in common.

—What's that?

—This idea that the women in your life need to be protected all the time.

Stan wandered back into the living room, thinking maybe he'd have a nap. Emily was in the vestibule untying her shoes. Frank hovered around her, trying to make light of whoever it was in the car.

—You should have brought him in for supper, said Frank.

—It's completely not an issue any more, Dad.

—I'm sorry to hear it. Hey, if you've got to insist on dating, how about you get yourself a guy with a better haircut?

—Actually, I've got an idea, said Emily. I'm sure I could get one of your rookies to take me out. That one that drove you home yesterday is really cute.

—Hey, said Frank. Listen . . .

Stan sat down in the recliner next to the cabinet stereo. He brought the footrest up and stretched his legs out. He didn't want Emily or Frank to see the smile he was wearing. How close he was, suddenly, to laughing outright. He let his head settle back and he closed his eyes.

He snoozed for an hour and was gradual about waking up. By then, the whole house was filled with the deep smell of the roasting turkey. Emily was sitting at the Clarendon upright.

—I hope I didn't wake you, Grandpa.

—I don't think you did.

—You were snoring like mad.

—Gentlemen like me don't snore.

Stan got up from the recliner. He wasn't sure if she'd been practising or not while he napped, but she put her hands to the keys and began to play "Jesu, Joy of Man's Desiring." In the kitchen, Mary and Louise were preparing the vegetables.

Frank picked at the turkey stuffing. When he saw Stan, he offered him a beer, and the two of them went and sat down in the screened-in porch at the back of the house. Cassius was loping around the yard, sniffing at the bird bath.

—Who was the boy in the car? said Stan.

—Bobby or Billy or something. He's been around a little bit, but he's nobody now. Just as well.

—She's got a good head, Frank. If she's going to university next year, you'll have to trust her.

—She'd be young. Just eighteen. It's still under discussion.

Stan stood up and watched his dog in the backyard. The dog dug under the cedar hedge at the back of the property until Stan called for him to cut it out.

—Stan, said Frank, I want to talk to you about Judy Lacroix. I want to know why you've got the interest in her.

—I'm the one who found her, Frank.

—She isn't the first dead girl you ever found.

—No.

—Stan, I know you might have had a look at the toxicology. I'm not going to make a big deal about it, but I have an idea of who might have showed you. That same person might just have put it back in the wrong place when Len Gleber went to file it. You know you don't have any official capacity.

—I don't need to be reminded.

—I know that. I suppose I'm just putting it out there.

—You don't think Judy was in any kind of situation that was over her head? There was a boyfriend, I heard.

—Yes, said Frank. Gleber interviewed him, the boyfriend. He's a low-life, Stan. A nobody. And I don't think he was quite the boyfriend she let on he was. I think he was taking advantage of a girl who didn't know any better, whenever he felt the need . . . Matter of fact, though, it surprises me and exasperates me a little that you know about the boyfriend too. How much more do you know?

—That business about the boyfriend is about all of it.

The patio door slid open and Louise came out. She said: Hi Dad, hi Grandpa.

—Grandpa and I are having a discussion, said Frank.

—Supper will be ready in five minutes.

—That's fine, said Frank. Be sure to knock first next time, you understand?

—Yes, Dad.

Louise went back into the house.

—Judy Lacroix killed herself, said Frank. She was a sad girl who should have been properly looked after, and she wasn't, and when she couldn't handle some of the ugliness this world has a way of dumping on people, she went and took her own life.

Stan nodded. He finished his beer. He looked to see what the dog was doing.

—It's a damn shame that you had to be the one to find her, said Frank. But you did find her and then you made sure the right people were in the right place. Thinking about it that way, I wish anytime a body turns up to the public, it's a retired cop who finds it. But now you don't have to worry about it any further.

—I'm not worried, said Stan.

—I hope not. Now come on. You know Mary doesn't like supper to be kept waiting. She's just like her mother in that way.

—Yes, said Stan.

Frank got up and opened the patio door and went inside the house. Stan followed.

Stan tried to put the conversation with Frank out of his head, but a few days after Thanksgiving his telephone rang. A woman's voice was on the other end.

—Is this Mr. Maitland?

—Yes, this is Stan Maitland here.

—Mr. Maitland, this is Ellie Lacroix calling. I wondered if you'd still want to speak with me.

He met with her at one o'clock that afternoon. They went to the Owl Café and sat in a booth halfway to the back. He had a roast beef sandwich and a cup of tea, and Eleanor Lacroix had a bowl of the day's soup. She just moved her spoon around in it.

—I apologize, Mr. Maitland.

—Call me Stan, and I don't know what you're apologizing for.

—How I spoke to you when you came to see me.

He put his sandwich on the plate and sat back.

—I know this has been a real upset to you, Ellie, but I also know that that's not why you weren't so quick to chat with me.

—That's true.

—I knew your family for a long time. It's only been the last twenty years or so, which at your age would seem a lot longer to you than it does to me, that I haven't had much of an eye on you.

—I don't know how old we were, said Eleanor. Maybe six or seven. You and another cop arrested my dad one night. We, me and Judy, we didn't even know what to think about that. We thought you were taking him to jail but when we got up the next morning he was there at the breakfast table. He looked like he hadn't slept all night.

—Your dad didn't sleep that night, you're right about that. He had a long walk back from where we dropped him off.

—Why would you do something like that, Mr. Maitland?

—Your dad, Aurel, he liked to have a drink, didn't he.

—He drank. But he never laid a finger on Judy or me.

—You can't say the same about how he was with your mother, can you.

Eleanor had the soup spoon closed in her fist. She lifted it in a strange way, as though to emphasize something, and then she put it on the table.

—I . . . No, I can't say that.

—That particular night he got very rough with your mother, said Stan. I don't know how much of this you might of known about or not, mind, but the neighbours called us. It was me and

Dick Shannon who went over to your place. Ellie, I was a cop for a long time. I did things, I don't know now if I was right or wrong or what-all, but I did things in a certain way that I thought was right. I didn't always care to see a man go to jail when I thought I could maybe help him come around to a better way of seeing things.

—So you hauled my dad out to some back road and kicked the hell out of him.

—No, Ellie. I never once had any kind of a battle with your dad. All I did was, I had a long talk with him and then gave him a good walk home to think it over. Do you remember him getting rough with your mother after that night?

—No, said Eleanor. I don't. Look, Mr. Maitland—Stan. My dad had a lot of problems. He used to have nightmares, from the war, I guess, although that was something he never talked about. I know he got shelled pretty bad and there were some scars on his leg. Anyway, he drank too much. He had a lot of trouble keeping a job. I know. I know. But the first thing I remember in my whole life, me and Judy are sitting on my dad's knee, and he's telling us the story of Baptiste and the Devil, my favourite. He could tell it better than anybody else. He talked French so fast you could barely understand him. I loved my dad.

Eleanor looked out the window. Stan took a bite of his sandwich.

—I never had much reason to come see your dad after that night. Which is why I didn't see you or your sister grow up.

—You want to talk about my sister, is that right?

—Yes.

—Don't you think I've answered all the questions the police had for me?

—Well, the only person's behalf I'm asking on is my own.

She nodded and said: Okay. But I want to know some things first, Stan. I want to hear your side. My dad used to say you had it out for our whole family.

—Is that what he said?

—He told me what happened with his older brothers. What do you have to say?

Stan put his hands together under the table. He thought how to weigh his response, then it came to him how they were in the wrong place for it altogether. .

—It's a nice day, Ellie. A little bit chilly but not so bad if you're moving. Would you care to go for a walk?

At the corner of Bayview Street and Chippewa Avenue was a three-storey brown-brick. Stan and Eleanor stood across the street. He pointed to the row of windows along the second floor.

—I had a boxing clubhouse up there. The parish priest, this was Father O'Leary, signed a lease on the room. Me and him, we both thought if we could give the boys from town some better things to do it would keep them out of trouble. I was twenty-four years old and I'd just finished my own boxing career and I came back here and I got hired as a constable pretty quick. When I wasn't being a cop, I was up there with O'Leary, who'd been a decent welterweight in the seminary. I was up there with him teaching boys from around town how to box. I don't know how it works for girls, but I think with a boy, he pretty near can't help it— when he's changing from boy to man, he's got a certain taste for breaking things. If you show him how to do it right, then it's a good way for him and his chums to have a couple go-rounds in the ring and get all that out of them, instead of later on that same night busting chairs or bottles over each other's heads. You see?

She looked speculative, said: Maybe. I don't remember me or Judy ever wanting to break bottles on people's heads.

—That's why I don't know how it is for girls. Anyhow, your uncle Darien was one of the best natural fighters I ever saw. Your uncle Remi was good too, but Darien was something. He was just barely a middleweight. They didn't have a whole lot to eat out at your grandmother's place, and your uncles never filled out right, but Darien still classed as a middleweight. He could throw these hooks like a machine gun. A lot of the other boys in the club quit sparring with him.

—I never met my uncles.

—I know you didn't. They've been gone a long time. Would you walk a ways with me? I guess you're not working at the bank today.

—No. Not today.

Stan took a last look at the windows where he'd trained local boys in the art of boxing. Then he and Eleanor walked along Chippewa in the direction of the river.

—I thought Darien had the makings of a professional fighter. He'd of been, oh, maybe seventeen at the time. Those were pretty lean years. Your uncle made a bit of a name for himself. The men on relief, they had a lot of love for a kid like Darien who came from nothing. They'd come out by the dozens, fifty of them, a hundred, to see him fight. We couldn't fit them in the clubhouse any more. Anyway, we got going so as I was coach and trainer and Father O'Leary was the manager. We brought on my old cutman. For a little while things were pretty good. Pretty good. Then there was this fight at the Orangemen's Hall in Orillia.

—Orillia, said Eleanor. Yes. My dad talked about that a little bit.

—Jack Watts, said Stan. He wasn't any kind of goddamn middleweight but he made the weigh-in for it. He had this haymaker he'd throw. I should of known better. It got to the fourth round and your uncle Darien was on the ropes and he dropped his guard. Just for a second. Watts hit him so hard he . . . well, that was the fight. The trouble was, your uncle got hit a lot harder than any of us knew at the time. He was never really right after that. I should of known better, Ellie. But I was thinking about winning. I guess maybe I wished it was me in the ring again.

They'd turned onto River Street and were passing Victory Appliances. On the other side of the street was the library. It was a squat building, with walls of thick limestone blocks and deeply recessed windows. A plaque describing the building's history was fixed to the wall beside the entryway. They crossed over and Stan led them up the stone steps and through the doors. The interior of the library smelled like dusty books. A directory was mounted on a pedestal just past the front doors. Stan consulted it, squinting, tracing his finger along it. He led Eleanor down a flight of stairs. They came into a room with filing cabinets and a row of microfiche viewers. He brought them as far as a door marked STAFF ONLY.

—We used to have our offices on the other side of this door. The holding cells were just past that.

They went back up to the main floor and found a reading room behind the fiction stacks. There was a window looking out of the back of the building. A short downslope to the river. He told her how there used to be a yard enclosed by a block wall out there. At one time it had been stables and then the yard was converted to a vehicle compound for the patrol cars.

—They used that yard, said Stan.

—What do you mean?

—For your uncle.

—When he died. And you were there.

—I didn't kill your uncles, Eleanor, I didn't. There were some hard years. The boxing clubhouse didn't last long after that fight in Orillia. Father O'Leary moved to a different parish and the man who replaced him didn't have any interest in boxing. I don't think we were two more months at it after that. The farm where your dad lived, your grandmother, your aunts, Darien, Remi, they couldn't afford to keep it going. They were in some money trouble. There was this one night Darien and Remi got into a fight with some boys at a dance. I brought them in. They came with me easy enough because they knew me. They got locked up in the holding cells. I was on the beat that night so I went back out. What ended up happening here was some kind of dust-up. Your uncles got out, and Darien, he shot the cop who was on duty. Charlie Rayfield was his name. Darien shot him with his own pistol. I don't know how much of this you might know.

—Some, she said. I know some of it. But this is different. Hearing it from you.

—Well, Darien shot this policeman and he and Remi walked right out the door. Pretty quick it was two boys who were in a hell of a lot more trouble than they'd thought of. It wasn't much more than a day or so before a half-dozen Provincial cops were up here from the city. They took over from us town cops. They hired on a bunch of local boys—men I knew, friends of mine—to help them track down Darien and Remi. There was one thing that the inspector figured out. Charlie Rayfield had a little .22 pistol he wore on his ankle and he'd fired a few shots off. The Provincial inspector, he figured maybe Remi or Darien had gotten shot on the way out, and if that was the case, maybe they didn't get so far as everybody thought.

—My dad used to say it was you.

—I know what your dad would of said. Thing was, I knew your uncles pretty well. I didn't want it to end in more shooting, and I figured with the Provincials looking for them, that's what would happen. So I went over to an old bootlegger's place I knew of, where your uncles used to like to go to have a drink. And sure enough, that's where they were. The inspector was right, Remi was shot. He was in bad shape, Ellie. He had a .22 bullet in his stomach.

—What did you do?

—What I did was I talked them into turning themselves over to me. They were scared. Remi was sick. But while this was happening, Charlie Rayfield died in the hospital. So the charge became murder. The way it turned out . . .

—Please. I want to hear it.

—Your uncle Remi died from blood poisoning. Darien got charged with murder. The murder of a policeman was a serious thing. He went to the penitentiary for a few years. Then in 1944, when your dad was serving in France, they brought Darien back here to town. Right back home. And just out there, where the yard used to be, that's where they did it.

—Where they executed him.

—Yes. He was the last person in the county to be put to death. I spoke to him, your uncle, the night before. He was scared, but not so scared as he could of been. Mostly he wished his ma would of come to see him. But things were different for her. She didn't have the farm any more. I was there the next day when Darien was hanged. And I was a cop for another almost thirty years after that but there's not a day that goes by that I don't think of that morning. Of your uncle up there on the platform. Every day, Ellie.

She was quiet for awhile.

—I don't know what to say, Stan. I knew some of this but I didn't know it. I guess I think for all my dad was or wasn't, how could he have two brothers who ended up like that?

Outside the window where the vehicle compound and the wall used to be, they'd landscaped a couple of footpaths overlooking the river. A man in coveralls came into view, raking leaves under a red maple. There were some odd characters who hung around the library in the afternoon. A man in a plaid jacket was snoring quietly in a study carrel. A man with mole eyes behind mended glasses was sitting at a table close by, bent over an anatomical textbook, looking at images of the female reproductive organs.

—It was all a long time ago, said Stan.

They stayed at the library for awhile and Eleanor held her end of their agreement. She moved into the telling as if it were something that lifted a burden from her. That she and her sister were twins did not give her any great insight.

—You can know someone better than anybody else knows her, and still you don't know her at all. How is it that everything went bad for her, but not me?

Nobody gave Judy's ailment a name for many years. Troubles with their father, Aurel, were enough. What had no name warranted no sympathy. It wasn't when their father died but when Eleanor went to college in the city that Judy suffered the most. Telling this to Stan, Eleanor had to pause between her words and look away. She said she felt guilty about that.

A doctor paid a visit and made a referral. The psychiatrist to whom Judy was referred gave her condition a name.

While Eleanor went to college, Judy went to a hospital east of the city, where she lived in a residence with some other girls. They were ex-junkies, they were girls with scars in their arms, they didn't eat right, they didn't say the right things. But Judy herself got along at the hospital after her first few months. There was a farm on the grounds. There was a new gymnasium. There were things to do with your hands and with your time.

Eleanor visited when she could. She was going to college and she was not far away. Some of these girls at the hospital were suicidal. They slugged through their time under a constant state of scrutiny.

—But Judy, said Eleanor, bad as she might get, she wasn't ever, like, she wasn't the kind to kill herself. That wasn't part of it. So that's why, Stan, that's why . . .

Judy was admitted to hospital again after their mother died. Eleanor, back home between terms, started going with Tommy Spencer. He was a local boy, his dad did roadwork contracting. Then the doctors at the hospital started releasing a lot of the patients to reintegrate them with the community. Judy was discharged two years ago, the same time Eleanor started at the National Trust. Judy and Eleanor moved together into their parents' old house, the house they'd grown up in. Eleanor's benefits covered a prescription for amitriptyline.

The pill was called Elavil and it kept Judy level. She put on some weight, but not much, and before that she was really too skinny anyway. She slept a lot. But for once she was even-tempered.

Still, Eleanor considered that Judy might grow bored. One thing about the hospital was that they kept you occupied. So Eleanor talked to Alda Shipley at Busy Beaver Janitorial, who'd had the cleaning contract at the National Trust for a long time, and for the first time in her life, Judy had a job. Busy Beaver was a bonded local outfit. They'd arrive in the afternoon before the branch closed and they'd clean until eight o'clock at night. The bathrooms, the carpets, the wastebaskets. Alda reported back to Eleanor that Judy didn't have much to say but she usually smiled faintly and she worked steadily and didn't object to any of the tasks.

Then Eleanor told Stan about the man who'd come into Judy's life. Around May or June, Judy started getting agitated. She was quick to put you off if you asked her anything. She would say, I'm fine, why do you want to know? It wasn't any kind of agitation Eleanor had seen in her before. Eleanor was already guessing what it might be.

And why not? Judy wasn't unattractive, and since the medication had taken the swings out of her mood, she was good company. She wasn't forthright about whoever the man might be and Ellie didn't press her, but then she happened to meet him at the bank one day in the summer. The Busy Beaver crew had started their work in the late afternoon. Eleanor had a dentist's appointment and was given leave fifteen minutes early. She went down the rear corridor and said goodbye to her sister and went out through the back door. She was halfway across the parking lot behind the bank when a man got out of a car and said: Hey, Judy.

This man was kind of singing an old song, *It's Judy's turn to cry, it's Judy's turn to cry. Judy's smile was so mean,* sang the man.

Eleanor guessed it took her coming closer, twenty feet or so, for the man to realize she wasn't her sister. They looked enough alike until you got up close.

—You've got to be Ellie, said the man. I'm sorry to have mixed you up.

Eleanor said it was okay, it happened from time to time. She let on that she knew about this man in Judy's life, that he wasn't something she'd only guessed at. So that was probably why he didn't tell her his name. Eleanor couldn't exactly say what he looked like. He wore jeans and a T-shirt, she remembered. Good for the weather but not like he'd come from an office or anything. He had sunglasses on, the kind with mirrored lenses. The car he was leaning up against wasn't anything special. He was older than Judy, maybe even ten years older, but otherwise he just looked like anybody.

He was nice enough. He seemed easy to talk to. He asked how Ellie liked working at National Trust and how she liked living in town. He smiled. Eleanor might have been late for her dentist appointment if Judy hadn't come out the back door just then. She was surprised. She chewed at her bottom lip and spoke in singular phrases, and the three of them—Eleanor, Judy and the man—made the points of a triangle as they stood talking to each other. So Eleanor, laughing a little, pleased for her sister, took her leave. As she was going she heard him sing it again, *Judy's smile was sooo mean*. And Eleanor heard her sister laugh.

That weekend they had a barbecue over at Tommy Spencer's house. Judy didn't bring the man and didn't make any mention of him. But then Eleanor got Judy to herself for awhile in the lawn chairs at the back of the yard. They watched Tommy horsing around with his brother's kids.

—So when were you going to tell me? said Eleanor.

—Tell you about what? said Judy, not meeting her sister's eyes.

It took a bit of pressing but Judy eventually told her. Once she got talking about him, she had a hard time stopping. The last six weeks or so, since the weather got nice, Judy had started walking to work every day. This was a big thing for her, a twenty-five-minute walk, but it was good exercise that was managing the weight the Elavil wanted to put on her frame. The midpoint of the walk was a little joint called Donut Line, and she'd started stopping there for an early meal before work. And this is where she'd met him.

Eleanor told Stan she could imagine it. Her sister at a table by herself. Bowl of soup, sandwich, day-old tabloid. There's this seasonal labourer who comes in around the same time every day for a coffee. This guy with the nice smile passes Judy at her table, the first time just saying hello, the next time asking how are you, and the day after that asking if this seat's taken.

The man's name was Colin.

It wasn't clear how long it had taken Judy to go on a date with him. Judy told Eleanor they went to the A&W mostly. They just talked. Colin was a good listener. He didn't ask a lot of questions, like how she was feeling that day, was it an up day or a down day. Judy would tell him all about how she liked riding on the train, like when she'd gone to and from the city, or how she'd loved it when her dad used to take them to the drive-in before he died. You couldn't go to the drive-in any more, of course, since it had burned down.

Eleanor wanted to ask Judy about the other dimension to it, but was embarrassed. Even now, telling Stan, she blushed fiercely. What else might be going on, other than chats in the A&W parking lot? But she made herself ask, and Judy stood up and said: Oh my God, Ellie. I'm twenty-eight years old. I know what I'm doing.

Eleanor only saw Colin once or twice more. Both times he was dropping Judy off at the National Trust. It seemed like a sign that maybe their lives were moving forward.

But then, around the third week of August, something happened. At work one afternoon, Eleanor didn't see her sister. Alda hadn't seen her either. Eleanor hurried home, found her sister in her bedroom, pale, haggard, as bad as she'd been in a very long time. She was unwashed and the room was musky.

It was Colin. Eleanor couldn't draw the particulars out of her sister but they didn't really matter. He'd been around for awhile and then he'd broken it off. He'd been casual about it.

Judy stopped eating, quit showing up for work. She quit taking her pills. She spent entire days inside with the blinds drawn and the television on. Eleanor called the doctor but he said little of substance. Judy wasn't aggressive or volatile. She was her own custodian as far as the law was concerned. Nobody could force her to medicate. They could only watch her. She'd been worse in the past, and she'd come out of that.

Eleanor told Stan that she didn't really think she could hold Colin to hard judgment for what became of Judy. Her sister had no prior experience with men. If a man wanted to take advantage of her, or just tell her this and that to keep her around for sex, she wouldn't know any better. And even if Colin didn't intentionally misguide her, Judy had probably made it a certain way in her mind and her heart that wasn't the same as reality. So Eleanor couldn't judge him too harshly.

Eleanor spent as much time as she could with her sister. She and Tommy cancelled a camping trip they'd planned for Labour Day. Then, the Tuesday after the long weekend, Eleanor came home from work and saw a dent in the front bumper of their mother's old car. Some bad scratches were raked into the paint. She found Judy on the back porch. Judy was different from how she'd been for the past ten days. She was smiling again. She looked half asleep. She looked like she'd resumed her medication.

Eleanor asked about the car. Judy told her sister a little bit about what she'd done, how she'd gone to a roadhouse where Colin liked to hang out. But this was the middle of the afternoon and he wasn't there. So she went to another place, a place he'd taken her a few times. A nice quiet place out at Indian Lake, twenty-five minutes east of town, where he lived in a motorhome, the kind you wish you could drive across the country in. Judy told Eleanor that she'd parked the car and gotten out and walked up the driveway. It was a long driveway. She'd come in sight of the motorhome. Outside, there was some *s-l-u-t* suntanning in a chair. Asleep, Judy guessed, because then when she heard Colin's voice calling this girl from inside the motorhome, calling her *baby*, calling, *Hey, baby, come on inside*, the girl in the chair didn't even move.

—You could tell just by looking at her what a tart she was, said Judy.

Judy turned around and walked down the long driveway and got back in the car and drove back to town. She cried the whole way. She hit a mailbox at one point but didn't care. She just wanted to go home.

Some real *s-l-u-t*, Judy told Eleanor. The flat way she said it, she might have been commenting on how the fall was right around the corner. She was feeling better now, she said. She had half a mind to get in the car and drive back out there and rain on the little party they were probably having.

—But you won't go, Judy, will you.

—No, Ellie. I'm staying right here.

—I keep thinking about how I shouldn't have left her for one minute, said Eleanor. But I'd made plans with Tommy that night to make up for the trip we'd cancelled. I thought Judy was okay because she was on her pills again, and would probably fall asleep early, and we'd be able to talk about it more in the morning . . .

Eleanor had been sitting at the table in the reading room with her cheek propped on her fist for quite awhile. No tears had been shed. She just looked tired.

—You couldn't of known, said Stan.

He didn't believe that. He could see Eleanor's lapse in judgment for what it was and he knew she would carry that with her for a long time to come.

—Do you remember what time it was you found her?

—Oh, said Stan. Had to of been ten o'clock.

—Three hours after the last time I ever saw her.

There wasn't much else to the story. Judy had left a note on the dashboard of the car. All it said was *I'm sorrey & I love you. Ellie.* Eleanor answered questions for the police and went through Judy's personal effects. She received cards in the mail. The women at the bank brought casseroles. If Eleanor never had another casserole again, she said, she'd be happy.

Stan walked with Eleanor back to where she'd parked at the Owl Café. She was driving Tommy's car. She'd gotten rid of the car Judy died in.

—What will you do now, Stan?

—I don't know, Ellie. First, I'll have a word with a couple friends of mine.

—Maybe there's nothing to know. Really. Maybe you shouldn't even trouble yourself.

—It's no trouble for an old guy with nothing much to do.

She opened her car door and said: Thanks for hearing me out, Stan.

—No. Thank *you*.

—I loved my dad, said Eleanor. I loved my dad, but he was wrong about you.

In the morning, Clifton took Lee with him to pick up building materials. The heavy labour at the cottage where they were working was wrapping up, Clifton said. He didn't know how much longer he'd need Bud or Lee on the site. Lee nodded, frowning.

—You're not losing heart, are you? said Clifton.

—I guess I liked the way things were going out at the big place.

—You're just supposed to keep heart as always. Think about

your Matthew. If you have faith as small as this mustard seed, you can say to this mountain, move from there to there, and it will be so. 17:20.

—Faith I got, Mr. Murray. A job is what I need to keep.

—Well, it so happens that I got the bid for another place. We'll be starting there soon enough, and I'll have enough work for you and Bud straight to Christmas if we're lucky.

Lee looked at Clifton. He was driving his truck very fast, weaving between other vehicles on the road. He was perched forward on the seat. Lee had never spent so much time alone with him.

At a little after nine o'clock, they pulled into the parking lot in front of Heron Lumber.

—I'll go in and give them the order, said Clifton. You go on into the yard and I'll meet you there.

Lee got out of the truck and went into the lumberyard adjacent to the store, lighting a smoke as he went. October was cold if you were just standing around. A kid in a Heron Lumber shirt came by and asked Lee if he was waiting on anything. Lee had just opened his mouth to answer when he heard his name being shouted. He looked, expecting to see Clifton. Instead, a wiry man was briskly coming his way. The man's hair had thinned and he had a burn-scar on the side of his face. He shouted Lee's name again.

—Speedy, said Lee. I'll be damned.

Speedy Simmons stopped short and scrubbed his hand across the front of his chinos and then offered it for Lee to shake. He said: Jesus Christ. I was in the parking lot and I thought that's Leland goddamn King. You've got grey hair, but. Hey, I didn't even know you were getting out. How long you been home?

—Six weeks or so, said Lee.

—Say, Lee, good for you.

Speedy was a face from the distant past. They'd run with the same crowd when they were teenagers, had spent a night or two sharing the drunk tank. Now they made small talk for five minutes.

Lee told him about his place downtown and about working for Clifton Murray. It wasn't clear where Speedy was working. He'd been at Heron Lumber to buy tools, he said, when he saw Lee in the parking lot. Then Clifton's truck appeared behind them. Clifton leaned out the driver-side window, looked at Lee and clapped his hand against the door.

—I better get going, said Lee.

Speedy offered his hand again. He said: You bet, Lee. Say, it was really something to see you. I'll come look you up sometime soon, we'll play a game of pool or euchre or what-have-you.

Clifton fretted over an invoice while Lee loaded materials into the back of the truck. Among the materials was a selection of oak and maple with which the kitchen cabinets were going to be made. Lee ran his hands over the wood. He could picture the cabinets as they took shape and came together. He knew that feeling of satisfaction.

When they were loaded, they got back into the truck and drove out of the lumberyard. Clifton was in a talkative mood: There's a tailor I got to stop at quick. Next month, my niece is getting married. A wedding in November—some of the gals say it's nice, some can't figure it out. I don't know. This is my brother Irving's daughter. Were you ever married?

—No.

—Oh.

A few minutes later Clifton broke the quiet again: So you know a thing or two about cabinetmaking?

—Say again? said Lee.

—Isn't that what you told me?

—Yes, that's true. When I was living in the St. Leonard's house in the city I was working at a shop that built office furniture. All the woodworking stuff, that was mine to do. I built a lot of desks—

—Desks aren't the same as cabinets. And what was this Saint—Saint who?

—St. Leonard's Society. They ran the halfway house where I was living.

—St. Leonard. Was this some kind of Catholic outfit?

—It wasn't Catholic. It was just named for him. For Saint Leonard. If I remember right, he was a guy from the old times, a monk, like, who freed a number of prisoners and took them to live with him out in the woods away from people. Taught them things and so forth, taught them how to be productive.

—Hmm. Long as you keep in mind the real way to salvation.

—I do, boss. Every day.

They drove in silence for some minutes more, until Clifton abruptly said: But I'll admit, mister man, you are a hard worker.

That afternoon, Bud was lively. He wanted to know had Lee seen the Maple Leafs kick the heck out of Buffalo the night before. They were cutting and packing fibreglass insulation into the exterior walls. Lee's skin was itchy. He and Bud both had bandanas wrapped over their mouths and noses. His eyes were stinging.

He turned back from the wall to cut a new piece of insulation. Clifton had given them a kitchen carving knife to use. The fibreglass dulled the blade quickly and they had to sharpen the knife frequently.

—You want to watch a game, you let me know, said Bud. We'll go to my friend's place. He's got a big colour TV.

Lee nodded. He was thinking about Speedy Simmons, thinking about the old days. His youth, what there was of it. There was Speedy, there was Jim Robichaud, Terry Lachlan, some others. None of them came from much, and nobody in town thought they had much ahead of them either. They battled constantly with kids of better means. At age twenty or twenty-one, Jim Robichaud had the idea that they should start an outlaw motorcycle club—he'd seen *The Wild One* a few too many times—but none of them, as far as Lee knew, ever actually ended up with a bike. Not in those days, anyway, even if they tried to dress the part. But there were lots of good times with those boys. They worked what straight jobs they could get, not ever really worrying about whether or not they kept the job for long, and whenever money was really scarce, they stole cars for a man two towns away who bought them at a good premium, or they moved crates of stolen liquor and counterfeit cigarettes for some people Speedy knew. They drank hard and fought hard and looked out for each other, and anyone who wasn't a cop did not fuck with them. For the most part.

—Smoke? said Bud. It's the hour.

—Yeah. Good idea.

They went outside and pulled their bandanas down and lit their cigarettes. Lee leaned against the wall and set to sharpening the knife they were using to cut the insulation. They watched Sylvain. He had begun work on a path that would lead down to the lake. He was crouched on a bed of gravel, eyeballing a string-line down the centre of the path. He'd brought on a kid from town to work with him. The kid was moving the string in slight increments side to side.

Bud puffed out smoke. He said: That insulation makes me feel like I got the clap. But all over instead of just my privates. Actually, that reminds me of a good one. This mom, she finds her kids playing doctor on the back porch, and she says to them, When Daddy gets home you're going to get a good licking! Which is what—Oh, wait. Damn.

—I'm going to get you a joke book or something, said Lee.

—I know so many good ones but I frig them up every time.

Sylvain barked at the town kid: Were you born like this or what?

Then he stood up from the string-line and started walking towards his truck. As he passed Lee and Bud, he said: Another smoke break, eh, boys?

—I see you got yourself a helper, said Lee.

—I'd hire you two if I wanted to lose money till next summer.

The familiar feeling overtook Lee quickly. He pushed away from the wall and flung his cigarette down in one motion. He turned the carving knife, held it up, and then pitched it into the ground a pace away from Sylvain's boots. The blade didn't catch the dirt and the knife bounced aside.

—Do you have a fucking problem with me?

—Lee, said Bud.

—Shut up.

But Sylvain just clicked his tongue against his teeth. He took on a slow smile. He reached out and clapped Lee on the arm: Mon frère, a long time I was worried about you. Now, I don't worry.

He carried on towards his truck, laughing. Bud skirted around Lee and picked the carving knife up from the ground. Lee balled his hands into fists and squeezed them and then let them go slowly. He took a long breath and held it in the pit of his stomach and then released it. It had been a long time since the anger had taken hold of him like it just had. He tried not to think about that too much.

—Oh boy, said Bud. Oh boy. Okay. I guess we can do more work now.

—I'm going to have another smoke.

—It's . . . you know, one an hour.

—I'm going to have another smoke. Do you want one?

He offered his pack and Bud took one.

When Sylvain came back from the truck he tipped Lee a wink as he passed them by, and then he yelled at the hired kid to quit screwing around.

That evening Lee took Helen to the Chateau Royale steakhouse on the other side of the town docks. As they went inside, she was smiling at him over her shoulder. His fingertips were in the small of her back. They were greeted with smells of searing meat, and they were shown to a table towards the rear of the dining room. Helen looked at the table and looked at the back of the restaurant and she voiced a faint, thoughtful sound, as if something were on her mind. Whatever it was, she didn't say it.

Lee hung his jean jacket on the back of his chair and sat down. The steakhouse's red interior walls were hung with paintings of castles, pastoral scenes, bullfighters. Just above their table was a picture of a lone parapet on a hill.

—I've never been here, said Helen.

—Me neither. I walked by it a couple times. I thought it looked like a good place.

A waitress came and asked what they would have to drink. Helen asked for a white wine. Lee asked for a Coca-Cola. The waitress left them.

—You could have a glass of wine with me. White wine is like not drinking at all.

—That's okay. I'll stick with the cola.

—Look at where we are.

—Where we are?

—Look at where we're sitting. I mean, really.

—This place is alright. It's nice. They got all the right smells for me.

The waitress came with their drinks on a tray. Helen gestured for Lee to order first. He asked for a striploin well done and a baked potato. Helen ordered the surf 'n' turf. She winked at him, told him sometimes you just had to spoil yourself. They lit cigarettes after the waitress had gone again.

—How was work? said Helen.

—We put up insulation all day. I had to have a cold shower for the itch to go away.

She nodded, drank her wine.

—I saw a guy I knew, said Lee. A long time ago. Before I went up. He didn't look much different. We talked a bit. I don't know what he's doing. Probably got hitched and had some kids.

—Do you wish that was you?

—What?

—Do you wish you'd gotten hitched and had a couple kids?

—I don't know, said Lee. It's an idea I never gave any thought to. Who'd want me as their old man?

—Parents, well, it takes a certain kind, doesn't it. Look, Brown Eyes, if you're meant to have a family, you will. Everything happens for a reason. Karma.

—My sister and her kids, I don't know, it seems like a lot of craziness to have kids tearing around all the time. But I guess I don't mind it, either. It's kind of what you're supposed to do. Some of the cons I was in with, they had their wives and their kids come to visit them and whatnot. It would have been good to have that . . . Anyhow, look, I'm not saying I'm dying to have a family. All I'm saying was I saw that guy. His life went one way and mine went the other.

The waitress came with their suppers on wooden cutting boards. Helen asked for another glass of wine. Lee broke open his potato and started to pile it onto the steak. He piled the vegetables on as well and drowned it all in A1 sauce.

—Oh, said Helen. Really.

He looked up at her. The cutting board before her was loaded with steamed vegetables, an eight-ounce steak, and four shrimp. She'd cut off a chunk of the steak and was holding it up for him to look at.

—Does that look rare to you?

—It's pink, said Lee.

The waitress returned with Helen's wine.

—This is not rare, said Helen. I asked for rare.

The waitress set the wine down.

—I'm real sorry about that. I'll get it taken care of.

The waitress took Helen's meal and went back in the direction of the kitchen. Lee sat for a moment and then put his knife and fork down.

—You may as well go ahead, said Helen. You must be hungry. Doesn't look like they messed yours up too bad.

Lee started into his supper. He talked around mouthfuls of food: My sister and her husband said they want to meet you. They want to meet this gal I told them about.

—This gal, is that right? Anyway, I see you haven't given up on the idea that somebody might try to snatch your food. Look at that, you're halfway through already.

—I was hungry.

He felt her foot against his leg.

—I can see that. So do your sister and her husband drink? Or are they straight-arrows like you?

—Straight-arrows, huh. No, they don't drink either. I thought I told you, he's a pastor. He preaches at, what's it called, Galilee Tabernacle.

When Helen's supper came back she made the waitress wait till she'd checked the meat for rareness. Then she ordered another glass of wine.

She was barely starting her meal as Lee was finishing his.

—That was good, said Lee.

—You eat everything. You eat the fat.

—Hey, you take a look at what they fed me for seventeen years. You'd eat everything too. I'd eat that damn bone if I could. How's yours?

—It's alright. Annoying to have to take two tries, but anyway.

—Well, take your time.

Lee looked around the half-empty restaurant, looked at the picture of the parapet. He sipped his Coca-Cola.

—You never gave much thought to a family?

—Wasn't what the universe had planned for me, said Helen.

—I see. Did you want dessert?

—Oh my God, no. I had a doughnut at lunch.

When Helen was finished the waitress came back to collect the cutting boards.

—Was there anything else I could get for you folks?

—I don't think so, said Helen.

—I'm really sorry about that steak.

Helen looked up at her and smiled, said: Do you think I don't know how this works, hun? You take people like me and my gent here and you sit us right back by the restrooms. I know how this works.

—Ma'am, I'm sorry. I don't have any idea what you're talking about.

—How about just getting us the cheque.

—Right away, said the waitress.

She returned with the bill and was gone again. Helen tapped out a cigarette. Lee took the bill and looked at it and hoped nothing showed on his face.

—You don't understand, said Helen. It's okay. I keep remembering how things are different for you—you haven't had the chance to see how so many people treat each other disrespectfully and all that. You want to go straight to your place?

—What else did you have in mind?

—Getting out of this snob-hole for starters. Get a drink at the Shamrock maybe.

He clapped his hand down on the tabletop: I'm not going to have a goddamn drink!

—Okay, Brown Eyes, said Helen.

People were looking at them. Lee lowered his face, stared at the tablecloth.

—Look, should we get going?

—I have to powder my nose, said Helen. I hope you don't leave her a tip.

She got up and headed to the ladies' room. Lee attended to the bill with cash from his wallet, conscious as ever of how much money he was spending. Then he looked over. He had a straight line of sight down the rear passageway where the washrooms were located. Helen had her head halfway out of the ladies' room door. She was gesturing emphatically for Lee to come.

He got up from the table and headed her way, said: What's the problem?

She pulled him in and closed the door. She was on him like a predator. Nails, teeth, tongue, taste of wine on her breath. The washroom was a space for individual use. Small and cramped, pink, the sink mounted to the wall. It smelled like cheap deodorizer.

—Somebody's going to know we're in here.

—I don't care. I wouldn't come back here. Snobs. Pricks.

She turned around and held the edge of the sink in one hand and balled her skirt up in her other hand. Her underpants were down around her ankles.

—Come on, said Helen.

—Bend over a little more.

—Careful where you stick that thing.

She reached around behind her and took firm hold of him and guided him in. She bent over farther and the angle was better. For a moment he did nothing. Then he grasped her shoulder. He took her roughly, one knee into the back of her leg as if he might trip her. He could see the sink threatening to come loose from the wall. Her nails pierced hard into the bare flesh at the tops of his legs. Afterwards, she preceded him out of the washroom, recomposing her hair as she went. He was certain all eyes in the dining room would be on them, but no one paid them any attention. He gathered his jacket from the back of the chair.

Outside all she said was: I'll sleep tonight.

She took his arm and they walked down the street. At one point she stumbled on the curb and dropped her purse. He squatted down to retrieve it and there in the street light he saw a drop of semen on her cowboy boot, like a crude pearl inlaid in the synthetic leather.

It was one of the few evenings Pete spent at home. He was sitting on his bed reading a paperback but he was unable to concentrate on it. His thoughts kept finding their way back to Emily. The last time he'd seen her was the morning after the party two weeks ago. He thought of Billy disappearing with her into a bedroom somewhere.

—Shit, said Pete.

—I heard that.

Pete's half-brother Luke was at the door.

—You heard that? said Pete. Well, if you snitch on me I'll cut your head off and hang it from the wall as a warning to other snitches. Come in. Close the door. What do you want?

—What's a Jew?

—What's a Jew? You know what a Jew is.

—Jesus was a Jew. But the other Jews killed him. We learned about how all the Jews are guilty of it.

—Look, said Pete. You know that store in town where we bought your sneakers? Remember the guy that worked there? Mr. Gold?

—Yes. He had glasses.

—That's right. Anyway, Mr. Gold's a Jew.

—He is?

—Yes. Mr. Gold. Do you think Mr. Gold personally killed Jesus?

—I don't know.

—Yes you do. You're not using your head, Luke. What do you really think? Did Mr. Gold at the shoe store personally kill Jesus?

—No. But Mrs. Adams said all the Jews are guilty of it.

Pete sat back in his chair. A nasty feeling went through him.

—Mrs. Adams, said Pete.

—My Sunday School teacher.

—When did Mrs. Adams become your Sunday School teacher?

—When we started this year.

—Well, Luke, it's possible that your Sunday School teacher is full of shit. You have to be careful. Not all grown-ups are right just because they're grown-ups. Or because they're Sunday School teachers. Would God give you a brain if he didn't want you to use it?

—No . . .

—No is right.

The boy loafed about, frowning at the carpet and at Pete when it seemed Pete was looking elsewhere.

—What's on your mind, Luke? Really?

—How come Uncle Lee went to jail?

Pete straightened up: Well, Uncle Lee did a pretty bad thing.

—What did he do?

—I don't know for sure, but it was really bad.

—Peter . . .

—You want to know, Luke, because you're eight and when you're eight you want to know everything. But—and you're going to be mad at me saying this—you're too young to know, Luke. I don't even know. But it was a really long time ago and Uncle Lee's different now.

—He's a good guy?

—Yes. Is there anything else on your mind?

—No.

—Good. Now get out or I'll sell you to the gypsies. I wouldn't even get two bucks but I'll sell you anyway.

Luke slouched out of the bedroom. Pete sat on his bed and chewed through another ten pages of the paperback. By nine-thirty the house was quiet. Pete rose from the bed and opened his wallet and counted out twenty-five dollars in rent money. He went out of his bedroom. His grandmother was in her chair in the living room, beside the radio. She often listened to evangelical cassettes that she got through the tabernacle library but now she was asleep.

Barry was in his office with his study bible open on his desk. He had a yellow legal pad he wrote his sermons on. Pete could see Barry's tight handscript, almost glyphic, words and sentences, bible references written in bold. Pete tapped the door frame.

—Peter, said Barry.

Pete gave him that week's twenty-five dollars. Barry took the money and counted it and put it in a little strongbox inside his desk.

—I'm grateful as always, said Barry.

—What's the sermon about? said Pete.

—Think of your Romans. 12:16. That we should not think of high things but of keeping company with the humble. It's the kind of thing that makes me think of Lee.

—You think Lee thinks of high things?

—What? Oh no. I think Lee is a lesson in how we ought to interact with each other as servants of Christ. Serving Lee has helped me learn a great deal.

—Serving Lee.

—Was there anything else, Peter? I've got a lot of work to do.

—One thing. Mrs. Adams. She teaches Sunday School.

Barry pressed his hands together: Sheila Adams, yes. I've got a lot of work to do.

—Do you . . . I mean . . . Did she get some kind of training before she got to be a Sunday School teacher?

—Peter, would you speak plain?

—Oh, ask Luke. I'm going to bed.

The next day was quiet at the Texaco. At half past three, Pete stocked up the jugs of washer fluid on the service island. Duane was in town for a doctor's appointment.

It was the kind of workday when the hours went by slowly but when Pete got home he would wonder where it had all gone. Once, when he was new, a customer had driven away from the pumps with the gas nozzle still in the filler neck at the back of the car. The hose pulled off the pump and flapped like an obscene rubber tail. Gasoline sprayed everywhere. A woman walking by just stopped and stared. She was smoking a cigarette. It was an hour or two before the customer returned, whipped into a rage. He went on about how they all would be held financially liable for the damage to his car. Even then, new as he was, Pete guessed you couldn't go long here before you were a veteran.

After he'd restocked the washer fluid, Pete went to change the trash bags in the washroom. He put on a pair of dish gloves they kept along with the other maintenance supplies. The gloves were pink and felt clammy inside. Pete was just stepping out with the bag of trash. He didn't even see Billy.

—Hey, man.

—Jesus Christ, Billy, you scared the hell out of me.

Billy was leaning against the back wall of the store.

—What are you doing out this way? said Pete.

—I got my brother's car. I kind of felt like driving around.

Billy spat out a little wad of saliva. He looked away at the bracken on the far side of the property: Emily, man. I don't even know.

—What happened?

—Oh, what does it even matter.

Billy spat again. He kicked at the gravel. Pete felt an instinct to reach out, put a hand on the shoulder. He was halfway to doing this before he recalled that he was still wearing the pink dish gloves. Instead, he said: I'm sorry to hear that, Bill.

Even as he said it, he felt the lie for what it was. He was sorry that his friend was hurting, but he could not even pretend to feel bad that Emily had broken it off. He wondered what this meant, what this told him about himself. He cleared his throat and looked at the sky, looked anywhere but at Billy.

—Everything happens for a reason and all that other shit my brother's wife always says, right? said Billy.

—I'm working tomorrow but not the next day. If you want we can get drunk.

—Yeah, maybe. You know what? Maybe when you skip town I'll come with you. Fuck it.

—You bet.

No, Stanley, said Dick. Like I said before, this Gilmore, he's not anybody at all. He told Len Gleber that the work he had was groundskeeping around EZ Acres down the highway. His story checked out fine. He told Gleber when it got cold he might head down to the city.

They were sitting in the front of the unmarked patrol car, rubbing the chill out of their hands in front of the heater. Stan's truck stood alongside the unmarked car and both vehicles were parked outside of Western Autobody. A cold autumn storm was brewing.

Dick went on: As far as it looks, all this guy did wrong was have another gal on the go. I'm glad Eleanor talked to you. Not just because of her sister but because of all the rest of it. Aurel and the brothers.

—I'm glad she let me tell my side. I think she's had a lot of sadness in her life.

Dick had a cup of coffee he'd brought with him from the garage. He tasted the coffee and then he cracked open the driver side door and poured it onto the wet pavement.

—One thing Eleanor said was how ordinary he was, said Stan. She said he didn't look like he worked in an office or anything like that but otherwise he was just ordinary.

—Ordinary, said Dick.

—They never look like anyone in particular, not like in the movies.

—You remember back when Fran and me were living in the city, said Dick. I never loved it at that time and I don't miss it one goddamn bit. But you remember I was on the Metro force. I was doing prisoner transfers from the provincial courthouse downtown out to wherever those sons of bitches ended up. There's not so much I care to remember, because when your job is to drive those kinds of men around, those men who rape or steal or harm children or kill for money, you're best to not pay them much mind. They don't deserve it. But I do remember one from all the men I transported, I remember one above all the others. Because he didn't have none of that desperation about him. He was just ordinary.

—Who was this?

—I don't have any memory of his name, though I suppose I read it a time or two on the paperwork or in the newspapers or on the radio, because his name was around for a little while. He was just a man with a plain face. We were taking him to Kingston. He'd worked in an Italian restaurant. He was a cook in the kitchen. He lived with his wife in the east part of the city. And one day this ordinary man, well, he goes into work, into the kitchen, and gets the biggest carving knife he can find and goes on into the manager's office and he sticks that carving knife into the manager's throat and cuts it wide open. Just like that, this manager sitting at his desk with his head, you know, hanging backwards just by the bones. Anyhow, the man went home on the streetcar and when he got home he got another carving knife from his own kitchen and tried to do the same to his wife. He would of, too, if he didn't cut her arm open first. They said he slipped in her blood and hit his head on a chair when he went down. The gal got herself out of there. God knows what she must of thought of the turn of events. I never even heard him raise his voice, is what she said at the trial, and that was all the witness she ever beared against him. Anyhow when the city cops—boys I knew, some of them—got to the house, the man didn't resist at all. They found him, they said, holding a towel full of ice to the back of his head. You know what he said on trial? He said the manager just talked too much. He said the gal talked too much too. He said he couldn't stand everybody talking all the time. On the day we moved him to Kingston, this cook, he just sat there quiet as you like and watched out the window. It was around Cobourg or so, and I remember we were slowed right to a stop with some roadwork. Bill Finley, the chap riding shotgun, was dead asleep. So I catch myself looking at the cook in the mirror, just how goddamn ordinary he was. I must of looked away for a minute and then I looked back again and the bugger was looking right at me. Right at me. He says what we're doing is a good thing. I should of paid him no attention, but him looking at me, it caught me off guard, and I says to him, Why is that? And he smiles and he says because he's not ever going to stop. He says there's too much talk in the world and he's not going to stop till he cuts every tongue out of every head he finds. Right around then, Finley waked up and he saw this man was talking so he slammed the cage with his hand and told him to keep his goddamn mouth shut. Which is what I should of done in the first place. Or just paid him no mind at all.

Dick was looking out over the dashboard. A leafless privet hedge was moving in the wind in front of them.

—I don't believe there are too many of them out there, said Stan. Or at least I don't want to believe it. I think like you say, most of them get rabid because of desperate times. Thirty-eight years and I don't remember but maybe one or two times I dealt with a person that had it that way right down to the core. The couple times I did think I saw it in somebody I always came away thinking I didn't have the real makings to do much about it. I was always afraid of that.

—The only time I thought I was looking it in the eye was that cook in the rear-view mirror. I shouldn't of even paid him any heed at all.

—Listen to us. We're a couple of miserable old bastards. Anyhow, the vet said he'd be done with Cassius at three.

—Hold up, old man. I'm not done with you yet. I can tell you one thing maybe you'll find interesting. Len Gleber thought Judy's boyfriend might be hard to track down. So Gleber went over to EZ Acres. The manager had to radio for him, walkie-talkie, but the boyfriend came after five or ten minutes. The boyfriend told Gleber he was real sorry about Judy but he thought she'd made more of it than he had. Said he hadn't seen her in a couple weeks. He didn't think he'd go to the funeral because he didn't want to cause any more upset to Eleanor, but would Gleber pass on a couple words of sorry. They looked into him after that and they didn't come up with anything. He'd been working at EZ Acres for about three months, according to the manager, mostly part time.

—You're going to a lot of work to tell me what you've already told me, said Stan.

—Well, look here. Gleber happened to see the boyfriend getting into a car after he interviewed him. Gleber didn't see the driver, and it wasn't a minute before the car was gone, but Gleber had a rookie he was training and he thought he'd get the kid to run the plates. So the kid runs the plates on the car and what he gets for the registration is Alec Reynolds.

—Alec Reynolds, said Stan. I remember the name . . .

—He's been in long-term care a few years. Dementia, all the rest of it.

—The car's hot?

—No. Alec's only living next-of-kin is a niece. Arlene Reynolds. The girl's name was registered on the insurance. When I got Gleber to talk about it last week, and I had to be careful about how I was asking these questions, he mentioned this girl's name. I did a bit of looking on my own. She lived in Montreal for most of the last ten years and came back here in the spring. But that's all. She doesn't have a record or anything. Maybe she's the other girl Judy saw.

—Didn't Alec Reynolds have a place on Indian Lake?

—The marina in the north end, said Dick. Far as I know the bank hasn't foreclosed on it yet but that can't be long off. The store's been closed up for six years, easy, as long as Alec's been in hospital.

—Eleanor talked about a place her sister had gone to try to track down the boyfriend. A motorhome was what she said.

—Motorhome—could be EZ Acres, where he was working.

—Could be.

—Goddammit, Stanley, what do you have in mind here?

—I don't know. I suppose I just want to meet him. Have some words with him. I want to see what there is to see about him. Anyhow, Frank gave me a warning at Thanksgiving. I don't want you to do anything to run foul of him.

—Oh, he suspects I've been poking around. But he hasn't come right out and said anything.

—Still.

—What's the worst he could do, fire me? I'd be away hunting moose so goddamn fast your head would spin off. I'll give you a ring, Stanley. Fran says she'd like to have you over for supper.

—I'll see you soon, Dick.

Stan got out of the unmarked car and the rain came down on him. He climbed into his truck and started the ignition and the heater. Nothing made his joints ache like cold rain. His knuckles, his hips. He sat cursing while the truck warmed up.

After Stan got up the next morning, he went down and did half a dozen rounds on the heavy-bag. It took some time to work the stiffness out of his joints. He'd spoken on the telephone to his sister in the evening after he'd brought Cassius home from the veterinarian. She was his only living sibling, seven years his senior. She lived out west and he'd last seen her when she came out for Edna's funeral. They talked about the weather and health and grandchildren. She asked about the house and he told her he thought Frank and Mary might buy it from him. They agreed it would be nice to keep it in the family.

After Stan had cleaned up from his exercises, he lifted up Cassius's ears and put in the drops that the veterinarian had prescribed. Cassius bore the indignity without complaint. Stan got a chunk of cold steak out of the refrigerator and gave it to the dog.

He left Cassius at the house and ran some errands in town. By midafternoon he had parked his truck near a marshy inlet on the northwest side of Indian Lake. He got out and walked up onto a pressure-treated birdwatching platform framed over the cattails. He had with him a pair of Bushnell 10x42 field glasses. He steadied his elbows on the rail and looked through the field glasses, north, to the bay at the top of the lake.

A rocky shore. One or two cottages closed for the winter. If Stan was correct, Alec Reynolds's property was marked by an eroded concrete pier at the base of a high feature. There'd been a gas pump up there. Stan could make out part of what had been a small store and restaurant behind where the pump had been. The windows were boarded over and much of the building was lost from sight by a growth of spruce. Where the land climbed up behind the building, Stan could just discern the roof of a storage shed or barn.

He got back in his truck and drove around the gravel township roads north of the lake. He kept driving until he saw what he thought was the same roof he'd seen from the lake, the storage shed or the barn. It was a hundred yards south of the road, with bush intervening. Stan drove slowly until he came to a possibly corresponding driveway. It wound out of sight through the trees. He stopped the truck for a moment's consideration.

A short distance back the way he'd come, the township road passed over a culvert. There were no other driveways between there and the one he reckoned led to the marina. Just past the culvert, a small clearing had been cleft into the bush. It was a good enough place to park. He got out of his truck and walked into the bush. Everything was still wet from yesterday's rainfall but the trees were not as thick as they had looked from the road. Up ahead, a creek was curving tightly through the trees and beyond that was the abrupt face of a rocky rise. Stan made his way over the fallen leaves. He came to the creek, which was wider than it looked, but he managed to cross it without any trouble. He went up the rise and when he came to the top he was breathing hard and the stiffness was back in his hips. He leaned on a tree to get his breath.

At the top of the rise was a thin treeline. Beyond the treeline, fifty yards of open ground led to the building he'd been seeking. It looked like a large shed for wintering boats, and on the far side of the shed he could make out half of a camper. Farther down, the roof of the store was just visible where the high feature dropped back to the lake. Stan unslung the field glasses from his neck and scanned the property. Nothing moved.

At last he trekked into the open field. The uncut grass hissed as he came to the back of the storage shed. The wall was windowless. He moved to the corner and peered around. The driveway from the township road came out of the trees and into a widened terminus between the storage shed and not one but two campers. One camper was a thirty-foot silver Airstream. The other was a battered Prowler, no more than nineteen feet long. The windows in both campers were dark.

Stan went to the door of the Prowler and knocked on it. Waited, knocked again. He went to the Airstream and knocked on the door. There was a window set in the door but a curtain was drawn behind the glass. He knocked again. After some minutes had passed and nothing happened, he tried the Airstream door and found it locked fast. He went back to the Prowler and found it locked as well.

Across from the campers there was a man-door in the side of the storage shed. Stan crossed the driveway. The man-door, at least, was unlocked. He went in. There wasn't much to see in the wan and dusty light. An empty interior. Hard-packed dirt for the floor. Two walls had been framed out of the back corner of the shed to make a large locker, crooked with age. The locker was perhaps eight feet by eight feet. There was a hasp for a padlock fixed to the locker door-frame but no lock was in place. Stan opened the door. The dark inner hollow could be illuminated by a forty-watt bulb overhead—you just had to turn the bulb in its socket. The yellow light it threw brought out the cobwebs and made eerie shadows, but the locker was empty. He darkened the bulb again.

Outside, Stan went down the slope to the back of the store. He felt certain he had some memories of this place when it was operational, summertime, kids with ice cream cones. The rear windows of the store were boarded over and *No Trespassing* was spray-painted on the plywood. The back door was locked. He did a circle of the building. The spruce on the headland had not been thinned in some time and grew close to the walls. Out front, Stan came to the pad where the gas pump had been. The wide panorama of Indian Lake lay beyond. The water licked against the short concrete pier below the pad. One front window of the store was unboarded. He cupped his hands around his face and looked through the glass into the darkness, saw the shape of a counter, a table with chairs stacked on it.

Stan crossed back through the property and walked the driveway through the trees to the township road. By the time he reached his truck he'd worked up a thin sweat. Sitting behind the steering wheel he tried to decide how he felt. Absurdity hovered close but there was more to it—what Eleanor had said her sister had told her about a place by the lake, and how that fell into place with the property he'd just wandered about. The vague signs of life around the mobiles and the storage shed. In his mind, he'd made a picture of the man, Colin Gilmore, who'd come and gone from Judy's life. And he thought how he was mocked by this, his own undertaking, when the pieces didn't even hint at a whole. Edna occurred to him again, what she would say about this. But behind Edna came an image of Judy Lacroix dead in the back of a car and, years ago, her uncle Darien turning at the bottom of the hangman's rope.

Perhaps he couldn't put it all into words—for Dick, for Frank, for the ghost of his wife—but he was gripped by it all the same. He was not going to stop now.

I'll be goddamned.

Speedy had said that a few times, each time shaking his head. He was driving them south out of town along the highway for a short stretch. His car was a Mercury Monarch, a wreck on four wheels. The springs were pushing through the upholstery. Between I'll-be-goddamneds, Speedy talked at a rapid rate about the woman he lived with, who he said was half wagon-burner and was therefore prone to going on drinking benders where she'd find herself in another town altogether. Lee smoked and listened. He had a low throb in his back and his shoulders from work that day. They were finished at the lakeside cottage and had spent the day cleaning up the job site.

—But I'll be goddamned, Lee. When was the last time we drove anywheres like this?

Before long, Speedy brought them to a truck stop off the highway. Down the other end of the lot was a concrete roadhouse that a neon sign advertised as THE NORTH STAR. The parking lot was perhaps half full.

—This is a good old place, said Speedy.

Lee took in the sight of the roadhouse through the windshield. He was quickly agitated. He said: Speedy. I can't be around here. I don't drink at all. I've been sober going on four years. When you came by you just said there was a place you wanted me to take a look at.

—A place to look at?

—That's what you said. I figured you meant a job site or a house that needed to get fixed up. I didn't think you meant nothing like this.

Speedy looked incredulous in the dashboard lights.

—Well, shit, Lee, I didn't know about the soberness. Listen. Let's just pop in for a minute then. Usually they got a band going. Plus, I got some buddies out here.

—I don't know.

—Lee, you crazy old bugger. Come on, ten minutes. Have a 7UP, see some music. You probably need to just get loose.

Speedy was already getting out of his car. Lee opened his mouth to summon Speedy back but he ended up saying nothing. He got out of the car and they went across the parking lot. There was a doorman who knew Speedy by name and he showed them into the roadhouse. The inside of the place was bigger than it had looked. A row of booths lined the far wall and tables were arranged around a riser. They'd stood jack-o'-lanterns around the stage and hung some dejected rubber bats from the ceiling. A lone man with an electric guitar and an amplifier was doing a decent cover of "Sundown." There were townies and truckers, and someone Lee recognized from the lumberyard. Speedy stopped briefly at the bar. There was a girl pouring some drinks and a man whom Speedy called Mike. Speedy ordered a draft of Molson and Lee ordered a Coke and then they sat down in a booth and watched the musician.

—Speedy, said Lee.

Before Speedy could reply, the girl came from the bar with their drinks on a tray. She had blond hair and a sexy sway.

—Always good to see Speedy, said the girl.

—Arlene, this is my pal, Lee.

She smiled, offered her hand for Lee to shake. When she left them, they watched her go until she was behind the bar again.

Speedy leaned over to Lee: What would I give to put the cock to her.

—Speedy, do you know what my parole officer would do if he knew I was here?

—Well, you don't see him nowhere, do you?

—No, but.

The Coca-Cola had come in a sleeve-glass with scoured sides. Speedy picked up a salt shaker from the other side of the booth and tapped salt into his draft.

—And the music's not half bad, said Speedy.

—No. Christ. It's not that.

—We won't stay real long. If I finish this beer and I haven't seen my friends, we'll get going, what do you say? There's a topless place other side of Animosh.

—Who are these friends of yours?

—Just some ordinary old boys.

They sat back, watched the musician for a few minutes. When they were eighteen or nineteen, Lee and Speedy and Terry Lachlan had broken into the office of a man who owned and operated a quarry southeast of town. The quarry-man was a European immigrant named Szabo, and it was rumoured that he was a Nazi war criminal on the run, but even that was a pretty thin pretense for robbing him. Rather, if Lee remembered correctly, they'd heard from Szabo's son, who was not on good terms with his father, that the quarry-man kept a substantial amount of cash in a safe in his office. So Speedy, Lee and Terry Lachlan had gone at night, kicked the door open, found the safe, wheeled it out on a furniture dolly, loaded it into a borrowed pickup truck, and driven away. The whole affair had taken fifteen or twenty minutes, which Lee later figured was way too slow, had anyone been observing them and called the cops.

As it was, the break-in went unreported, whether because Szabo was actually a Nazi war criminal fleeing justice, or, more likely, because the cash kept in the safe was income he hadn't claimed the taxes on. Either way, after Lee and Speedy and Terry had finally pried the safe open, they found themselves each three hundred dollars richer. Lee didn't think he'd done anything more serious before breaking into the quarry-man's office. The stolen cars and counterfeit cigarettes all started after that.

Now he needed to find or do something to take his mind off both the past, and where he was in the present. He thought maybe conversation would work. He turned his glass on the tabletop and said: Anyhow, what've you been doing? You got a trade?

Speedy touched the burn on the side of his face: No. I'm on disability.

—For what?

—For awhile I had a bit in a welding shop. This one time I was cutting up a steel I-beam with a burning bar. You ever see one of them cocksuckers, a burning bar? They'll burn through anything, Lee. Steel, concrete, any fucking thing just like that. Some of the slag got blown back on my face. But here's the beauty, Lee. The foreman and the manager got their asses chewed because I wasn't wearing a mask when I got burned. The court settled pretty sweet for me.

—Jesus. You could of got blinded.

—Sure, but I didn't. Anyway it's no trouble no more. I got some various business interests. I never liked having to answer to a buck or a foreman.

When the conversation lapsed, Lee was aware of how unsettled he'd become. He could feel a pulse in his eyes. Speedy was about halfway through his draft. The musician wrapped up a song and told the room thanks.

Then a big man was standing beside their table. His head was bald but he had a thick beard and he was wearing glasses that were an odd contrast to the rest of his appearance. The big man leaned his fists on the tabletop.

—How's she going, Maurice? said Speedy.

Speedy and the big man shook hands.

—This is my pal, Lee, said Speedy.

—So this is Lee, said Maurice.

They shook hands.

—You say it like you know me, said Lee.

—Speedy told me a little about you. All good things. You're among friends. Come on, let's go to the back. You want a beer, Lee?

—I'm okay.

Maurice led them to a passageway on the far side of the riser, past a door marked LADIES, a door marked MEN, and finally to a knobless door at the back marked OFFI E. He pushed the door open and led the way into a small room. Against one wall stood metal shelves bellied under the weight of potato sacks and tins of cooking oil and boxes of empty liquor bottles. Beer kegs were stacked in a corner and there were two windows set high in the wall. There was no desk but there was a Formica table and a mismatched collection of chairs. At the table a man was tapping a pen on a crossword puzzle torn from a newspaper. He didn't have any particular look about him, but somehow he seemed at odds with the townies and the blue-collar hang-abouts out in the main room. Before him in a tumbler was a mixed drink, and when he saw them coming he smiled brightly.

—Well. How are you, Speedy?

Speedy said hello and introduced the man at the table as Colin Gilmore. He stood up to shake hands with Lee.

—All is well, Lee, said Gilmore. Any friend of Speedy's is a friend of mine. Speedy, what do you say you visit with Arlene, get your glass filled back up.

Maurice let Speedy out and then he closed the door and leaned against the wall. Lee again felt the pulse in his eyes. He sat. Gilmore offered up a pack of Camel cigarettes. Lee withdrew one and Gilmore lit it for him.

—I know Roland Poirier, said Gilmore. You'd remember Rollie, wouldn't you?

—Yeah, I knew Rollie, said Lee. But that's a few . . . that's more than a few years ago.

—Rollie's been having a hard time lately. He got in some trouble out in New Brunswick.

—I heard something like that, said Lee. Gambling or cards or something.

—Yes, cards, gambling. All the vices. But he put in a pretty good word for you. I said, Roland, when you were a guest of the Queen, did you know a fellow named Lee King? He did, he said. He said you helped him out when he had some trouble with a couple of boys inside. Also over a card game, I understand.

—That's twelve goddamn years ago.

—Never mind how he can't gamble for shit, Roland's a good judge of character. He said you were a reliable kind of guy. Serious. That's what I like in a friend.

—In a friend, said Lee.

—Speedy says you're looking for work.

—Well, Speedy told you wrong. I got a job.

Something passed between Gilmore and Maurice, wherever Maurice was. Behind Lee.

—Sure you do, said Gilmore. That isn't to say you might not be enterprising.

Lee wanted to turn around and look behind his chair. To see wherever that big man was. He remained looking straight-on, but not without effort.

—Look, buck. Me and Speedy. I haven't seen him in seventeen years.

Gilmore was exuding sympathy, a joke shared between them. He said: Speedy's a busybody, pal, you know? Right now he's almost at his full potential. I say almost because Speedy has a set of skills that make up for everything else he got shortchanged. It's not quite the same with you, Lee. You're your own set of skills. From what Roland Poirier told me and, to be honest, from what I can see from meeting you.

—I don't know what you're talking about.

—I can make it clearer, said Gilmore.

—Here's the thing, buck. I got a job, I got a place, I got a girl on the go. Opportunity and all the rest of it, I don't have any interest.

Gilmore grinned a salesman's grin. He sipped from his mixed drink.

—I think I'll get out of your way now, said Lee.

He got out of the chair. Maurice hadn't moved. He was still leaning against the door. He had his glasses off and he was rubbing one of the lenses with a Kleenex.

—Hope we'll see you again, said Gilmore.

—Sure, said Lee.

Maurice put his glasses back on and opened the door. He said: Take care.

—Yeah, said Lee. So long.

In the passageway, Lee pitched the butt of the Camel cigarette to the floor. Speedy was at the bar talking to the bartender, that girl Arlene they'd been served by earlier. Lee saw Speedy turning to look at him as he went by but he crossed the floor and went into the vestibule. The doorman was telling a couple of kids that they couldn't come in. There was a bank of pay telephones. Lee picked up a receiver and pushed a dime into the slot and dialed Helen's number. It rang a dozen times before he put the receiver back in the cradle.

Speedy had appeared in the vestibule, carrying a refilled glass of beer.

—Lee, come on. Let's go back inside and run us down a couple chicks.

He reached out to take Lee by the sleeve. Lee shoved him hard against the wall. The doorman turned to see and the kids went wide-eyed.

—Speedy, you dumb motherfucker.

—Lee . . .

Lee moved past the doorman. The kids made way for him and he hustled down the front steps. He didn't know if Speedy was following him or not but he went quickly across the big parking lot. Some distance away, the lights of a rig were moving onto the pavement from the highway. A row of overnighted tractor-trailers stood like dormant beasts. Lee turned and Speedy had not come out of the roadhouse. The neon sign above was crude against the night sky.

All that was past the trucks was a store with sundries and a counter of day-old doughnuts. Lee bought a cup of coffee and went back out. He made his way back up the highway, putting his thumb out whenever headlights appeared behind him, and about half a mile along, a man in a Buick stopped. The man said he didn't mind giving a fella a lift, but that he had a twelve-inch length of iron pipe under his seat, if Lee was the kind of person who didn't have the right idea of how far charity extends.

Even after Lee was back in town, he didn't uncoil. The windows at the Owl Café were dark. He went to the Corner Pocket and got a table and played a couple of games by himself. He'd been there about forty-five minutes when he put his cue down and went over to the counter and asked for a Coke. The barman popped open a can and filled up a glass for him.

—Good to have you back again, said the barman.

—Yeah.

A man came up and returned a rack of balls, paid off his table. Lee drank the Coke and set the glass down.

—Another?

—Yes.

The barman popped open the can. Lee pressed the heels of his hands into his forehead. His eyes were pulsing again. The glass was just half full when Lee told the barman to stop pouring. The barman looked at him.

—I was thinking, said Lee. Maybe you could put a couple splashes of rye in there?

—

Halloween came a week later, falling on a Friday. From street light to street light went the children in their costumes, carrying shopping bags full of take. Lee and Helen went to the liquor store and filled out a selection card and came out with a couple of bottles of whisky. Lee felt like a big man. He'd spent a few days fretting over Speedy and their trip to the roadhouse, but by the same token he was pleased with himself. Anybody who said he couldn't go straight, well, they could fuck off, now more than ever.

He and Helen walked along Princess Street. They passed one of the bottles between them, whisky mixed with cola, hidden inside a paper bag. Lee took a swig. If he could stand his ground with some serious men like Speedy's friends, then he didn't think he'd have any problem handling a drink a two. He felt like he was actually in control of what was happening around him, what was happening to him. And he was proud of that.

Three kids in monster costumes went running past them. When Lee himself was a little kid, he'd dressed for Halloween as the Lone Ranger, year after year. A mask and a gun, which, thinking on it now, made him laugh. He'd been out to Barry and Donna's house for supper the night before, and Barry had told him that he and Donna weren't letting Luke and John go trick-or-treating for Halloween, because they didn't think a festival celebrating the devil was something you wanted to have your kids take part in. Instead, they were going to a sleepover at Galilee Tabernacle, where each child came dressed as a biblical character and there was a contest for the best costume. Pete, who was also there for supper, suggested that the boys go to the sleepover dressed as Cain and Abel, with Abel murdered and the Mark of God on Cain's forehead. Lee laughed, but Barry just changed the subject.

Lee and Helen made their way back to Lee's place. She made popcorn on the hot plate and he mixed them some drinks and they watched a Hitchcock film—*The Birds*—on his TV. As they sat together, he looked at her from time to time, wondering what she'd been like as a young child.

Monday came and Lee was swinging his hammer. He was destroying the kitchen in a solitary island residence on Lake Kissinaw. The cupboards and counters were to be torn out. The bathrooms would go next. They would rip up the floor tiles and carpeting. The building and the island had sold for $60,000 to a man named Forsythe and his wife, who were said to live in New York State for most of the year. Clifton had gotten the bid for the renovations they wanted. Lee swung his hammer, caught the edge of a shelf, tore it out. A few feet away, Bud was working a crowbar on the kitchen counter.

At seven-thirty that morning they'd left in Clifton's barge from the public landing. Clifton called his watercraft a barge but it wasn't much of one. It was a dented twenty-foot steel push-boat with a flat bottom. The drop-gate in the bow didn't work properly and was welded shut. It took them half an hour to cross the lake. Salvaged planks had been retrofitted in the barge as seats, and it was Lee, Bud and a man Lee hadn't met yet riding along. Clifton helmed the barge, which plodded along, weighed down with lumber, a covered stack of pine, and a portable Monarch cement mixer. Lee didn't want the others to take notice of how he was hunched forward with his fists pursed together. Moving over open water was chilling him to the bone. A T-shirt and work-shirt underneath his jean jacket were not going to be enough against the weather much longer. He craved a cigarette.

The barge tracked along a narrow hogback and then hooked into a calm back bay. The biggest island in the bay was sixty yards end to end, covered by white pines. The side of a boathouse was visible where the island tapered down to a rocky shore. Clifton guided them to a dock. On the shore, a material delivery had preceded them by a day or two: a couple of yards of gravel and three tons of Sakrete dry cement mix in forty-pound bags. Once they were tied up, Lee hopped out and got the blood moving in his limbs. He lit himself a cigarette and offered one to Bud, who shook his head and hustled past him onto dry land. Clifton mugged at Lee but didn't say anything. A short path led past the boathouse to the cottage that Forsythe had purchased. It was a dejected storey-and-a-half structure, once whitewashed. A deck attached to the side of the house was severely out of level.

Clifton looked at Lee, striding along the path beside him. He said: Forsythe's wife said she dreamed about this place. What do you make of that, mister man?

—Long as it keeps us going through the winter, boss, anybody can dream anything they want.

Lee didn't know why Clifton was asking for his judgment. And the man was roused, more than usual. It wasn't half past eight before Clifton invoked words of God and idleness and loosed Bud and Lee on the kitchen.

The new man who'd come out with them was named Wally. After one of the counters had been torn free of the kitchen wall, Wally appeared with a tape measure to take some measurements. He jotted numbers down on the exposed wallboard where the counter had been. Then he left the kitchen, taking Bud with him. Ten minutes later they came back from the barge with a table saw. Lee saw them setting it up in the living room.

At lunchtime they sat around the fireplace. The flue whistled and moaned.

—So you're a cabinetmaker? said Lee.

—That's right, said Wally.

—Lee's a carpenter too, said Bud. He got his trade. He could do up some beauty cabinets. For sure.

—Hot dog, said Wally. Where did you apprentice?

They were looking at Lee.

—Go on, Leland King, said Clifton. You shouldn't hide nothing.

—Say, never mind, said Wally.

—Prison, said Lee.

—Oh.

—That's where I got my trade. Anyhow.

—Tell me what you think, said Wally.

He handed Lee a manila file folder. Inside was a set of plans for the kitchen. The cabinetry was all to be face-framed and constructed from the pine they'd brought.

—It looks good, said Lee. What do they call it . . . modern.

—If they stain the pine right it will come up nice.

—Sure it will, said Lee.

—Not quite like whacking together some desks, said Clifton.

—I guess not.

—Lee has come a real long way, Wally. Words and deeds and prayer, every day. Right, Lee?

—Every day, said Lee.

—We might even see you at Galilee Pentecostal one of these days, said Clifton. You too, Bud. Even you, Wally.

Wally took the plans back from Lee. He said: My wife and I like the United Church just fine, thanks.

Clifton was getting into it. His posture was erect: The United Church, that's where—

—Clifton, said Wally, I'm thinking about something my dad used to say. All things in moderation. Religion too. You go all you want to your church and I'll go to mine. In the meantime we'll talk about hockey.

Wally stood up to stretch. He took a few strides across the living room floor and went outside through the kitchen door.

Clifton shook his head.

—A lot of guys just don't want to hear the truth.

By mid-week, a great deal of scrap material had been culled out of the house. They cast the fibreboard and wiring and pipes into a midden they had dug on the back of the island. All the scrap lumber was brought down to a rocky flat along the shore. They primed the scrap with gasoline and set it alight. Bud tended the fire. He poked it with a shovel and hopped around like some kind of one-man pagan ceremony. Lee remained in the house, either helping Wally feed pine through the table saw or keeping the sawdust swept up and the tools organized. His own tool belt stayed folded neatly in a corner where he could keep an eye on it. Even Clifton was working. He was in the bathroom, putting solder on the new copper pipes.

At the end of each day when the light was fading, they took their things down and stood with Bud on the point. The coal bed gave off tremendous heat and the idea of barging out across the cold lake was a dismal prospect. Maybe even Clifton thought so, because they would stand around for awhile, instead of leaving. Nobody said anything. They just watched the red patterns shifting in the coals.

When Saturday came, Lee had a late breakfast at the Owl Café. Helen said she was going to be doing a tarot reading with some girlfriends that night but could see him the next day. If he wanted, of course. Lee walked breakfast off by going to the Woolworths around the corner from the National Trust. He tried on a Carhartt jacket. It was stiff denim lined with quilted flannel and it was so warm that it brought sweat out of his skin as he looked at himself in the store mirror. He moved the zipper up and down. He looked at the price tag and looked away, and then he carried the jacket and a wool toque and a pair of lined work gloves up to the cashier.

Your jacket, said Irene. It looks sharp. Don't you think, Barry?

—It looks warm, Brother Lee.

They were at the hospital Saturday afternoon. The cancer ward was small and smelled new. They sat in a waiting area not far from the radiotherapy suite, Lee and Barry and Irene, and despite how warm the new jacket was making him, Lee was somehow reluctant to remove it. He was getting the feel of it on his body.

A nurse came and told Irene they were ready to see her. The nurse helped her to stand up. Lee stood with her, holding her by the arm. The nurse gave him a bland smile.

—No worries, said Barry. These gals know what they're doing.

Lee lowered himself into his chair: I'll be here, Ma.

The nurse showed Irene out of the waiting area. Barry watched them go and then turned to Lee.

—I arranged a little time with her doctor if you want to meet him.

The oncologist was a small brown man whom Barry introduced as Dr. Vijay. His manner was prim and dignified and he did not shake hands. He offered them seats in his office.

—You are Mrs. King's son?

—That's right, said Lee.

—Thanks for seeing us on a Saturday, said Barry.

Dr. Vijay lifted his hand in the air and moved it side to side. He was looking at notes on a clipboard.

—Since the ward opened there are three thousand people in this region who come here for care. So I do not have much in the way of a weekend. But I am happy, Mr. King, to tell you a few words about your mother's illness. Carcinoma, do you know this?

—Lung cancer, said Lee. Same as that one-legged kid who tried to run across the country.

—That one-legged kid, as you say, said Dr. Vijay, he suffers from osteosarcoma. A cancer that has spread from his leg to different parts of his body, including his lungs. What your mother has, Mr. King, is carcinoma. A cancer that has formed directly in her lungs. Your mother was a heavy smoker, yes?

—She smoked. Same as anybody else.

—The tumours in her lungs are almost certainly a result of heavy smoking. I am not making any recommendations to you,

Mr. King, but you might want to give that some thought if you are also a smoker.

Lee was unsure how to respond. He looked to Barry for any sign of comradeship but Barry had his plain face on. Lee shifted his jaw. Dr. Vijay flipped a page on the clipboard.

—As it is, your mother's treatment seems to be progressing as well as can be expected. The third stage of the sickness, which she was diagnosed with in August, did your family explain this to you?

—They said she has a year to live, said Lee.

—Yes, that's the estimate. I don't want to give you any false hope. Still, she is responding well to the radiotherapy.

—She's got this faith, said Barry abruptly. She knows Whose Hands she's in.

—Yes, said Dr. Vijay, and he cleared his throat.

Faith was a funny thing for Lee. He'd been told how faith was shaped and what it looked like and how he could resolve himself to it. One time the prison chaplain drew from Revelations, how when a child of God walks away from the Lord, the Lord will yet reach to call him home. The chaplain said how when the call came it was faith by which it was heard. How faith was like a telephone. Lee had heard how the call was to come into your heart and thus deliver you.

After the visit to the hospital Lee went back to Union Street. He got supper at a small diner he hadn't visited before and then, walking home, he saw Speedy cruising that part of town in his wreck of a car on God knows what kind of errand. Speedy saw him and stopped the car and said it was good to see him, never mind the way they'd parted at the North Star. Speedy wanted to know what Lee was up to that night. They went to the Corner Pocket from there. The conversation with Dr. Vijay stayed in Lee's head but after a couple of drinks he felt alright.

He'd been a drinker through much of his prison sentence. There were cons who made a wicked homebrew out of fruit scraps and whatever else they could get their hands on, sometimes potatoes. If it was a bad brew, it could blind you, or worse. But if it was a good brew, and it was generally alright, it could help you forget where you were for a little while. It could help you feel big if you needed to. He'd sobered up later, after he'd been working steadily in the woodshop for a few years and the possibility of an early parole had started to take shape. Writing back and forth with Barry had helped. His sobriety put him in good stead with the parole board once his time to be heard came around, but they did not impose it on him as a condition. Maybe they'd thought he could go straight. Maybe they'd seen that in him, even before he'd seen it in himself.

—Lucky to run into you this aft, said Speedy.

Lee chalked the tip of his cue and drank his rye and cola. He broke the balls on the table and studied where they'd moved to.

Speedy talked about the latest spree his woman had gotten involved in. Across the poolroom was that sharp-featured man again, shooting pool with a buddy. When Lee saw the man, he felt a niggling pull of familiarity.

—So how's this gal of yours?

—What?

—Your lady friend, said Speedy.

—She's good. She's doing some kind of card game with her girlfriends tonight. They read cards that tell you this or that about a person. Their fate.

—There's just all kinds of crazy nonsense out there.

Lee deftly beat Speedy. They had some more drinks and played a few more games. Speedy maundered on about other topics. He asked Lee how work was going. Lee told him about the island where they'd torn out the kitchen.

Speedy did not remain much longer. He stayed only long enough that Lee wondered if it had been deliberate that they'd met up in the first place. Lee was a little bit drunk, loosened up. But he could feel clearly that Speedy was up to something.

—Say, Lee, how's about we go run us down some better action than here.

—I don't know what kind of better action you got in mind.

—Some of them friends of mine.

—What, those boys I met?

—Sure. On a Saturday they like to have a bash out there. What do you say.

Lee bent over his cue and tried a bank shot but he scratched it.

—I guess I'd just as soon stay around here, said Lee. You know.

—Sure, Speedy said after a moment. Well, you know where we're all at. If you want to steal a car and come on out. I'm only kidding you.

They shook hands and Speedy gathered his jacket and left. Lee put his cue down on the felt and went over to the bar. He and the barman exchanged some words of conversation. Lee got another drink. He wondered briefly how it might be out at the roadhouse, he couldn't deny that, but he was also relieved that Speedy was gone.

He went back to his table and racked himself a new game. Then the sharp-featured man and his buddy drifted over to him. The buddy had black grease lining his fingernails and was wearing a Penzoil jacket with a name tag on the breast that read *Clark*.

—How about a game? said the long-haired man.

—There's two of you.

—We'll take turns. Us and you.

—What, you want to stake some cash on it?

—Let's play a friendly game first, said the man. Then we'll see if we want to stake some cash on it.

They set the balls and Lee lined up his cue and broke. The sharp-featured man was studying him intently. Lec took a long drink and rubbed the back of his neck.

—Do I know you? Are you one of the subtrades that Clifton Murray brings around?

—I seen you around, said the man. Once at the Owl Café.

That was it. Plain as day—the long-haired man, down-filled vest, snapping his fingers to try to get Helen's attention, the first day Lee had met her.

—Oh, said Lee. Okay.

They played halfway through a game. They were not bad but Lee was better. He was down to the last two stripes and the eight ball and there were still four solids on the table. The two townies finished their jug of beer and the man with the Clark name tag went over to the bar to get another.

—I seen you talking to Miss Helen at the café, said the sharp-featured man.

—Is that a problem?

—No. Why would you think that?

Clark returned with the jug of beer. Lee clipped the cue ball hard. He took a quick look around the poolroom.

—I think you're by yourself, said the man. How is Helen treating you anyhow?

—Kind of my business, don't you think?

—She was treating me pretty good for awhile.

—You're starting to get on my nerves, buck.

—Well, I wouldn't want to do that.

Lee breathed. Then all at once he dropped his pool cue on the tabletop. He said: Fuck this.

—Hey now, no reason to get like that.

The two townies were grinning. Lee walked over to the bar, feeling the pulse in his eyes. He sat on a stool and paid off the table and ordered another drink.

—You know them guys? said Lee.

—Who, said the barman. Over at the table you had?

—Yeah.

—I've seen them around, I suppose.

A man came up and asked the barman for something and Lee worked on his drink. After a few minutes he looked back over his shoulder. The sharp-featured man and his buddy were gone.

Lee left the Corner Pocket a little before eleven o'clock. He went out the back door and hopped over a concrete knee-wall and cut through the lot of Dutch's Chevrolet Pontiac Buick, New And Used. He turned up the collar of his new jacket and it was only because he stopped to light a cigarette that he saw them coming for him.

Their motions were reflected dully in the flank of a used Skylark. They were coming quickly down the narrow space between the cars. He turned just in time to see the man with the Clark name patch bearing down in the lead, swinging something. Lee bobbed sideways and the thing Clark was swinging crashed into his clavicle. Pain flashed down through his body and his arm went numb and for just a second Clark and the sharp-featured man, crowding in behind him, looked like maybe they weren't sure what they were doing. Then Clark took another step and just as he put his weight down, Lee swung his steel-toe boot into the side of the forward knee. Clark dropped and let go of what he'd swung. A long wool sock with a pool ball rolling out of it. The ball rolled to rest against the Skylark's tire and the sharp-featured man gaped at it. Lee kicked him in the groin. He dropped noiselessly and Lee kicked him again, first in the ribs and then across the jaw. Lee was breathing heavily now and was acutely aware of the pain in his shoulder. He looked. Clark was kneeling on his good knee, groping for the pool ball. Lee stomped the man's fingers against the pavement and bent over him and punched him a number of times in the face. The man fell over.

Lee slammed a dent into the Skylark with his boot. It seemed there wasn't enough air he could pull in. The men on the ground were breathing but they weren't making any motions to get up. Lee walked backwards until he was out of sight of them.

When he got home he turned on the lamp and looked at his hand. His knuckles were swollen but not opened up. His shoulder was tender where the pool ball had struck it. He took off his new jacket and laid it on the table and inspected it closely for damage to the fabric, for blood. There wasn't any. He hung the jacket in the closet. He went to bed and lay awake for the rest of the night.

A few days later, after work when Lee was walking home with a bag of groceries, he became conscious of a vehicle tracking along beside him. At first he thought it was the police car again but then he saw it was a GMC Caballero. The vehicle angled to the curb beside him and the driver-side window came down. That big man with the glasses from the roadhouse. Maurice.

—Looks like you could use a lift.

—I'm okay. My place isn't real far.

—If you say so.

A pause.

—I'll see you, said Lee.

—Hold up, said Maurice. Word was you had some trouble on the weekend.

—Whose word is that?

—Doesn't matter. Just thought you'd like to know there isn't nobody going to be talking about it. Like so it would get back to the cops or your parole officer.

—I don't have trouble with anyone.

—No, that's true. You don't. And if you did have trouble with anybody, say, a couple shithead town boys, then maybe you'd like to know these same shithead town boys have had certain things told to them.

—Okay, said Lee, not knowing what else to say.

—Shitty how them things happen to a guy from time to time, said Maurice. You sure you don't want a ride?

—I'm okay.

—See you around, Lee.

EZ Acres was five miles down the highway south of town. The sign at the gate showed a cartoon fat-man snoozing in a hammock. The park had thirty-five campers sited on the shore of a circular catch-basin called Lake Albert. The office was one of three permanent buildings on the property. The park was seasonal and Stan didn't know if anybody would still be around or not, but as he walked towards the office, a husky rose from the ground and barked twice.

A short woman with cropped grey hair came around from behind the office and told the dog to shut up. She had a splitting maul over her shoulder. She said: Can I help you?

—I guess you folks are closed up, said Stan.

—We open again on Victoria Day.

The husky trotted over and hung close to the woman's leg.

—I thought you'd maybe be able to point me in the right direction, said Stan.

—What direction would that be?

—A friend of mine, he's been in the hospital for awhile. He's not in good shape. His doctor wanted to have a word with my friend's niece who's been keeping an eye on his property. It's been hard to get a hold of her, the niece, but I heard she had a friend who worked here.

—Well, there's nobody here now. Just me. We had two or three guys on seasonal but I let them go when we shut down after Thanksgiving. What was his name?

—I believe it's Colin Gilmore, said Stan.

—Right, Ballin' Colin. Last time I seen him was a week ago when I had a couple hours' work in the hydro-cut. I don't know if he's still around or not, but up the highway there's a truck stop where they got this roadhouse. The North Star. You know it? Colin was drinking there when he was around.

Stan thanked her and started to head back to his truck. He got on the highway and drove to the North Star. He knew of it but he'd never had reason to visit it before. He parked at the back of the lot and got out. A cool breeze was carrying small sharp granules of dirt across the asphalt. Stan went up to the front door of the roadhouse and went in. Past the entry, the interior was garishly lit by overhead lights. On the riser at the back, a man was plugging an electric guitar into an amplifier. The drone of the amplifier filled the whole room. Closer to the front door a man with his cuffs rolled up to his elbows was unstacking chairs at a table. The bar was shuttered. The man looked at Stan.

—Bar opens at seven. The band goes on at eight.

—Okay, said Stan.

—Which is to say we'll see you then.

Stan went back into town and had supper at the Owl Café. He took his time reading the newspaper. The minutes were a long time passing. After seven o'clock he got up from the booth and went over to the counter to pay. The big-haired waitress was distracted, involved in some conversation with an angular man, wearing jeans and a Carhartt jacket, down at the end of the counter. The man she was talking to, there was something familiar about him. Stan had seen him before, but he couldn't think where or when. The man noticed Stan looking at him and he said something to the waitress. She nodded and came over to collect Stan's bill.

There was a pay phone at the back of the diner. Stan dialed Dick's house and Fran answered. She said she was happy to hear from him, said how they would have him over for supper anytime.

—Dick's not home, is he?

—I'm sorry, Stan. Dick's down at the drill hall with Richard Junior. Brian's getting sworn in to the Air Cadets tonight. Dick's wearing his Europe medals for it. Do you want me to tell him you called?

—No, that's fine, Fran. So long.

It was close to eight by the time Stan was back at the truck stop. There were some rigs pulled into the lot for the night and a dozen or so cars and pickups parked in front of the North Star. Inside, it was cigarette smoke and music from the jukebox. Thirty or thirty-five patrons. The band was clustered in discussion at the back of the riser. They were talking to the man with the rolled-back cuffs Stan had seen when he'd come in earlier.

For the first time it occurred to Stan that he had no idea what he'd say if he actually made Gilmore's acquaintance. Maybe it was just a matter of knowing the face attached to the name. Stan took a stool at the bar. The sheer weirdness of this situation overcame his thoughts. A drunk barfly two stools down gave him a big friendly nod and offered a hand to shake.

—These boys put on a good show, said the barfly. Just you wait.

The bartender came down to Stan. She was young and had a streetwise comeliness to her. Stan could see how she lifted her eyebrows a little when she took him in.

—What will you have?

He ordered Coors in a bottle. Draft didn't agree with him any more. She came back with a bottle and set it on a coaster in front of him. The barfly two stools down pushed a bowl of pretzels in Stan's direction.

—Say, said Stan to the bartender. Does a fellow named Colin Gilmore hang around here?

She didn't have to say anything. Her face gave it away.

—Maybe, said the bartender.

—I'm over from EZ Acres, just wanted to pass a message on to him from the manager.

—I don't know if he's here tonight.

—If he is, said Stan.

She nodded. She coasted back down to the other end of the bar.

A few minutes later, the front man of the band took his guitar and stood to the microphone. The jukebox cut out. The barfly leaned over and patted Stan on the arm and gave him a thumbs-up. The band launched into some rock 'n' roll piece. Stan nursed the beer he'd ordered. Speculating. The roadhouse was all possibility. But what was he really going to say?

The band had played through their first song when Stan became aware of a man who'd sat on the stool immediately to his right. The man was leaning back against the bar, one arm stretched along the bevelled edge. He had a slim build and a thick head of hair, jeans, engineer boots, a dark T-shirt, but otherwise he was as they'd said. He was anyone.

—If I happened to see one older gent like yourself in a bar or if I saw a hundred it would never look quite right to me. But maybe that's my own kind of prejudice.

—You'd be Mr. Gilmore?

The man laughed a little: I'll go with that. *Mr.* Gilmore.

He took his arm off the edge of the bar to shake Stan's hand.

—I'm Bill, said Stan.

—How do you do, Bill. Are you enjoying the music?

—It's a year or two after my time.

They shared a thin chuckle at that. Stan had put himself in a corner and he knew it. The last of his beer had gotten warm and he didn't have much taste for it. He quarter-turned on the stool to better converse.

—Mr. Gilmore, I'm a friend of a family you might know.

—Okay. So you're not from the trailer park.

—No. I'm friends with the Lacroixes. Would you have a word with me about Judy?

Stan wasn't sure what effect forthrightness would bring, but Gilmore remained good-natured. He said: Wasn't that a goddamn shock.

—Yes, said Stan. Nobody thought Judy would do that. But we guessed you might of been the last person to see her alive and we just wanted to know if you had any thoughts on it. On how she was acting.

—I'm sorry to say, Bill, but I didn't see her for a couple of weeks. We kind of parted ways. I didn't know about it till I heard around town. So sad.

—Yes.

—I have to use the men's room. You think up some more questions if you want.

Gilmore patted Stan on the shoulder and got down from the stool. He went to a rear corridor past the riser. Ten minutes later he hadn't come back. Stan looked around. He saw the girl behind the bar making a telephone call. She was looking right at him. When she was finished, she came to ask Stan if he wanted another beer. He told her no thanks and asked what he owed.

—A dollar-fifty, said the girl.

—You wouldn't be related to Alec Reynolds by any chance, said Stan.

—He's my uncle. Do you know him?

—Not well. I hear he's in the hospital.

—Yes, said the girl. A long time now.

Stan nodded. He put some money on the bartop.

He went into the rear corridor and looked in the men's washroom. There was a fat townie at one of the urinals. Stan went back into the corridor and went down to the door at the end with OFFI E lettered on it. There was no knob on this side of the door and it didn't move when he tried to push it.

—There's a reason we keep the office locked.

The man with the rolled-back cuffs was in the corridor behind Stan. Stan apologized, said he was lost. He went past the man and back into the bar but the man followed him out and took his sleeve.

—How about I just show you out of here. Come on.

—How about you take your hand off my arm.

—Come on. Nobody wants any trouble.

He gave Stan's sleeve a tug. Stan pulled his arm away and took handfuls of the man's shirt and pressed him against the wall. Through his teeth, Stan said: I wouldn't let the white hair fool you.

But then a big bearded man with a bald head and a pair of glasses appeared, moving fluidly for all his size. He wrapped his forearm around Stan's neck from behind and jerked him backwards and at first Stan kept his grip on the man with the rolled-back cuffs and they all moved together. Then Stan let go of the man he was holding and clawed at the arm around his throat. The big man holding him wasn't saying anything at all. Stan kicked out one leg and succeeded only in knocking over a table in front of them. A couple of drinks jumped off the tabletop and splashed down the front of his trousers. By now the band had quit. People were shouting and getting out of the way. The big man hauled Stan across the floor. Stan was spitting between his teeth and his vision was greying out.

A moment later, he was being moved out into the coolness of the night. The big man held onto him until he'd pulled him down the front steps. On the flat ground of the parking lot Stan was forcefully let go. He stumbled about, bent double, gagging air. He grasped hold of the side-view mirror on a pickup truck. When he was able to stand straight again, he saw the big man poised halfway up the steps to the roadhouse. The faces of a few townies were crowding out of the front door above.

—You son of a bitch, said Stan.

He took a step forward. He was so angry that he was grinding his teeth together. The wrath was all the worse for how his body wasn't responding as it used to. But the man on the steps, the faces in the door, they weren't looking at him. They were looking at something behind him. Stan turned.

Two cops, young, unknown to him, were coming across the parking lot.

For a full minute, Frank didn't say anything. He was wearing jeans and a sweatshirt. They'd called him in from home. Stan was the only one in the holding cell at the back of the detachment.

They'd taken away his belt and his shoes and his keys and his wallet and his little penknife.

Frank turned to a constable standing beside him. He said: Open it up. Give him his things.

Frank's office was at the back of the detachment. He kept it neat. There were school portraits of Emily and Louise and a candid photo of Mary. On one wall, Frank had framed letters of thanks from civic groups. He leaned forward on his desk.

—How often do you think the goddamn North Star calls us to send a car out, Stanley? Just how often do you think that happens?

—They called you, did they?

—They called us and said there was some old drunk making rude comments to the girl behind the bar.

—Whatever you want to say about it, Frank—

—I don't even know what to say. Never mind what might have happened to you. Three years ago a man got kicked in the head out behind that shithole, they had to airlift him to Sunnybrook. He died a week later. So tonight the dispatcher gets a call from the North Star, sends a car, and by the time they get there who do they see getting launched out. Some old drunk.

—Do I look like some goddamn old drunk to you?

—First off, you smell like hundred-proof. And second, when the boys brought you in, they thought you'd peed yourself.

—What? A goddamn drink got spilled on me . . .

—Stanley, this is unbelievable.

—Don't you see, Frank, the kind of people Judy Lacroix was tied up with? It seems to me you're not paying attention to this.

—You're absolutely right. I'm not paying attention. I've put more horsepower into it than it deserves and everything keeps coming up empty.

—This Gilmore—

—I don't care, Stan. I don't. I'm sorry to have to put it so blunt but you are not employed in the service of the law any more.

—I don't know why you think you've got to remind me.

—I say again, you are not a police officer.

They'd kept the pitches of their voices reined in but there was colour in their faces. Frank leaned forward with his forearms spaced out on the desk. He said: Look. Think of the position you're putting me in. And if that doesn't mean anything to you, think of the position you're putting Dick Shannon in, every time you ask him to get you something you don't have any claim to any more.

—Dick's got nothing to do with any of this.

—We have a good relationship. Don't put any strain on it by talking to me like I'm stupid. I am not stupid, and I do not want to have this conversation again.

Stan felt ashamed and tired. There wasn't anything about Frank's position that was unclear. Still, Stan couldn't say it. His silence would have to suffice as acquiescence.

—Go home, Stan. Your truck is outside.

Before Stan left, they agreed that nobody else in the family needed to know. Word would get around among the men they knew, but Mary and the girls didn't need to know about it.

When he got home later that night, he couldn't get any of it out of his head. For the first time, it felt like he was looking fully at his own desperation and foolishness and loneliness. He'd never felt more like an old man, long past his usefulness. The dense shadows in the room seemed to be crawling, seemed to be closing in on him. It was as long a night as he could remember.

Finally, he got up and turned on the light in the hallway and got back into bed.

—I'm sorry, he said. I don't know what else I can do.

By Friday evening the weather had become cruel. Wind barrelled over the pavement behind the variety store. Pete had come from work. He parked his car and got out, carrying a shopping bag. He hustled upstairs and knocked on Lee's door.

—What's happenin', Pete?

—Hey, Uncle Lee. Mom sent some leftover pot roast.

—Come in, buck.

Pete went into the crooked little apartment. The television was on and cigarette smoke was thick.

—I didn't know you got a TV.

—I bought it awhile ago. I never used to like it. But I also never used to have any money to buy something like this. Who knows. Some of the shows I've seen are alright, and sometimes they have movies.

Pete still didn't understand Lee. For most of his life, Lee had seldom been mentioned. Irene had photos of him squirrelled away somewhere but his mother did not. She had Luke and John write to him at Christmas every year, but otherwise practically never mentioned him. Pete had had no idea what Lee looked like until they met in September, and even now he was a mystery. It was hard to imagine that they had any family connection at all, really, that they shared blood. There was no way Pete had found of putting himself in Lee's shoes.

Part of it was that he didn't know what Lee had done. It was serious, whatever it was, but the crime itself remained unknown. Rape? Murder? High treason? Whatever it was, and in spite of his curiosity, he did not want to think about it. He'd come to like Lee—this strange newcomer in his life, who was tough and hard, yet, at the same time, oddly soft-spoken.

Pete had thought he would deliver the leftovers and be on his way but he ended up staying to watch television for awhile. And then something unexpected occurred: Lee went to the refrigerator and came back with a couple of beers. He gave one to Pete and he had one for himself. Pete held the beer can he'd been given. He opened it, listened to the fizzle. Lee was watching the television. Pete took a drink. They watched *Sanford*. When it was finished Lee got them a couple more beers and said should they see about supper.

—Unless you have to go somewheres, Pete.

—I'm not in a hurry.

—Not going to see a girlfriend or nothing?

—No.

—Well, let's have us some of this pot roast.

Lee heated the meat and the leftover vegetables on his hot plate. He brought a bottle of ketchup out of the fridge. They ate while they watched *The Dukes of Hazzard*. Lee was doubtful about the events of the show. He kept asking how the fuck that would work or why wouldn't they just shoot the goof. Finally he looked at Pete and said: See? Bullshit.

—You bet, said Pete. Say, how about the lady you were going with?

—Helen? All good, as far as I can tell. She's her own kind of gal. Sometimes we'll get together maybe three or four days out of the week. Sometimes once. You can't ever tell.

Pete wasn't sure how it happened but they were into their third beers. *The Dukes of Hazzard* ended and a television movie came on.

—I heard you quit going to Barry's church, said Lee.

—Yes. I did.

—Didn't you go there your whole life?

—Just since I was eight, when mom met Barry. But since then? Almost ten years, every Sunday. We weren't living in town when Mom met him. We lived in North Bay, actually, just Mom and me. I was born up there. But Grandma was still here, and a neighbour of hers had got her going to the church. Barry was a junior pastor back then, and he was single. I don't know exactly how it worked—I was too young to figure it out, really—but Grandma got Mom talking to Barry, and before long Mom came back here and brought me with her. We lived in Grandma's apartment for about a year. Man, that place was tiny. Then Mom and Barry got married, and they got the house where we are now, and all of us moved out there.

—Well, said Lee.

Lee didn't prompt him further, but after two or three minutes, Peter said: Maybe you think I'm, you know, that I'm going to go to hell. Because I quit the church. Maybe you think Barry's right about how people have to get born again and again. How Christians have to bring people in and convert them. So I'm sorry if this offends you but I don't believe any of it. I didn't go to church one Sunday, and I'll tell you why, but hang on, and Barry gave me a look but he didn't say much. Three weeks in a row I didn't go and then he brought it up. At dinner one night. I said I didn't want to talk about it. But Barry said spiritual things are what a family talks about with each other. Which is bullshit because we don't talk about anything ninety percent of the time, but whatever. He pushed. So I came right out and said I didn't plan to go any more. That I didn't believe it. Barry got upset. He said, did I know what I was doing about my salvation? And I told him that's not something he needs to worry about, but he said he would be and that he'd be praying for me. Mom had to get up and go into the kitchen.

—Pete, I wouldn't ask you to spill nothing you don't want to.

—Well, can you promise you'll keep something between us?

Lee put his hand out. Pete shook it.

—You talk about what you want to, Pete. I won't break any trust with you.

—Okay, look. Sheila Adams, she teaches Sunday School. She's ten years older than me. Last year, I was . . . you know, sleeping with her. She's married. She wasn't then, but she was engaged. I hadn't ever slept with a woman before. But I'm getting ahead of myself. From the time I was eight till last spring I was at church, like I said. Every Sunday. But I think I knew for a long time that I didn't belong. At the church, when the people get going, it's what Barry calls the Baptism of Fire. They speak in tongues and put their hands in the air and act crazy. But you want to know something about it? It never once worked for me. I never had the Baptism of Fire. I wanted it, I really did, but I never had it. A few years ago, I even quit pretending, quit faking that I was having the Baptism just so I'd look like everybody else. We'd be there at church, and while everybody else was with the spirit, I'd just daydream. Sometimes I thought about girls from school. If I really had guts I would have faced the facts and quit a long time ago. But I didn't. I kept thinking I just had to hold out, open myself to God, pray more and do this and do that and then I'd feel the grace. I did stuff with the youth group. Why not? I never had a lot of friends at school. The youth group, we'd do retreats, we'd do lockdowns at the church—

—Lockdowns?

—Yeah, said Pete. Lockdowns are sleepovers at the church. Not lockdowns like you'd think of from jail, I guess. Sorry. Anyway, stuff with the youth group was alright. It made it so things at home were easygoing.

Lee nodded.

Pete was past sober and loose-jawed. He went on: Last fall, Sheila Adams started helping out. She wasn't the youth pastor. She was the coordinator. I think she made the title up. I think she was bored. The guy she was engaged to was an engineer at the chemical factory. He was away for awhile, down in Central America, on a mission to help people purify their water. It was with the International Pentecostal Church. Sheila was at home, bored, so she started coordinating with the youth group. I knew her from around. She was young, she was kind of foxy. But I also knew her because of how into all of it she was. Talking in tongues, moving around, the whole bit. Sometimes she'd cry in a service. Cry and laugh at the same time. Look. It doesn't make a lot of sense. I don't know why it was me that she picked. Maybe it's because I was the oddball. Who knows what goes through women's heads.

—You'd never had sex with a woman before?

—Never. Here's how it went. I told you about those lock-downs? We did one for New Year's Eve. It was all pop and chips and games. About eleven o'clock my friend Billy and a couple other guys came by outside. I got out a window and smoked some grass with them. Then I went back inside. After midnight I was a little weirded out so I went walking around the church to clear my head. Sheila was in the office. She had a key, I don't know why. She called me in. I thought she knew I'd been smoking grass and she was going to let me have it, but . . . there wasn't much talk. She closed the door and it just happened. Just like that. I was looking over at Barry's desk the whole time, which was maybe five minutes. That was how it started. January. She'd need something, she'd need help over at her house. She'd give me a lift home from meetings. Once I skipped class and we did it in the afternoon. I thought I was in love with her but I guess I knew I wasn't. Whenever we actually talked about anything, all she ever said was, that's nice, or that's interesting. And if it was something complicated, she'd say, look in the Bible. But she wanted to have sex all the time, and I was happy to give. It was all I could think about. But then in March, Sheila found out her fiancé was coming home a couple months early. He'd gotten sick down there. He'd lost a bunch of weight. She told me we had to stop seeing each other. She said she was grateful for all the times I'd helped her out around her house. In a way I think she didn't believe any of it actually happened. Me, I was a mess. I didn't know how to deal with it but I knew I couldn't say anything. I knew if even one person had any idea, how fast it would get out. Church people love to talk. I knew if it got out what it would do to us. I didn't really care . . . about Barry. But Mom and Grandma, Luke, John, I care about them.

—You did just right, said Lee. So you quit going to church on account of this girl?

—Not right away. Sheila quit coordinating the youth group. I quit going to events. Her fiancé came back from his mission and there was this big Welcome Home for him at the church. He was skinny and his skin was yellow. I was mad. I was so goddamn mad . . . But then we were at church this one Sunday in May. We were at church and everybody had the Baptism of Fire, hands in the air, talking in tongues. I saw Sheila, and she was right into it as usual. But the thing was, the face she was making, while she was blabbing out all these old languages, the face was the exact same as when she'd be having sex. Exact same. I don't know why but I thought that was one of the funniest things I ever saw. I thought I was going to laugh my guts out right there in church. And then I knew. I knew how come I never had the Baptism of Fire. I didn't go to church again. I quit school a couple weeks after that. It was the same there, Lee. Bullshit, all of it. I knew if I was going to head out west I was going to need to save some money. That's all I've cared about ever since.

He'd halfway finished his beer. He was blinking against Lee's cigarette smoke.

—Maybe I am passing up my chance for salvation. Maybe I'm going to hell. But I never chose to see through it all.

—I'm not sharp like you are, said Lee. I read the Bible a few times and I think there's some real good stuff there. But they say God loves everybody. He cries if a bird dies. Sure. But then the same God would send somebody like you to hell forever? Just on account of you don't get the call, same as some other people? I'm not sharp like you are, but I never got anybody, like a chaplain or a pastor, to work out that question so it made any sense.

—You don't believe in hell?

—Sure I do. I seen it with my own eyes. It's right here in the world where people make it for each other.

Lee didn't know what advice he could give to Pete, if Pete was even looking for advice. Lee had known, of course, that Donna had left town to live somewhere else for several years, that Pete hadn't been born here, but that was a different subject entirely.

They got a little drunker and they watched the television

movie for awhile. Just a few beers remained. Pete said he didn't think he could drive home until he sobered up.

—You'll end up in the goddamn ditch, said Lee. Stay here.

Lee got a deck of cards and dealt it out onto a TV tray. He said he was going to teach Pete a kind of poker called Fishing Hole that he'd learned inside. You could play with as few as two players or as many as seven. Everybody would ante in and then the whole deck got dealt and each player's cards got tallied up for points against whatever hands he might have been able to make. Sometimes a certain guy would book a regular game and would be able to rake a small profit. They played a few rounds. Pete felt like he'd been inducted into a secret order.

—Did you always do carpentry? said Pete. Like, before?

—No. I did a few building jobs here and there in town with some guys I knew, but when I went up, I wasn't anything at all. I got my trade after I got there.

—Right away? said Pete.

—It wasn't right away, no. I'd been in there almost ten years.

—Oh.

They played another round of Fishing Hole. They were using pennies and nickels and cigarettes to make their bets. Lee was winning, and he took one of the cigarettes he'd won and he lit it. He took a drag and let out a stream of smoke.

—Joe Holmes, a con I knew, he was in the woodshop. He sort of got me interested in it.

—He was, what, your cellmate?

—No, we weren't two to a drum. Joe Holmes, I just knew him. When he was a kid he used to steal cars. He got sent to the reformatory, got out, stole cars again. After awhile the Crown got tired of him taking up space at the reformatory so they locked him up for good. But he wasn't a serious guy. He wasn't a fighter or a scrapper or nothing. He'd been in the woodshop for a few years when I knew him. Everybody thought working in the infirmary was where it was at because it was an easy go, but Joe liked the woodshop. He was kind of a trusty. The screws listened to him if he had something to say about the manning in the shop, and they didn't give him much headache. And Joe, he just liked seeing things come together. That was all. He said he never knew that before he was inside.

—Do you still talk to him? Is he out?

— . . . No, said Lee. Say, did you know about the riot in 1971?

—I was a kid. It was just after Mom met Barry. Grandma got real upset when the riot was on the news. I don't remember much more than that.

—The riot, right, I was there inside when it happened. There was this con named Dave Dempsey. He was a goof, Dempsey. He'd gotten sent up for kicking the shit out of his woman. She was a couple months pregnant when Dempsey had at her and she lost the kid. They nailed him hard for that. He was twenty years old, skinny, blond. To look at him when he got there—this was maybe 68 or 69—you'd think some old daddy would snap him up just as quick as can be, but Dempsey made himself useful. The real serious guys, they just put up with him. When they needed a guy to do something, Dempsey was who they used. And anyway . . . Dempsey and Joe Holmes . . .

Lee butted out the cigarette on the TV tray.

—You know what, buck, never mind.

Pete blinked sluggishly.

—What?

—None of that shit matters any more.

—I don't know about that.

—I do, said Lee.

—So . . . Uh. I have to use your bathroom.

Pete went into the bathroom and closed the door and Lee could hear him dry-heaving and washing his face with cold water, and then Pete stumbled back into the living room.

He stayed the night at Lee's. Lee set up the pullout bed and told Pete to sleep there. Pete was too drunk to argue. For himself, Lee aligned the couch cushions against the wall next to the television. But for a long time, while Pete groaned with the spins and tried to sleep, Lee sat at the window, watching the street. Remembering.

Nobody had bad blood with Joe Holmes, that was the hell of it. But the riot was a strange time. It brought out what was lurking in the hearts of a lot of men.

It lasted four days. By the end of it, the army had set up camp outside the penitentiary and had readied their machine guns. All they were waiting for was the order. Lee was up at the top of the dome, laying low. In the beginning he'd had a hell of a good time with everybody else, tearing it all apart, lighting fires. The best time in years. But then there were certain boys who wanted to talk about rights this and rights that. And there were other boys who wanted to hold court. What that meant was tying up all the rapists and perverts and snitches and going to work on them with fire and iron bars. One man who'd fondled some schoolkids had his eyeballs gouged out and his ears melted. Lee knew some of the boys holding court. Dave Dempsey was one of them.

When they were sure the end was near, boys in ones and twos and in groups were going out to give themselves up. Some were in bad shape. Hungry or beaten or dehydrated. About five in the morning on the fourth day, Lee came down to give himself up. He wasn't interested in prisoners' rights. He was even less interested in getting chewed up by a machine gun.

Down on the bottom tier it was dark and wet with piss and water. There were fires burning. There were some men who couldn't move. Out of it there came Joe Holmes, huffing and puffing from the chronic lung trouble he had. He was making his way out.

And then out of nowhere, Dave Dempsey. What was he doing? It looked like he was hugging Joe Holmes from behind, hugging him, saying, How does that get you off, baby? Then he dropped something and in the firelight Lee saw it was a screwdriver red with blood, and Dempsey just turned and walked away same as if he was on the sidewalk doing his shopping.

Joe was down on his knees when Lee got to him. He was bleeding bad. He'd been stuck half a dozen times around where his kidneys were. His eyes rolled.

—Let's get you out of here, Joe. Christ.

—It's clear, said Joe.

—Come on with me.

—Can't you see how clear it is?

After the riot Dave Dempsey and some of the others got packed off to the new super-max pen. If Dempsey ever had a reason for sticking Joe, he never said. Word got back to Lee that all Dempsey ever said was he should have stuck him in the neck. He laughed when he said it, Lee heard. Dempsey was a goof and full of shit. He got thrown off a tier a few years later, and was paralyzed.

Joe Holmes was in the hospital for a long time. Afterwards they had to commit him to a psych ward because he'd stopped talking. He just wandered around and never said anything. Joe Holmes who stole cars and went up and learned what it was to put something together with his hands. Joe Holmes who didn't have bad blood with anybody.

You see that and you know for the first time what a thing of randomness is. You know how even if you have your affairs under control, there's something else at work, something that's aware of you. And it waits, until just the right time, and it steps out of the dark, just long enough to take shape and act and then disappear again.

In the early morning Peter drove them to the Owl Café for breakfast. Helen was not going to be working until later in the afternoon. Pete pushed his French toast around on his plate.

He was in rough shape. At six-thirty, Bud's car was outside. Lee clapped Pete on the shoulder, told him he'd see him again soon. He picked up his lunch pail and his tool belt and went outside.

Bud and Lee drove north to the public landing. Under a single street light, they could see Clifton waiting for them on the pier. He was not supposed to be at work with them today because of his niece's wedding. Wally was nowhere to be seen.

They got out of Bud's car. Bud locked it.

—Leland King, said Clifton. We have a problem.

Lee stiffened a little. Was this a problem with him? Did Clifton know, somehow, about Lee having some drinks again, or about the fight he'd gotten into outside of the poolroom? Warily, Lee said: What's the problem, Mr. Murray?

—Our good pal Wally decided to forget what side of the bread is buttered. You hear?

—I'm not following you.

—Wally's walked off the bloody job, Lee. You don't just get paid to do odd jobs. You get paid to think.

Lee nodded. It was nothing to do with him, after all. He said: So you're not going to the wedding.

—My faith can move mountains but there's some things even out of my reach. This is your chance to make good on what you say you can do. I want the kitchen cabinets up before you leave today. Bud can do the piers. Understand?

—I understand. I'll get them cabinets up. You'll—

—At the end of the day I want the rest of the concrete mix and the mixer brought back. Jeff'll be out here with a truck to pick it all up. You and Bud can help him.

—No trouble, Clifton.

—This is it, mister man. This is what I need from you. Get to it.

Bud had piloted the barge before, so Clifton gave him the keys. Bud perched himself behind the wheel. Then they were moving away from the pier while the sun rose behind murky clouds.

The island seemed particularly quiet with only Bud and Lee there. They got the generator going and started the cement mixer. They smoked with impunity. Bud disappeared under the building to work on the piers.

In the kitchen, the new counter was built but there were two cabinets that remained to go up. Lee found the cabinet plans and laid them open beside the table saw. It was cold but his palms were moist. He buckled on his tool belt and he took out his pencil and put it behind his ear.

Then he got going. He pulled sheets of pine and marked out lines and measurements. He measured twice. He labelled each piece. He set the fence on the table saw and then he threw the switch, listened to the blade spin up. He fed the first sheet through. The blade on the saw was new and the cuts it made were completely smooth. Lee cut out shelves and cut dadoes and rabbets for the joints.

Late morning, Lee went out to piss. It was still very cold. The house had been brought back to level by a collection of railroad ties and kickjacks while new concrete piers were poured. This was what Bud was doing. Underneath the house you couldn't bend up higher than your waist and Lee didn't envy Bud at all. He made sure Bud was okay for smokes and then he went back into the kitchen.

They had a quick lunch in the living room. Bud was surprised at Lee's work. He said Wally or any of the other inside guys never moved that fast. Lee let the observation stand but he was secretly pleased.

After lunch he got going again. He put the carcasses together and put the shelves in. They fit smoothly. Wally had left a bottle of glue on the new counter. Lee took it and beaded glue where the shelves and panels fit together. He found a box of finishing nails and a punch. He tapped the finishing nails into the pine and then fingered putty into the holes.

The cabinets were to be hung on French cleats, which he

ripped out from two-by-fours on the table saw. He fixed the first one up and checked it for square and levelled it. He stood back to look.

Joe Holmes was on Lee's mind as he worked, Joe talking about things going together. Otherwise, Lee had little to think about. Not Helen, not his mother, not his sister, not money, not anything in his life that had brought him to this.

After Lee hung the second cabinet he realized it was past three already. The cedar in the yard was skittering against the kitchen window-glass. He put on his jacket and went outside onto the deck. The wind had picked up. He turned his back to it until he had a cigarette lit.

After three calls, Bud came out from under the building. He was crusted with raw earth and liquid concrete. Lee squatted and offered him a smoke through the boards.

—How's the pier?

—Just about done. How's the kitchen where it's nice and warm?

—Second cabinet's up.

—Not bad for a Saturday.

—Not bad for a Saturday.

Lee had to relight his cigarette. The wind was moving faster now, building up a great black reef of clouds. The evergreens were leaning. They were little more than an hour from dark. The light was pallid and the wind knifed through Lee's clothes.

—I think we're getting some mean weather.

Bud looked off to the northeast. He dug in his nostril with his thumb and said: You think so?

—That could be snow. We should pack up.

Bud licked his teeth.

—Okay. Let's get going. That pier is nothing I can't finish Monday.

—How many bags you got left?

Bud glanced under the building.

—Maybe thirty of the bastards.

—Clifton wants the extra ones back at the shop tonight.

Bud kicked a stump and called Clifton a mean old bastard. Lee went into the kitchen and put away the tools and swept up. He ran his hands along the cabinets.

The weather was getting worse. Most material could stay on the island except the mixer and the remaining bags of Sakrete. There were twenty-eight bags and Lee and Bud piled them in the barge. They brought the mixer down and strapped it next to the console. They collected their pouches and lunch pails.

—A couple days ago I seen this chick in the grocery store, said Bud.

—You what?

—I seen this chick in the grocery store. A mother. She's got these five little brats. All of them are running around, screaming, bumping into old ladies. Just tear-assing around. Finally the mother, she loses it, and she screams at them, screams, I knew it, I should have swallowed you all!

Lee looked at him for a long moment. Bud was able to contain it briefly and then he was laughing. Lee laughed with him.

—That's the first one I ever heard you get right.

—That's a good one, isn't it?

Bud went to the console and turned on the motor. Lee untethered the barge and hopped in. There was no snow yet but the clouds had a smudged quality that troubled him. Bud navigated the barge in the direction of the hogback south of the islands. Their motion was ponderous with the weight of the concrete mix they were carrying. Bud pushed the throttle forward. Lee put his toque on and hunched inside his jacket. The late autumn treeline on the hogback was colourless but there were two glaring gaps where the foliage had been razed away from new lots. He could just make out the orange stakes of the property boundaries.

The barge angled around the hogback and into the open lake.

—Jesus Christ. Lookit it out here.

Outside the bay, the open water was breaking hard. It crashed at the steel hull. Lee turned his head to watch forward and his eyes filled with spray. They were five hundred yards off Echo Point to the east. From there it was another four hundred yards south to the public landing. There were lights scattered around the north shore but he could see nothing of town in the south.

Bud's face was bright red and the concrete dust was running in veins off his head. They crossed a hundred yards out into the open water and the hogback became indistinguishable from the shore behind them. Bud grinned around his cigarette and gave Lee the finger. Just then, a plume of water broke over the starboard gunnels and doused Bud from head to crotch. It put the cigarette out. He stood there blinking, his middle finger still lifted. A second wave boomed against the side of the barge. Lee strained to see ahead of them.

The frigid wind was blowing harder, chopping the water. Whitecaps peaked around them. Lee looked back around and immediately he saw sheets of water coming in over the transom in the aft. Two or three inches of water were sloshing around his boots. A horrible feeling filled him. The barge slugged forward, water sluicing in on all sides. Lee dove onto the Sakrete bags. He took them up one at a time and threw them overboard, desperate to lighten the weight they were carrying, Clifton be goddamned. The bags were monstrously heavy. He stood with legs spread wide, trying to keep his balance, casting the Sakrete bags into the dark waves.

Bud shouted something. He pointed. A curtain of falling snow was sweeping across the whitecaps. They could see it closing in.

Lee lifted and threw as quickly as he could, feeling the strain in his forearms. Something pulled in his midsection. Half a dozen bags remained and then the snowfall was on them. It blanked out the shore in all directions, leaving them in a white netherworld.

Lee threw the second-last and then the last bags overboard and stood mute until the barge lurched and he was thrown against the mixer. His shoulder blades smashed painfully into the rim of the drum.

A light resolved out of the snowfall to their front. Bud was bent at the console, his lips pulled back from his teeth and his hands clamped on the steering wheel. He angled the barge towards the light. The silhouettes of conifers began to take shape. It was Echo Point and they were coming up on it fast, no longer so weighted. The west face of the point was bare rock where the waves smashed up and sprayed apart.

Bud heaved the wheel hard right and Lee fell back into the cement mixer, feeling it shift against the tethers they'd tied it down with. Neither of them had seen the marker bouncing in the waves, marking a shoal. Bud had turned them right on top of it. The propeller and hull barked against rock, and the impact was tremendous. Lee cartwheeled overboard. The cold of the water struck his head like a hammer blow and there was water in his nose and his mouth and he was looking stupidly into the black. He could not determine up from down but his boots were drawing him in one particular direction. He pulled the opposite way.

When he broke through the surface of the lake there was no feeling in his hands or in his face. He could hear the motor revving some distance away through the eddying snow. He thrashed about, calling for Bud. Lee's boots were touching the shoal below. He saw a grey beach south of the point, not far away at all, where the water was sheltered almost to stillness. The barge was raking towards the sand, propelled at an oblique angle by the damaged motor. He couldn't see Bud.

Lee swam for it, clawing the water until he struck on sand. He hauled himself up onto the beach. He was shaking all over. He got to his knees, fell sideways, got back up. Up on the point was the profile of a building. A single window-light. Lee heard a dog barking. Sixty feet away in the other direction was the barge, resting partway out of the water. He could make out one upthrust leg of the mixer.

He moved haltingly down the sand, holding his hands in his armpits. He was frigid to the core. He called Bud's name. He sloshed back out into the water to the depth of his knees and laid his unfeeling hands on the gunnels.

—Oh, Bud. Oh come on, man.

There were eight inches of water in the bottom of the barge. Bud was face down beside the console, pinned beneath the drum of the mixer.

—Bud, you dumb motherfucker.

The dog barked again. Lee looked back and saw a man and a dog resolving out of the snowfall. Lee leaned over the gunnels and jabbed the kill-switch on the console. He reached down and took hold of one of the legs of the mixer. He could not feel it and it wouldn't move and Bud did not move beneath it.

Emily was napping in her grandfather's house when the storm came up. She had come out in the early afternoon to help him stack firewood. For the last week there'd been some tension at home, something that had happened between Grandpa and her dad, but nobody was talking about it. In any case, the old man needed help around the house and was being too headstrong to ask, so Emily had come out on her own.

They'd stacked wood all morning. After a late lunch, with a fire in the woodstove and the house warm and dry, she'd gone into the front room, closed the door and lain down on the couch and fallen asleep. When she woke, it was near dark through the windows and the snow was blowing sideways on the wind.

Something had woken her. Maybe the dog barking. She sat up and stretched. There were photographs of her grandmother's cousins, Margaret, Bette, Ida. She could remember her grandmother naming them. Telling their histories. Next to the cousins was a photograph of Great-aunt Rose, who was still alive, whom Emily and her mother would visit this year before Christmas.

The piano was in the front room. Emily remembered her grandmother placing her hands—she wasn't yet five years old. C chord, D major, E major. Doesn't that go together nice? The foot tapped along. Grandmother smelled like lavender. In her absence, the room smelled like dust.

There were books of music stacked on top of the piano. One was a United Church hymnal. On top of the stack was Erik Satie. Grandmother had liked Satie best. She said how he didn't have so much to say in his music and what he did say was pretty simple. When you thought about that, wasn't that good? More with less.

Emily held her hands above the keys for a moment and then she began to play. She played Satie and the snow fell against the window.

The piano music came from somewhere in the old man's house, muted through the walls but plainly audible. Before the piano, there had been the sound of the old man's voice speaking on the telephone on the other side of the kitchen. Then the old man had gone back outside.

Lee was hunched in front of the woodstove, clad in dry clothes the old man had given him. They were too big for his frame but too short for his arms and legs. He was wrapped in a wool blanket and the old man had had him put on a dry toque and clean wool socks. Lee listened to the piano. The tune was not anything he'd ever heard.

Stan came back into the kitchen, Cassius following. The dog was agitated and whiny until Stan stayed him with a gentle hand on his head. Stan took off his jacket and his gloves. Then he paused, listening to the music. He spoke quietly: She's awake, then. My granddaughter was having a nap. If she's up, I'd just as soon let her be. I don't want to upset her.

Stan had brewed a pot of tea before he'd made the telephone call and gone back outside. He filled two mugs. He mixed three spoonfuls of sugar into the one he brought over to Lee. Stan sat down.

—There's an ambulance on the way. It may take a little time to get out here. There've been a couple car accidents in town with the snow . . . I brought your friend up and covered him. There's nothing more I can do. I am sorry.

Lee nodded. He couldn't stop shaking.

—I told him we should leave the job site. I wanted to go before it got dark.

—Never mind that, said Stan. This isn't anything you can hold yourself to.

—It was my idea to leave.

—Maybe, said Stan. And there's nothing I can say but it was an accident. My name is Stan Maitland, by the way.

—I'm Lee.

Stan nodded. Even if Lee had been paying attention, Stan gave nothing away just then.

—What were you boys doing? said Stan.

—We were working. Bud was under the house making it level. I was in the kitchen doing the carpentry.

—Carpentry, said Stan.

—Doors, windows, joining. Cabinets. It's my trade.

—I was never much of a carpenter myself. About every time I swing a hammer it's my thumb I hit.

—What do you do? said Lee.

—Not much of anything any more. I try to keep this place from falling down.

—How long have you lived here?

—On and off my whole life. It was my brother's house for awhile. My dad built it. That's almost a hundred years ago. I lived here with my wife until she passed on.

Lee lifted his tea and drank. For once he did not want a cigarette at all.

—It's real sugary, he said.

—You'll need the extra kick to help you get warmed up.

Stan guessed Lee was at least mildly hypothermic, as well as in shock. Cassius lay down under the table. Neither Stan nor Lee took conscious note that the piano music had quit.

—It's a business about getting old, said Stan. You start to wonder how long anything you leave behind will last after you're gone. Like a house, say. Probably not all that long.

—It doesn't matter. You go when you go and nothing you leave behind matters no more.

—I suppose maybe you're right. Maybe there's even some comfort in that.

—Sometimes it stops mattering even before you go.

—Well, I don't think it's any good if a man ever gets to that point.

Lee gathered the blanket around himself. He couldn't seem to think straight, couldn't set his mind to the events of the last hour. He liked Bud, Bud was okay. Now Bud was gone, but how could that be? He'd never been so confused in his life.

—Here's something I want to know, said Lee.

—Yes?

—If everything I ever done, if this is what it brought me to, is it maybe that I never had a choice in it?

—I don't know, said Stan. Do you think so?

—No. I don't think so. No matter how I try, I can't see how that would be so.

After Emily finished with the piano she went out of the front room and through the hallway. The door to the kitchen was closed. She used the washroom on the ground floor and when she was in there she could hear Grandpa talking to somebody in the kitchen. Their voices were pitched low. She couldn't make out the words.

The washroom had a small window looking down through the trees to the little beach below the point. She was drying her hands when she noticed the barge out on the sand.

She came out of the washroom and almost went into the kitchen. Then, as she thought again of the barge, curiosity got the better of her. She got a blue afghan off the couch in the living room and wrapped it around herself and put on her shoes and slipped out the front door. She followed the path down through the trees. The snowfall was slowing down and the twilight was strange. The dark water against the beach was calm but out past the point she could see the whitecaps. In the grey sand was a confusing mix of tracks. Something looked to have been dragged. She went and looked in the barge. She looked at the water in the bottom. She saw how the toppled-over cement mixer had been moved aside. Snow collected on her hair and eyelashes.

—I remember you, said Stan.

—Do you.

—Yes. In truth I do. I was a cop for many years.

Lee didn't say anything. Stan had given him a leftover grilled-cheese sandwich to eat and he'd managed a few bites of it.

—I'd heard that you'd come back, said Stan. I don't know if you remember or not, but I was the man who drove you down to the provincial jail. You weren't all that old—

—I was twenty-two.

—Yes. Well. I was old then but you weren't. I thought about that at the time.

—I was old enough.

—How long has it been?

—You mean how long did I do? Seventeen years.

—It's a long time, said Stan.

—The Crown wanted to hang me.

They were quiet for a full minute. Stan at the table, Lee as close to the woodstove as he could get. Just then the mud-room door opened and Cassius stood up. Emily came in from outside, wrapped in the afghan, with snow in her hair.

—Emily, said Stan.

—Grandpa. There's a man down by the basement door. He's under a tarp and he's—I think he's deceased, Grandpa.

She was so factual about it. *Deceased,* she'd said. She was concerned but not panicking. She looked like it was out of the range of what she could figure out. Cassius went over to her and she knelt down and embraced him.

—There was a bad accident, said Stan.

The man in the rocking chair, this man she did not recognize, who was wearing a toque and was draped in a blanket, whose posture and absurd appearance was telling her what Grandpa was not, this hard-looking man, she could see his hands shaking.

—Goddammit it, said Lee. I just can't get warm. Not at all.

The weather cleared by late evening. Pete went in through the emergency doors of the hospital. He was hungover, still wearing the work clothes he'd slept in. The emergency room was sparsely filled. A woman was holding a towel against a cut on her forehead. She looked annoyed more than anything else. A boy with his father was coughing steadily. Pete went up to an orderly at a desk.

—Can I help you.

—I got a call from my mom.

—You got a call from your mom.

—My uncle was in some kind of a work accident. They brought him here. Leland King is his name.

—Yes, said the orderly. Wait here, please.

The orderly made a call. Pete sat down. The woman with the cut sighed loudly. Then a cop came into the emergency room and spoke to the orderly. The orderly gestured at Pete. The cop came over and Pete stood up.

—To confirm, said the cop. This is your uncle you're here about.

—Yes, Officer.

There was something unreadable on the cop's face. He said: Your uncle. Leland King. He was in a work-related accident this afternoon. He's banged up. Has mild hypothermia. They're going to keep him here overnight.

—Jesus, said Pete. Can I see him?

—You want to see him?

—Why wouldn't I?

The cop shrugged.

—Well, you can't see him, said the cop. The doctor said he's resting now. He's okay, your uncle. But the other guy . . .

—The other guy. Bud?

—What a situation they got themselves into. Of course, Leland King is the one to turn out okay. Funny how that goes.

The cop was almost grinning. He turned around and went back into the interior of the hospital. Pete watched him go. Then he went over to the orderly.

—Listen, can you tell me anything?

—I can't let out any information other than to say they just want to keep him here under observation.

—Is there a phone I can use?

—Pete?

He turned from the orderly's booth and Emily was standing there. He tried to make sense of her.

—Emily.

—I had no idea he's your uncle. I just heard your name from one of the constables. It happened near my grandfather's place. Oh my God, Pete. Your uncle's friend died.

—Jesus Christ. This keeps getting worse.

Emily laced her fingers together and looked at the floor. When she looked at him she smiled wearily, said: My grandfather took care of most of it. I'm just tired at this point. I don't think I've ever been so tired. The only thing I can think about is going to bed. Is that pretty terrible?

—No. I don't think so.

—It's good to see you, Pete.

—You too. Under the circumstances and all. I haven't seen you in awhile.

A white-haired man, broad-shouldered despite his age, came into the emergency room. He was carrying a wool jacket. Emily introduced Pete to Stan. Stan nodded.

—Your uncle's going to be fine. You don't need to worry.

—So I hear.

Stan put his arm around Emily's shoulders. She folded against him and yawned.

—I'll take you home, said Stan. And you, Pete? Do you need a lift anywhere?

—No, I have a car here. I was going to see my uncle but they said to come back tomorrow.

—He'll be alright.

Stan told Emily he would be in the truck and he shook Peter's hand again and left. Emily hung back a moment.

—I have to go, Pete.

—I know.

—It would be nice to see you again soon.

Emily went out and Pete watched her go. Then the woman with the cut on her forehead called out that at some point she was going to need some goddamn assistance. Nobody was listening.

THREE

NOVEMBER TO DECEMBER 1980

The accident on Lake Kissinaw was big news for the remainder of November. There was a police investigation and then a Ministry of Labour inquest. Stan's and Lee's names were kept out of the paper but for a few days all you would see were pictures of Bud and his despairing widow. He was not buried. He was cremated and his ashes were spread at a campground he'd gone to every May long weekend for the last ten years.

Lee did not go to the memorial. He'd been very fond of Bud, but the thought of people, almost all of whom would be strangers, standing together, looking at him, whispering his name, knowing that it was he who'd been with Bud at the last moment, was too much to bear. He went up to the poolroom instead, and had a few drinks and shot a few games, and then went home and watched the hockey game on his TV.

By early December, six inches of snow had come to stay. Lee came into the hospital through the visitors' entrance and went directly into a smoking area encased in glass. He nodded to an old man in a wheelchair who was smoking through a tracheotomy. Lacklustre Christmas garlands hung from the walls. Lee lit a cigarette.

Two hospital volunteers were sitting at a desk near the elevators. They were both old, a woman and a man, she with white-blue hair and he with liver spots on his bald head.

—I'm here to see Irene King, said Lee.

They peered at him. The woman painstakingly consulted a list of patients in a three-ring binder. She said: She's in room 3B. Amiens Wing.

—I know where she's at. I've been here a few times since she got here.

They gave him a visitor's pass. He felt them watching after he'd passed by. He hadn't been in any state of mind to pull together his observations in the short time he'd spent here following Bud's death, but he felt a revulsion towards the hospital, he suspected because of its institutional nature.

It was in the hospital that he'd been interviewed about the accident by the police and by an investigator from the Ministry of Labour. His parole officer, Wade Larkin, had come for the interviews. It hadn't taken long to clear Lee of any culpability but that hadn't left him any more at ease. Clifton was in more trouble, and as his part in the investigation wore on, work had ceased.

Lee took the elevator up to the third floor. Up here were a number of other terminally ill persons. Irene shared her room with an old woman named Mrs. Petrelli, who was dying from pancreatic cancer. She did not speak English and she became talkative only when her son came to visit in the early afternoons. The remainder of the time, she watched the TV in the corner of the room, soap operas or news broadcasts. Irene reported that Mrs. Petrelli had had night terrors on two occasions, had screamed until the nurse came. Mrs. Petrelli's son said his mother was bombed in Italy as a teenager in the Second World War. Most of her family was killed.

Irene was sitting up in bed wearing a nasal tube, her supper tray on a bed table in front of her. The meal was chicken and peas and it reminded Lee of the meals in prison. He sat down beside her. Under the bed, just at the edge of sight, was a catheter pouch full of urine.

—Did Barry or Donna visit today? said Lee.

—Barry said he would come by.

The television chattered. Mrs. Petrelli moaned.

—You shouldn't have to share a room, said Lee.

—It's okay, son. Unless she has her nightmares.

—You should have your own room. Goddammit.

—Lee, now.

He held up his finger.

—Wait, Ma.

Lee went out of the room and found the duty station, where a nurse wearing a cardigan over her scrubs was bent over a clipboard. Lee leaned on the edge of the desk. The nurse asked in a flat voice if she could help him.

—I want my mother to have her own room.

—To whom are you referring, sir?

—Irene King.

—Is there a problem?

—She shares a room with a lady who doesn't even speak English. My mother is real sick. She should be in a more comfortable way. She shouldn't have to worry about sharing the TV with nobody or getting woke up in the night.

—I hate to say but it's not so quick a process. Bed space is always an issue.

—Well, what can you do about that?

—I can recommend a hospice or in-home care.

—Something I'd have to pay for, in other words.

—That's correct. But I assure you, sir, the comfort of all patients here is very important to us.

—She should have her own room.

—It would be nice if this hospital was twice the size it is, I agree.

Irene had been in the hospital since the last few days of November. Lee had gotten a call from Donna, relayed upstairs through Mr. Yoon. Later he'd heard the whole story from Pete, how Pete had come home late one night from work and found his grandmother on her knees in the bathroom. She was trying to cough quietly. There were bright spots of blood in the sink and in the toilet and on the floor.

Dr. Vijay called it hemoptysis. Some of the cancerous blood vessels had burst in her lungs. The doctor did not think it was necessarily severe, and said it would likely subside on its own. But they needed to discuss a more aggressive treatment, he said. In the meantime, she was to be kept in the hospital.

When Lee went back to the room, he saw that Barry had arrived. Barry had stopped to speak some words with Mrs. Petrelli, standing by her bed and holding one of her skinny hands.

—Si chiamano figlio mio? Egli ha sposato un ebreo.

—God bless you, said Barry, patting her hand.

—Barry, said Lee.

—Hey, Brother Lee.

They went to Irene's bed. She was looking out the window and her breathing sounded like dirt caught in the gears of a machine. Barry was about to speak but Lee spoke first: We're looking at getting you your own room, Ma.

—Lee, said Barry.

—That's what we're going to do.

—Well, said Barry.

They stayed for awhile. Barry talked about his sons, about Donna, about the Christmas outreach programs Galilee Pentecostal had organized. Meals for the infirm, a gift drive for the empty-handed. Lee sat with his face planted on his fist. He watched how Barry was solicitous in the telling. He badly wanted a cigarette.

—It makes me proud, said Barry.

Irene and Barry were both looking at him.

—Say what?

—I was saying it makes me proud, Lee. How you've been keeping your faith since the tragedy. You'll be back on your feet before you know it.

—You done well, son, said Irene.

—I think maybe it's time for a prayer, said Barry. He turned to Mrs. Petrelli and asked would she join them in prayer.

—Chiamare l'infermiera. Io sono affamati.

Barry took Mrs. Petrelli's hand and he took Irene's hand and he held them. Irene reached her other hand out to Lee and he took it in both of his own. Irene squeezed her eyes shut. Mrs. Petrelli gaped. Barry lowered his head.

—The burdens that are put on us, there's nothing that's not intended to strengthen us in Your service.

—Dear Jesus, said Irene.

—The body gets weak but the soul gets stronger.

There were tears collecting at the sides of Irene's shuttered eyes. She whispered: Oh dear Jesus.

Lee watched his mother, wondering what these words were doing for her. He thought about the Bible, he thought about some of the verses he'd learned, or at least some of what he'd heard chaplains saying—hope in hard times, deliverance in the face of death. They spoke of God as the high tower, God as shelter from the wicked, God as the shield, God as the sword, God as the one who would escort you up from your earthly pain to heaven, where you would be pain-free for the rest of eternity. All you had to do was have faith. But faith in what? In these words? Was his mother squeezing her eyes shut from the words alone? Because all Lee could hear were the words, and they'd never sounded so hollow.

—Amen, said Barry.

—Egli ha sposato un ebreo, said Mrs. Petrelli.

Ten minutes later Lee stood to go. He kissed his mother's

forehead and smoothed back what remained of her hair. He went out and looked at the duty station, but the nurse was gone. Barry caught up with him at the elevator.

—Brother Lee, thank you for coming. It means so much to her.

—It would mean more if we got her into her own room.

—Honestly, I was a little surprised when I heard you say it. I thought we agreed on the arrangements.

—I agreed till I saw the room lately.

—Bed space is a major issue here, Lee.

—Don't worry about that, Barry. I'll find something to take care of it.

Barry clasped his hands together and smiled tightly: Can we agree it's something to discuss with Donna?

—We can agree.

—Good. Are we still seeing you for supper next Thursday?

—I'll be there. I'll introduce you to my lady friend.

—We'll be happy to meet her, said Barry.

—I'll see you soon.

—Lee, there's one other thing.

—What's that?

Barry pushed a pamphlet towards him.

—It's something to think about. Everybody is here to help, Brother Lee.

Barry went back to Irene's room and Lee got into the elevator. The pamphlet showed a drawing of a figure contemplating a bottle. It advertised Alcoholics Anonymous. The meeting was held weekly at the Charles Grady Memorial Community Centre. Lee wondered if Barry had even noticed that part. Probably not. He managed a thin chuckle.

He carried the pamphlet with him into the smoking section in the cafeteria. He had a smoke among the ill and the dying, the relatives, the attendants. He put the pamphlet on the table and took his leave.

As he went outside, he thought of the call that faith was supposed to be, the call in your heart. He'd thought he'd heard it once or twice, perhaps, but now, everything that had gone before was doubtful. Everything, it seemed, was just words.

The sun was going down, making long shadows of the gas pumps. Duane was finishing with a customer and Pete was in the store. He kept looking at the clock on the wall.

—You seem like you're in a hurry tonight, said Caroline. Big date?

Pete shifted his feet.

Caroline nodded: If it's a date, you'll have to tell us about it. Go take Duane a hot chocolate. Yes, you can have one too.

Pete went to the coffee stand and mixed powdered hot chocolate and hot water into two Styrofoam cups. He sealed the cups with plastic lids and went outside. The air smelled of cold concrete. He gave one of the hot chocolates to Duane. Duane spat a wad of chewing tobacco into an empty pop can.

—Thanks, said Duane. Feel like working, you dog-fucker?

—Not really, said Pete.

—I thought not. Hey, you know this guy?

Duane was pointing. A Camaro was parked across the lot. Billy was coming towards them at a brisk pace.

—What's up? called Billy.

Pete crossed the distance to meet Billy halfway.

—What's up? said Billy.

—I don't know. What's up?

—You tell me, you fucking traitor.

Pete did not reply. The heat through the Styrofoam cup was creeping into his fingers. Billy's face was pale and etched.

—Where are you going tonight, Peter?

—I guess you know already.

—You fucking traitor.

Billy's voice was gaining an edge. He was so angry that tears had formed in his eyes. He knocked the hot chocolate out of Pete's hand. It hit the ground and the lid burst off. The hot chocolate steamed on the dark pavement.

—Say something, Peter.

—I don't know what to say. It just . . . doesn't have anything to do with you.

Billy pulled his fist back but then Duane swept between them, barrelled up against Billy, pushed him away. Billy kept calling Pete a fucking traitor. Pete happened to glance over at the store. Caroline was watching from the window. Duane walked Billy backwards, speaking to him all the while. There was no real fight in Billy anyway. There was only hurt etched on his face.

—You're a fucking traitor, Peter.

A few feet farther on, Duane released Billy. Billy pushed Duane away and shook his shoulders. He pointed at Pete and said they were done. Then he slouched away in the direction of his car. Pete and Duane looked back at the gas pumps but no customers had come in the meantime.

—You okay? said Duane.

—I'm fine.

Pete bent down and numbly retrieved the Styrofoam cup. They walked back and Pete dropped the cup in a garbage can. His hands were shaking and the image of Billy's hurt face seemed to have been burned into his mind. If there'd been anything to do or say before, the opportunity was lost now.

By this time Caroline had come outside. She came right up in front of Pete, not standing as tall as his chest.

—You, mister, keep your personal shit away from here. I'm trying to run a business. Understand?

—I'm sorry, said Pete.

She went wordlessly back to the store.

Duane leaned against one of the pumps. He looked amused. He said: A girl between buddies, I'm guessing.

—Everything changed when I met her. I just wish he could have seen that at the time.

Pete drove into town. He was stiff inside a brown tuxedo and dress shirt he'd rented. He didn't know why, exactly, but he swung past Lee's place first. For advice of some kind, perhaps? There was also a desire just to see the man, given the accident he'd survived a few weeks previous. But at Lee's place, the windows were dark. That seemed to be the case lately. Maybe he was on one of his long, town-wide walks, hunched into his coat, smoking a cigarette. Pete drove on.

The address Emily had given him was the house of her friend Samantha, who lived on Harding Crescent, up near the golf course. It was a nice part of town. Snow lay on lawns and rooftops and the tops of hedges. There was light in the windows of Samantha's house. Pete parked behind another car. A corsage of small roses he'd purchased sat in a box on the passenger seat. He took it and got out of the car and crossed over to the porch.

Samantha opened the door. He had a vague memory of her from the party at Nancy's house in the fall—she'd spent the night conspiring in the kitchen. Samantha was wearing a purple formal gown and was heavily made up. She nodded, and she called out to Emily that Pete had arrived, but Emily had already appeared in the hallway.

She looked coolly elegant, much as she had the first time he'd ever seen her, in the church when she'd played the piano. She was dressed in a pale satin dress, fitted in the bodice, bare across the shoulders. She was smiling as she came forward, and Pete felt his breath catch in his throat. She smelled like lilacs, and when she said hello there was peppermint schnapps on her breath.

Pete held up the corsage. Emily told him to come in, that they'd go soon.

Samantha was in the living room with her boyfriend, Doug.

Doug's tuxedo trousers were short by a full two inches, and he'd paired white sports socks with the brown leather shoes he was wearing. Doug and the girls finished the drinks they'd been working on and they all went out and got into Pete's car and set off for Heron Heights. Doug pawed at Samantha in the back seat. She was slapping his hand and laughing. They passed a mickey of rum between them and offered it to Emily. She had a sip of it, made a face, and passed it back. The corsage was pinned over her breast. She was wearing snow boots, but had brought along a pair of high heels to wear at the dance. Pete kept looking at her out of the corner of his eye.

They'd spent much of the past two weeks seeing each other. She'd called him at work one day, a little while after he'd seen her at the hospital. She'd admonished him for not calling her. The first two times they'd spent together, they barely touched. He'd not dared to put words to what might be happening. He avoided Billy entirely. Then, on a weekend afternoon, he and Emily had gone walking by the river and she'd stopped abruptly and said he'd better give her a kiss.

In the car now, Emily asked Pete how work was. He answered briefly, agreeably. He didn't say anything about Billy's visit.

They arrived at Heron Heights at a quarter past eight. Pete had only gone to a few dances at his old high school. He'd never gone to a formal.

They got out of the car, Samantha and Doug in the lead. Emily looped her arm through Pete's. She said: Do you think a Christmas formal is too much? I feel like I at least have to make an appearance.

—We'll have fun, said Pete. Will we see your other friends?

—One or two of them. There's been some drama.

—Drama.

—I don't like drama. But if you're a girl you can't get away from it. I envy you. Boys don't become dramatic. Boys just hit each other like cavemen when they get mad.

They went into the school lobby. There was a national flag and a portrait of the Queen and a bulletin board. Music was coming through the doors to the auditorium. The students' council had set up a reception table. A girl at the table greeted Emily and Samantha and Doug by name and asked Peter if he was Emily's guest. She crossed their names off a list and told them to not forget about the photographer.

The auditorium was dark, hot and half filled with young people uneasy in their fancy dress. Paper snowflakes hung from the ceiling. Some teacher chaperones policed the scene, prowling for booze. A local disc jockey had his equipment set up on the stage. He had stacks of LPs in milk crates and was just now drawing a record out of a sleeve. Nobody was dancing.

People spoke to Emily and Samantha and Doug. Pete was introduced. They spent some time idling about in their foursome and Emily was never far away. Fingertips on Pete's hand or a tug at the edge of his jacket. He wondered at it. She told him when a good song came on she wanted him to dance with her.

After awhile, they went to a classroom where a photographer had set up his camera in front of a muted backdrop. Pete and Emily took up a position. The photographer came over and adjusted their pose, angled them towards each other. Pete's free hand traced patterns on the small of Emily's back. The photographer scooted back behind his camera and told them to smile their million-buck smiles.

Emily murmured: Is this completely ridiculous?

—It was your idea.

She pushed her back against Pete's fingers.

The flashbulb went off and the photographer told them that was just great. Emily took Pete's arm and they stepped away from the backdrop. Pete wondered vaguely what might become of the photograph.

Back in the auditorium, the music was slower. Couples were pairing up to dance. They spied Doug and Samantha out on the floor, turning slowly. Doug looked half asleep.

Emily led Pete out and they started to dance, and then over her shoulder Pete saw a small group of the people he'd wondered about. There was Nancy. Some other girls were with her. There was Roger. He was leaning against the edge of the stage. Beside him one of his mates was saying something into his ear. Roger had his head tilted the better to hear, and both he and his friend were looking at Pete. If Emily had seen any of them, she gave no sign of it.

When the song ended, Emily and Pete headed back to the chairs at the edge of the room. Sweat and perfume and cologne hung in the air. Doug had disappeared somewhere but Samantha had come with them. She said she needed more rum, would Emily go with her to the bathroom.

—Am I just going to leave Pete here? said Emily.

—We'll only be two minutes, said Samantha. Can you take care of yourself, Pete?

—I'll be fine, said Pete.

Emily put her lips against his ear. Her breath was warm. She told him she would be back and she kissed him on the cheek and squeezed his hand. Then she was gone.

Pete was very hot. He made his way over to a refreshment table along the far wall, beneath a banner of the school mascot, a snarling cartoon Indian brave. Snacks were arrayed on the table around a big punch bowl. He poured a cup and drank it. The punch was not spiked but it was queasily sweet.

Nancy came up to him from somewhere. It was all on her face and in her voice. They said hello to each other and then asked the cursory questions people are required to ask—what have you been up to, what's new? Her tone was clipped: How come you never called on me?

—I don't know, said Pete.

—I thought you were nice. I don't fool around with just anybody.

—I don't know, Nancy. I'm sorry.

—Was it because of Emily?

—What?

—You thought I couldn't see it? Well I've got one thing to say to you. Be careful.

—What?

—You think Emily doesn't have big ideas about her life? No offence, but you're a dropout. Don't say I didn't warn you, Peter.

She seemed like she was waiting for a rebuttal. Instead, Pete went back over to the dance floor, tipping down the punch on the way. It almost made him gag.

Emily and Samantha had returned and sat in the chairs. Pete came up to them and Emily stood up and kissed him. He could taste rum.

—Is it just me or is it roasting in here?

—I'm boiling, said Pete. Actually, I think I'll go splash some water on my face.

Pete went down the corridor outside of the auditorium. He found the boy's washroom and went in. He was alone but for one pair of shoes glimpsed beneath a cubicle.

There was a round stone sink in the middle of the floor. Pete looked at himself in the stainless-steel mirror over the basin. He adjusted the stiff lapels of his rental tux and loosened his bow tie a little bit. He scrubbed cool water into his face and into his hair. Then he heard the door open and close. He knew who had come before he even saw them.

—Look who it is, said Roger.

He had a friend with him. Pete straightened, water dripping off his jaw. They had come around to the side of the sink, casually. Roger spat on the floor.

—Are you having a good time?

—The punch is too sweet, said Pete.

He had nowhere to go without having to go around them. They exchanged a look and then they smiled at him. It was their advantage and they knew it, and Pete wondered exactly how bad this was going to be.

But then the cubicle opened. A kid with long hair and an ill-fitting suit took two shuffling steps out. His face was dead white and he was smacking his lips.

—Buddies, said the kid. Buddies.

The kid swayed. He dropped to one knee and vomited onto what must have been Roger's father's oxfords. A stench of stomach acid and raw alcohol filled the air. The kid shuddered and vomited again. Roger's face went bright red. He tapped out a peculiar dance to extricate himself from the waste on his feet. His friend looked like he was getting close to retching himself, going pale, staring, taking great gulps of air.

Pete stepped around them and went into the corridor. A moment later, he could hear voices lifting in outrage. He was ten paces away when he heard the washroom door clap open. He chanced a backwards look and saw Roger's friend jogging into the corridor with a hand clasped over his mouth.

When Pete re-entered the auditorium, the heat was almost forceful. There was a slow song playing again and Doug and Samantha and everybody else were up dancing.

Emily came up behind Pete and took his arm. She was frowning. When Pete looked past her shoulder he saw Nancy in the near distance.

—Are you okay?

—I'm fine, said Emily.

—Well. Do you want to dance?

—No. I want to get out of here. This is ridiculous.

—What about your friends?

—They'll be fine. Doug lives a block away and that's where they're going.

—Okay. Do you want to go home?

—Oh my God, Pete. I didn't get dressed up to be home by ten. Let's go do something. Come on.

Emily told Samantha that they were leaving. She linked her arm into Pete's and they walked out. He was relieved. He got his car started. Emily thought for a minute and then she told him exactly what she wanted to do.

It was a house league night but there were a few lanes open for the public. They switched their boots for the rental footwear. They bought colas and hot dogs and went to their lane and bowled badly. The house league teams were drunk, shouting at the balls thundering down the hardwood. Pete and Emily were objects of some amusement in the clothes they were wearing, but nobody bothered them.

Pete sat in one of the plastic chairs at the head of their lane. Emily took up a ball and launched it with unnecessary force. It curved into the gutter. She turned back around, laughing. Pete watched her with complete wonder. The sight of her in that moment was taking hold of him. Her eyes were big and clear, her skin was pale, and her mouth, usually set cool to match the way she carried herself, was pulled open in a wide smile. Through the times to come, whenever he thought of her, this was how she would appear.

By midnight, Pete's car was parked close alongside a snowy meadow north of Echo Point. Lights passed infrequently along the highway. The back door of the car opened and Pete emerged, wrapped in a wool blanket, and jogged over the snow in his work boots. He went out twenty feet and opened the blanket only wide enough to pull off the condom he was wearing. He flung it away and urinated into the snow and jogged back to the car.

The car engine idled and the heater blasted away. Emily was sitting in the back with her legs up on the seat. Pete turned the engine off and got into the back seat with her and draped the blanket around them both. For some time they were quiet. The windows were foggy. Emily traced her initials.

—My grandpa's place is close to here.

—Yeah?

—It's the house on Echo Point. Right where . . . that boat crash happened. Your uncle.

—Where my uncle's friend got killed.

—Yes. Grandpa's lived there a long time. The house was in his family before that. He wants my folks to take it from him. My mom was an only child.

—How long ago did your grandma die?

—Two years ago. It was in the spring. She had a stroke and she died right in her garden.

—Jesus. That's terrible.

—I think it's kind of nice in a way, said Emily.

—Nice?

—She loved her garden. It was a beautiful morning. I remember because they called me into the office at school and I was looking out the window when I took the phone. Here's my dad telling me, and I'm looking outside and thinking what a beautiful day it is. I didn't get upset at all. Not until I got to the hospital and saw Grandpa. She was gardening when it happened, which was her favourite thing to do, and she just lay down right there. We should all be so lucky.

—My grandma is dying of lung cancer. She's been sick since the summer. She smoked a pack a day for her whole life and finally she quit, maybe two years ago. But she was too late. She's got a tumour in her lungs. They can't do anything for that at her age. You know what I'll remember best? Go get Granny her menthols, Pete. I grew up hating the smell of cigarettes. I hate them now.

The cold was creeping into the car. Emily moved closer against him. There was nothing to see outside the car, nothing of their surroundings.

—Was your granddad always a cop? said Pete.

—Yes, forever. He was sixty-two when he retired. I think he

had to at that point, legally and all, but it was hard for him. But when he was really young, twenty or so, he was a boxer. Grandma used to tell me about it. They had these old newspaper pictures. This handsome boy wearing funny trunks, with a funny haircut. A moustache. Got his dukes up. I couldn't recognize him at all except for the eyes. It's hard for me to imagine that time in his life.

—Was he a cop here in town?

—Always. Here's something. The last guy they executed here? Grandpa arrested him. The man had killed another cop. They executed him, out behind where they have the library now. Grandpa never talks about it. I only know because my mom knew. She told me about it once when we were visiting her aunt. We took the train down to the city to visit, and on the way back Mom told me a lot of things I never knew. It's funny what happens when you grow up. How you learn about things in the lives of the people you love. The big things, the bad things. They happened before you even existed.

—You find out and it changes things.

—I guess.

—You don't think so?

—Well, I think with the people you love, unless you find out they're murderers or something, you still love them. It's just you find out they're actually people. They're not giants any more.

—My uncle is a murderer, said Pete.

—What?

—I can't say for sure. There aren't many things other than murder that you do that long in jail for. But I can't say for sure because nobody in my family talks about anything except Jesus. My grandmother is dying and nobody talks about that. My real dad ran off somewhere before I was born and nobody talks about that. My uncle was in jail for seventeen years and definitely nobody talks about that. Half of what I make at the gas station goes to Saint Barry for rent—he counts it every time—

and you don't hear anybody talking about that. I don't even talk about it. If it weren't for Jesus I would live in one quiet house. Are you cold?

—Yes, a little.

He reached into the front and started the car for the heater to blast again.

—You know what they told me about sex? said Pete. They left a booklet on my bed. I was twelve. It was called *The Christian Path to Growing Up*, and it was a booklet full of reasons why if you beat off or if you neck with a girl you're going to hell.

—My mom told me everything, said Emily. I could have done with just an explanation. I didn't need her to talk about techniques.

—That's better than a booklet about the evils of necking, believe me.

—Tell me how evil necking is, said Emily.

She moved against him, shifting out of the blanket. Her pale body moved fluidly in the dim light. She kissed him with her tongue inside his mouth and her fingers tracing along his cheek.

There was nothing to compare this feeling with.

He wanted her to be vulnerable, wanted her to need him as much as he felt he was beginning to need her. He was even willing to believe that it was so, that she did need him as badly. She moved on top of him and slid her hand down his stomach.

—Do you want to go again?

—Yes, said Pete. Anything for you.

—Good. After that, you'll have to take me home so I can go to bed like a good girl.

A few nights later, Pete picked up Lee and Helen after work to take them to Donna and Barry's house for supper. Lee had dressed in what he had for a formal occasion, jeans and a collared shirt and his Carhartt coat. Helen wore big hoop earrings and a leather jacket over a tight-fitting dress. Lee held the door for her and she got into the passenger seat. He got into the back.

Pete had assembled a picture of Helen from what Lee had told him, and in person she was not far removed from what he'd imagined.

—Haven't I heard a lot about you, said Helen.

—Hi, said Pete. Hey, Uncle Lee.

—Hey, Pete.

They drove out to the house.

—This is a nice-looking joint, said Helen. Why don't you move out here, Brown Eyes?

—It's filled up with people out here is why, said Lee.

They were halfway up the walk when Donna opened the front door and stood there thinly against the backlight, wearing grey slacks and a cardigan. Lee went up first. He and his sister embraced stiffly and he went to kiss her on the cheek but she had already turned her head. Helen came up the steps and took both of Donna's hands. Pete could see his mother's shoulders climbing in defence.

—Hello, said Helen. What a big beautiful property you guys got out here.

They were shown into the living room. Helen was as misfit a figure as Pete could imagine, but she seemed oblivious to it. Donna served them hot apple cider. Lee took Helen's jacket and showed her to the couch. Irene's recliner remained vacant. The Christmas tree was crooked. Donna went into the hallway and tapped on Barry's office door.

—He'll be out in one minute, said Donna. He's working on his sermon for Sunday.

Donna came back into the living room and Pete brushed past her to the office door. The door was open a few inches so he opened it fully and stood on the threshold. Barry was at the desk with his study bible open beside him.

—Just a moment and I'll be out.

—Take your time, said Pete. My mother is only half panicked. You've got a couple minutes before she loses her mind completely.

Barry put on a look of forbearance: What is it, Peter?

Pete took the week's rent out of his wallet. Barry darted a look into the hallway. Then he composed himself again.

—You're a day early with that, said Barry, taking the money.

He counted it carefully and stowed it in the strongbox in the drawer. Peter craned his neck to spy a bible quotation Barry had transcribed and underlined on his legal pad. It was about the angel appearing to the terrified shepherds, bidding them be unafraid, for that day a child was born.

—Do you believe that about the angel coming down to talk to the shepherds?

Barry blinked, tugged at his ear: Why wouldn't I?

—I'm just curious.

—How God calls us is up to God. That's exactly what I'll be talking about on Sunday. It would be good to see you there. It would be good for your mom to see you there.

Pete went back into the hallway. When he was going back through the living room, John and Luke were being presented to Helen. They were both wearing the dress shirts they wore to church, pressed and tucked in, and they had identical left-sided parts in their hair.

—Couple of little heartbreakers, said Helen.

Donna served a roast ham with peas and a macaroni salad. Lee and Helen were seated next to each other across from John and Luke. Barry sat at the head of the table. Pete and his mother took their usual places. The spot for Irene at the other end of the table remained conspicuously empty.

Barry said they would pray first. They held hands around the table and Pete watched them bow their heads. He was holding

John's hand. The boy had his eyes pinched shut. Barry told the Lord thanks for the food and the fellowship of family. Across the table, Lee's eyes were closed. Helen was looking at Pete, grinning.

Amen was said. Donna served their plates.

—Would you tell us about yourself? said Barry. We've heard a little bit.

Helen shrugged, hand to her chin. The boys stared at her.

—I didn't come from around here. I don't know anything about this town to tell you the truth. It's funny how we end up in certain places. I went to college for a year or two, this was, like, '67 . . .

She laughed as she spoke. Barry smiled sociably. Donna and Lee were both staring into their meals, slicing through their ham with something approaching savagery. To see them, you would conclude, finally, that they were sister and brother.

—I travelled for awhile with these Hare Krishnas, said Helen. We shared everything. They were real good people. Then I went back to the city in about 1972. The city was where the action was.

She told them more, a rambling stream of words interrupted by the odd giggle. It was difficult to understand what had driven her to the city, but she told them she had a son.

—He'd be about your age, said Helen to John.

John gaped at her. Lee sounded as if he'd caught something in his throat. He coughed and cleared whatever it was, and slowly set into his ham and his peas again.

—Does your son go to school here in town? said Donna.

—Oh no, said Helen. I don't . . . He doesn't live with me. But the way it goes, things have a certain way of working out, you know? Like, to everything there is a season and a purpose.

—But you were in the city, said Donna. How'd you end up here?

—You got a lot of questions, said Lee.

—That's okay, said Helen.

But Donna had put her knife and fork down on either side of her plate: I'm sorry, I didn't mean to be nosy.

The boys stared around the table. Barry chewed methodically.

—It's fine, said Helen. Come on, Brown Eyes, she's asking me about myself.

—I didn't mean to be nosy, said Donna again.

—It was a man, hun. Isn't it always a man for us gals? Anyways he's not my problem any more. I don't even know where he is.

—I see.

—And he owed me money, but, oh well. Maybe Lee should go have a chat with him. Tell him what's what.

Silence fell like a shroud. They all went on eating, pretending nothing had been said.

At length, Barry cleared his throat: I've seen Clifton at church. It's a difficult time for him but he's handled it well.

Lee chuckled dryly: And he wasn't even in the god— He wasn't even in the boat when it happened. Good for him. I wonder if he's helping Bud's wife to handle it, too. He's sure done a lot to check up on me.

—He always mentions what a hard worker you are, Lee. You really did impress him.

—Well, how about that.

Helen had caught John staring at her. She crossed her eyes and puckered her lips together. The boy blinked down at his plate. She told him he'd catch flies with his mouth open like that.

—I made a cobbler for dessert, said Donna hastily. She got up and started to clear the plates.

—I'll help you, said Helen.

—No, I have it.

But Helen had already lifted her plate and Lee's from the table. She laughed: Oh, hun, I've been a waitress for a long time. Stuff like this is one of the two things I'm any good at.

—

A short while later, Pete was on the telephone in the hallway.

—I'm going to be in town later tonight. I want to see you.

—Pete, it's a weeknight. My dad is home. Is something wrong?

—No, there's nothing wrong. I just want to see you is all.

—I want to see you too. Okay. I'll go out for a walk. Eight-thirty. I'll be walking on my street.

He hung up and went back through the living room. Barry was conducting a bible lesson with Luke and John. He was speaking about the Magi. Pete could only see the backs of the boys' heads and the expressiveness on Barry's face as he entreated them. Lee was sitting in the recliner. He was flexing his hand into a fist and studying it closely. Releasing, flexing.

In the kitchen Donna was holding a dish, paused in the act of drying it. There had been times in Pete's life when he had found her like this, unmoving and blank in the midst of some chore.

Helen was sitting on the counter, discussing gossip from the Owl Café. Donna stood static, holding the dish like a plate of armour over her heart.

—And the man she shacked up with? said Helen. Hun, you wouldn't believe.

—Mom, said Pete.

He put his hands on the dish and tugged and for a moment Donna's hands clutched it. Then she released. Her eyes moved to her son. She put a hand to the side of her face and then she turned around to what remained on the drying rack. She said nothing.

—Pete even helps out in the kitchen? said Helen. I bet every girl in town is kicking down your door.

She flashed a brazen wink.

When Pete went back into the living room, Barry was telling the boys how King Herod was in a murderous rage. The faces of the boys were rapt, imagining the sight of infants being put to slaughter. Lee looked bored.

—Uncle Lee, said Pete.

They all looked at him. Barry paused mid-story.

—I'm going to drive into town in a minute or two, said Pete.

—I'll grab Helen if she can stop yapping, said Lee.

The guests said their goodbyes, Lee curtly and Helen with the same rambling exuberance she'd shown through supper. Donna did not come out of the kitchen. Barry saw them to the front door. He told them he'd be happy to see them at church.

They got into Pete's car. Pete was tense and he did not know why. Every darkened field he passed he found himself looking for avenues of escape, as if it should be a sudden and uncalculated move. Helen laughed about something.

—I didn't know you had a goddamn kid, said Lee.

—That was another life, said Helen. It doesn't matter any more.

They came into town. Lee told Pete to take them down to his place. The trees in the lakefront park stood like black bones against the snow.

—Funny, said Lee. I never thought about it before, but if any-body asked me I couldn't tell them where you live. I got no idea.

Helen laughed: Oh my God, Brown Eyes.

Pete pulled in behind the variety store. Lee said that he would see him around and got out of the car. Helen patted Pete's knee.

—So nice to meet you.

Pete watched them. Lee dug for his keys and Helen hitched at her pantyhose and stepped side to side in her shoes. She swatted Lee's backside. Lee looked at her and she shrugged.

Emily was walking on her street. She had her head held high and her hands in her front pockets. She got into Pete's car and she kissed him, cold lips and warm mouth.

—I'm glad to see you.

—I'm glad to see you too.

—I can't stay out for long. Five minutes.

—It's okay. Five minutes is enough. How are you?

—School today was asinine. I feel like my work here is done, you know?

—I know. I've felt like that for a long time.

—What does it matter. Christmas break starts next Friday.

He could listen to her forever. Her hand was on his except when she lifted it to emphasize a point. Once again, nothing else in the world mattered. He wondered how, fifteen minutes ago, he'd been thinking about escape.

—I have to go away this weekend, said Emily.

—You do?

—Peter, you look broken-hearted.

—No . . .

—I am a little too. We could have gone bowling again.

—Where are you going?

—Our annual trip to the city, my mom and me. We'll do our Christmas shopping. We've been doing it almost as long as I can remember.

—Where will you stay?

—In a hotel. Very fancy. Or maybe not, I don't know. It's close to downtown. Somewhere you can see the CN Tower and the lights and everything else. This is the first year we're bringing my sister. But let's talk about next Tuesday.

—Next Tuesday.

—You're invited to dinner.

—Where?

—My house, Peter.

—With your folks?

—Who else? Do you accept?

—I do, said Pete. For sure.

When she kissed him, he could feel her tongue moving and then she grinned against his mouth. He drove her down to her house. She kissed him once more and she got out of the car. At the front door she turned and waved at him and then she went inside.

Pete drove around for awhile before he went home. His mind was at ease, which was funny to realize, since half an hour ago he'd been thinking about a sudden and uncalculated escape from everything. But now, the smell of Emily's perfume or shampoo lingered in the car. As he drove, Pete found himself reconsidering his plan to move west. Maybe he had a reason to stay here, after all. Maybe he would rent an apartment in town, like Lee's. Maybe, for once, everything was okay.

Pete left work in the middle of the afternoon on Friday to take some magazines and evangelical cassettes to his grandmother at the hospital. Later, he would think that Roger and the others must have followed him, looking for an opportunity. The gas station was too busy, too exposed.

He did not park in the visitors' lot at the hospital, where they charged a toll. Instead he parked on a gravel patch at a small construction site a little way down the street. Then he went down the sidewalk, through the hospital entrance, and up to see his grandmother. He didn't stay long—she was drugged and sleepy. He delivered the items he'd brought, and he stood looking at her and fighting the constriction of his throat.

He was going back across the gravel patch, thinking about Emily, and how the city had taken her away for the weekend, when the boys jumped him. They'd been waiting in a wood-panelled station wagon. They piled out and set on him hard from all directions before he could even make sense of what was happening. He felt knuckles slugging the side of his head. Someone punched him above his right eye. Someone kicked him in the thigh and he stumbled, and they pushed him over into a ditch alongside the gravel. He raked damp snow off rotting leaves as he slid down. He could feel his forehead swelling.

Roger stood on the edge of the ditch and told Pete to stay the fuck away from the Heron Heights girls.

—Four of you, said Pete.

Roger came down and kicked Pete in the stomach, driving the air out of him. He thought he might vomit. Then Pete heard the station wagon pulling away and they were gone. He hauled himself up. There were leaves clinging to his back, leaves in his hair. Nobody had been around to see anything. He managed to get himself into his car, where he sat for a long time, beaten, ashamed.

The radiator made soft clanking noises. Early headlights moved through the predawn outside the window. Lee was sweat-sodden on the pullout bed. First he dreamed the old dream, the boarding house basement, the crippled caretaker shuffling towards him. Then he dreamed he was in solitary confinement in the penitentiary. Brick and steel, enclosed on all sides. In this hole there was no door.

Workless afternoons prior to his hospital visits, Lee would walk the town. It was a strange time for him, when idleness gave way to dark thoughts. Bud frequently occurred to him, the jokes he'd get wrong, and particularly the image of him face down in the bottom of the barge. He thought also of Donna, and found himself looking for things he might get the family for Christmas. Donna used to make Luke and John write to Lee annually, this time of year. Once, a couple of years ago, they'd written about Lee spending Christmas Day with them sometime in the future, after he would be released. The idea had appealed to him, more than he cared to admit, but he hadn't yet been invited. He didn't know how to ask.

Everywhere around him was the bustling industry of the holiday season, the store windows packed with signs peddling sales, the ceaseless clatter of Salvation Army bells. Lee went about in his work boots with his collar turned up.

One day, Lee went into a furniture store he'd passed many times. The showroom was warmly lit with crafted desk lamps. Every article of furniture was made of unvarnished wood. He was drawn to a dining room table, ten feet by five. The tabletop was an inch and a half thick. He ran his hand along the rasping smoothness of the naked wood. A grey-bearded man appeared from somewhere.

—All our pieces are handcrafted, said the man. This table is solid oak.

—You make this? said Lee. It's a hell of a nice piece.

—Thank you. We like to keep our prices negotiable too.

—I got Christmas coming up. I got some people to buy for. Where does the price start out before you negotiate it?

—This table starts at three hundred dollars.

Lee laughed dryly. He seemed unable to withdraw his hand from the sanded tabletop. He cleared his throat and said: Actually, I was wondering if you ever hire. I'm a carpenter myself.

The bearded man nodded.

—For the most part we're a family business. And to be honest with you, we're a little slow-going right now. But I'd be happy to put your information into our files.

With some reluctance Lee withdrew his hand from the table.

—You got the time by any chance?

The bearded man had a silver timepiece on his belt. He brought it out. With his timepiece and his beard he was like something out of the olden days: It's two o'clock, said the man.

—Two o'clock. Well, I've got some things to do.

What he had to do was meet Wade Larkin at three o'clock. After the barge accident and the Ministry of Labour inquest, Larkin said he wanted to meet with Lee more frequently, once every three weeks or so, especially since Lee was out of work. They were set to meet, today, in the same spare municipal office where they'd always met, and this appointment would be the last Larkin would see him before Christmas. Not that the meetings ever amounted to much. Larkin couldn't do anything to get Lee a job, or get Irene into her own room at the hospital. He would just ask his questions and nod and make notes in his notebook, and confirm, as always, that Lee had Larkin's business card in case of any trouble. At least today Lee would be able to tell him that he'd tried to get a job.

Lee went to the front door of the furniture store. He paused, looked back over his shoulder at the table: I do think that piece is a beauty.

—Thank you, said the grey-bearded man. Happy holidays.

Lee went back onto the street. He bought a pack of cigarettes and some lottery tickets from the pharmacy. He wanted to buy some booze, as well, before the liquor store closed. He had just enough time, perhaps, to pick up a bottle of rye, walk home and stash it, and arrive at the meeting with his parole officer empty-handed.

That night Speedy was on the drums at the North Star. The band he was playing with was driving through Rolling Stones covers. People whirled. Garish coloured lights beamed through the smoke.

Lee and Helen had had a few drinks, and he was feeling good. Helen said she'd had no idea he could be so goddamn fun. Lee had seen Maurice over near the bar, eyeing the dance floor. Maurice nodded to him. In a booth, Helen sat across from him with her chin propped on her hand, smiling. She'd worn a chambray shirt unbuttoned low enough to show the deep crease between her breasts. She had her foot up between Lee's thighs.

In the adjacent booth sat Gilmore and Arlene. Gilmore leaned over the plywood divider and clapped Lee on the shoulder and asked if they were enjoying themselves. Lee said they were. It was

Speedy who'd gotten them out here. Lee had had some drinks with Speedy a few nights earlier and he'd told Lee a band he jammed with was going to be at the roadhouse—would Lee and his lady friend come for some rock 'n' roll? Lee was feeling now like a big man.

Gilmore dropped back into his own booth.

—I didn't know you had friends out here, called Helen.

—I've got a few.

She gave his thigh a friendly dig. He looked into the crowd and saw strangers moving to the music.

The band took a break and Lee got up to go to the men's room. He studied the graffiti over the urinal. Someone had written *Sally D Is A Cocksucker.* There were black hairs on the drainplate.

He came out. Gilmore was waiting in the passageway, leaning on the brickwork with one hand in his pocket.

—Looks like you're having a good time, said Gilmore.

—We're having a good time, yeah.

—What would you say to going for a ride?

—You want to go for a ride someplace?

—Have a smoke.

Gilmore took out his Camel cigarettes and offered one to Lee.

—I told you before, said Lee.

—I know you did. It's just a ride is all it is.

—Where is it you want to go?

—I have a business associate I'd like to visit. All you're along for is just another pair of eyes and ears, that's all.

Lee took a long drag: Eyes and ears, said Lee.

—In business there's a matter of appearances.

—You keep using that word, *business*.

Gilmore laughed: Yes, I do.

He had a fifty-dollar bill folded between two fingers. He tucked it into Lee's breast pocket. He said: On good faith, Lee. It was a hell of a bad accident you were in a few weeks ago. A raw deal for a dependable guy. I want to see better things come your way.

—What about my lady friend?

—Come.

Gilmore showed Lee to the booth where he'd been sitting. Helen was in the booth with Arlene. They were laughing. Arlene looked up when she saw Gilmore.

—You keep Lee's lady friend company, said Gilmore. You hear me?

—Yes, daddy.

—You're going somewheres? said Helen.

Lee looked at the tabletop. Helen reached her arm behind him and patted his butt.

—Well, go on, Brown Eyes. Just give me a bit of money, will you?

He gave her a few dollars. He and Gilmore walked out shoulder to shoulder like old comrades. Out in the parking lot, Maurice was waiting at his Caballero.

—You were pretty sure, said Lee, quietly.

—Pretty sure about what, pal?

—That I'd come with you.

Gilmore just smiled.

They drove all the way back to town, to a row of frame houses along the rail line. The house they parked in front of had paint peeling from its siding. No sooner had the car come to a stop than two barking Rottweilers materialized behind a chain-link fence penning in the backyard.

A door opened on the crooked porch and the shape of a man shouted at the dogs. He came out and stood on the porch and looked at the car.

—Come on, Lee, said Gilmore.

Maurice did not get out of the car. Lee felt uneasy. During the drive into town it had occurred to him that maybe this was some affair of old blood, though he couldn't think of who or what, but maybe this was a house he would go into and not depart from.

The man on the porch was wearing unfastened work boots and a T-shirt, despite the cold. He was short but he looked like he pumped a lot of iron. He merely nodded when they came up. The dogs behind the fence seemed half berserk. Gilmore and Lee were led into a kitchen. The room was crammed with junk on the counters, engine parts, a twelve-ton jack. Through an opening, they could see into a living room where coloured Christmas lights were strung around a shuttered window. A young child was parked on the living room floor, watching a movie on a black-and-white cabinet TV.

The man closed the door to the porch. Turned the deadbolt.

Gilmore sat down at the kitchen table. He pushed aside a telephone from which a snarl of wires had been partially eviscerated.

A woman in a wheelchair rolled through the opening into the kitchen. She was thick-bodied, with grey hair in braids. Her legs were gone below the knees. She pulled up to the table. The man in the T-shirt leaned against the wall behind her. He glanced back into the living room, perhaps to check on the child.

—Gilmore, said the woman.

—Happy holidays, Jean.

—You got a new friend.

Gilmore looked back over his shoulder at Lee, smiling: Where are my manners? This is a good friend of mine. Say hello, Lee.

Lee nodded to the woman. She looked him up and down. There was something shrewd about her, calculating.

—You might think we came because of the Christmas season, said Gilmore. Friends calling on each other to spread cheer and all that.

The woman chuckled: The way you talk, Colin, I almost got the idea you think I'm just some young hussy.

—Jean, I wouldn't think that of you for one second. Not one second.

Gilmore brought out a thick sheaf of money held together with a wire clasp. Lee saw twenties. There might be a thousand dollars in there. Gilmore held the money out to Jean and she took it and counted it.

—On good faith, said Gilmore.

—You'll have the van before Christmas. The electronics too. The other things, I got here.

She gestured with her head. The man opened a door off the kitchen where Lee saw steps leading to a basement. The man went down.

Lee found the woman studying him again. He wondered once more, was this old blood, was he maybe going to be taken down to the fruit cellar and shot in the back of the head? He'd heard of such things happening, cons with serious history getting out of the pen, only to be found dead a short while later. He was digging deep to remember who he'd had particularly bad blood with. There were any number of names from his first five or six years—but that really was a long time ago, and he didn't think any of them had ended up here, in his hometown.

Just then the child appeared in the kitchen. A little red-headed girl, maybe six years old. She came and stood beside the wheelchair and regarded Gilmore and Lee. The woman put a hand on the little girl's head.

—And how are you, half-pint? said Gilmore.

The little girl shrugged: I'm okay.

—Beautiful, said Gilmore.

The man came back upstairs carrying a canvas duffle bag. There was something long and thin pushing out the side of the bag. A golf club, perhaps, but Lee doubted it. The man set the bag on the table in front of Gilmore. Gilmore unzipped the bag and glanced inside and zipped it back up before Lee could see what it held.

—Good, said Gilmore. Of course, there won't be any need.

—The Bible says hear no evil see no evil, said the woman.

—Sure it does. It also says a man can get up and dance three days after you nail him to a chunk of wood.

Midmorning the next day, Lee woke with a bad hangover. Helen was snoring. Lee got up and for some time stared into the mostly empty refrigerator. He had enough food for today, that's all. He thought of the money Gilmore had given him.

He boiled water for coffee and fried some eggs. His recollection of the rest of last night was dim. After they'd left the house in town they'd driven back to the North Star. He'd danced with Helen for awhile, he could remember that. Then there was a fight. Some townies, some hatchet-faced woman screaming at them. The woman jumped on a man's back. Lee remembered Maurice wading into it, moving his big fists in steady articulations, but Gilmore had disappeared altogether. Lee had been bumped by a stranger, whom Lee then struck under the eye and in the side of the head because the stranger looked like he might be thinking about it. Lee remembered the hatchet-faced woman sitting spread-legged on the concrete floor, shrieking curses. He'd walked off into the dark then and he couldn't remember much more. A car barrelling through the night. Cigarettes. Helen's hand squeezing up his thigh. It was Speedy's car. What hour?

Lee piled eggs and toast onto two plates and brought them to the pullout. Helen was blinking at him. The sheets were twisted around her.

—Eat. There's coffee.

—Aren't you a dear.

He sat beside her with his legs up and his plate balanced across his thighs. Helen still had mascara in shrouds around her eyes. She smiled dizzily.

When they'd finished eating, Lee took their plates and stacked them on the countertop. He lit two smokes and gave her one.

—What I'm not real excited about is working tonight, said Helen.

—I'll bet.

—So what kind of business opportunities?

—Business opportunities?

—Your friend Colin was talking about business opportunities.

—That was all talk.

—I'm guessing he didn't mean real estate.

Lee stabbed his cigarette out: How about you don't need to ask.

—Suit yourself.

A moment passed.

—I didn't mean to snap at you, said Lee.

She yawned and stretched her arms: Forget it. Come here and rub my shoulders.

First, Lee turned on the television. There were Sunday morning church shows. He turned it off and went over and sat on the couch-back behind her and rubbed her shoulders. They were quiet. Then she fondled him through the thin fabric of his undershorts.

—What do we got here?

When they woke again it was early afternoon.

—Some things I've been thinking about, said Lee.

—What's going on in that cute head of yours?

—Some things about me and you.

—Okay, said Helen.

—Well, things aren't always going to be like this.

—What is *this*?

—My situation.

Helen rose up from the pullout. She went into the bathroom and Lee could hear her urinating.

She came back out, saying: Can't we talk about this later?

—What's wrong with right now?

—My head hurts. I don't want to talk about these serious things.

Lee was going to say something but there was a knock on the

door. Helen covered herself. Lee pulled on his jeans and the shirt he'd worn last night. The money was still in the breast pocket. He opened the door to Mr. Yoon.

—Phone for you, said Mr. Yoon.

Lee turned to Helen: Don't go anywhere.

Lee followed Mr. Yoon down into the store. Mr. Yoon's wife was tending the cash-out. A plastic nativity scene had been set up beside the register. Mr. Yoon led Lee to the office at the back. The telephone receiver was overturned on the desktop. Lee looked at Mr. Yoon until Mr. Yoon tightened his face and backed off to inspect cans of soup on a shelf. Lee picked up the receiver.

—Hello.

—Lee, Clifton here.

—Clifton.

—Listen Lee . . . That thing with Bud was a mess. The Ministry is fining me two thousand dollars. Two thousand, mister man, what do you think of that. But listen, I got some work coming up. I want to get on with it after Christmas. If you want some inside work, I got it. Some cupboards, some trim. Maybe three weeks solid.

Lee held the receiver. He traced his thumb along the edge of the desk.

—Lee.

—Yeah, Clifton.

—Thought the line cut out.

—So that thing with Bud was a *mess*, Clifton?

—Lee—

—Go fuck yourself. You think I ever want to kiss your ass again?

He hung the phone up. He came out of the office and passed Mr. Yoon.

—When do you work again?

—I have some things, said Lee. Not for that bastard, though. I gave you this month's rent. You'll get next month's.

Back up in the apartment, Helen had put on her bra and panties and was pulling on her pantyhose.

—What are you doing?

—I have to leave more sooner than later, said Helen. I have to work.

She went into the bathroom and redefined the edges of her makeup. She sang some words from a radio song. She came out and put her clothes on.

—Do you think that Oriental will have to call a taxi for me?

—Maybe, said Lee.

She picked up her purse and looked through it: How do you like that. Brown Eyes, do you have any cash?

Lee took his wallet off the dresser and opened it. He did not want to but he counted. Seventeen dollars. Plus the fifty in his shirt pocket. He gave her five dollars and felt the money moving out of his hand. Before long she was standing in the doorway.

—The café is going to get real busy with the season, said Helen. So how about I'll call you.

In the early dusk, Lee went down to the store and bought a can of Stagg chili. He cooked it on the hot plate and opened a beer. There was a science-fiction movie on television—the one where Charlton Heston had to fight a bunch of talking monkeys on horseback. Lee had seen this one when he was in jail. They'd shown pictures in the chapel.

All at once, Lee tensed up and launched the beer can at the wall. It bounced off, leaving a mark on the plaster, and what beer was in the can sprayed onto the floor.

Pete went to supper at Emily's house on Tuesday. He hadn't seen her since she'd gone to the city with her mother. They'd had one conversation on the telephone to confirm the dinner invitation. He did not mention having been jumped by the boys she knew.

In the driveway of Emily's house was a police cruiser, a hard-angled Ford LTD. There was also an old GMC pickup truck and a small Volvo. A holly wreath hung on the front door of the house.

Emily's sister, Louise, opened the door when Pete knocked. The first thing he heard inside was the piano. He knew the tune but it took him a moment to name it . . . "O Holy Night." The pianist wasn't confident yet, and the notes were hesitant and loud.

Mary Casey appeared to welcome him. Pete hoped the swelling on his brow had gone down enough not to be noticeable, but he saw how Mrs. Casey's attention flicked quickly to the wound. Then she smiled.

Pete was shown into the living room. It was warm and there were a lot of gifts stacked under the Christmas tree. He could see Emily at the piano bench, her back straight. He wanted to touch her. Mrs. Casey told Pete to make himself at home and then she leaned over Emily and said that her friend was here. The back of Emily's head moved but her hands stayed at the piano keys. The melody she was playing was recognizable but not graceful.

Pete had barely lowered himself to the couch before he stood again, for Mr. Casey appeared in his uniform trousers and slippers. He was carrying a drink that smelled like rye and Coke. Behind Mr. Casey was Stan Maitland, holding a beer.

Mr. Casey offered his hand in one firm shake. He saw the swelling over Pete's eye. Pete knew he did.

—This has got to be Peter, said Mr. Casey.

—Thanks for having me, said Pete.

Stan told Pete it was good to see him again—that last time wasn't so good, was it.

—How is your uncle getting along? said Stan.

—He's fine, I guess. That accident was bad.

—Was that when the man died out at Grandpa's house? said Louise.

—Louise, said Mrs. Casey.

Mr. Casey nodded at Pete: Your uncle, Leland King.

Emily stopped playing. One chord struck hard, reverberating. She turned around on the bench.

—Hi, Pete. I hope you're hungry. It's spaghetti night.

At supper, Mrs. Casey asked Pete if he would have a glass of wine. Mr. Casey answered for him, said Pete didn't need any wine if he was to be driving later. He said Emily didn't need any wine either. Emily and Pete had been seated together at the table. Pete did not want to keep stealing glances at her but he could not help himself. Once they were eating, Mr. Casey asked his daughters about school that day. They answered shortly, succinctly, school was good.

—Just a couple days till vacation.

—Yep.

Mr. Casey pointed with a piece of garlic bread, said: What kind of bonehead parties do they have planned for the weekend?

—I wouldn't even know, said Emily.

—How about you, Pete?

—I'm not much of a party kind of guy.

Mr. Casey grinned: Not big on the drinking and scrapping?

—Frank, said Mrs. Casey.

Stan touched his napkin to his lips. There was something unsaid in the air. He chopped through his spaghetti and chased each forkful with beer.

—Mr. Maitland, my uncle told me a little bit about your house.

Stan looked up: Did he?

—He said it was on a real nice piece of property. Good view of the lake. I've probably seen it at one time or another but I can't think of when.

—From time to time I think I could hire some help out there, maybe an afternoon or a day. If ever you have a bit of time to spare. It's an old house and it's hard to keep up by myself.

Emily ate quietly, steadily. Her silverware made clipping sounds against her dish.

—Your mother, Pete, said Mr. Casey. What does she do these days?

Pete hadn't realized his mother was known to Mr. Casey. He wondered vaguely how.

—She stays at home. Looks after my brothers. When we moved here from North Bay, she got a job as a secretary at the chemical factory, but they laid her off. That was four years ago.

—And your dad, he's a pastor, right? Out at that Pentecostal church?

—Dad, said Emily.

—It's okay, said Pete. Yeah . . . my dad is a pastor. I didn't know you knew them.

—Not really well, said Mr. Casey.

They did not ask him anything further. After supper, Stan was quick to collect his coat. He said he had the dog to get home to and he asked if Pete would let him out of the driveway. Pete went out and backed his car onto the street. He passed the old man as he was heading to his truck.

—Good to see you, Mr. Maitland.

—Is your uncle working?

—No. He hasn't been able to get anything. He tries, you know. Tries to find work . . . but, so far . . .

Stan nodded. He said so long and got into his truck.

When Pete went back inside, Mr. Casey gave him strict orders to have Emily back by eleven. They went out and got into his car. He kissed her before anything was said. Then they were driving.

—That was not how I wanted it to be, said Emily. I did not want everybody to be mad at each other.

—I thought maybe it was me.

—It wasn't you. It was my grandpa and my parents. Fifteen minutes before you got there, my dad broke the news to him.

—They're not going to take the house?

—No. They're not going to take the house. And there's more.

There's been something wrong between my grandpa and my dad for a month. I wish they'd just come out and say what it is.

—Oh, said Pete.

She was quiet for the rest of the drive. They went to the cinema out by the shopping mall and she insisted mildly that she would pay. She bought tickets for *The Empire Strikes Back* and bought popcorn and soft drinks. They went into the theatre. She allowed him to take her hand and he tried to think nothing of it. Pete lifted her hand to kiss it. After the film started she took her hand back to eat with.

Later, coming out of the theatre, they talked about the movie on their way back to the car.

—Did you want to drive around awhile? said Pete.

—Just drive around?

—Or go somewhere?

—And do what, Pete?

She was looking at him with a touch of amusement. He felt very small.

—I haven't seen you in a week.

—I should probably go home. My dad will be waiting up.

—Okay.

She watched out the window while he drove. There was a faint reflection of her face in the window-glass. When they got to her house, there were lights in the living room window. She allowed herself to be kissed a little. She touched the swelling over his eye.

—I do not understand boys at all.

—I didn't think it would be so noticeable.

—It was. But don't worry about it.

She allowed him to kiss her again, then she said: I should go in now.

—Did I say something wrong? I didn't go looking for a fight with your friends, if that's what you thought.

—You didn't say anything wrong, Pete, and I know you didn't

go looking for a fight. They are not my friends. They're a bunch of spoiled brats. I can't wait to be done with them all. Anyway, thanks for taking me out.

She was getting out of the car.

—Well, said Pete, should we plan something?

—It's a busy few days. I have to play piano at the Christmas Eve service and I haven't even practised. You heard it when you came in. It sounded horrible.

—It didn't sound so bad.

—I need to practise more. I have to go . . .

—Emily, for Chrissake. What's going on?

She paused with the door open. The cold flowed into the car. She sat back down on the passenger seat. She said: I think tonight wasn't a good idea but it was too late to take a step back from it. That's my fault, Pete, and I apologize.

—I don't understand.

—We're just moving a little too fast.

—I thought we were having fun. I thought you miss me when we're apart.

—I really have to go.

—So what now?

—I'll call you.

And she was gone. She went up the driveway and into her house. He saw the silhouette in the living room window and then put his car into gear. Nothing seemed quite real. There was a weight on his chest. As he drove away from her house, he could still taste her on his lips.

Two days passed and Emily didn't call. Late Thursday, Pete was in the booth between the pumps, watching vehicles on the bypass. Duane had the day off and Caroline was in the store. Pete hunched down in his winter coat. The cold in the booth was a qualitative thing. The cold could be addressed.

From time to time he would touch his eyebrow to bring the pain, which had subdued to an ache. He ate half a sandwich. Then he heard the bell and saw a police cruiser pulling up to the pumps. Pete went out, knowing who it was before the window rolled down.

—Hey, Mr. Casey, said Pete.

—A top-up is all I need.

As far as Pete knew, the local detachment had a service contract with one of the other petroleum companies, so if Mr. Casey was at the Texaco station, it was because he'd gone out of his way. The tank was topped up in a minute.

Mr. Casey paid cash. He was casually watching the sunset through his windshield. Pete struggled for something to say: Thanks again for supper the other night.

—I guess you know where we stand. Most times I don't get involved in her business. But I know about you. I know what you are.

—Mr. Casey, if you mean my uncle . . .

Mr. Casey looked at him directly: I know exactly what you are. She's got too many good things going in her life for you to make a jackpot of it. You'll just want to look for another kind of girl, one who's more your sort. I won't have you hanging around my property or my daughter. It's no goddamn good for anybody.

Pete studied the scoured pavement: I don't think that's going to be a problem.

—That's right. That's exactly right.

The patrol car pulled out of the station and back onto the bypass.

Pete found himself pacing the apron. He stopped once and touched his eyebrow. It did not hurt enough. He pressed it with his thumb. He could leave. He could leave right now. There wasn't enough money but when was there ever enough money. Instead, he sat back in the corporeal cold of the booth as the dusk gathered.

The question remained. It had always been there.

—

Later, Pete took his supper break at the hospital. By that hour his family had come and gone and his grandmother was watching television. Pete watched with her for awhile, nursing a hot chocolate he'd bought in the cafeteria. Mrs. Petrelli was gone. Departed from the world, about a week earlier. The bed was remade and vacant, ready to take on a new occupant. There was nothing to suggest Mrs. Petrelli had ever been there.

Irene asked in halting words how was work and when would he be going back to school. He told her what he always told her. Then he asked her the question.

—You know that, Peter.

—I just thought maybe you remembered something. Or maybe I forgot something you or Mom told me once.

—He wasn't nobody at all. Come and gone. Left a young girl pregnant . . .

She lifted her hand and gripped his wrist with surprising strength. She whispered: Don't you go treating girls that way.

—I won't, said Pete.

—I know.

Irene's eyes gaped at him. He smiled for her and wondered was she afraid of this, the long business of dying.

It was after midnight by the time he got home from work. The only sound was Luke grinding his teeth. Pete got into bed. He read a paperback until his eyes burned. He shut off the light but did not sleep. He saw Emily in the bowling alley, in her formal dress, laughing. It was four o'clock before he fell asleep.

—We've been through this before. You carry that number over, you add it, and that's how you get the answer.

—I don't understand.

—Yes, you do.

Pete watched them from the kitchen doorway. Late-morning sunlight banked in through the window over the sink. The boys had their notebooks open before them. Luke had his pencil in his fist and was glaring at an arithmetic lesson. John saw Pete and fixed him with a stare. A bubble of snot pushed out of the boy's nostril each time he breathed.

Donna noticed him at last. She paused with the dog-eared curricula notebook in her hands. Then she told the boys to keep at their sums and asked Pete if he wanted breakfast. Pete sat down at the table with his brothers, asked them how the lesson was going.

—Hard, said Luke.

—Hard, said John.

The boy still had the mucus in his nostril. Pete told him to blow his nose. His mother brought him oatmeal with brown sugar and a cup of tea. Pete knew he should be hungry but he wasn't. It was as if his belly was obstructed by a thing just starting to take shape.

Donna picked up the curricula book.

—Okay. We were at times tables.

Pete put his spoon down. He said: Hey, boys. Can you go into the living room for awhile?

The boys looked at him.

—We're doing lessons, said Donna.

—Just for a few minutes.

The boys looked at their mother. Her thin shoulders drooped. She made a shooing gesture and they hopped off their chairs.

—No, take your notebooks. This isn't playtime.

They bounded into the living room.

—Peter, do you know how easy it is to get behind in the lessons?

—I want you to tell me what we never talk about.

—What?

—I want to know about my dad.

—You know about that.

—No. I don't know. We never talk about it.

John's voice rose in outrage from the living room. Donna stepped to the doorway and looked out at them. She raised her voice: Let go of your brother's head. Now.

—We never talk about it, said Pete. I want to know.

—There's nothing worth talking about. He was nobody.

—Goddammit, listen, Mom. What's it got to do with the cops? Is Uncle Lee involved?

She stepped forward and slapped him, but drew back immediately, with all her fingers splayed and her lips quivering. She hadn't struck him hard but his face felt branded all the same.

Pete rose from the table. He carried his dishes to the sink and washed them. He was slow in his motions. Everything, every feeling he'd felt over the last few days, over the last month, over the last year, seemed to be coming together into a single, slow-burning flame. It was a sensation he didn't even have a name for, but he felt the heat of it in the bottom of his gut.

Donna moved backwards to give him a wide berth. She spoke quietly: He was just a loser. How do you think it felt to be me? Why do you think you didn't live here for so many years? I couldn't be here, Peter. I couldn't.

Pete nodded. Hot water flowed over the bowl and the cup. Steam lifted through the sunlight.

—Peter?

—Never mind.

He turned from the sink and went out of the kitchen. He didn't know if the boys had seen anything but they were sitting on opposite sides of the couch, conspicuously silent.

By half past noon, Pete was in town. He drove past Heron Heights, where a number of students were moving between the parking lot and the school doors. Emily was nowhere to be seen. What

Pete did see was the wood-panelled station wagon. It drove past him into the lot and parked. Roger and one of his friends got out and walked into the school. Pete watched them.

Pete drove back downtown. He parked at the A&P and walked over to the variety store and went around back and rang the buzzer to the apartment. No one came. He went into the store. Mr. Yoon was stocking the refrigerator.

—You see my uncle?

—Not working today, said Mr. Yoon.

—You know where he's at?

—He just walks around sometimes. I see him. Or he goes and plays pool. Bar around the corner.

—Okay.

—When is he going to work again?

—I don't know.

Pete drove to the Corner Pocket, the only poolroom on the block. There was a small parking lot in back. He went in through the back door. The place was nearly empty this time of day. The man behind the bar was wiping down the sides of a jar of devilled eggs. The radio was on, or the jukebox, but Pete could only discern the dry sounds of the drum track. Finally he spotted Lee at a table across the room.

Lee was lining up a shot when Pete came over. Four empty beer bottles stood on the rail behind him. He was working on a fifth.

—Uncle Lee, said Pete.

Lee banked the six-ball into a pocket. He said: How are you, Pete?

—If I ask you something, will you level with me?

Lee leaned the cue against the side of the table. He took a drink of beer.

—What are we talking about?

—I want you to tell me what nobody else will.

—You're not making any sense.

—Look. You know that cop? Frank Casey? He came to my work. He says he knows what I am. *What* I am, he said, whatever that means. I've never even gotten a speeding ticket. So what is he talking about?

—That son of a bitch is a ball-breaker, Pete. He's giving you a hard time because of me.

—That's not it. There's something nobody will tell me. My mom got real upset when I started asking—

—Don't bother your mother about it.

—And Grandma won't tell—

Lee slammed his beer bottle down. The noise drew casual glances from the few hang-abouts in the place. Lee pressed his finger into Pete's chest.

—Do *not* bother your grandmother with this shit. Do you hear me?

Pete stared back. He felt blood come into his cheeks: Fuck this. One more person. The sooner I'm done with all of you the better.

He turned and went out the back door.

The afternoon was all the brighter for the brief minutes he'd been inside. He was opening his car door when he heard Lee say his name. Lee was standing at the back door of the poolroom.

—Maybe nobody tells you because they figure you don't want to know. This was a bad thing, buck.

—Yeah?

—But I know what it's like to be on the outside of everything. So I won't lie to you. I won't do that. But what you have to know is nothing will be the same if I tell you.

—I want to know, Lee. I can't live my whole life like this. Maybe I used to think it didn't matter, but it does now. People around me have made it matter, but they haven't wanted to give me a choice in much of anything. So I'm choosing to know. I don't know if you understand what I mean, but I'm choosing to know.

—Well, like I said, I won't lie to you.

Pete followed Lee back inside to a table near the jukebox. On the wall above was a faded print of dogs shooting billiards. Lee went to the bar and came back carrying four beers. He gave one to Pete. Pete nodded at the bartender.

—He won't mind?

—I'll talk to him if he bitches. But he won't. If I wasn't having a drink, I don't think I'd be able to get into any of this. If you're going to hear it, you'll want to have a couple too.

They drank in silence for a little while. Lee lit a cigarette. He said: You're eighteen.

—Yeah. I am.

—Eighteen, that means you're a man. Eighteen years ago I was twenty-two. I was on trial for capital murder. Six months was all it took. You're born in, what, July? '62? Well, July '62 I'd already been inside for three months. Your grandmother sent me a snapshot of you in the hospital when you were born. There was this Indian in jail that I had some trouble with when I was first there. He thought he was a big man and he thought I was just some young goof. He got a hold of some of my stuff and he burned it. That picture was part of it. He did this when I was working in the mailbag shop, which is where all the new fish go. I don't know why. But later on I got my chance at him in the shower. I did twenty days in the hole for what I did to him, but that big dumb Indian, anytime he saw me after that, he stayed away. I'm already off the subject. Look. When your mom and me were kids we didn't have it too easy. I know everybody says that. But our old man—your granddad—even though he worked all the time, we never had enough money. I don't know why. Maybe he could earn money okay but he couldn't save it. He wasn't bad to us, never beat us up or nothing, but I never knew him either, not really. When I was still pretty little, the old man had three heart attacks. He still didn't quit working. The fourth heart attack killed him flat out. That was the end of that. The store went bankrupt and a year later we were on the dole. Do you know all that?

—Not like this, said Pete.

Lee finished his beer and started on another.

—Well. We lived in a boarding house on the other side of downtown, north of the river. Merritt Street. I think about that place a lot, I don't know why. I went to see it awhile back but it's different now. Your grandmother helped clean the place to take down the rent she was paying. And your mother wasn't always so serious, Pete. Did you know that? How she is now, I wouldn't of even known her. So quiet. So wrapped up. But she wasn't always so serious.

—I don't remember her ever being anything else. There were times when I was younger, I'd see her just staring off into space. Just blanked out.

—When she was young she was a lot of fun, and she was real pretty. A real knockout, they'd say. She didn't care that she barely had two changes of clothes. She got along good with practically everybody. She was the only person, the only person . . . I mean, she cared for me. I was her older brother, the loser, the small-time hood, but none of that bothered her. I used to be afraid I would, you know, disappoint her, but I'd get drinking or doing something stupid, and no matter what, she was always there to pick me up and drive me wherever it was I needed to go, or if I needed to come back home for a little while, she'd give up her room and sleep on the couch . . .

Lee was peering into the tabletop, moving his beer bottle back and forth between his hands. Pete drank down his own beer. He left the dregs in the bottom of the bottle. A man weaved into the men's room nearby and by the time he'd come out Lee had still not resumed.

—Lee, said Pete.

—You know that hockey arena in town?

—The community centre, sure. Charles Grady Memorial or whatever.

—And you never played hockey?

—Never. I took some skating lessons when I was little, but I wasn't any good.

—Well. Chuck Grady was a hockey player from town. He played forward. He had a hell of a name for himself. He was playing Triple-A when he was sixteen and he got scouted for the National League by the time he was your age. I knew this because everybody in town knew it. Chuck had a brother named Simon, about a year or two younger than him, and when Chuck was back in town you'd always see them two together. The Grady boys. There wasn't a teenage girl around that him and his brother couldn't get into. Chuckie Grady. He started sniffing around your mother. She was going with a guy—I can't remember his name, but what does it matter—and she didn't care about hockey and she had no interest in Chuckie Grady. But him and Simon would cruise by the boarding house every now and then. They had this, what was it, a real flashy car. T-Bird, if I remember.

—T-Bird? said Pete.

—Yeah. A T-Bird. Their old man owned the dealership.

—Jesus, said Pete.

—What?

—Nothing. Never mind.

—Well, I figured I'd let Chuck and Simon know that your ma wasn't interested in them. I saw Simon one time at a party and I let him know he didn't need to have anything to do with her. Ha. A week later I was pretty drunk, coming out of a dance hall, or maybe the bowling alley, and Chuck and Simon and a few of their pals were waiting for me. They stomped my ass into the ground pretty good. I guess they figured a greaser hood like me shouldn't be speaking up for his sister.

He'd taken to studying the tabletop again. After a moment, he went on: I'd been on a real tear for a few days, way out on Indian River. Me, Speedy Simmons, Jimmy Robichaud, a couple others. It was maybe September. I came back to the boarding house at night. I wasn't supposed to be living there any more—I was in my twenties—but I couldn't hold a job down for real long, and I'd been evicted from the place I was living. I remember that night because it was late, eleven o'clock. I had Jimmy Robichaud's dad's Buick, which we all just kind of used when we needed to. Anyways there I was near the house and that fucking T-Bird is going the other way real fast, and I thought, there's the Gradys cruising again. But when I got to the house, your mom, she was just sitting outside on the porch. She . . . she had no shoes on. She was barefoot. Her legs were all scratched up.

Lee peeled the label off his beer bottle. Pete's mouth was bone dry.

—I never figured out why those two guys thought she'd just keep her mouth shut, said Lee. I thought about it a long time. But you know? They were right. She did. Far as I know I'm the only person she ever told it to, and I think it was on account of I saw their car and I saw her sitting there on the porch. The only time she said a word of it was to me that night. How she was walking home from the grocery store where she worked. How they came by and saw her and picked her up, she said, and this was maybe nine o'clock at night in the fall, so it was full dark, and then they didn't drive her straight home. She didn't talk a lot more about what happened after that. Not to me. Not even when she got called up as a witness for the defence, and I was sitting there with those charges laid on me. She just looked at the floor when the lawyer asked her. Did you know Charles or Simon Grady? She said, no, sir. Not at all, sir. I guess they all knew a lot more about shame than I ever did, which is why they knew she wouldn't say anything. I don't know what Chuck and Simon did when they went back into town, and after that night Simon was never able to talk clearly anyway. He couldn't even be called as a witness. See, I don't know where they went after they left her. I only know I got to their house before they did. When they got home it was around midnight and I was there already.

Pete started to get up from the table. He felt queasy.

—Sit down, said Lee.

—I have to go.

—Sit your ass down, Peter. You wanted me to start talking about this, well, I am. The Crown wanted to hang me for it. You can't duck out now.

Pete sank into the chair.

—Jimmy's dad was a framer on a building crew, said Lee. He had a framing hammer in the trunk of the car. It was twenty-two ounces. I didn't say nothing to Chuck or Simon and they never got any words out themselves. The whole thing was done and over in less than a minute and I drove away. I threw the hammer down a creek. But the thing is, Simon Grady was still alive. That's something I didn't think of at the time. When I left them, they both had their heads pretty messed up. I . . . I know I used the claw a couple of times, anyway. But I was also young and pissed off and drunk. Stupid. Simon Grady was still alive, but he was all messed up. He never got right again.

—I feel like I'm going to throw up.

—They gave me twenty years. They talked about some of the chicken-shit stuff I'd been picked up for before, and they called a few witnesses who said I had prior history with the Gradys. And me, us, whatever you want to call it, I just told the court I didn't like them bothering my sister. If she couldn't talk about what they'd done to her, I couldn't speak for her. Mom knew, and I think some people in town might of had the idea, but it never come out in the newspaper. Just how the local hockey hero got murdered in cold blood. They called it envy. The first chaplain, when I was inside, he called it covetousness, and he showed me in the Bible what that was.

Pete stood up again. He was unsteady and feeling sick to his stomach. He said: I don't understand at all why you . . . why you'd come back here. Why you'd do that to us.

—To us, said Lee. Is that right? You're the man of the family now? You're the big man?

—I've got to go.

—Well, one more thing, big man. I'm sorry you had to find out from me, like this. I'm sorry your mother won't say nothing, specially when I think of all the time I sat in jail. I'm sorry for all that wasted time. I'm sorry for what's gone down since I got out, like Bud, for example. I'm sorry that Simon Grady is a halfwit because I didn't have the sense to make sure I finished it. But I'm not sorry for what I did. I never will be. I can see that. Clear as anything.

—What gave you the idea you could decide that?

—What gave you the idea I couldn't?

He drove the streets. He hadn't eaten all day. He clenched the wheel until his hands hurt. The flame in his gut had turned into a fire, and it was spreading through every part of him. Every thought in his head was a wordless, desperate scream. In the late evening he pulled up a few doors down from Nancy's house. He could see the cars in the driveway, the station wagon among them, and all the lights in the windows, and people moving about on the porch. He got out of his car and crossed the yard.

Pete went into Nancy's living room. There had to be fifty people there and it was hot and cloudy with smoke. Nancy must have seen him as soon as he came in, because she appeared almost immediately.

—What are you doing here?

—I'm looking for somebody.

—Emily's not here.

—I'm not looking for her. I won't be long.

—Hey, said Nancy. Look . . .

He brushed past her. She grasped his arm and he pulled away. He walked through the kitchen and the dining room. Nancy fell into step behind him.

He found Roger in the den at the back, the same place he'd been when they first exchanged words. He was with a few of his friends and some girls. They were playing quarters on the coffee table.

Roger's head turned. He looked drunk.

Pete kicked the chair out from under him. Roger went down and Pete jumped on top of him. He pinned him down with his knees. Roger had his arms raised to fend the blows as they came. Around them, voices cried out. Pete felt a hand grasp a mitt-ful of his collar and he half turned and punched somebody in the testicles. He was punched hard in the side of the forehead. The world spun. He was hauled backwards. He could see Roger crawling away on his elbows, crablike. Roger's nose was bleeding onto his shirt.

Pete was on his knees and he was up and down and up again. He held his own. In the end, he was dragged out of the house. He staggered off through the front yard and paused under a street light. Roger came out and stood on the porch, crying out that he would kill Pete. There were neighbours peering out their win-dows and doors. Pete didn't say anything. He walked back to his car and got in and turned the key in the ignition.

Streets rolled out in front of him. He drove along the lakeshore. He drove up the hill, drove past Galilee Tabernacle, drove out to the CIL factory, to the shopping mall, drove back down the hill, sped along River Street. He saw the place where Emily had told him he'd better kiss her. He kept going, but there was only so far you could drive before you were covering the same streets again. He was shaking coldly, seeing the red and green lights around win-dows, the store signboards saying MERRY CHRISTMAS, the wooden crèches out front of the churches. Everything seemed cheap and cruel. He hadn't balanced any account, and he couldn't possibly go home.

Once more, Lee went to look at the boarding house. When he got there, he stood with his fists pocketed. Then he went up the driveway and around to the back of the house, watching the windows all the while. The back porch was still there but it had been bolstered with pressure-treated lumber and repainted. He went around the porch and followed the steps down to the basement door. The steps and the door were exactly as he remembered them.

He was reaching for the knob when he heard the porch door open and close above. He looked up, blinking against the sky, and could see the side of somebody's head, could see gloved fingers moving along the deck rail. There were two of them. One asked the other where they should go for lunch and the other said downtown.

Lee didn't move. He was in plain sight if the men above looked down. But a moment later they were gone in a car. Lee waited a little longer. Water dripped from an icicle overhead. He tried the basement door and found it locked. He tried it again. He pushed the door with his shoulder. It did not budge. That was that.

He went back up the steps and around the side of the house and back to the street.

In those days long past, if he had happened to glimpse the crippled caretaker outside in the yard, he was not afraid of the man at all. He wondered what had become of him.

You know, I've seen the old boarding house a few times. You ever go back there?

—Not so's I remember.

—You remember that day when Dad died?

—Would you change the channel?

Lee went to the television. He changed one soap opera for another until Irene nodded and said: I like this program.

—Down the basement of that house they had a big coal furnace. I saw it the day Dad died.

—Mrs. Pound didn't want any kids down there.

—I remember. I went down there anyways. I never liked anybody telling me what I couldn't do.

She lifted a finger from the bedrail and poked the side of his hand with it. Her skin was tight across her skull. She breathed. Her eyes flashed in their dark hollows. Her voice rasped at him: That was a long time ago, Leland.

—Yes.

Lee looked into the other half of the room. No one had come yet to occupy the other bed. His mother had gotten her own room after all.

—Barry thinks you've been drinking.

—He said that?

—He worries about you.

—He doesn't need to worry so much.

—He worries about Donna. He worries about the little boys. Peter.

An unpleasant feeling went through Lee at the mention of Pete's name. He'd been drunk when he told Pete the truth. He didn't know if he would have told him otherwise, although it bothered him to think how the great shame remained a secret even now. It more than bothered him—it made him angry. He flexed his fist and pulled his eyes away from his mother's and looked at the TV for a little while. He didn't know if word had gotten out to the rest of the family yet that he'd told Pete the truth, and he didn't know what it would be like for him to see Pete again. Maybe it would be easier not to see the kid at all any more.

And besides, nobody had said anything to him yet, about coming over on Christmas Day.

He leaned over and adjusted the blankets on Irene's bed. He said: Well, Barry doesn't need to worry about me.

She groped for his hand. She smiled: I know. I told him. He doesn't need to worry about me neither. I'm close. Called up to Jesus. He doesn't need to worry about me at all.

The Owl Café was turning a brisk trade. There was a hiss of frying in the kitchen. The cook sweated in his whites and turned plateloads of food onto the wicket. The radio played an endless list of Christmas songs. Voices were layered in conversation and there were boxes and bags full of gifts piled into booths. The waitresses moved about quickly. Nobody paid attention to the bell-chime as the front door opened.

Helen served a bowl of soup to an old deaf man at the counter. When she turned she saw that Lee was down at his usual place, sitting with his hands folded on the countertop. He was alone, as always.

She went down to him.

—Hello, Brown Eyes. Haven't seen you in here in a little while.

—That's true.

The cook spoke through the wicket: Helen, your fried chicken's up.

—It's real busy, Brown Eyes, said Helen. Maybe later on.

—I want a cup of coffee. Maybe I'll order some lunch.

She brought Lee a mug of coffee. He emptied two sugars into it and stirred in some cream.

Helen took a plate of fried chicken from the wicket and delivered it to a woman down the other end of the counter. Lee watched her. The place was busier than he had ever seen it. Near Lee, a man was trying to flag Helen down to pay his bill. Helen came and took the bill and returned the man's change. The man left her two quarters. She moved a strand of hair from her forehead and asked Lee if he was hungry.

—Am I hungry. Why not. I'll have the BLT.

She wrote the order down and posted it on the wicket. Lee lifted his coffee. He watched her work. The old deaf man had finished his soup. Helen cleared away the bowl. The old man counted coins out of a leather change purse and laid them on the counter. He stood up from his stool and shuffled out of the diner.

The cook called to Helen that the BLT was up. She brought the plate to Lee and refilled his coffee. She had her other hand knuckles-down on the countertop. Lee closed his own hand over hers.

—Haven't seen you.

—I've been busy.

She pulled her hand away. The people sitting around them were making an effort not to notice.

—I'll check on you in a bit.

—Wait, said Lee. What time do you get done today?

—It's real busy. I don't know what time I'll finish. I'll check on you in a bit.

She moved back down the counter again. Lee raised his hand, called to her:

—Hey, miss. There's a hair in my sandwich.

She returned to him. He was grinning.

—It's real busy, Lee.

—Let's just make some plans.

Helen pressed both hands down on either side of Lee's plate and pitched her voice low and lethal: If you've got to know, Lee, you talked about all that serious shit. You and me, serious. You think that's what I wanted to hear? You can't even keep a goddamn job. Now why don't you eat your sandwich and pay your bill and get back to whatever it is you were doing.

She went back down the counter, moving with her shoulders lifted. Not three seconds later there was the noise of crockery breaking. All conversation in the café came to a halt. Lee was standing when she turned. She could see the shards of his plate and the mess of the food on the floor. He drove the coffee mug forward off the counter. The mug burst on the floor as the plate had.

Helen could feel all the eyes on her. Lee's hands were opening and closing. He bared his teeth and said: You're nothing but a cheap goddamn bitch, you know that?

The cook came out of the kitchen and stood with his arms crossed. Lee hauled his billfold out of his pocket. He flung a handful of change and one-dollar bills onto the counter, and then he turned and went out of the café.

The bell on the door chimed his departure. A woman in a booth laughed once and then clapped her hand over her mouth. The radio was still playing Christmas carols.

The old men convened at Western Autobody. They stood in the office, Stan, Dick, Huddy, some of the others, drinking coffee, watching the garage. Bob Phillips and the other mechanics had two cars raised on the lifts. The pneumatic wrench whined. The old men in the office exchanged bits of gossip from the last week. Dick and Stan leaned against the wall together.

—I'll be working Christmas Day, said Dick. I'm coaching the new kid. He's a bit of a mouthpiece. Always knows best, that kid.

—Reminds me of you, said Stan.

Through the window, they watched Bob as he tightened the lugs on a tire on one of the lifted cars. After awhile, Stan said he should be getting on.

—Where do you have to be? said Dick.

—I'm going up to the shopping mall. I have a present to buy for Louise. I've got something in mind. She likes to go fishing and she likes to know the names of everything, every goddamn bird and bug you can imagine.

Huddy was putting his hearing aid back in. He peered at them, said: Birds?

Stan went out to his truck. Dick caught up with him.

—Stan, are you in town on Christmas Day or are you staying out at the Point?

—I'll come into town to see Frank and Mary and the girls. It's easier than them coming out to me.

Dick went and started the unmarked car and Stan started his truck. Then Dick came over and leaned on the side panel.

—Stanley, I overheard Frank on the telephone with Mary. I know about the house. I'm sorry.

Stan nodded. He said: I know. But it's . . . Mind you, it's a few years off yet. Anyhow, I've got some things I want to do with it, some new doors to hang. I never was much of a builder. It takes me a long time to do any of that. But time I have. Time I have.

—It's a good old house.

—I know. So you're working on Christmas Day?

—I am, said Dick.

—I'll come by after I'm done with the family. You leave the new kid on the desk and we'll go get some lunch. We'll find someplace that'll be open.

—Okay, Stan.

Stan found a book called *The Young Naturalist* at the bookstore in the shopping mall. He turned the book in his hands. He opened it and read a passage on the denning of beavers. The woman at the checkout asked him if it was a Christmas gift and he said it was and she asked him if he would like to inscribe it. She offered him a pen. He printed: *Louise, here is a good book about nature. You & me can learn together. Happy Xmas, Grandpa*. His printing looked peculiar to him. There was sway in the letters. He paid for the book and the woman gift-wrapped it.

Stan had seen Eleanor Lacroix the day before yesterday. She'd called and asked him to meet her in town. They'd met up for a cup of coffee at a small diner near Stan's old boxing clubhouse.

They talked for half an hour or more—mostly Eleanor did the talking. She and her fiancé, Tommy, had a vacation they were going to leave for the next day. She had to get away, she said. She couldn't imagine Christmas at home without Judy around.

Stan nodded. He told her she looked like she was doing well, which was true. There was colour in her face again and she'd put some weight back on. He'd only ever been able to say he'd come up short looking into Judy's former boyfriend. He was sorry. He was goddamn sorry there wasn't anything more. He was sorry for a lot of things. He did not elaborate on this. He just listened as Eleanor told him about her vacation plans.

Outside the diner, she got a rectangular gift-wrapped object from her car.

—Thank you, Stan. For everything.

—It was nothing, said Stan.

—Maybe you think that. But it's not right. Because what you did is you cared. I won't ever forget that.

Eleanor put her arms around him and kissed him quickly on the mouth.

—This is for you, said Eleanor. I couldn't really think of anything but then I found this.

She gave him the gift-wrapped thing. It felt like a book. All he could say was, Happy Christmas and so long.

Later, after he'd gotten home, Stan unwrapped it. It was a big hardcover book. *The Illustrated History of Canadian Boxing*, published by the Canadian Amateur Boxing Association. Eleanor had bookmarked a page a third of the way through, and though he'd never seen the book before, he had a sense of what might be on the page. He was correct. Himself, nineteen years old, poised on the mat with his gloves up. He thought maybe the picture had been taken in Parry Sound shortly before he'd gone professional. If it was the Parry Sound fight, he'd won it with a knockout in the fifth round. He couldn't remember much about the opponent, neither his name nor his face, but he'd worked the man into the ropes with body blows until the man dropped his fists, and then he'd fired his right cross into the man's jaw and watched him fall sideways. The fight was in a fairgrounds tent and the mat was canvas stretched over hay bales. Hard as rock. But there he was, little more than a boy, living a part of his life he could scarcely remember now.

In the shopping mall corridor, Stan saw a man clad in a canvas jacket and dirty jeans and work boots. Leland King. Lee was carrying a box under each arm and in one hand a paper bag. They were coming directly towards each other.

—Lee, said Stan.

—Mr. Maitland.

—Christmas gifts?

—Yeah. My sister's two boys. Do kids like these types of things any more?

The boxes Lee had contained two model airplane kits, a B-17 and a Lancaster bomber. Both kits were 1:48. Lee opened the paper bag and Stan saw tubes of glue, a wheel of paints, and a set of camel-hair brushes.

—I used to like these things, said Lee. What do I know about kids?

—I'd say a couple boys would like it. Say, Lee, I saw Peter not too long ago.

—Peter, said Lee, speaking the name as if he didn't know it.

—He's a good kind of a guy. When he talks, you can see he's sharp.

—He's so sharp he quit school. That's how sharp he is.

—I think he's been seeing my granddaughter, said Stan. Anyhow, he says you're getting by okay.

—Sure I am. At least I'm not working where somebody gets drowned on the job.

Stan made himself laugh at that. He said: It's good to see you, Lee. I can't imagine the boys not liking those airplanes. So long.

—See you, said Lee.

Stan ran a few more errands around the mall. He bought extra batteries and candles in case he lost power out at his house. It was snowing lightly when he went out and got in his truck, and driving back in the direction of town he spotted Lee at the bus stop, waiting for the half-hourly town bus. There was no one else waiting. Across the way was a vacant house with plywood tacked over the windows and the porch collapsed, and behind it a hundred acres of overgrown and snow-dusted pasture. Stan stopped the truck and called to Lee, asking if he would care for a lift back downtown.

For a moment Lee did not move and Stan thought he might not come, but then he stood and pitched away the cigarette he was smoking. He jogged forward, carrying the model kits and the bag. He climbed onto the passenger seat and sat his purchases on his lap.

Stan put the truck in gear and moved back onto the road.

—I hear your mother is in the hospital.

—They found two more tumours in her lungs.

—It's an awful goddamn thing.

—They can't do much at her age.

—They can make it comfortable, said Stan. My wife . . .

But Stan didn't finish that. He found he had little to say to this man on the subject of his wife.

—For awhile she had to share the room, said Lee.

—She doesn't have to share any more?

—No. The other lady died.

—I see.

—So far they haven't given her anybody new. She's got the TV to herself.

—All this getting old, Lee, it's a goddamn job all by itself.

—Longest sentence you can do, I guess.

Stan put the windshield wipers on to sweep snowflakes off the glass. Downtown, there were many people on the sidewalks, moving in and out of the stores. People carrying boxes and bags. Lee studied one of the model kits. A bomber moving through the air far above a patchwork of fields, a smiling pin-up girl painted beneath the plane's forward windscreens. Stan said again how any boys would love to have model airplanes to build. Lee nodded.

It was good until they were two blocks from Lee's place. They were on Union Street, between the postcard storefronts. Then they stopped at a pedestrian crosswalk, and there before them, being led by the arm by his father, was Simon Grady. He walked at a doddering pace. He had a toque on his head and it hid the indented scars where the flesh had split from the impact of the framing hammer. He was led along, grinning blithely.

Simon and his father disappeared into a store.

—Think I'll get out here, said Lee, quietly.

—I can drive you the rest of the way.

—I'll walk.

Stan nodded. Snow was collecting on the windshield. The wipers swept the glass. Lee gathered his purchases and got out of the truck.

Stan watched Lee move off down the hill. Then he put the truck in gear and moved up. He beeped his horn and reached into the glovebox for a pen. He scrawled his phone number on an old business card that advertised a man in Novar who'd restored Stan's woodstove. He rolled down his window and Lee looked at him.

—Look, said Stan, I've got some things I need to do at my house. Some doors to hang, some windows to fix. There's a bad squeak in the floor in one place. I can do some of it but I could use a hand. Maybe a week or two of work, what you think is fair. Give me a ring after Christmas if you want to talk about it.

Lee took the business card. He looked at it. He brought out his billfold and stowed the card inside. Stan pulled away from the curb. He had kept himself from looking at Lee when they'd seen Simon Grady a few minutes earlier. He thought again of the young man he'd driven down to the provincial jail, shortly after Charles Grady had been killed and Simon Grady had been put in the hospital, comatose, with his head stove in. The trial had divided the facts of Lee's crime into blacks and whites, but even in those days Stan had had no faith in blacks and whites. There was always the grey, and in the grey was where the truth often resided. The death of Judy Lacroix had only reinforced that belief, and he'd done what he could, and he'd come up short.

Stan looked in his rear-view mirror. Lee was still standing on the sidewalk, staring at nothing in particular.

Pete stayed at the Shamrock Hotel for a few days. He ended up there late in the night after he'd left Nancy's house. There were a few nice hotels in town, a very nice one near the golf course. But he'd never set foot in a hotel in his life, certainly not in the nicer ones, and he doubted he had the means or the appearance for them. At midnight, the sign at the Shamrock still said OPEN. The people in the adjoining tavern ignored him.

The desk clerk told Pete it would be ten bucks a night. Pete thought about it. He said he'd pay the first night and then daily thereafter. The clerk was disinterested. He had Pete sign a register and then he gave him a key.

The room was up on the third floor. A shared bathroom was down the hall. There was mismatched furniture and threadbare carpeting. An ugly painting of a sailboat. A small black-and-white television. The sheets on the bed were faded but they seemed clean. He lay on them, dense with exhaustion. Through the wall someone was arguing. Emily seemed an occupant of another world entirely. He fell asleep with the TV on.

At work at the gas station Pete watched for police cars, certain that it was only a matter of time before they came to have him account for what he'd done to Roger. To have him account for who and what he was.

—You're way out in space, said Duane.

—I'm sorry.

—Listen, man, these gasoline fumes. They'll burn your head.

—Never mind, said Pete.

Duane appraised him with bemusement. A car came and Pete went to attend it.

At two o'clock Caroline came out and told him he had a phone call. Despite himself, his pulse was accelerating. But the voice was not Emily's.

—Listen, said Donna. Where are you?

—You're calling me at work.

—How come you didn't come home?

He was alone but he still cupped his hand around the mouthpiece: How could I do that? How could I come home after?

—I'm sorry I hit you, but all this stress. Grandma.

—I know, Mom. I know what I am. Lee told me.

When at last she spoke there was a tremor in her voice: You don't know anything.

—Yes, I do. I do. But it's not your fault. How can it be?

— . . . Peter . . . Oh Jesus. Would you just come home?

—I can't do that yet. I can't. I'll call you tomorrow.

The call ended.

He passed Caroline as he was coming out of the office. Caroline said his name. She looked like she was weighing her words.

—Are you good to work Christmas Eve?

—Yeah.

—Noon till close. Maybe eleven or midnight, depending.

—Okay.

—Good.

They were busy for the next hour. When finally there was a lull, Duane ambled over, drawing tobacco out of his chew tin.

—Do you want some of this?

—Have I ever? said Pete.

But he took a pinch of tobacco out of the tin. He saw Duane's eyebrows lift under his toque. Pete tucked the chew behind his lip. The flavour of burnt cherry was not unpleasant but instantly his head was spinning like it would lift off his shoulders. His mouth filled with juices. Duane offered a Styrofoam cup for him to spit into. Pete tried to hold his head steady.

—Don't whatever you do swallow it, said Duane. Let it do its work for you. Anyway, man, your face.

There were fresh bruises on Pete's face from the night before. His ear was a little swollen. Nobody had said anything yet.

—I fell down the stairs.

—Look, if you got trouble with anybody, don't be too proud, right? Let me know.

Pete spat again. All the colours and sounds were too vivid.

—Thanks.

—Don't be too proud, Pete.

Over the next two days, he made himself somewhat comfortable at the Shamrock. Down in the tavern the food was not bad. He ordered a steak. He ordered a beer as well but the barman just laughed and poured him a ginger ale. Pete sat eating his steak. The only Christmas decoration in the tavern was a plastic Santa Claus in the corner. There were six or seven other people at the bar or at tables, keeping to themselves, smoking. There was an older woman who reminded him of a thinner version of Lee's lady friend, with the red-painted lips and big hair, and Pete wondered what it would be like to take her up to his room and do things with her.

In the late evening he watched the television until he fell asleep. It was the only thing that could really dull his thoughts.

On Monday morning Pete stood in the shower before he went to work. Parts of his head and face still hurt. His work clothes were piled on the vanity. They'd need to be laundered soon. Somebody came into the bathroom and used the urinal and went back out. Pete didn't give that much thought until he'd dried off and dressed and was heading downstairs to pay the clerk for another night. He discovered his wallet wasn't in his pocket. He went back up and checked the room, checked the few possessions he had with him. His wallet wasn't up there either.

He found that fury and helplessness were almost indistinguishable. All the more so for the desk clerk's impassivity.

—Did you get a look at the guy through the shower curtain? So should I call the cops to just turn the whole place upside down? I feel for you, kid, but what do you want me to do?

—God fucking dammit, said Pete. All the cash I had was in my wallet.

At least he still had his car key. He sat in his car in the small lot next to the hotel. He felt like crying.

At lunch, Caroline sat at her desk. Pete stood across from her. Caroline nodded slowly. She said: Well, I can't say I'm real surprised. But can we talk about it again after New Year's? Fix a date then?

—Yeah, said Pete. We can do that.

—You work hard, Pete. It'll be a shame.

She made motions to signify that their business was concluded, but he stayed.

—Was there something else, Pete?

—I just wondered if I could use the phone for a second.

—Yeah, of course you can.

She left him to it. He called home and was mildly surprised that it was Barry who answered.

—Peter?

—Hi, Barry.

—Peter, it's good to hear your voice. I've been doing a lot of thinking. I thought about Colossians, and how it says if anyone has a quarrel against anyone else, as Christ forgave so should we. I've been thinking about that.

—Oh yeah?

—There's an open door here for you, Brother Pete. You know that. Your mother—

—Barry, I know. Look. I'll be home tonight.

He'd been out on one of his town walkabouts. He'd stopped at the Brewers' Retail and picked up a case of beer and he'd bought smokes as well and had come up the stairs with the beer under his arm. He put his key into the lock only to find his door already open.

Gilmore was sitting on the corner of the pullout, watching the television. He looked up, smiled.

—Lee. Don't block up the doorway, pal.

Lee heard his toilet flushing. Maurice came out of the bathroom. Lee took measured steps into the kitchenette. He set the beer on the counter.

—How did you get in here?

—You left your door unlocked, said Maurice. You don't remember?

Lee closed the door.

—Did the landlord see you?

—That old slant? said Maurice. He didn't see nothing. And yeah, I could drink a beer.

Lee took a beer out of the box and gave it to Maurice. Maurice took it and prised up the ring-tab with his finger. The sound of the can opening was clear even over the TV. Maurice drank and Lee watched his throat move.

Lee tried to be casual. He went over and took hold of the swivel chair at the window. He moved it forward as if he might sit across from Gilmore—but he didn't sit, not yet.

—I get the feeling you didn't just come to say hello.

—The time's come, Lee, said Gilmore.

—What time?

—We talked about opportunities.

—I told you.

—Sure you did. But it's in your voice, Lee. In the way you say it. I can hear it as plain as anything. Look around. You think you fit?

—Are you making rent this month? said Maurice.

—What business is it of yours?

Gilmore leaned forward, elbows on his knees: We're your friends, Lee. We're the people who know what a solid guy you are.

Lee squeezed his hands together. He breathed: So what is it? What are you talking about?

Gilmore leaned back. He smiled at Maurice, Maurice who was looking at Lee. And Gilmore told him what the business was. Not the specifics, but enough.

He did not say which bank it was exactly. Not how they'd studied it, but how long they had studied it, which was several months. Watching, waiting. It would be done overnight. No requirement, he said, for ugliness. No requirement to stick hardware in anybody's face. No requirement to rush the job. He spoke of all the cash being turned around this time of year, laid up in deposits from stores. When? Christmas Eve. The day after is a holiday. Won't anybody have an idea about it till we've been and gone. Forty-eight hours will have passed.

—Jesus, said Lee. I have no idea about any of this. I was never a bank man.

—And you don't need to be. All you've got to be is the six. All you've got to do is keep your eyes open and keep your cool. What you're good at. We'll do the heavy lifting.

The take would be more and more than enough. There'd be no requirement for ugliness. And you will eat the labour of your hands.

—Why? said Lee. Why now?

—Because the time has come. I've been sitting on my ass in this town since March and now the time has come. One night of work. That's all.

—And what, you just came around thinking I'd agree?

—You already agreed, Lee. You've been in agreement for a long time. All the time you spend walking the streets. Doing nothing for anybody. What that is, is you throwing your lot in. You know it.

Lee sat down at last. His hands formed patterns on the tops of his thighs. He thought about the air in the room and how it moved and was recycled man to man. He watched Maurice cross the floor and stand by the window, lift the dirty blinds, glance down at the street. The fading daylight was ashen.

—One night of work, said Gilmore.

Lee looked at them, one to the next. He looked at them for a long time. Then it was in the motion of his head, however slight. All things came to that.

Gilmore leaned forward again.

—Say it.

—Say what.

—Say the words, pal.

—You want me to say it?

—Call me old-fashioned but there's a certain thing about a verbal contract.

He flexed his hands. He could feel his pulse right down to the balls of his feet.

—Fuck it, said Lee. Everything. Yes.

—Good to hear, pal.

Gilmore offered a handshake. Maurice gave Lee a phone number on a scrap of paper.

—Call us tomorrow.

Lee nodded. He put the scrap of paper into his billfold, next to the business card with Stan Maitland's number on it. That encounter seemed to have happened to a different man altogether.

—It's good, said Gilmore. How you've thrown your lot in. Soon you'll find yourself a man of means. Give that some thought.

—The rest will happen fast, said Maurice.

His visitors did not remain for much longer. It was better that they did not linger. It would introduce doubt and they must have known it. As surely as they'd known what his response would be.

He went to the hospital, up to the Amiens Wing. He was making his way down the corridor, conscious of his steps, conscious that things were happening, when the older of the two little boys ran down the hallway ahead, coming from the direction of the washrooms. The boy did not see Lee. The boy ran through the door of Irene's room.

Lee came to the door. It was open six inches or so. He looked through the narrow space. Donna and Barry and the two boys. Irene wearing a respirator. He watched them and he remained unseen. After a moment he turned and left.

Back at his apartment, he looked at the model kits he'd bought for the boys. The purchase was pre-emptive on his part, the invitation having never come, but he hadn't wanted to be caught empty-handed.

Not that it mattered now. He thought about stuffing the two bombers into the garbage can, but he couldn't bring himself to do that. He left them where they sat, and he got himself a drink and sat down to watch television.

But then he saw something that he had overlooked. The mark on the wall, some weeks old, from when he'd launched the beer can against it. He wetted a rag and scoured the mark. The scuff came out but an indentation remained.

He was tired, heavy in the bones. He'd walked to the hospital and back. This made him weary, but it wasn't the only thing.

Because Gilmore was right. All other considerations aside, Lee was tired because he was greatly relieved. Relieved to let go of these motions he'd been forcing himself through. Relieved to see that thing—that thing he couldn't name—stepping out of the dark once again, taking shape, letting him know he hadn't been forgotten.

It was clear now. Everything was clear.

FOUR

DECEMBER 1980 TO MAY 1981

On the afternoon of the twenty-fourth, there was a light snowfall. In the shallows of the lake the reeds were clenched by thin black ice. Stan went about his ablutions and put on his suit. When he entered the kitchen, he heard scratching on the back door. He opened it and Cassius came in. The dog's fur was crisp and cold. He padded over to the woodstove.

Stan put on his overcoat and galoshes and went out carrying the good leather shoes he would wear for the evening church service. The trees creaked overhead. Snow shrouded Edna's garden. There was nothing to say where she'd leaned over and died one morning. At times, it seemed she was something he could only grope for in the dark. Stan got into his truck.

At seven-thirty, Pete was parked in his car looking at the United Church. Snow wheeled down out of the sky. Pete sat until the last of the Christmas Eve churchgoers went through the door and then he waited a few minutes longer.

He would have to be back at the Texaco for nine o'clock. Caroline had given him two hours' leave. She'd asked why and he told her he was going to church, and she gave him a doubtful look but did not say anything further.

He'd made one stop before church, perhaps as a gesture of appeal. He did not know. He'd parked out front of the variety store. The light was on through the blinds in Lee's window. Pete got out of the car and went through the alley to the parking lot.

There was a big Dodge van parked close to the Dumpster. One of the side-view mirrors was wrapped with duct tape and part of the windshield was cracked. The hood of the van was open. A man was bent over the engine, working by flashlight.

Pete was about to go up to the apartment when he heard his name spoken. He turned and saw that it was Lee working on the van. Lee was shrouded inside his coat and he was holding a spark plug and a dirty rag. He was backlit by the flashlight, which was resting on top of the heater. Cigarette smoke lifted around him.

—When did you get a set of wheels? said Pete.

—I'm hanging onto it for a buddy of mine. What are you doing here?

—If you can believe it, I'm going to church.

—What are you doing that for?

—Emily is going to play piano for the service. I don't care. I want to hear her. If I have a chance to see her, I'll tell her I'm leaving town after New Year's.

—The time's come, has it.

—It has, said Pete.

Lee just nodded and said: What are you doing here?

—I was passing by . . . Look. I gave it a lot of thought. A lot of things are fucked up and . . . Well, they're just fucked up. I'm sorry about what I said, about why would you come back here and all that. I'm not the big man, Lee. I'm not anything at all. Anyway, I thought I'd see maybe if you weren't doing anything if you might want to come along when I go see Emily. Maybe you can keep me from making an ass of myself.

Lee drew on his cigarette. He turned the spark plug in his fingers and worked it with the rag.

—Go away, Peter. I don't want to go to church.

—Lee—

—Listen, don't come around here no more. You don't have to be sorry for what you said because you were right. I am no good, and it was stupid of me to come back here. If I can get my shit together, I'm not going to stay much longer, either. For now, the best thing is if we just stay out of each other's way. I don't want anything to do with you. With any of you. Do you hear me?

Pete stood for a moment. He felt cold right to his bones. Then, without thinking of anything he could say he turned to go. Lee had already bent back over the van's engine.

The encounter was still stinging him as he went into the church. The entryway was vacant. Through the doors into the sanctuary, he could hear "Good King Wenceslas" being played on the organ.

He went through the doors and found himself at the back, behind all the rows of pews. The place was crowded. In the pews closest to the front, he could see the shoulders of suits and evening dresses, of coiffed hair, of perms, the well-to-do families. In the middle pews were the elderly, mostly blue-haired women, sitting upright and dignified. And in the pews at the back were the meagre and the odd. Some were families. Some were single mothers. There were children with cold sores and bad haircuts. There was a weird little drunk Pete had often glimpsed collecting empty bottles to take back for the deposit.

He moved up a few rows and sat in an empty spot beside a lone man in a ski jacket who was gazing at the floor. At the front of the sanctuary, Pete could see the organ pit and the organist, and next to the organ on a riser was a baby grand shining brightly.

It did not take long to spot her family. They were near the front. He could see the back of her parents' heads and Stan Maitland's thick white hair. And closest to the aisle, Emily herself, her dark hair, long and straight. The shoulders of her cardigan.

The service commenced with a choral procession. The choirs wore red and white gowns and came down the aisles. Their voices rose: *Through the cloven skies they come with peaceful wings unfurled . . .*

The choirs passed by at his elbow, adult child adult child. A fat man in his gown went past and behind him was Louise Casey. Pete could hear her soft soprano. She saw him seeing her, then she passed by. He watched her go. He saw Emily's face turn to smile at her sister, but she did not turn enough to see Pete at the back.

The minister came behind the choirs. He sang in a warbling baritone, not quite in tune. The choirs moved into their lofts and the minister took the pulpit. He spread his arms and said: Welcome all, on this holiest of nights. This was the night when the shepherds keeping watch over their flocks were visited by an angel who said to them, Do not be afraid. I bring you good news . . .

The minister led them through some readings and prayers, calling on the Lord to remember the sick and the poor. Christmas is so joyous, he said, for so many. And so hard for so many others. The congregation sang some of the old carols: "It Came Upon a Midnight Clear" and "The First Noel."

Pete stood and held a battered red hymnal at his waist. He sang perhaps every fifth word, hummed through the rest. Instead of a sermon, there was a re-enactment of the nativity. Children in the costumes of barnyard animals, in brown housecoats with shepherd's crooks, in wire-frame angel's wings. A young couple also in brown housecoats, with dun-coloured scarves over their heads, came down the aisle. They carried a sleeping baby. When they approached the altar, a child playing the part of the innkeeper turned them to the side. The child boldly waved his finger. The young couple went among the animal costumes and crouched down awkwardly. Joseph's forehead was shining beneath the scarf. They were visited by the shepherds, pantomiming their wonder. They were visited by three children in purple bathrobes and plastic crowns, the Magi, bearing gift-wrapped boxes to lay before the baby. The baby woke and started to bawl. His mother smiled nervously.

—Behold the King of Kings, said the minister.

The couple took their crying baby out of the sanctuary and the costumed children went to rejoin their families in the pews. Pete thought about Galilee Tabernacle, what would be going on there. They had a Christmas Eve service as well, and usually also re-enacted the nativity. Pete himself had been in the re-enactment a few times when he was younger. One Christmas, when he was ten or eleven, he'd played the Angel of the Lord, speaking to the shepherds. He was vaguely amused by the memory. This time last year, he'd been sitting with his mother and grandmother and his little brothers while Barry led the worship. What had he been thinking about? Maybe he'd been stealing glances at Sheila Adams, as he was stealing glances at Emily now. Without question, he'd known himself to be just as much an outsider there as he did here.

Next in the United Church service was a candlelight communion. The lights in the sanctuary were dimmed, and then Emily was going up to the front. She took a seat on the bench of the baby grand. She started to play slowly, "O Holy Night." She moved slightly as she worked the keys, her shoulders and her head sliding forward and back, her feet moving on the pedals. The notes were bold and strong. As the music built there was movement up at the front. Church ushers moved into the aisles, passing out white candles. Following the ushers came the minister. He was carrying a lit candle and was using it to pass the flame along to the candles of the congregants closest to the aisle, who in turn would pass the flame to their neighbours. Small points of light fanned out through the choir loft and through the sanctuary. Behind the minister came two more ushers carrying the collection plate. All the while the piano melody climbed. The lead usher came to Pete and offered a slender unlit candle.

—Peace be with you, said the usher.

Instead of taking the candle, Pete stood up and looked once more to the front. Then he turned from the usher and went back down the aisle to the doors.

He was about to go down to the street when someone said his name.

Stan Maitland was sitting on a deacon's bench against the entryway wall. Pete hadn't noticed the old man leaving the sanctuary.

—Mr. Maitland.

—You're not going to stay to the end of the service?

—Well, I could ask you the same thing.

Stan sat back against the wall and smiled. He said: We're both a couple of truants. I slipped out five minutes ago.

—It was warm in there, said Pete. A lot of people.

—I started out Catholic, said Stan. I was an altar boy. If I think hard I believe I can still say the rosary in Latin and French both. But my wife, before she was my wife, when I first took a shine to her, this was her church. She taught Sunday School and she played piano for the choir. Thirty years she played. They named a room after her . . .

—Emily talked about her a few times. Said she learned to play from her grandmother.

—Yes, that's true. Her grandma knew she had it right from the beginning.

—You missed hearing her tonight.

—It was too hot in there for an old bastard like me. If you want to know, Pete, a good many Christmases I used to work. A lot of Christmas Eves. I always thought it was a funny night to work, a funny kind of night for people to get up to this or that.

Pete put his hand on the newel post at the top of the banister. He wanted the relief of the cold outside.

—Well, Mr. Maitland—

—One time on Christmas Eve we got a call to a car accident. This would of been 1960 or so. So I drove out there with Dick Shannon. This young fellow, he'd robbed a liquor store in another town. He'd made it all the way up here before he wrapped his car around a telephone pole.

—Was he okay?

—He shouldn't of been, but he was. He was thrown out of the car and into the snow and that had to be what saved him. He was pretty drunk when we got out there. He was sitting on the snowbank on the other side of the road. Just sitting there, having himself a Christmas Eve snort of Scotch. Watching.

—Watching what?

—Well, it was snowing that night, same as it is tonight. And this boy had a trunk full of stolen liquor. When he crashed the car, the liquor caught on fire, and then the upholstery in the car caught on fire, and then just about the whole car itself. When me and Dick got out there, strange as it might seem to you, I thought that was one of the prettiest things I ever saw. All that fire in the middle of the dark and the snowfall.

Pete looked down at his boots.

—I should get back to work.

—Careful driving.

—See you around, Mr. Maitland.

Lee was sitting at the bar in the Corner Pocket. He was on his third beer. A cigarette was perched on an ashtray before him.

Events were moving quickly. He'd spent much of the past two days in the storeroom at the roadhouse, where he'd been brought in on certain aspects of the plan. Gilmore had not been specific, but he'd let on he'd done other bank-jobs before, in the Maritimes, mostly in Quebec. He'd come to believe that daytime stickups ran too much risk. An overnight job was how to go. Patience was his watchword. Lee had the sense that Gilmore had been laying low for a time. He also sensed that Gilmore wasn't even the man's real name, but what did that matter. Work was work.

Gilmore was the overall planner. Maurice was to take care of the internal alarm system, and provide heavy lifting when it was needed. What heavy lifting consisted of was not explained to Lee, but they'd told him again they did not foresee any trouble. Maurice was spending all of the twenty-fourth doing surveillance on the intended location. Speedy was to put his welding skills to the vault. They would go through the wall. Speedy was proud of this. He'd said with an oxygen lance he could cut through anything and, perhaps unconsciously, he'd touched the scar on his face.

And Lee. The eyes and ears. The six. The man for the odd jobs.

Much of the security of the plan rested on monitoring a police scanner and on watching the street. They were to be three hours from start to finish. The police could be there in four minutes. If anything was coming, they were all to drop what they were doing and go their separate ways.

—Quickly but not running, Gilmore had said, you get it? If it's the street, you just go back down the alley and go home. If you're in the van, you just get out and leave it where it's at. Same thing. Split. We all go in different directions.

—And?

—And what? Wait. Keep quiet. Give it a few weeks. What nobody's doing, Lee, is any time. Nobody's going up.

Gilmore said there was ten thousand dollars in it for Lee, maybe twelve, maybe more. They would hit the deposit boxes, but there would also be cash in the vault that stores had deposited, last minute, before Christmas. He reminded Lee that it was the season of giving.

But the take would have to be moved first so it could be laundered before they divided it up. And here was the last piece. They weren't going to drive the take anywhere. At seven-thirty on Christmas morning, a friend of Gilmore's would land his Cessna Skywagon just outside, right down there on the ice. From there they would fly, all of them, with the take, to the lake country east of Maniwaki. And then by car to Montreal, where Gilmore knew some people. In Montreal they would get the take laundered, see what was happening on the news, and then split up. After that, Lee could take the first-class coach on the passenger train. Gilmore wanted to know if Lee had ever done that, taken first-class anywhere?

Lee drank his beer and asked the barman for another. He had still not been told what bank it was going to be.

Earlier that day, Lee had surprised himself by sleeping in, dreamlessly, waking late in the morning. An hour after he'd finished his breakfast there was a knock on his door. His visitor was the same young man he'd met before, the man whose wheelchair-bound mother had given them the canvas duffle bag.

The man had a Datsun crew-cab in the parking lot. They got in and drove wordlessly to a garage in the industrial park on Douglas Avenue. Behind the garage was a fleet of various cars and trucks, mostly derelict. There was no one in the yard, but the back of the garage was open and Lee thought he spied some movement within.

The man parked the Datsun out front and he and Lee walked around to the back, where the cars and trucks were.

—This is your place? said Lee.

—A friend of mine owns it.

—So you have something for me? said Lee.

—It's over here.

The man led Lee past a stripped car and a damaged pickup truck to a '74 Dodge B100 van. There was a crack in the windshield and one of the side-view mirrors was mended with duct tape. The van had been painted in a kind of matte grey that Lee associated with warships. Or institutions. The man opened the side door. One bench seat. A lot of space in the back.

—Just like Gilmore wanted, said the man.

Lee nodded. He lit a smoke and offered his pack. The man, watching him, took one and lit it. Then he opened the passenger door. The transmission was an automatic floor shifter. The upholstery was old blue vinyl.

—See the radio?

Set in the dash was the faceplate of an AM/FM radio.

—It's the scanner, said the man. We have the bands for the cops. I was sitting in here listening to the cocksuckers all morning.

The man showed Lee how the scanner was wired to its own battery, hidden at the back of the glovebox, so that it could be used while the engine was off. The rest of the van was in as good shape as it needed to be, but Lee thought he might have a look under the hood anyway, later, when there was nothing much else to do but wait. The man gave him the key.

Driving back to his apartment, Lee tried to determine how he felt, but he had no answer. The one thing he could be sure of was that there was nothing and no one he could invest his certainty in. He could only go forward, alone.

Lee ordered another beer. It was nine-thirty at night. He and the barman made idle conversation. For some reason Lee was thinking about how there'd always been cockroaches in his cell in the pen. He'd never been able to get rid of them.

Not much later Speedy came in through the back door.

—Hey, friend, pour me a drink. It's Christmas. I want to get right frigged up. I'm only kidding. I just came looking for Lee.

Lee paid for the beers he'd had. He had less than twenty dollars left to his name. He followed Speedy outside. Even at this relatively early hour the street was quiet. They walked to the variety store parking lot.

—There she is, said Speedy, looking at the van.

—The brakes are touchy but it speeds up better than I thought. I never drove automatic before.

—I'll drive. I know where we're going.

—Not to the North Star?

—No. We're done there.

They drove east on one of the side roads past the shopping mall. Speedy fiddled with the radio until Lee told him it had been replaced with the scanner.

—How long? said Lee.

—Fifteen minutes till we get there. Not long.

—No, how long did you know?

—How long did I know what?

—Speedy, do you have any fucking sense? How long did you know what Gilmore was planning?

—Oh. Well. Gilmore talked to me about it in August or thereabouts. He knew about me from around. When he heard I used to be a welder, he came to talk to me about the opportunity.

—August. How come it took so long?

—They needed the time to be just right. They were going to do it earlier, maybe September. But then this one night, after Labour Day, I was out there—the place we're going now, Arlene's uncle's old place—and some crazy little broad shows up and starts yelling at Gilmore. It was almost funny, Lee. She was mad as hell because I guess she'd found out about Arlene. Gilmore manages to talk this crazy broad down a bit, and he gets into her car with her, and off they go. Then I didn't see the boys for a week or two.

—Who was the girl?

—She was just some broad from town. Kind of had problems, I guess, but you wouldn't know that if you just saw her. She wasn't deformed or nothing. She worked at . . .

Lee saw Speedy was staring hard at the steering wheel.

—Where did she work, Speedy?

—Well, she was a cleaning gal at the bank. After hours. Gilmore would visit her at night sometimes.

—And what, she's not around no more?

—No. She was real upset about Arlene and Gilmore. She killed herself. Problems, Lee. Nice girl, but. Anyway, Gilmore and Maurice cooled it for a bit after that. They almost quit the whole idea. But then they started talking about it again. Maurice wanted to do it just three of us but Gilmore thought we needed one more. Around then was when I ran into you at the lumberyard. Funny how those things work out.

Lee watched the road through the dark before their headlights. During his first meeting with Lee, hadn't Wade Larkin mentioned something about a girl who'd killed herself? It had been a meaningless question then, but thinking about it now made Lee feel unsettled and strange. The thin snowfall glittered where the headlight caught it.

The grounds of the marina looked deserted when they arrived. Speedy had told Lee a little of the history, how the property belonged to Arlene's uncle who'd been in a care home for many years. Arlene used to visit when she was a kid but hadn't been here since. She'd known Gilmore in Montreal and they'd come out here in the spring, was all Speedy knew. He didn't have any idea how Maurice and Gilmore had come together.

In the dark, it was difficult to make out the lay of the property, but after they'd turned off the side road, they followed a long driveway hemmed in by pine trees. Then the headlights shone against a wood-frame storage shed on one side of the driveway and two camping trailers on the other, an Airstream and a Prowler. Speedy stopped the van in a small patch where the snow had been cleared. They got out. The land dipped sharply and a footpath led through the snow. Forty yards farther on, they came to a building perched on a headland over the lake.

The windows were boarded over but faint edges of light came through from inside.

The door in the back of the building opened. Gilmore stood there in silhouette. He was wearing a dark jacket and treaded boots. He said: Come in out of the cold, pals.

He led them through a storeroom to what had at one time been a general store and a small restaurant at the front of the building. There were four or five tables with chairs overturned on them. On one of the tables was a rusty metal tool box. There were wooden grocery shelves all stripped bare. There was a range and a round-top Kelvinator propane fridge. At the front of the restaurant, a pay telephone was mounted on the wall.

Two overhead lights were on. If nothing else, the place still had hydro. A space heater in one corner was pumping out warmth.

—You got the van? said Gilmore.

—I got the van.

—And the scanner?

—It works. I'll show you.

The telephone rang. It was an alien sound, startling. Gilmore looked at his watch. He looked at Lee.

—Take the call, Lee.

The phone rang a second time. Lee went and picked up the receiver. One of the front windows was unboarded. He could see himself in the dark glass.

—Hello?

A pause, then: Lee. It's Maurice. Is Gilmore there?

—He's right behind me.

A long hiss of static, and then Maurice said: Well, tell him there's nothing different.

—He says there's nothing different.

—Nobody's been there since they closed at four, said Maurice.

—Nobody's been there since four.

—Tell him to call again at midnight, said Gilmore.

Lee told him and Maurice said he would. After the call ended, Lee went back over to the table.

Gilmore said how Maurice had set himself up in a room on the fourth floor of the Shamrock Hotel. He'd been able to watch the bank and the alley behind it all day. Based on these details, Lee had a feeling that the bank they were going to was the National Trust—but so far, no one had said it outright.

—So what's next? said Lee.

—We load up.

Up in the storage shed, Gilmore showed them to a locker framed into the corner. He unlocked the padlock and opened the door. He turned the overhead light bulb to light up the enclosure and what it contained.

There was a canvas duffle bag packed with tools: crowbars, sledgehammers, a power drill with a concrete bit. A second duffle bag was packed with a welding mask and leather coveralls. There was a milk crate containing four Truetone walkie-talkies. The biggest part of their inventory was a homemade burning-bar rig. It consisted of a dolly with an oxygen cylinder strapped to it. Attached to the oxygen cylinder was a hose and a regulator and beside the dolly were five lances bundled together. They were made out of old salvaged iron pipes, each about four feet long, with one end threaded to fit the oxygen hose. The lances could be lit with a portable Victor torch set, the kind you might carry around in the back of a truck.

Lee looked at what was before him. These were tools and he was conscious of the surety in them, of their seriousness. Things were happening now as though they were always meant to happen this way.

They loaded the tools and the bags into the back of the van. The lances were very heavy. When they were finished they pulled a canvas drop cloth over the load.

Speedy went back into the shed as if he'd forgotten something. Gilmore was examining the scanner. Lee lit a cigarette and came around the front of the van and leaned beside the door.

—I suppose maybe you've seen the inside of this bank.

—You think we'd be moving on it otherwise?

Lee couldn't help but prod Gilmore a little further, he didn't know exactly why. He said: Did the cleaning girl show you in?

Gilmore drew slowly back from the scanner. He said: The cleaning girl.

—The one who killed herself.

—What happened to just watching, pal? Just being our eyes and ears?

Lee lifted his shoulders: I'm going into the shed. I don't have much love for the cold. When do we get going?

—Twelve-thirty, Lee. Rest up. You have all your questions answered?

—I just want to be sure what I'm dealing with. That's all.

When he went back inside the shed, he saw Speedy squatting in the middle of the dirt floor, oddly simian. He was doing something with his hands. Lee came up on him.

—Fucking Christ, said Lee. What is that for?

Speedy was pushing bullets into a magazine. A Browning 9mm automatic was balanced on his boot.

—Just for security is all, said Speedy.

Speedy was talking quickly. He fumbled a bullet on the top of the magazine and it bounced on the frozen dirt below. He retrieved it and pushed it at the top of the magazine but it wouldn't load. He looked contritely upwards at Lee.

—I think she's full.

The Texaco had not had a customer in close to two hours. In the store the radio was playing "O Come, All Ye Faithful."

Duane was into a car magazine. Pete was looking at the newspaper. Caroline came out from the office with a mickey of rum and a carton of eggnog. She put them on the counter and she mixed three drinks in paper cups.

Outside they heard Jake Brakes, and through the snowfall they saw the lights on the back of a bobtail rig that was slowing down at the edge of the apron. But the rig didn't pull up to the pumps. They heard its air brakes squeak and then heard it gear up again. The lights moved off towards the highway.

—Gentlemen, said Caroline. How about a Christmas cheer?

—Fuckin' A, said Duane.

She swatted his hand. They each took a cup and raised it.

Then the door opened and a small figure came in, bundled in a hooded coat. The snow on her shoulders was already melting. She pulled the hood down and smiled.

—Hey, Pete.

Pete was slow to reply: Emily . . . It's almost midnight.

—I hitched a ride with a trucker.

Pete and Duane and Caroline all looked at each other.

—How come everybody thinks I was born yesterday? said Emily. Jeez. What I would like, if you don't mind, is something to drink. I'll pay for it.

—No you won't, said Caroline. Come on, have a cheers.

Caroline poured another drink and Emily came and sat with them. She put her coat onto the stool beside her. She was still wearing the cardigan he'd seen her wearing at the church. Her snow boots came up to her knees.

—Merry Christmas.

They raised their glasses. Emily reached over and took Pete's hand. Her fingers were cold but he could feel the blood pulsing back into them.

They stayed only for the time it took to drink the eggnog and then Caroline told them to leave.

—Go on, she said. Duane and me'll close up.

—You sure? said Pete. Duane?

—Fuck you, Pete. Merry Christmas.

Pete warmed up his car first and then he drove them back into town. Emily closed her eyes as soon as she sat down, and she took his hand when it was not working the gearshift. Only when he'd stopped in front of her house did she come around.

—Park in that driveway, said Emily. The Jacksons' house, they're on vacation.

—Park?

—We're not staying in the car, Pete.

He drove to a house a few down from hers. Several inches of snow had accumulated.

—Aren't your folks home?

—Of course they are. It's Christmas Eve. But it's the one night a year my dad relaxes. He had three rye and Cokes after church and he was sound asleep by nine-thirty. My mom went to bed at ten. And anyways, she's on my side. She sees what my dad doesn't. Come on.

They entered her house quietly. The living room was dark except for the lights on the Christmas tree. They went down into Emily's bedroom. The reading lamp was on. She had him sit down on the corner of the bed and she went out and closed the door behind her. He looked at a portrait of her grandmother she had on her desk. When she came back into the room, she was carrying two mugs of hot chocolate. She gave him one and she kissed him and she sat down in a rocking chair.

—I saw you play piano at your church tonight, said Pete. I wanted to stay and talk to you but I left before it was over.

—I know. Grandpa and my sister both said you were there. I had to see you, Peter. I had to talk to you. I'm sorry for how it all happened. But I can't stop thinking about you.

Pete put the mug down between his knees. It was difficult to look her in the eye. He said, quietly: Do you know about me?

—I know now. My dad knows. He told my mother. He thinks he has to shelter me from these things. True things. But like I said, my mother understands.

Shame flowed through him. He closed his eyes, said: She told you . . .

—Yes. She said it's why your mom moved to North Bay to have you, why you lived there for a few years. But, look . . . none of that is what makes you who you are now. It's just where you came from. You're a good person.

He took a deep breath and opened his eyes again. He said: Did you hear what happened at Nancy's house?

—Ha, yes I did, said Emily. Nancy and I aren't speaking much these days, but Samantha was there. She couldn't wait to tell me about it, how you came in by yourself, walked straight into the back room, and beat the hell out of all of them.

—It didn't exactly happen like that. I'm surprised I made it out of there in one piece.

—I'm surprised it didn't happen sooner. I hope you won't think I'm terrible if I say Roger Amos might have finally got what he deserved.

—I guess so, said Pete. It was stupid. I wasn't thinking straight. It was the same day . . . I found out about myself.

—You really never knew, did you.

—No.

She put her hot chocolate on the corner of the desk. She leaned forward and took his face in her hands. She kissed him again. Her mouth was soft and warm. She withdrew and sat back in the rocking chair.

—What went wrong with us? said Pete. Was it finding out about me?

—I don't care about that, Pete. Look. For a long time I've felt like I was done with school and everybody here in town. It's too small here. People are too small, you know? I fast-tracked this semester and I'm going to go to university in the fall. A year early. We looked at the university while we were in the city. We saw the music college and met the dean. It's amazing there, Pete. It's everything I want. That's what the problem was. It reminded me I didn't want to care about anybody. I wanted to be able to get up and leave. I thought if I got away from you it would make it easier. But I was wrong. I've been thinking about you the whole time.

—It's strange that you say that. One time you asked me what my plan was. Do you remember?

—Yes. You wouldn't tell me.

—Tonight I came to your church to do just that, to tell you. But I didn't know how, so I left. Anyway, since I quit school I've been planning to go out west. As far as I can. Right out to the ocean, I guess. Because I know what it's like to feel like it's too small here. I've known that for a long time. I told them at work that I was going to leave after New Year's. But, now, with you . . . I don't know what to do. I don't know anything.

—I don't know either. But . . . let's think about that later. It doesn't matter for now. It's just good to be with you again.

They were quiet for a little while. Then Emily asked him, gently, how, exactly, he'd found out about his past. She quickly added that he didn't need to talk about it if he didn't want to, but he realized that he did. He said: Well, I kind of dragged it out of my uncle last Friday. He was drunk. He probably wouldn't have told me otherwise, and I think now that I put a lot on him when I got him to tell me. I've only seen him one time since, and it was earlier tonight. He told me to stay away. He's drinking again, and he's out of work, and he told me the truth about my life. So I know he's on the outs with my mom and Saint Barry. I know how they are.

—Didn't you tell me it was Barry who got him set up here? Got him a job and everything?

—That's true, said Pete. But I think Barry sees angles in things like that. There's an old drunk I see downtown sometimes. I think

I saw him at your church tonight. He goes around with a shopping cart and picks up empty bottles to take back for the deposit. I think Barry is kind of like that. His old bottles are the Lees of the world.

—Barry seems to be doing more than most people, who barely ever give a shit in the first place. I love my dad, I do, but if he had his way, people like your uncle would never ever get out of jail.

—Well, I don't know what I think about that, either. This is what makes it hard about Lee. I want to be on his side again, and I wish I could tell you that I am . . . But I don't know. I just don't know.

She leaned forward and said: You should give him another chance. And more importantly, you should give yourself a chance, Pete. No matter what, there are lots of people who love you.

—I'll be alright, said Pete. Things can't get much more fucked up than they are now. Maybe they're already looking up.

They finished their hot chocolates. She stood up and took his mug and put it on the desk, and then she sat down on his lap and kissed him deeply. They broke apart. Pete touched her hair.

—I guess your dad would kill me if he knew I was here.

Emily grinned: You and me both, buddy.

—Well, maybe I should go.

—Do you want to?

—No, said Pete. Not at all.

—Good.

She kissed him again. She settled her hips against his. He hadn't thought it possible to be rid of the shame and uneasiness, but as she moved on top of him, he started to forget everything. Even if it was just for now. He was trembling all over.

She got up and went over and stood beside her bed, looking him in the eye. She unbuttoned her blouse, and then she reached up under her skirt and drew down her nylons and panties and stepped out of them. She lay down across the bed and reached out to him.

They were back in town shortly after one o'clock in the morning. It had to be the National Trust they were hitting. Lee was sure of that. They drove past Woolworths and past the cheerless frontage of the Shamrock, where the tavern was still open. Speedy turned the van at the bottom of the street and then doubled back up a laneway behind the buildings. The parking lot behind the bank was closed in on one side by a line of poplars and on the other side by a loading dock. A windowless steel man-door was set in the back wall of the bank. Speedy parked the van against the poplar trees. Gilmore switched on the scanner. They waited, listening.

There was little talk on the scanner. Some cop reported he was returning to the detachment. The dispatcher acknowledged. The words were dense with static.

They'd been there about fifteen minutes when they saw Maurice coming up the laneway. Gilmore looked at his watch. Maurice crossed over to the van. He opened the passenger door. Gilmore nodded to him.

—What a shitbag dump that hotel is, said Maurice. I didn't see nothing down here all night.

—Good. Let's go.

They distributed the walkie-talkies and tested them. Speedy was sent down the alley where he could watch the street. They waited. Then Speedy's voice rasped out of the walkie-talkies.

—Come in, boys. I'm watching the street.

Gilmore told him to check in again every fifteen minutes.

Maurice got into the driver's seat and backed the van across the parking lot right against the wall of the bank. They turned the ignition off and listened to the scanner for five minutes. Then Gilmore got out. Maurice told Lee to get up behind the steering wheel. Gilmore had the side door open and was digging around in the tool bag. He came out with a can of Styrofoam on a spray gun. Maurice got out and boosted Gilmore up onto the roof of the van. His footsteps thumped above. Lee stuck his head out the window and angled the mended side-view mirror upward so that he could watch.

The bank's exterior alarm box was fixed to the wall five feet above the back door. Gilmore, standing on top of the van, fed the spray gun's nozzle through the grill of the box. He emptied the can. This was something he'd done before, Lee could see. When he was finished there was foam bulging out of the grill. The foam would hold the clapper fast so it couldn't strike the bell if the exterior alarm was tripped. Maurice, meanwhile, had drawn a crowbar out of the tool bag. He helped Gilmore come down and he told Lee to drive five feet forward.

Lee moved the van and put it into park. He turned it off and listened. The door at the back of the bank was directly behind the van and out of sight to him. Gilmore had come up to the passenger window. He stretched his legs as if preparing for a sport. He opened the door.

—How about a smoke, pal?

Lee gave him one. Five minutes later, Maurice came back, holding the crowbar in one hand.

—It's open.

Gilmore nodded.

—Let's go, Lee, said Maurice.

Lee got out of the van. The door at the back of the bank was open. It was dead black through the space. Up above he could see ridges of spray Styrofoam swollen out of the alarm box. He found that he was intensely aware of everything, of every sound, of the fabric of his clothes. Lee and Maurice hauled the burning-bar rig out and carried it into the bank. They lifted out the lances and moved them inside. Before they took out the tool bag, Maurice reached into it and dug for something. Gilmore came and leaned on the side of the van. He might have been passing the time of day.

—This is where it gets long. Maurice will work on the interior alarms now. Wait a few minutes and drive up to the corner. All you have to do is watch and listen.

Speedy checked in on the walkie-talkie and told them the street was still quiet.

Then Maurice had the tool bag over one shoulder and was moving away from the van. His big frame was moving with his breathing. He licked at one side of his mouth.

—We're going in now. Every fifteen minutes on the walkie. Don't fall asleep.

Lee saw that Maurice also had hold of a shotgun. The barrel had been cut down to just above the pump. Maurice saw Lee looking at it.

—Listen, Lee. Don't get the idea that me or Gilmore haven't worked this through. We got everything planned out. That includes you.

They studied each other.

—I'm here to work, said Lee. Make some money. That's all.

Maurice wordlessly followed Gilmore into the bank.

Lee closed the back doors of the van and got into the driver's seat. He moved the van back to the poplar trees. He parked it and turned the ignition off. He checked that the scanner was on. He checked the walkie-talkie. He looked at his hands on the steering wheel. The cold was settling into the vehicle. Lee looked out the window again. They'd left nothing in the parking lot and the falling snow had already begun to soften their tracks. The back door was closed. There was nothing to see but the buildings and the blanched night sky. He had a cigarette.

Some time passed and they did a check on the walkie-talkie. Speedy said he could use a cup of coffee. Maurice came back on, with a slight hiss of interference, and told Speedy to shut the fuck up.

A short while later there was some talk on the scanner. From what Lee could tell, a cop was following a drunk driver. Lee listened with some interest and he told the others over the walkie-talkie. It was good to have something to pay attention to. Before long, he interpreted that the drunk had been pulled over and arrested and a tow truck had been summoned. He checked in again on the walkie-talkie. And then he went back to waiting.

The driver's door opened and Lee sat up. He blinked, unsure of his whereabouts. Cold air swirled into the van. Maurice had the door open. The shotgun was pressed to the side of his leg where it wouldn't be noticed from a distance. He spoke in a hoarse whisper.

—Go spell off Speedy.

—What?

—I said go spell off Speedy. In the alley. I'm done with the alarm. Speedy's got to start cutting now.

—The plan was I was up here, said Lee.

—Yeah, well, so far you're the one getting the easiest ride. Besides, looks like you can't keep awake anyways.

After a moment Lee climbed down from the seat. Up close he could see the way Maurice's head was moving side to side. Maurice was gripping the shotgun tightly.

—Radio check when you're in place. Keep your eyes open.

—Whatever you say, buck.

Lee made his way down the alley beside the bank. The snowfall had eased and the new-fallen snow lay clean, faintly glittering. Close to the street there was a doorway recessed into the building on the other side of the alley. It was here that Lee found Speedy. Speedy's hands were buried in his pockets. His walkie-talkie was set on top of a garbage can he was sharing the space with.

—You're to start the cutting now, said Lee.

Speedy shuddered.

—Lee. Okay. I just about froze solid down here.

Speedy pulled his hands out of his pockets. He had his pistol in one hand. Lee kept an eye on it.

—How long will the cutting take?

—Hard to say. Might be two feet right through. A hundred years? I'm only kidding. But you might be here awhile.

—You better get going, said Lee.

—I'll see you soon.

—Don't forget your radio.

Speedy took his walkie-talkie and went back up the alley. Lee checked in on his own walkie-talkie. He said he was in place and watching the street.

The lights had been turned off in the tavern up at the Shamrock. Lee looked down the street in the other direction. About two hundred yards away the street ended underneath a pulsing stoplight. He was a ten- or fifteen-minute walk from his apartment.

He hunkered back into the doorway and put his walkie-talkie down on the garbage can.

There was no wind, but it wasn't long before a chill began settling into Lee's extremities. His toque was pulled low and his collar was turned up. He moved on his feet. He kicked at the wall. It occurred to him that he could just turn out of the doorway and leave. That simple. But leave to what? To what purpose?

He lit a cigarette and watched the smoke go out before him. It dissolved in the still air.

At four in the morning, a patrol car moved past the alley. Lee lurked in the dark, watching the car stop outside the Shamrock. He was aware of everything again, of the close proximity of the concrete walls on either side of him. He lifted the walkie-talkie from the garbage can and spoke into it.

—I got a bull out here.

Maurice's voice came back: What do you see?

—One car. Stopped up at the hotel.

Gilmore's voice: Wait. Just watch them for a minute.

Lee had been fatigued before this. Now he was awake and aware of how cold he was. He turned down the volume on the walkie-talkie so it was just audible.

—There's nothing on the scanner, said Maurice. What is it, just one car?

—Yes.

—One, two cops, we can take care of if they come around back here.

Lee was going to say something. He pressed the send button on the walkie-talkie. But he said nothing. He moved the fingers of his other hand to get the blood flowing.

—Lee?

—Wait.

The patrol car moved again. Nobody had gotten out of it. The car climbed the rise. Lee watched it till it was out of sight. He counted to five and then to ten.

—They're gone now. They were just looking at the hotel.

—Keep watching, said Maurice. I want to know if anybody's coming back this way.

Lee wanted a cigarette, but his fingers in the gloves were too clumsy with cold. He put the walkie-talkie down. He pulled his gloves off and put his hands down the front of his pants. He pressed his fingers between his thighs. His fingers throbbed when at last the blood moved back into them.

Maurice called him on the walkie-talkie five minutes later to ask if the cops had come back, and Lee told him they had not. Ten minutes after that he put the walkie-talkie down on the garbage can. He ventured out to the front of the alley again.

Then he went out onto the sidewalk. He looked in either direction. Down street of him, the stoplight blinked like some endless portent. Without giving it much thought, he wandered out into the middle of the street and stood where the patrol car had left its tire tracks. He thought the end of the world might look something like this. Undramatic. Just emptied out. And he, the last man.

He went back into the alley, thinking his solitary thoughts.

The walkie-talkie was speaking, urgently but hushed because he'd lowered the volume. Lee picked it up and said he was listening.

Maurice: Lee, where the fuck have you been?

—I didn't hear you.

—Get back here. We're packing up.

He came into the parking lot, stiff with the cold. He could see Maurice loading the tool bag into the van. Speedy was in the driver's seat.

—Go in, said Maurice. You'll see the way. Quick. Sixty seconds.

Lee put the walkie-talkie into his pocket and went through the back door into the bank.

It was black through the door. There was a powerful stink of burnt things. He saw a flashlight flick twice, quickly, up ahead, offering just enough light to reveal the dimensions of a hallway. It was Gilmore. Coming close to him, Lee could sense the man laden with something. A duffle bag, perhaps, thick with contents.

—Take the flashlight. Go up around the corner and don't turn the light on till you're there. You'll see where to go. There's three more bags. Make it quick.

He took the flashlight from Gilmore and felt his way around a corner. He turned the flashlight on. He was in an office. To his left was the wall where the door to the vault was set. The door was untouched. They'd cut the hole beside it. He could see where they'd pulled the carpeting back so the molten concrete slag from the cutting would pool only on the subfloor. The hole itself was roughly three feet square. Everything around and above it was burnt, up to the ceiling tiles. Smoke was still dense in the room. If the interior alarm hadn't been successfully cut, Lee wondered who would have arrived first, the cops or the fire department.

The leather welding apron had been laid over the bottom of the cut. As Lee folded himself through, he could still feel heat baking off the concrete. The wall of the vault was eighteen inches thick. Where the rebar had been cut, the metal still had a cherry glow, and he was careful not to touch it. He prodded his foot down onto the rubble inside the vault. The air was almost unbreathable with smoke.

He stood up and shone the flashlight around the vault. There was smoke damage all over the ceiling. Dividing the vault in half was a barred gate but they'd hammered that open. He saw a metal table and floor-to-ceiling safe deposit boxes. Most of the boxes had been smashed open and pillaged. He saw old family photographs strewn about the floor, documents, deeds, promissory notes, insurance policies. He saw a broken urn, someone's ashes spilled out of it. The three remaining duffle bags were in the middle of the floor, stuffed full.

—Lee, goddammit. You got to move quicker.

Behind him Maurice was crouched on the other side of the hole.

Lee grabbed the first bag. Whatever it was packed with was dense and irregular and heavy. He pushed it through the hole. Maurice pulled it out of the way. Lee pushed the second bag to him. He went back for the last bag and then he looked over his shoulder. Maurice had his shotgun butt-down on the floor with the barrel canted forward through the hole.

—How about you get that gun out of the hole, said Lee.

—What? How about you hurry the fuck up.

—Maybe I don't like how you have that thing pointed.

—This isn't a goddamn game.

—I know.

But Maurice moved the shotgun out of the hole.

Lee hauled the third duffle over and pushed it through. He followed it as quickly as he could. All was dark except where the two flashlights lanced about like phantoms.

Maurice spoke close to Lee's ear: This is not a goddamn fucking game, Lee.

Lee hoisted a bag up over each shoulder. He could feel Maurice watching him. He switched off the flashlight and went back the way he'd come. The door was a faint outline up ahead and he was conscious of how much of his back was exposed to the man behind him. But he got outside without incident. Nothing had changed in the parking lot.

Maurice came out. He had the shotgun in his right hand and the last duffle bag in his left. The back door of the bank closed evenly in its frame, so that its breach would not be readily apparent. They crossed the parking lot towards the van. The engine started. In the haze of the brake lights he saw Gilmore hop out to open the back of the van. He and Maurice dropped the bags into the space behind the seat. The tool bag and the burning-bar rig were already packed under the drop cloth. They closed the doors. Maurice went ahead of Gilmore and got in the back seat. The van started to move forward.

That was it. All it had ever been.

Lee stood dumbly, watching them leave.

Then the van stopped. The back door opened, Maurice's face hung halfway out: Get in, Lee, get in the fucking front. What are you waiting for?

Lee jogged up and opened the passenger door and got in. He hadn't even closed the door before they were moving again. Lee looked up once and in the rear-view mirror he could see Gilmore and Maurice in the back. Maurice with the shotgun on his lap.

—What did you think? said Speedy. We were leaving you back there?

—Speedy, said Maurice. Shut the fuck up till we get back.

Lee said nothing. He took a cigarette out of his pack and lit it. He had three cigarettes remaining.

Pete woke up and saw by Emily's alarm clock that it was five o'clock in the morning. He pulled himself away from her warm body. When he'd finished dressing, she stirred and took his hand. She put it to her breast and he felt the nipple harden.

—Pete? Can I see you maybe this afternoon or tomorrow?

—I'd like that.

—Me too.

He made his way back up through the house and slipped out noiselessly. The sky had cleared and the stars were profuse. The branches creaked on the maples above and the snow underfoot hadn't been disturbed. He stole down the street to his car and let it heat up as he brushed off his windshield. He got into the driver's seat. He could still smell Emily on his fingers. He drew in the scent deeply.

He took the long way through downtown. The heater pumped out heat and the radio was on. It was well before dawn yet. He felt better. He passed the dark front of the National Trust and passed the Shamrock Hotel. He laughed a little. The few days he'd spent in the hotel seemed a long time ago.

He drove up Harris Avenue. He was coming to the intersection where the Union Street bridge crossed over the river and carried on to the highway bypass. The light turned red. He slowed down and stopped. He yawned. The radio told him to have a happy holiday and Pete drummed on the steering wheel.

Then he saw the van pass in front of his car, the van with the mended side-view mirror and the crack on the windshield. The van had the right-of-way at the intersection and it turned onto the bridge up ahead. Pete watched a cigarette butt come sparking out from the passenger-side window, over the guardrail, and down onto the frozen river.

They passed a handful of other vehicles on their way back to Indian Lake. Headlights appeared, bore down on them, and passed. When they arrived at the property, the lights were on in the Airstream. Speedy brought the van to a stop next to the shed. Arlene's hatchback was parked a few feet ahead.

They opened the van and got out. The door of the Airstream was open now and in the warm light they could see Arlene in silhouette, holding a robe around herself. She raised a hand.

—Do you think I'm glad to see you or what?

—Get your ass back in the bedroom, said Gilmore. I got something to give you.

—Oh, big talk.

Gilmore feigned a charge at the Airstream and Arlene scampered back inside, pulling the door shut behind her. Gilmore came back to the van.

—How about a cigarette, Lee.

In the dark, any man was just a shape bearing faint edges of ambient light. It was a moment before Lee said anything. His voice was pitched low: One of mine?

—Well, who else is the chain-smoker here? Tell you what, I'll buy you a deck or two in Montreal.

Lee offered his pack and Gilmore took one of the last three.

—I could go with one, said Speedy.

Lee gave Speedy his second-last and then took the last for himself. The cigarettes were lit and the smoke smelled good in the cold air.

There was work to do yet. Lee smoked half of his cigarette and then butted it on the side of the van. He put the remaining half back in his pack. He could not put any trust in words so he submitted to what he was told to do. They moved the tool bag and the burning-bar rig back into the locker in the corner of the shed. The five duffle bags they'd hauled out of the vault were moved through the doorway of the Airstream into a small galley. Arlene was leaning on the wall. Her robe was silk with Chinese dragons patterned on it, frayed about the hem. She smiled as she watched them carry in the take. Lee had no idea what it amounted to.

They went out and stood by the van. The airplane was to arrive before eight o'clock. Gilmore had spoken to his friend the day before and all was well, but if the plane did not arrive by nine, they would go north in the van. In the meantime that meant waiting.

Gilmore disappeared into the Airstream.

—You two can wait here, said Maurice. The van or the shed. There's no reason to go wandering around the property nowhere.

Speedy laughed: I don't know where the fuck we'd go.

Lee took out the remnants of his last cigarette and lit it.

—Lee? said Maurice.

Lee exhaled smoke.

—Lee, did you go deaf or something?

—I heard you, said Lee.

He opened the passenger door of the van and sat down. He looked at what was revealed by the starlight, looked at Maurice and Speedy moving into the shed. His last cigarette did not last long. He rolled down the window and pitched out the butt. If he closed his eyes he could see the van moving away in front of him.

He wondered if in times to come he might question whether things could have followed another direction. A short while later he shut his eyes.

The old dream: the concrete dark of the basement, the sight and sound of the coal furnace. The cripple with the spadeshovel. Only this time the cripple had a newer old face. Joe Holmes. The blood poured out of his side where he'd been stabbed with the screwdriver. He had the caretaker's limp. *You see how clear it is, don't you? Don't you see how clear it is?*

—

Lee was cold and stiff. The passenger door was open. The sun had not risen but the sky had lightened. Speedy was shaking him awake. He was stepping foot to foot, agitated, prodding the air with his 9mm.

Lee shot his hand forward and grabbed Speedy's wrist: What the fuck is wrong with you?

—Lee.

—Is the airplane here?

—Lee.

He let go of Speedy's wrist and pushed the man away. He said: Quit waving that fucking gun in my face.

—They got somebody here.

—They got what?

—Somebody here. Oh, man.

—A cop?

—Not a cop. They got a kid.

—A kid, said Lee.

He hopped down from the van.

—Just come and see, said Speedy. Oh, man. Arlene doesn't know nothing about it. She's still in the camper and Gilmore says—

Lee pushed past him. The equation was falling just short of a complete picture.

—Where is this kid?

—In the locker. Maurice was looking around, like keeping an eye open, and he finds this kid over by the trees . . .

They went into the shed, Lee leading. He crossed to the locker and pulled the door open. Gilmore was there. Maurice was a little deeper in, crouched down.

In the back corner of the locker they had him laid out on the floor, bound with duct tape around the ankles and wrists. Maurice reached out with the shotgun to prod the kid's ribs. The kid had a strip of duct tape over his mouth. His nose had been badly broken and was leaning sideways and both eyes were blackened and the top of his forehead had been split open, wide enough to show a pink slip of bone beneath. His face was curtained with blood.

When Maurice prodded him he shuddered. Maurice stood up. He said: Yeah, still ticking.

—What is this? said Lee.

Gilmore and Maurice turned back to look at him and Speedy. The expression on Gilmore's face was hard to interpret. Maybe vague distaste.

How could this be? How could *he* be here?

—What does it look like? said Maurice. While you thought you'd get yourself some goddamn sleep I went to watch our backs. And look what I found. Look what the fuck I found.

Lee worked moisture into his mouth: He doesn't look like nobody I know. Who is he?

—He's Peter, said Gilmore.

—Peter.

Gilmore pointed at the name embroidered on Pete's jacket.

—He didn't have a wallet on him, said Speedy.

—Peter, said Lee.

He saw Pete's eyes rolling in their purpled swells. The blood vessels of one cornea had all burst.

—Did he tell you anything? said Speedy.

—No, said Maurice. He doesn't have anything to say at all. Maybe you should get your torch going.

The eyes rolled.

—He's nobody I know, said Lee, and they looked at him.

He stepped backwards out of the locker. The other men resumed talking. Lee went across the floor to the tool bag and opened it and dug through it and came out with an eight-pound sledgehammer. He carried it mid-shaft in one hand and he went back into the locker. He shouldered his way between Speedy and Gilmore. He heard his name spoken. He pushed past Maurice and he stood above the kid.

—Lee, said Maurice.

Lee laid the sledgehammer over his shoulder and he leaned down. He tore the strip of tape off the boy's mouth. He heard him suck in breath. Two of his teeth were missing.

From beside him Lee could see Maurice taking a step backwards. He had the shotgun at his hip and was not quite pointing it and he was looking to Gilmore.

—You're nobody I know, said Lee.

He straightened up. He put both hands on the shaft of the sledgehammer. The cords in his arms drew tight. Through his gloves he could feel the wood grain in the hickory.

—You're nobody at all.

Lee brought the sledgehammer down. It moved with all the motion his arms could put to it, with its own weight carrying it. The steel head crashed into the frozen dirt six inches from Pete's skull. Fragments of earth cascaded into his face. He had his eyes and mouth squeezed shut. When Lee lifted the hammer, a grey dent was left where it had struck.

He turned around.

Speedy's hands were pressed against the sides of his head. Maurice was pointing the shotgun at Lee but he'd not yet pumped the action. He was looking from Lee to Gilmore and back to Lee. Gilmore himself was unreadable.

Lee went out of the locker. He threw the sledgehammer away from him. It hit the ground and bounced and came to rest. He could hear Gilmore speaking to Maurice:

— . . . your kind of shit to deal with. You figure out what this little sack of shit thinks he saw. And then you figure out what you want to do with him. The plane will be here in an hour. And nobody says a word, a fucking word, to Arlene.

Gilmore came out of the locker and crossed through the shed. He slowed as he passed Lee and the two of them looked at each other and neither said anything, and then Gilmore went back outside into the gathering daylight.

The locker door was partially ajar but all Lee could see through the opening was Speedy's back.

The business card he'd taken from his wallet was yellowed with age. It showed a cartoon man in coveralls holding an oversized wrench, and behind the man was a woodstove with two white eyes and a smiling row of teeth. *Gunter's Maintenance & Restoration—All Makes.* There was a phone number and a concession address in Novar. He turned the card over and read a different phone number handwritten on the back. He was in the store, holding the cold receiver of the pay telephone to his mouth.

The man on the other end of the line had not spoken for a long moment.

—Do you understand? said Lee. If I call the bulls and they come with all their lights and sirens and all that shit, then these boys will kill him. If you don't understand the rest of it then you have to understand that.

—I understand.

—Then . . .

—Yes. It's a ways from me. I'll need twenty minutes.

Lee closed his eyes.

—I'll see you.

He hung up. He breathed slowly. He walked a lap around the interior of the restaurant. He opened the rusty tool box he'd seen the night before. The box contained wiring tools: a cable ripper, a selection of marrettes, screwdrivers, needle-nose pliers.

On one of the stripped grocery shelves he found an old pack of cigarettes. There was one cigarette in the pack. It was stale and dry and the smoke moved briskly through it when he lit it. He looked back at the telephone.

There was what might have been an office through a door past the round-top fridge. The smell of mouse shit was sharp.

One window in the office was unboarded, and Lee looked out on the white stillness of the property. The rising sun was slanting crosswise through the spruce. He could not see the shed or the campers from here. He opened his wallet again and looked at what little remained. One thing was his parole officer's card. He balled the card up and threw it in the corner. Wade Larkin hadn't ever been much use in the first place.

Lee drew on his cigarette.

He came back out of the empty office and went towards the tool box on the table. That was when he heard boots behind him. Maurice was standing in the opening between the rear storeroom and the restaurant. The shotgun was laid over his shoulder.

—What are you doing, Lee?

—I came down here to warm up.

—To warm up. What are you doing with that tool box?

Lee went past him into the rear storeroom. Over his shoulder, he said: The heater in the van is broken.

He took two steps and then he started to run for the back door. Maurice swung the shotgun by the barrel and the butt hit Lee in the back of the head. He pitched hard onto the concrete floor. The tool box crashed open in front of him and the wiring tools and marrettes scattered out.

—What in the fuck, Lee? I told you not to come down here. And why are you running?

Lee's vision wavered. There was an immense throb pulsing out from where he'd been struck. The cigarette, pressed between his cheek and the floor, was searing his skin. He rolled his head off it. He got himself up onto his hands and knees and put his fingers down over a flathead screwdriver that had spilled from the tool box. Maurice stood beside him. He put the shotgun to Lee's ear.

Maurice started to say something but Lee snapped the screwdriver into Maurice's thigh and brought it back out. He surged up off the floor and into Maurice and both men scrambled backwards into the restaurant, coupled absurdly, grunting, seeking out soft parts with knees and thumbs. Maurice still had hold of the shotgun in one hand but he hadn't pumped it yet and his free hand was occupied with trying to crush Lee's windpipe or drive his fingers into Lee's eyes. Lee thrashed his head about. He pulled at any part he could get hold of. Maurice's weight was enormous. He guided them by sheer size, both bodies colliding into tables and shelves.

Then Maurice backed Lee into the range and pressed his whole weight into him. He drove his knee up into Lee's thigh and wrapped his hand around Lee's throat and squeezed. But now they were fixed in one place. Lee rammed the screwdriver into Maurice's neck, as many times as he could, as quickly as he could. Maurice's fingers released Lee's windpipe, and the big man moved backwards and found the refrigerator and sat down on the floor against it. He had his hand around his own neck now and he looked surprised. Doubtful. He was still holding the shotgun in his other hand.

Blood came out of Maurice's mouth and between his fingers. It was all over his shirt. Lee staggered upright from the range, gagging air back into his lungs. His hand was slippery with blood.

Maurice said a nonsense sound.

Lee dropped the screwdriver and dug under the counter until he found a threadbare tea towel. He wiped the blood from his hand. He fingered the swelling on the back of his head. Then he went over to Maurice and pulled the barrel of the shotgun. Maurice held on. Lee planted his boot on Maurice's arm and pushed, still holding the barrel, until the shotgun came free.

Maurice said the nonsense sound again. It might have been the word *you*. There was more blood than Lee could have believed possible. It was on the refrigerator and it was pooling on the floor.

Lee pumped the shotgun halfway, checking the gate to see the cartridge in the chamber, and then he finished the pump and thumbed on the safety. He knelt down a few feet in front of Maurice and leaned on the shotgun and continued to get his breath back. Lee watched until Maurice had stopped moving and all the sight had gone from his eyes. The blood still trickled out of him.

Lee got up. His head felt like a cracked bell and his left eye was blurred where Maurice had pressed it. His windpipe was burning. He went through the storeroom and looked out through the open door, across the rise of snow-covered property, to the shed and the van and the campers. Nothing moved.

He went out. There were tracks in the snow. His tracks coming, Maurice's tracks coming. Lee climbed the rise and turned the shotgun out in front of him. The treeline beyond the shed was a dark sketch between earth and sky.

He came first to the prow of the Airstream where the windows were shuttered. He could see the man-door into the shed, open and dark. He moved up on the stoop of the Airstream and tried the door. It was unlocked. He slipped inside. The galley was warm and smelled like cigarettes.

A passageway ran from the galley to the forequarters of the trailer. Just as he was about to step forward he saw Arlene come out of where he reckoned the bedroom was. She was wearing her robe and was combing her hair out of her eyes. Lee pointed the shotgun at her but she did not notice him. She went into the bathroom midway down the passageway and folded the door closed behind her.

Gilmore's voice spoke from the bedroom.

—In the fridge, said Gilmore.

—I will, said Arlene.

Lee went down the passageway to the bedroom. There was a double bed with the sheets pulled up from the corners. The duffle bags packed with the take were heaped one on top of the other beside the bed. Gilmore was sitting on the edge of the mattress, paused in the act of either pulling on or removing his jeans, glancing curiously at what was now filling the doorway.

—Lee, said Gilmore.

Lee shot him in the chest and Gilmore dropped down onto the mattress. His arms were outflung and his jeans were still around his knees. Stuffing from one pillow swirled to the bedspread and smoke hung in the air and there was a shrill ringing in Lee's ears. He pumped the shotgun.

He turned and went back down the passageway. Arlene was screaming in the bathroom. Lee opened the front door and went outside. The man-door into the shed remained unchanged and he kept it in plain sight.

He was on the bottom of the stoop when something slammed into the side of his abdomen and turned him halfway around. He became aware of a popping noise that broke through the ring in his ears. Once Helen had made popcorn on the hot plate and this sound was not dissimilar. He looked up.

There was Speedy at the back of the van, not coming out of the shed at all, and he was holding up the 9mm in both hands.

Lee fired the shotgun from his hip. The pellets punched into the side of the van. He pumped and fired again. Snow and dirt spewed up from the ground. Speedy had already turned and was fleeing. Lee walked towards the van, pumped the shotgun, fired again. Speedy was thirty yards away, running flat-out, head bent forward, not looking back. Lee pumped the shotgun and pulled the trigger and nothing happened. He had to lean against the van when he reached it. What was this thing bound around him? He looked down and saw a hole in his jacket, dark and small and singular, somewhat like a cigarette burn. He thought of the day he'd bought the jacket, the money that had gone out of his wallet. He looked up again and Speedy was out of sight.

Lee's breath plumed out. He took a step away from the van and he faltered. The man-door into the shed was on the other side of the van. He inclined his ear but could hear nothing through the ringing. No airplane, no woman screaming. Nothing of the boy.

Stan was two miles from the marina when he saw the man by the side of the road, waving his arms above his head. He slowed down and the man jogged forward. He slipped once on a patch of ice but kept his footing. He was a small man, moving quickly, and there was a scar on the side of his face. Stan glanced over his shoulder at the Marlin .410 he'd brought from home. It was laid behind the seat. The man came around the passenger side and Stan leaned across the seat and opened the door.

—What's the trouble?

—Just listen, said the man.

He was pointing an automatic pistol. Stan could smell the metal of it, the gun oil. The man climbed into the truck. Up close Stan could see fine scratches on the man's face and hands, as if he'd been running through the bush. His jeans were wet to the knees.

—Listen.

—I just stopped to see if you needed help.

The man wagged the pistol at him. His lips were pulled back over his teeth. He told Stan to shut up while he thought.

Stan looked in the rear-view mirror. The road behind him was vacant.

—Okay, said the man. We'll go back.

The man turned forward on the seat. There would be no other chance. Stan hit him with a hard right cross into the chin, felt the man's jaw move sideways against the impact. Speedy dropped his pistol in the footwell and toppled sideways out of the truck.

Stan started to move over on the seat and the truck lurched forward and he realized it was still in gear. He pulled the shift to park and slid across the seat and picked up the 9mm. The safety was engaged at the back of the slide.

He got out of the truck. There was a spot of blood where

Speedy had landed on his head on the road. He'd gotten up and was now shuffling away in an aimless, drunken fashion. Stan pointed the pistol at him.

—You son of a bitch. Stop walking.

Speedy stopped, turned around: You want to talk about this, man?

—Shut your goddamn mouth. Are you alone?

But then the unmarked cruiser came into view on the road behind them. It slowed to a stop and Dick Shannon got out. He'd unholstered his revolver.

—Stanley. What are you doing with that gun?

—This son of a bitch waved me down and then stuck this at me.

—Has this got to do with why you called me?

—I don't know yet, said Stan. There's a real jam of some kind. Leland King . . .

Dick came forward. He patted Speedy down. He told him he was arresting him for pointing a firearm, did he understand? Speedy said nothing. Dick handcuffed him and found Speedy's wallet in his hip pocket. He looked through it.

—Simmons, said Dick. Willis John. What's your story, Willis John Simmons?

—I have nothing to say to you.

Dick pushed Speedy down into the back of the unmarked car and closed the door behind him. Stan turned the 9mm and removed the magazine and ejected the chambered bullet.

—What's this about Leland King? said Dick.

Stan bent down and retrieved the ejected bullet. He offered the pistol and bullet to Dick.

—Lee King called me half an hour ago. He said he was in some kind of jam.

—What kind of a jam are we talking about?

—He said they robbed a bank.

—Jesus.

—They found a kid out there. Tailing after them maybe, I

don't know. Lee didn't have much time to talk. He said he figured if the police came with the sirens going, the kid was going to get killed.

—And why was Leland King calling you to talk about this?

—Christ, Dick, that doesn't matter just now. I know the place he called from. It's Alec Reynolds's place.

—Stan, this is some kind of a goddamn mess. I'll get some cars scrambled—

—The nearest tactical team is two goddamn hours away. I'm going.

—I don't want you to do that, Stanley.

—I think I know what kid Lee was talking about.

—You jackass, look how old we are. I have a crown of pork waiting for me when I get home. I'm telling you to wait right here.

Stan was already moving back to his truck. He heard Dick shout his name. Dick was standing alongside the cruiser with one hand lifted in a gesture of entreaty.

—Follow me, said Stan.

He drove his truck quickly down the road. He parked it in the clearing where he'd parked it before. The deadfall was cloaked under the snow. Past the culvert and a hundred yards farther down the road he could see the entrance to the laneway. He got out of the truck and took the .410 out from behind the seat. By that time Dick had pulled up behind him and was getting out of the unmarked car.

—Stanley, Christ. There's cars coming from every detachment from here to North Bay. The tactical team there is standing up. We can sit tight.

—I know where to go, Dick.

Stan could see Speedy in the back seat of the car. Stan looked at Dick. Dick lifted his hands and held them palm out.

Then Dick got one of the detachment's 12-gauge shotguns out of the trunk. He loaded it. Stan could see that his fingers were fumbling slightly. Dick left Speedy in the back seat, and then he and Stan went into the bush, backtracking the way Stan had gone before, taking deep steps through the snow. It was slow going. Up ahead was the shallow fold of the creek. Beyond that was the rocky slope. He watched the high feature for movement in the breaks between the trees. Dick thrashed through the snow behind him. He'd unholstered his pistol again.

They came to the creek. Stan slipped going down the bank and put one leg up to the knee into the freezing water. Dick hauled him back out by the shoulders.

—Look, said Dick, pointing.

Fifteen feet downstream there were fresh tracks coming crosswise down the slope above the creek. Right at the bank the snow was cloven away to the mud beneath, as if someone else had stumbled and fallen. The tracks resumed on the other side, heading to the road.

—He was in a hurry.

They stepped over the creek where it narrowed between two rocks. It was hard work climbing the slope past the creek, and they would be long in reacting if anyone appeared above. At the crest they leaned on tree trunks, sucking wind. Fifty yards across open ground stood the back wall of the shed. Nothing was moving.

They looked at each other and then set out across the field, moving abreast through the snow. The feeling had gone out of Stan's foot where he'd put it in the water. They stopped to study the tracks through the snow that Speedy had left as he fled. They watched the shed and the campers. They could see an import hatchback parked a little farther down the laneway. They came around the shed to the laneway and saw the van. There was an array of tracks in the snow. There were ejected 9mm casings, maybe six or seven of them, and three spent shotgun cartridges. They saw the buckshot holes in the side of the van.

—Airplane, said Dick.

—What?

Down past the store they could see the flat white surface of the bay. There was a small airplane, maybe a Cessna, sitting on the ice just below the drop-off, almost obscured from view by the spruce.

—None of this can be any good, said Dick.

Drops of blood lay in the snow, pink and oddly delicate, tracing a path around the van to the man-door in the shed.

Before there was opportunity to track the blood, they heard the Airstream door open up. A bearded man came out on the step. He had a detachable aviator's headset around his neck and he was bent under the weight of a duffle bag. The man was holding Arlene by the wrist. She was lurking in the doorway just behind him, wearing a slip and a jacket and snow boots. Her face was vacuous and makeup was smeared down her cheeks.

—Oh, said the bearded man. Fuck.

Dick pointed the 12-gauge and told the man to drop the duffle bag and to come down off the stoop with his hands plainly visible. The girl too.

—How many other people are in that trailer? said Dick.

The pilot looked at Arlene. She just stared at the ground.

—There's nobody, said the pilot. There's just us. Can we talk about this?

—You're goddamn right we can, said Dick. I'm very interested to know what you have to say.

Stan covered with his .410. Dick had a couple of plastic cable-ties tucked in his hat. He used these to bind Arlene's wrists and the wrists of the pilot, who stiffened angrily. He told them how there was some crazy asshole with a shotgun sitting in the shed.

—What are you boys going to do about that, is what I want to know? said the pilot.

—Stanley, said Dick.

But Stan was already moving to the man-door, seating the .410 into his shoulder and laying his finger along the side of the trigger-guard. He passed through the door frame and blinked to get the brightness out of his eyes. He saw the blood spotted across the floor. Something was hunched against the locker in the corner.

He crossed half the distance and the thing moved and it was Leland King, sitting with his legs forked out in front of him. He had a sawed-off shotgun across his lap. As Stan came forward, Lee made some effort to move the shotgun. He appeared to be incapable of fully lifting it. He just braced the stock against the wall beside him and hefted the barrel up on one knee. He held it for a moment and then he lowered it and let it slide out of his hands altogether.

Stan moved up and shoved the shotgun away with his boot. He heard Dick call after him from outside and he turned his head and shouted that he was alright. Up above, the trusses were creaking quietly. Lee had not bled through the hole in his jacket but he'd bled down his jeans onto the hard-packed dirt around him. He was pale as candle wax.

—Lee, said Stan.

Lee's eyes were fixed not on the old man but at a point in the middle distance. He spoke in a dry and cracked voice: One time I guessed I knew something.

—Tell me where the boy is.

—I guessed I knew something. But I wasn't right at all.

—Where is he, Lee?

—I was wrong about it the whole time. Everything. Maybe you think you can understand that. But you can't.

Lee lifted his hand and grasped the edge of the locker door. He was able to pull it open a few inches and then he dropped his hand back onto the ground.

Stan reached the .410 forward and hooked the foresight on the door and pulled it open. The door was heavier than it looked. He thought the boy was dead until he saw the eyes blinking on either side of the broken nose. The boy's mouth moved.

—You can't understand it, said Lee.

—I can understand it. All of it, pretty clear.

The man on the ground shook his head: No. There's nothing clear.

—He's alive, Lee.

Where he goes, I won't see him.

But already the old man was turning away, calling to his friend outside. What remained for Lee was that which lingers through the smallest, loneliest hours. Rising, stirring, stepping out of the dark, calling his name.

It had always been there.

The new year came and there was a great deal of talk in town and there was talk through the months that followed and the talk was inflated and inaccurate and everybody claimed ownership of some stake in it, somebody they'd known. A vast number of persons claimed to have witnessed the robbery itself. Or at least to have heard it. Or at least to have known somebody who had witnessed it or had heard it. In the retellings, there were thousands of gallons of blood spilled out at the defunct marina on Indian Lake. There was a battle among the perpetrators and a war with the police that lasted half a day. Spring came and the snows receded and the leaves budded pale on the trees and the birds returned and the days grew long. The scope of what people talked about began to swell beyond the limits of the town, which itself had begun to fade back into the ordinary once again.

On the face of the headstone was her name, *Edna Eunice Maitland*, and the years she'd lived, and an engraved epitaph:

That bells should joyful ring to tell
A soul had gone to heaven,
Would seem to me the proper way
A good news should be given.

Beside the epitaph, there was a simple depiction of a stand of birch trees and a path winding among the trees and out of sight. Patterns of light and shadow shifted on the stone from the tree above, which was not birch but white ash, newly flowered. She was three years interred in the earth and beside her was the plot the old man had arranged for himself in times to come. In the fall, Mary had dug a small flower bed in front of the headstone and planted hyacinth bulbs in the soil and they'd bloomed well.

Now that the good weather had arrived, he could come to visit more often. There was much to tell her and only standing there could he say it. Not that words were necessary. Mary's health, Frank's health, the news from the last letter he'd received—two weeks ago—from her sister in Toronto. Emily would be there come September and she said how she would go to visit her great-aunt every few weeks. That was worth telling. Very much. And how today when he left the cemetery he was going to pick Louise up from school and go out to the stand on the west side of Indian Lake to see what birds they could name. In the cab of the truck he'd brought along the 10x42 field glasses. He did not think when they got there that he'd even cast a glance at Alec Reynolds's property to the north.

There was more. He looked away from the words on the stone, the image of the birch trees and the winding path.

There was the house. Sold not three weeks after he'd had it listed. A young couple from the city with two kids, looking for a summer cottage. They'd spoken of the view and of the flower garden in the dooryard, despite the weeds that had grown in it. And they asked him if they could buy the piano in the front room. He told them no. The piano was not for sale. But they could have it free for the asking.

He'd found a place in town. A small townhouse on the end of a row. It backed onto a long grove of trees on the edge of the golf course. He could take the dog walking. He could leave the house on Echo Point for what it was, timber and stone and nothing more. He thought he could.

He also thought about the affairs over the last several months, but he did not dwell on them as much as he had expected he would. Frank had congratulated and thanked him in a civic ceremony, but had almost nothing to say about it in private. They had, however, gone fishing a few times—just the two of them, and at Frank's invitation—after trout season opened in April. Dick Shannon, who'd also been part of the civic commendation, had put in his retirement paperwork a week later.

The incident itself—the robbery at the National Trust and the bloodshed that had followed—wasn't something that could be put to rest simply by awarding civic commendations, or by telling and retelling it in newspapers and on the national news. The incident defied categorization. Sometimes what came back to Stan was sitting at the roadhouse with the man who'd called himself Colin Gilmore, Gilmore leaning back against the bar, saying, *You think up some more questions if you want,* before he got up and disappeared. The truth was, Stan hadn't known what to ask the man then, or what to say to him. He didn't know any better now.

And Leland King, who'd survived, had nothing to say. Nothing by way of explanation, nothing in his own defence. Maybe Lee thought the world had finished listening to him a long time ago. He was probably right.

Lastly, there was the question of Judy Lacroix, whether she had or hadn't taken her own life. Nobody would ever know, and nobody could ever make it right. But it didn't trouble Stan as much as it had in the fall, even though he still thought about her. And he still thought, every day, about her uncle Darien, turning at the bottom of the hangman's rope. He knew that Darien

Lacroix would be his to think about, no matter what, for as long as he had thoughts in his head.

But he'd done what he could, and that had to stand for something, in his own heart if nowhere else. He'd even had supper on two occasions with Eleanor Lacroix and Tommy Spencer. Eleanor was pregnant.

The breeze stirred and moved the hyacinth blossoms and turned the water that had run from his eyes down the seams of his face cold. He lifted a hand and rubbed back the tears and he told Edna so long for this week.

He walked back down the gravelled footpath to where his truck was parked in the lane and as he came close to it, Cassius sat up in the bed and looked at him. He opened the door and got in and turned on the truck. He was about to put it into gear but he didn't. He got out again. He went around to the tailgate and lowered it and told the dog to get down. The dog hopped down and stretched and then looked at him.

Stan closed the tailgate and walked up to the passenger door and opened it.

—Get in.

The dog looked at him.

—Get in, you stubborn bastard.

The dog whined once and then sat back.

—Look. I can't lift you any more.

It took some coaxing and patting the seat before Cassius stood back up and reared and jumped and scrabbled his way into the cab. He got up onto the seat and turned around and looked at Stan for further guidance, unaccustomed as he was to the front of the truck, but Stan only closed the door and came around and got back in the driver side and closed his own door. Then he put the truck into gear and carried on with his afternoon.

To look at the sky above the cemetery, you might think it had never been any different.

FIVE

JUNE 1981

It was the slow onset of a summer evening when he watched the announcement on the evening news. He was sitting in a restaurant at the Pine Tree Motor Inn in Marten River. This, the first evening of his journey. He was eating a hamburger and french fries. The news came on the black-and-white television behind the counter and the newsman first said good evening and then he said Terry Fox had died that day in the early morning hours. The woman behind the counter did not stop what she was doing, cleaning silverware with a vinegar-soaked cloth. On the television a nurse at a B.C. hospital gave a statement. Then a doctor spoke and then they returned to the newsman and to other affairs. The woman behind the counter went to rub a spot off a glass cakebell.

Later that night, Pete lay in the back of his car listening to rain drum on the roof. He'd parked at the edge of a farm field and it was very dark outside, but for a purple stutter of lightning. He found he was listening for some sound or sign of something. Maybe for the radio to come on spontaneously.

Many nights, now, he lay awake. He'd very nearly suffocated, between the broken nose and the tape over his mouth. The back of his throat had filled with blood. Sometimes he had nightmares: the sledgehammer falling above him. The nightmares came and went and he woke gagging for breath and clawing at whatever part of the sheet had fallen over his face.

But this night on the farm field outside Marten River was different. He was not disturbed at all. He just was. And maybe he was awake to consider that.

The girl said her name was Veda and she was a few years older than he was. Whatever she was travelling with was packed into a nylon World Famous knapsack with leather straps. When he first saw her, he thought she was good-looking. When he saw her close up, he saw how her fingernails were chewed down and ragged. Her legs were long and brown. She was wearing tennis shoes.

He met her in a laundromat in New Liskeard. The radiator in his car had cracked earlier. It could be repaired that day but it was going to take a few hours. He was anguished at the hole the repair made in his wallet. Then he gathered some clothes to wash. It seemed premature to be doing laundry this early into the trip. He'd only set off from home at noon yesterday.

He saw her when he came in, loading clothes into a washing machine. Then she went out of the laundromat without looking at him. Half an hour later she came back. She was carrying a big soft drink cup. The only other person in the laundromat was an old woman dozing by the front window. He'd caught a slight reek of cooking wine when he walked past her.

The girl set down her soft drink and took her clothes out of the washer and loaded them into a dryer. Then she was looking at him. He looked back down at his book. When she'd loaded the dryer she moseyed over his way, chewing on the straw in her soft drink cup. She came with casual boldness, as if they'd been familiar all along.

—It's fucking hot outside.

—I know it, said Pete.

—Listen, can you tell me where the bus station is?

—I don't know. I'm not from here.

—Well, isn't that my luck.

She dragged over a plastic chair and sank down into it. She did so as if suddenly exhausted, as if she'd just climbed a hill. She sat with one leg over the armrest. Hesitantly, Pete introduced himself.

—Hi, Pete. I'm Veda.

—Veda . . .

—You say it like you never heard it before.

—I don't know if I have.

—Well, my dad was a hometown kind of a guy. But my mom, she's a woman of the world. It's the kind of thing she knows about.

—Veda. Okay.

He liked the way her name sounded.

They made conversation for thirty minutes, waiting on their clothes and then lingering after their clothes were finished drying. She spoke a little about university in Montreal. He could tell she was making tracks from something, but what this was, he couldn't put together yet. She'd apparently arrived in New Liskeard yesterday afternoon, when he was still on the road to Marten River. He had the sense she was out of money.

—I'm going back to Hearst for awhile, said Veda. Going back home. It's my dad's place and it'll do till things get back on track. Dude, if I had a tail, it would be between my legs. Put it that way. Anyways, where are you going, Pete?

—I'm going west.

—And how long are you going for?

—However long they'll have me.

—Sounds like quite a move. But hey, dude. Shit like that I can respect. Anyways, if you're going west then it seems you'd be going through Hearst on your way. Six hours from here.

—I get the feeling you're proposing something.

—I won't fuck with your radio.

—Okay, said Pete. You can ride with me.

They left New Liskeard early the next morning. He picked her up at the campground where she was staying. Veda packed her tent into her knapsack and got into the car.

—I'm going to say what ten billion girls have said before me. You seem like a nice guy. We get on the road, in your car, don't turn evil on me, okay? I've got an eight-inch switchblade in my bra and I'll stick you if I have to.

They had breakfast at a gas bar on the edge of town. It made him think of the Texaco. With everything that had happened, it had been necessary for him to stay on at the Texaco for some months longer than he'd intended, once he'd been able to resume working again. His last day at the Texaco had been the twenty-fifth of June. Duane had walked him to his car, smiling his townie smile.

—You take it easy out there, Pete. You're a bit of a shit-magnet.

—I'll do what I can. I'll send you a postcard.

—You probably won't.

Behind them a car was pulling onto the apron.

—One of us has to get back to work, said Duane. See? Some things never change.

They shook hands and Duane turned and sauntered back towards the pumps. There was an oil rag hanging out of his back pocket and in the other pocket was the round shape of his chew tin. A few days later, Pete was on the road.

Once he and Veda had finished breakfast and started driving, she fell asleep and she didn't wake again until ten o'clock. She smacked her lips and looked around.

—Where are we?

—We just passed a place called Tunis.

—Tunis.

—There wasn't much to it.

—I know it. I know Tunis.

This was pretty country, with great stretches of bush separating the villages and towns they drove through. They passed fields where the long grass was fiery with hawkweed and devil's paintbrush.

—It's your dad's place in Hearst?

—Thanks for reminding me. I wasn't thinking about anything and it was nice.

—Hey, sorry.

—Oh, don't fret it. My dad, he's a good guy. But, like, he's a hometown guy. The farthest he's ever been is Sudbury and he is A-OK with that. And Hearst, I just . . . Hearst is Hearst, right? One time I heard this comedian say that the thing about a small town is once you've seen the cannon in the park, you've seen all there is to see. It'll do for a little while, until things get evened out.

—Things in Montreal?

—Yeah, in Montreal. And other places. Here, for starters.

She was tapping the side of her head.

—I hear you, said Pete.

—So this is the part where . . . ?

—Where what? What part?

—The part where we exchange our stories.

—I was just making conversation.

—Exchange our stories and figure out what they mean. When you're on the road, everybody you meet is going somewhere to get away from something.

—I'm not getting away from anything.

—Don't bullshit a bullshitter, Peter.

—I'm not.

—Come on, what was your issue? What did you do? Who did you lose?

He looked over at her. He looked back at the road. The last time he saw Emily, she'd been kind. She said they both knew what was inevitable. For Christmas, she'd gotten a leather coat and she looked really good in it. For reasons he couldn't understand, Pete resented the coat more than anything, more than any of what was said about how they had to part. She could go in peace, but if it were up to him the coat would be torn to rags.

To Veda, he said: Well, I lost my grandmother about six weeks ago. I lived with her my whole life. She died of lung cancer.

—Hey. I'm sorry. I didn't mean to push you with my craziness or anything.

—It's okay. You asked.

—Can I ask you something else? Do you think it means anything?

—My grandmother dying?

—Yes.

—It means about as much as the next thing.

—You're keeping something back, aren't you. You've got some information up your sleeve. That's cool.

—Jesus. Look, are you hungry?

—I'm getting to be.

They had an early lunch in Smooth Rock Falls. Veda told him a little bit about Hearst. A logging town. Her father was a sawyer at a mill. Theirs was one of the few families in town for whom French was not their first language. She'd grown up with a lot of native kids and she spoke of a few who had taken their own lives. But she said there were worse places to have to hide out for awhile. She said Hearst had its charms.

—There's this giant crosscut saw people take pictures of. You'll see. You can stay for Canada Day. My dad is always happy to entertain. He doesn't need much of an excuse.

They got going again. Sometime after Cochrane, he looked over and saw she'd kicked off her tennis shoes and leaned her seat back. Her feet were white against the brown of her legs. One of the toenails was black. As they drove, she took out a small zippered pouch and opened it and brought out the makings of a joint and rolled it.

—I'm guessing you're one of those people who want things to mean something, she said.

—I'm not sure what you mean by that.

—I'm not so, you know, good at saying what I think. So never mind.

—No no, said Pete. Tell me.

—Well, that one thing happens and it means something. Or, let me see if I can explain this better: one thing happens because something else happened before it to make it happen.

—But doesn't that make sense? You know, one thing leads to another. Like, I could stick my leg out and I trip you, you fall down. That's one thing leading to the next.

—Yeah, then I get up and I bust your nose. Again, by the looks of it.

Without thinking, he touched his nose. It had reset crookedly. He was never sure how apparent it was to people who saw it.

—What was it? said Veda. Hockey?

—No.

—Anyway, that example, that's all that is. You can't look for a bigger plan there.

—Well, yeah. I guess there's nothing bigger in that. Okay.

—So do you believe in God?

—Do I what?

—It's an easy question, dude.

—I don't know. I haven't really thought about it.

—Well, that's disappointing.

—Yeah, well, the house where I grew up, there was a lot of talk about God all the time. And not much talk about anything else. I think whatever it is I do believe is kind of based on the opposite of everything that was talked about at home, because all I could ever think about was what didn't add up and where the holes were. And, no, that's not me saying I don't believe in anything at all, either. I don't know if that makes any sense to you.

—It makes enough sense for now. Okay. You haven't let me down as bad.

—I'm glad I got your approval. But is this something you believe in? God?

She shrugged. It was a full, exaggerated roll of the shoulders. She crossed her eyes and said: I don't know about God but there's always the bet.

—The bet?

—This French guy I knew, he told me about it? So basically there's a coin toss and you got to bet on it, heads or tails—this is what he told me—and if you bet on heads, or God, you win everything. All that stuff about heaven, right? But if you bet on tails, that there isn't any God, and you lose, you lose it all.

—This doesn't seem like much of a bet, really. Why would you make this kind of a bet?

—Well, it goes like this. If what you stand to lose is everything, and what you can win is also everything—or, well, heaven—you have unlimited reasons to make the bet.

Veda lit the joint. She took a few hauls and handed it over to him. He toked and coughed and passed it back.

—I just don't know if I'm convinced, said Pete. This coin toss. Anything about believing. My stepdad is a pastor and he and the people at his church have a whole lot of answers that work fine for them. But they never worked for me. It took me awhile to realize that. And you talk about just believing, well, I'm not convinced.

—Me neither. Like if God's up there, how can everything in life be so shitty?

—I guess that's assuming that you and me and everybody else should be happy all the time. If he's up there, maybe that's not what he even has in mind. Us being happy all the time.

—If.

—Yep.

—We're about half an hour away, said Veda. This is country I know. It's been awhile since I saw it but I know it. Anyway it's hot as hell. I want to go swimming first. Come on, I'll show you a good place up here. But you got to be man enough.

—Man enough. What do you mean?

—You'll see.

She told him to turn off the highway onto a side road. Scarcely more than a gravel trail through the bush. The side road tapered past a few properties and went on for awhile and came finally to a dead end at a railbed.

They got out of the car. Pete stretched. When he turned around he saw she was removing her shorts and her T-shirt. She was wearing a swimsuit underneath. She caught him looking. All she said was: Summertime in this country—it's a day wasted if you don't swim, you know?

The Adidas shorts he was wearing would do as a swimsuit. He hesitated for a moment and then took off his own T-shirt and tossed it onto the driver's seat. The sun was hot on his shoulders and the back of his neck.

She led him down the tracks, telling him it was an abandoned line. As they walked, she brought out another skinny joint and they smoked it. A sign standing to the side of the railbed exclaimed NO TRESPASSING in letters partly obscured by rust. They rounded a final bend and the bush receded on slabs of exposed bedrock. Up ahead was a wide blue creek and spanning the water was the bulk of an old train trestle. The girders were gaunt, all browns and blacks. It had to be forty feet from the girder framing the top of the trestle to the surface of the water.

—That thing? said Pete.

—You bet. Best view in the world up there.

Pete looked into the river below. The water was the same breathless monochrome as the sky. But where it flowed under the trestle, the water was shadowed in depths of green-black. He watched as a long walleye arrowed lazily into the shade. It lingered and then it darted away. Pete felt reluctant to look at the trestle itself.

—Well?

—What do you do, you just climb it?

—Right up the side. All us kids have been climbing that thing as long as I remember. I might have been eight years old first time I jumped off.

—You're fucking crazy.

—Oh . . . I wondered if you'd be man enough.

—I'm not sure why you think this has to be a test of whether I'm man enough.

—But isn't that how it works for men? Physical challenges and all that?

—So they tell me.

She was ambling over to the angled upright. She stepped out of her tennis shoes.

—Anyways, good fortune comes to those who prove themselves.

—What is that supposed to mean?

But she'd already begun climbing. She moved like a spider, hands gripping the wings of the I-beam, toes curling on the rounded bolt-heads. She scaled the upright and moved fluidly over the triangular brace at the top.

Pete stepped across the concrete pad where the upright was anchored. He took off his sneakers and stashed his car keys in one of them. He grasped the sides of the girder. He could feel his sweat gelling against the rusty metal. He climbed. As long as he stared directly ahead, he was okay. But looking left or right, to where the surrounding landscape stretched away, he had flashes of acrophobia. It lit small fires in his fingers and toes. He was breathing hard. He came to the brace and made the final bodily twists onto the skyward face of the girder.

He lay airless on the sun-blanched metal. His feet stuck out over the edge behind him. The beam wasn't two feet wide. To his right was a frightening drop to the ties and rails. To his left was an even longer fall to the river.

Pete raised his head. He was sweating into his eyes, clinging to the hard surface beneath him. Veda was fifteen feet farther down the beam and she was sitting. Pete crawled out to her.

—There you are. Sit up, will you?

Pete laboured into a sitting position and groped for the edges of the girder.

—I like it up here, said Veda. It's so quiet. It's a good place to get my head together.

—It's alright as long as I don't look around too much.

—Just enjoy the view.

—I'm trying.

—It's a couple of years I've been gone. We used to come up here all the time.

—You were never afraid?

—Of heights? No. Never of heights. Heights were always, you know, whatever.

—Yeah. Just like that.

—I loved it in Montreal. God I loved it there, for what it was, for the time I was there. But it didn't have any good quiet places like this. Like . . . I think most dudes say they love a girl but by love they mean have. You know. Possess. All those songs, right? All those poems. *I want to have you, I want you to be mine.* I'm not any good at being possessed. But I'm not any good on giving up on men either. They all just interest me too much. That's my problem. The possessing thing, calling it love, that was his problem.

—So it *was* a boyfriend.

—That sounds so cute. It's more like how sometimes you know how it's going to end up. Sometimes you want the pain of it. Right off from the beginning.

—He broke your heart and you skipped town?

—That's way over-exaggerated, dude. I didn't say I got my heart broken. But me and him, let's say I just got my heart right tired out. And when that happens and the going is good, you know, you got to get a move-on.

—I think I know a thing or two about that.

—Don't think it was all at once. I went east first. I was in Halifax for a couple months, working at a hotel. Then I got a job at Mont Tremblant. I was in Ottawa. But, like I said, I just got tired out. In my heart, if you can see what I mean at all. So I'm going home. I am flying the white flag. I got my hands up and I'm coming out. Don't shoot, you bastards.

—It's not your whole story, said Pete.

—It's whole enough. How bad do you need the names?

—Good point.

They lolled quietly, letting the hard sunlight work on their skin. If he moved his hand to a new position the steel was almost too hot to touch. The hot metal made him think of the bitter cold floor inside the storage locker, how all the feeling had gone out of his hands and feet and ears. In Pete's waking vision, the hammer was falling even now. He let one hand go from the edge of the girder and he looked at the rust lined into his flesh.

—My uncle is a killer. He killed a couple of men not so long ago. And a long time before that, he killed another guy, a guy who . . . Well, it doesn't matter now. A guy who my uncle thought had it coming.

Veda was looking at him. Her hair was sweat-slicked across her temples and her shoulders were bright with the sun.

—Hey, man. Listen—

—I won't talk about it if you don't want to know.

—I didn't say that.

He told her everything. He considered leaving out some details but he did not. He told her of his life and he told her of the months and weeks and last days leading up to the morning of the falling hammer. He told her of the time that followed. Barry who prayed, the boys who stared, his mother whose face became a barren thing, moonscape where two vacant eyes sat in deep craters. His grandmother who could not say anything at all, who just receded more and more into the rhythm the machine dictated for her. She lived longer than anyone thought she would. A measure of months. When she died, it was at night and none of them were present.

—And this guy, your uncle?

—He's alive. Like, he shouldn't be. But he is. It missed his spleen. The bullet. Missed his liver.

As he spoke, he held his hand up, flat, palm down. He moved the hand slowly in front of them. He had no idea what he was trying to communicate by the gesture. Something ballistic. He let the hand back down to grip the girder.

—He was in the hospital for a long time.

—And, what, did you see him?

—No, said Pete. I never did. Now he's back in jail. I've spent a lot of time trying to figure him out. I can't. I don't know if I ever will. He's a killer . . . But if it wasn't for him, I wouldn't be alive. I wouldn't be sitting up here talking to you. Those men would have broken a hole through the ice and sunk my body to the bottom, or God knows what they would have done. But that didn't happen because of what my uncle did. Try telling me what that means.

She didn't say anything. She just sat there for a little while, squinting her eyes and flexing her toes. He'd speculated there might be release in the telling, but there wasn't. Maybe it would take some time to feel it but for now there was just the day and the heat and somewhere the knowledge of every day that had gone before.

—So, said Pete.

—You're alright.

—What?

Veda put her hand on his face, on his nose. Traced with her fingers the crookedness of the bone.

—You're an alright kind of guy.

—This is something you just thought of?

—Mm, maybe. Anyways, come on.

—You want to go?

—The jump is always the best part.

—Right.

She stood up.

—There's things we've got to get to, Pete. Things waiting for us. And today the getting is good.

She jumped off the edge of the beam. She fell soundlessly and crashed through the surface of the river. There was a brief time that she was out of sight, Pete watching for her, and then she surfaced. She kicked out a ways and turned on her back in the water and waved to him. She called his name.

After a short time, he climbed slowly and deliberately to his feet. He was giddy with the height. The view was vast and lonesome. He drew breath from the hot air and he saw in the southwest where rain clouds were gathering slowly, towers of cumulus piled to the sun, old as anything.

Pete bent forward. There was a last moment of contact with the hot steel and then there was nothing but gravity. He looked down, and just before he hit the surface of the river, he saw himself, a fast-moving shadow, rushing up feet-first to meet him.

ACKNOWLEDGEMENTS

The author wishes to express his gratitude to the following:

Douglas Abbott
Phyllis Bruce
Catherine Bush and the University of Guelph MFA
in Creative Writing
Roger Caron
Phillip Halton
Martha Magor Webb
Michael Winter

A NOTE ON THE TYPE

This book is set in Berling, an old-style roman created in 1951 by Karl-Erik Forsberg for the Berlingska Stilgjuteriet foundry in Lund, Sweden. The face has a Scandinavian sharpness and clarity, and it features unusually shortened descenders—an adaptation to the greater frequency of descenders in Swedish.